T0015797

ALSO BY LINDA CASTILLO

A SIMPLE MURDER

A Kate Burkholder Short Story Collection

Linda Castillo

St. Martin's Paperbacks

This is a work of fiction. All of the characters, organizations, and events portrayed in this book are either products of the author's imagination or are used fictitiously.

First published in the United States by St. Martin's Paperbacks, an imprint of St. Martin's Publishing Group

A SIMPLE MURDER: A KATE BURKHOLDER SHORT STORY COLLECTION

For information, address St. Martin's Publishing Group, 120 Broadway, New York, NY 10271.

www.stmartins.com

ISBN: 978-1-250-78361-5

Our books may be purchased in bulk for promotional, educational, or business use. Please contact your local bookseller or the Macmillan Corporate and Premium Sales Department at 1-800-221-7945, ext. 5442, or by email at MacmillanSpecialMarkets@macmillan.com.

Printed in the United States of America

St. Martin's Paperbacks edition 2021

10 9 8 7 6 5 4

Contents

LONG LOST

There are some things that never grow old. The brilliant autumn foliage that blankets the rolling hills of Ohio's Amish country is one of them. It's mid-October and the northeastern part of the state is a shimmering collage of orange, rust, and red. I've driven this road countless times in the years I've lived here, but I never tire of it. Every pilgrimage differs in some profound way so that I drink it in with a perspective that's breathtaking and new. The way the light slants across the trees, turning the foliage to fire. The way the morning mist hovers like smoke over the forest floor. The unexpected sight of an Amish farmer and his team of draft horses harvesting corn. The spectacle of fallen leaves caught in an eddy and scattering across the asphalt like small creatures trying to escape the impending winter.

My name is Kate Burkholder and I'm the chief of police of Painters Mill, Ohio, a small farming community nestled in the heart of Amish country. I'm sitting in the passenger seat of state agent John

Tomasetti's Tahoe and we're bound for two days of R&R at a small bed-and-breakfast an hour from where I live. I should be relaxed and looking forward to some much-needed downtime and the chance to spend some quality time with the man I love. If only life was that simple.

I've lived too many years to suddenly come down with a case of nerves over spending the weekend with a man I've known for almost three years now. I'm not prone to bouts of anxiety or angst. Tomasetti is, after all, my best friend. He's my lover and confidant, and a man I admire greatly. We've worked some difficult cases together—murder and kidnapping and all the depraved things that go along with those kinds of crimes. Still, inexplicably, the thought of spending two nights at a cozy bed-and-breakfast without the buffer of work scares the living daylights out of me.

Perhaps because deep inside I know the tension running up the back of my neck has little to do with the weekend ahead, and everything to do with the evolution of a relationship I value more than my own life. The next two days promise to take that relationship to the next level, a *new* level I have little experience with, and I'm not sure I'm up to the task.

"You're brooding awfully hard about something."

His voice draws me from my thoughts. I glance over at him and I'm moved not only by the sight of him, but by the depth of my feelings.

"I'm not brooding," I tell him. "I'm contemplating. There's a difference."

"If I didn't know better, I might jump to the conclusion that you're having second thoughts about this."

"You're not calling me chicken, are you?" I ask.

He slants me a smile. "I would never disparage a woman who can outshoot me."

The words elicit a grin. "I think I can handle a weekend alone with you. I'm just . . ."

"Nervous?"

The word sounds juvenile and makes me feel just a little bit foolish. I want to tell him nerves are for schoolgirls, something I haven't been for a very long time. "I'm not used to taking time off."

He cuts me an amused look. "Or sharing your bed with a man for an entire weekend."

"There is that."

"If it's any consolation, Chief, this is new ground for me, too."

"So at least we're on an even playing field."

The banter is like gentle fingers kneading the back of my neck and I feel myself begin to relax. "I'm glad I have you to help me keep things in perspective, Tomasetti."

"Anytime."

We crest a hill overlooking a lush, forested valley, and we're met with a shimmering ocean of red and yellow and gold. Maples and black walnut trees shimmer like faceted gems as they rush by my window. We reach the valley floor and cross an old steel girder bridge tattooed with graffiti that spans the

Rouge River. We pass an Amish buggy and then a rustic sign directs us toward the Maple Creek Inn.

"Here we go." Tomasetti makes a left onto the narrow gravel lane.

Ancient trees close over the Tahoe, blocking the bright afternoon sun. To my right, the slow-moving water of the river keeps pace with our vehicle. I glimpse tendrils of woodsmoke above the treetops and then the old farmhouse looms into view. It's a large, two-story Victorian with a redbrick chimney and tin roof. A porch adorned with hanging ferns and clay pots filled with cheery yellow mums wraps around three sides of the house. Pretty red Adirondack chairs beckon one to sit and watch the river. There's more seating on a paved patio just off the porch where several benches surround a huge bronze chiminea.

Tomasetti parks in a gravel area at the rear marked with a battered wooden GUEST PARKING sign. "Might take awhile to get used to all this peace and quiet," he comments.

"Spoken like a true city boy."

Giving me a wry smile, he shuts down the engine and we get out. I'm met by crisp fall air and a cacophony of birdsong. There's not a cloud in the sky, but the thick canopy overhead turns the light murky. I smell the river now, a pleasant mix of moist air, wet earth, and foliage.

Tomasetti picks up my overnight bag and then slings his own over his shoulder. We cross the gravel lot and take a pavestone path to the front of the house.

"I'm told there are trails along the river," he tells me. "And a couple of restaurants down the road. I thought we'd explore the woods and then drive into town for some lunch."

"Sounds great."

The scent of the woodsmoke pleases my olfactory nerves as we take the steps to the porch. Tomasetti opens the door for me and we enter a large front office that looks more like the living area of some 1890s farmhouse. The aromas of hot cider and cinnamon lace the air. A braided rug that looks Amish-made covers distressed hardwood floors. To my left is a good-size room with floor-to-ceiling windows that look out over the dark water of the river. A fire crackles and pops from within a massive stone hearth.

A gray-headed woman in a blue dress, white apron, and gauzy *kapp* stands behind a counter, an old-fashioned landline phone wedged into the crook of her neck, a hotel register open in front of her. The *kapp* tells me she's Mennonite. She makes eye contact with me and smiles, raising a finger to let us know she'll be right with us.

Tomasetti sets our bags on the floor. A man with a full beard that reaches his waist comes in from another room, his arms filled with firewood and kindling. I guess him to be about sixty years old. He's wearing dark gray work trousers with suspenders, a gray work shirt, and a black barn coat with a flat-brimmed hat.

"Ah, customers! Didn't see you come in." Kneeling next to the hearth, he stacks the wood on a wrought-iron rack. "Welcome to Maple Creek."

Tomasetti introduces himself and the two men shake hands.

"I'm Harley Hilty. My wife and I own the place."

I extend my hand and he gives it a solid, friendly shake. "It's beautiful."

"Fannie and I love it here. She inherited it from her *grossdaddi* thirty years ago and we've been fixing it up ever since." He brushes wood dust from his coat, chuckling. "It's a full-time job," he says and addresses the woman behind the counter. "How long have we been running this place now, Fannie?"

She hangs up the phone and comes around the counter. She's a plump woman of about sixty with ruddy cheeks and the chapped hands of a hard worker. "Oh, I'd say going on twenty-three years now." She crosses to me and we shake hands. "I'm Fannie."

"Kate Burkholder."

She tilts her head and eyes me with curiosity. "Now there's a nice Amish name for you."

"I used to be Amish." I say the words in Pennsylvania Dutch.

"I see." She arches a brow, and I can't tell if it's in judgment or if she's merely acknowledging my words. "You left the fold?"

I nod, wishing I hadn't said anything. This weekend is about Tomasetti and me. I don't want to worry about our hosts condemning me for my choices. To my surprise, she nods and offers a smile. "We were Swartzendruber, you know."

"Too strict for our liking," Harley puts in.

"We're Mennonite now." Fannie crosses to a small coffee station and pours cider into four mugs.

I nod, letting that bit of information soak in. The Mennonites and the Amish share a long and complex history that goes back over three hundred years. Today, the two groups share many similarities with regard to theologic views and cultural heritage. But the differences, particularly between the Swartzendruber Amish and the Mennonites, are profound. The Swartzendruber group is the most conservative, with stringent rules against technology. All but the most conservative of Mennonites—the Old Order Mennonites—utilize modern conveniences, including cars, electricity, and even computers and the Internet.

"Don't recall seeing you folks here before," Harley says. "This your first visit?"

Tomasetti nods. "I was out at one of the travel websites and one of your guests mentioned something about this place being haunted."

The couple exchanges a grim look I don't understand. The Mennonite man covers the awkward moment with a chuckle. "Well now, we don't really talk about that too much." His eyes flick to his wife and he lowers his voice. "But there have been a dozen or so sightings of her since she went missing."

"Her?" Tomasetti asks.

"Harley Hilty, don't go scaring the guests already." Straightening, Fannie turns and carries two mugs over to us. "All that talk of ghosts. That's just a load of horsefeathers."

"Fannie doesn't believe in ghosts." Harley points out the obvious.

"You just hush about all that." The Mennonite woman shoves a steaming cup at me. "I've got a cinnamon stick if you'd like."

The aromas of cider and nutmeg tease my senses as I take the mug. "This is perfect. Thanks."

"There's an apple orchard behind the old barn," she tells me. "My *grossdaddi* planted all those trees fifty years ago and they're still producing the best McIntosh apples I've ever had."

"The couple that was here last weekend saw her in the orchard," Harley says.

Fannie makes a sound of annoyance.

"You mean the ghost?" I ask, trying not to feel foolish.

Tomasetti picks up the pen and begins filling out the registration form. "Everyone likes a good ghost story."

"Pure silliness." Fannie shakes her head. "And disrespectful of the dead if you ask me."

Harley picks up his mug of cider. "I seen her myself a time or two."

I look from husband to wife. "What happened?"

Looking a little too excited, Harley explains. "A young woman by the name of Angela Blaine stayed here not long after we opened. She was a sweet, pretty thing. But I knew she was running from something. Or someone. Had that scared look about her. You know, in the eyes." He shrugs. "Anyway, she checked in for two nights. Paid cash. And never checked out."

"Disappeared into thin air." Fannie grimaces. "At first we didn't know if the poor thing left or if something happened to her. A couple of days later Harley was out walking by the river and found her clothes." Shaking her head, the woman crosses to the counter and steps behind it, as if she wants nothing to do with what will be said next.

"They were blood soaked," Harley whispers.

"That was when we called the sheriff's office," Fannie puts in.

"A few days later Angela's mother filed a missing person report." Harley slurps his cider hard. "What kind of mother waits that long before reporting her daughter missing?"

Despite my efforts not to be, I'm intrigued by the mystery. "Did they find her?"

"Not a trace," Harley responds. "Aside from those bloody clothes, anyway."

"Did the sheriff's department search the property?" Tomasetti asks.

"The entire hundred acres," Harley replies.

"Brought in bloodhounds and organized volunteer search parties. Folks went out on horseback. No one found a trace."

"We followed the story through the weekly newspaper." Fannie looks down at the register before her and scribbles something. "Saved all the articles." She opens a drawer, pulls out a frayed manila folder and sets it on the counter. "She was pretty as a movie star." Sighing wistfully, she peels open the cover and looks down at the yellowed clippings.

I find myself staring at the grainy photo of a fresh-faced girl with brown hair, huge brown eyes, and an engaging smile. A mole on the left side of her chin only adds to the allure of her face.

I glance over at Tomasetti, but I can't tell if he's intrigued or indifferent or somewhere in between, like me.

"I see you're a policeman."

I glance over at the counter to see Fannie looking down at the registration form Tomasetti just completed.

"I'm with the state," he tells her. "BCI out of Richland." He looks at me. "Kate is the chief of police in Painters Mill."

Harley nods. "I bought a horse there a few years back."

"We've never had policemen stay here before." Looking intrigued by the notion, Fannie opens a drawer, pulls out a set of keys, and dangles them at her husband.

"Oh. Right." Harley grabs the keys, crosses to me and picks up my overnight bag. "If you're ready I'll show you to your room."

I set my mug on the counter. "The cider was wonderful, Fannie. Thank you."

Harley takes us up a steep and narrow staircase to the second level. We pass three rooms with tall, paneled doors. He stops at the fourth and bends to use the key. "It's our nicest suite," he says, opening the door and stepping inside.

The first thing I notice is the fire crackling in the hearth and the faintly spicy scent of potpourri. An intricate Amish quilt of red and blue and green covers a king-size bed. The headboard and furniture are antiques, the mahogany-brown stain contrasting nicely with beige-colored walls.

"It's a lovely room," I say.

Beaming, Harley goes directly to the closet, removes a luggage rack, and sets my overnight bag atop it. "We usually charge more for this one, but since we're not busy this weekend, we figured you should have it."

"We appreciate that." I wander to the window and discover a breathtaking view of the river.

Tomasetti sets his bag on the bed and I catch a glimpse of his shoulder holster and pistol beneath his jacket.

"You folks going to want some lunch?" Harley asks as he starts toward the door. "Fannie's quite the cook."

"Actually we were going to check out that steak house in town," Tomasetti tells him.

"Ah, The Oak is an excellent choice." He lowers his voice. "Just between us, their prime rib is better than my Fannie's." He goes to the window and opens the drapes further. "When you leave, just make a right on Rouge Road. The Oak is about two miles down on your left, right next to the bowling alley."

He starts toward the door. "Let us know if you need anything."

"Thanks," I tell him, and then he's gone.

Across the room, Tomasetti begins to unpack. "You know we're not going to get involved in that, right?"

"You mean the missing girl thing? Of course not." I unzip my own bag and begin putting my clothes into the bureau. "We're here for some R&R, not a twenty-two-year-old cold case."

"Exactly."

Tomasetti and I opt for a walk along the river before driving into town for a late lunch. Donning our hiking boots and jackets, we find the trailhead behind the house and within minutes we've been swallowed by thick woods. The calls of cardinals and the chatter of sparrows follow us as we make our way down a wide dirt path. The smell of fallen leaves, and the muddy scent of the river hang in the still air.

I glance at Tomasetti and I see he's as caught up in the beauty of our surroundings as I am.

"Nice idea, Tomasetti," I tell him. "It's beautiful here."

He casts me a half smile. "You're not feeling stressed out by all this serenity, are you?"

"Not a chance."

Taking my hand, he pulls me around to face him and kisses me. It's a small thing, the slightest brushing of lips, but my heart begins to pound, and I'm amazed that even after three years of knowing him, he still does that to me.

After a moment, he pulls away and stares down at me. "Every time I look at you, the things that happened three years ago . . . it gets easier."

He's referring to the murders of his wife and two children by a career criminal. It was a horrific tragedy that nearly killed him, too. He's come a long way since then, but sometimes the rage and the grief still eat at him, like a cancer that's fooled him into thinking it's gone into remission only to flare up when he least expects it.

"You're healing," I whisper.

"You've been a big part of that, Kate."

"Thank you for saying that."

He grimaces. "I don't know if this makes sense, but there are times when I can't remember their faces or the sound of their voices. That scares me because there was so much good. I mean before . . . I don't want to lose that. I don't want them to disappear."

"They'll always be part of you."

16 *Linda Castillo*

"One of the hardest things to accept when some-one you love dies is that life goes on. It's like a river that never stops."

"Tomasetti." I set my hand against his jaw and turn his face toward mine. "They'd want you to be happy. You know that, don't you?"

He gives me a wry smile. "I think they'd approve of you, Kate."

The words warm me with unexpected force and for a moment I have to blink away tears. For the first year or so that we were involved, he kept that part of himself—that dark, killing grief—locked away inside a place I could never reach. I know it was wrong, but there were times when I felt as if I could never compete with the kind of love he had for them or heal the gaping wound left on his heart. Sometimes I felt like an interloper.

"I hope so," I whisper.

"I mean it." Never taking his eyes from my face, he brushes his lips across mine. "I know this hasn't been easy for you. I know *I* haven't been easy."

"I've never been one to walk away from a chal-lenge," I tell him. "Especially when I want something."

He smiles at me, then takes my hand and we start down the trail. We've walked about a quarter of a mile when I realize the path is now running paral-lel with the river. Another hundred yards and we're walking along the riverbank.

Tomasetti's stride falters. "What's that?"

I follow his gaze. Next to the trail, something yellow and red snags my attention. "Not sure."

We approach the object. Nestled within the tall yellow grass between the trail and the river is a small shrine of sorts. I see faded silk carnations and fern leaves tucked into a vase. A good-size stone has been set partially into the ground. The façade is etched with a simple inscription: *In loving memory of Angela Blaine.*

"Maybe this is where they found the clothes of that missing girl." Tomasetti looks out across the churning black water as if expecting to see her standing on the opposite bank.

"I wonder who put it here," I say, thinking aloud.

"Someone who cared about her." He tosses me a wry smile. "Or maybe Harley put this here to keep the legend of their ghost alive."

I elbow him. "Has anyone ever told you you're cynical?"

"Just about everyone."

It's a silly, charged exchange. But it's fun and we grin at each other like a couple of idiots. "What do you say we get back to the B and B and then grab some dinner?" he says after a moment.

"I think that's one of the best ideas you've had all day."

Half an hour later we're standing on the sidewalk in front of The Oak, which is erected inside a refurbished railroad car and wedged between an Irish pub and the Buckeye Lanes bowling alley.

"One-stop shopping," Tomasetti mutters as he opens the door for me. "Bowling, food, and booze."

"And not necessarily in that order."

The aromas of grilled steak, baked potatoes, and yeast bread greet me when I step inside. A short waitress with red hair and big round glasses converges on us with a smile and takes us to a booth. We sit facing each other, a candle flickering on the table between us.

"I'm Sandy," she says as she snaps down two menus. "You folks visiting from out of town?"

"Painters Mill," I tell her. "We're staying out at the Maple Creek Inn."

"Oh! You're them cops."

Tomasetti gives her a how-the-hell-did-you-know-that look. I smile because, a small-town native myself, I know how quickly news travels.

"We are," I tell her.

Tomasetti picks up the menu. "Cops on vacation."

"I hear you're interested in the Maple Inn ghost."

"Well, not exactly . . ."

The waitress continues as if she didn't hear me. "Angela Blaine's mama worked here for almost six years. In fact, Patsy was working here with me the day her girl went missing." She sighs wistfully. "She's been dead going on two years now. Lifestyle finally caught up with her, I guess. But she was my best friend and I can tell you she suffered a lot when little Angie disappeared. Everyone thought she was a bad mother. Granted, she had her problems." The waitress lowers her voice. "She liked pills, booze, and men, which is a bad combination if you ask me."

I sense Tomasetti holding his tongue; he's no fan of gossip, especially when the subject of said gossip isn't around to defend herself.

"I hear the prime rib is good," I say, hoping to ward off an unpleasant exchange—and any more talk about the missing woman.

"Best in town." Oblivious, the waitress pulls out an order pad. "Angie was a sweet kid. Pretty and smart, such a happy little thing. It's a damn shame what happened to her. Seems like yesterday that she was running around here, changing out the salt and pepper shakers for her mama." She clucks her tongue. "Everyone knows that son of a bitch Tucker Miles done it. And he got off scot-free. Just ain't right."

Tomasetti sets down his menu a little too hard and gives her a direct look. The waitress doesn't seem to notice.

I set my hand over his. "We'll have the prime rib," I say quickly.

"Awesome." She grins and scribbles on her pad. "You want horseradish with that?" Her grin widens. "Guaranteed to burn your lips off."

I hear Tomasetti mutter something beneath his breath and I say quickly, "On the side."

"Coming right up." Giving us a final grin, she rips the top sheet from her pad and hustles away.

The prime rib lives up to its reputation, and Sandy was right in that the horseradish is hot enough to burn off your lips. It's a good thing Tomasetti and I like it spicy. When we're finished, he leaves her a decent tip and we head toward the door. We're nearly there when I hear, "Hey, you cops!"

Turning, I see our waitress rushing toward us, a wad of what looks like newspapers in her hand. "Glad I caught you before you got outta here," she says breathlessly.

Tomasetti looks longingly at the door.

I look down at the papers in her hand. "What's that?"

"These are all the newspaper clippings from when Angela went missing," she says. "With you being cops and all . . . I thought you'd want to see them."

"We're not interested," Tomasetti says point-blank.

Undeterred, she focuses her attention on me. "A lot of people around here thought them Barney Fifes down at the sheriff's department didn't do a very good job of looking for her. They thought her mama was a piece of trash. Half of them damn cops had been in her bed and most of them paid for what they got. That don't mean that innocent girl was like her mama and it doesn't mean she don't deserve justice. Take my word for it, they wadn't nothing alike."

Feeling as if I'm somehow betraying Tomasetti, I take the papers.

"Hold on a sec." Sandy pulls the pen from behind her ear and scribbles something on her order pad. "I know you ain't interested, but if you change your mind, this is Tucker Miles's address. Piece of shit lives in that old trailer home on the edge of town. Drinks all day and don't work half the time." She rips off the sheet and shoves it at me. "If you go out there, I wouldn't turn my back on that ball-scratching son of a bitch. He'll stick a knife in it or else shoot you."

I take the sheet and tuck it into my pocket without looking at it. "We're probably not going to get involved."

She tightens her mouth. "Well, I'll feel better knowing I tried."

She turns to leave, but I stop her. "Who put that marker out there by the river?" I ask.

"I did," she tells me and walks away.

"Kate, we're not going to get into this murder thing." Tomasetti slams the door of the Tahoe and we sit there a moment looking at each other.

"I know," I tell him.

"We have two days here. I'd rather spend them in bed with you than tromping around some damn trailer with a psycho inside."

"I agree completely."

"Then stop looking at me that way."

"What way is that?"

"Like justice matters, goddamn it."

Frowning, he starts the engine. Neither of us speaks as he idles through the parking lot and turns onto the highway. In the opposite direction of the bed-and-breakfast.

"I thought we were going back?"

"Detour."

"Where to?"

Sighing, he tosses me a yeah-right look. "The Willow Run RV Park is right down the road. Since we're only a couple of miles away . . ."

I nod, trying not to smile. "So we're just going to talk to him, right?"

"And try not to get our asses shot off."

It only takes a few minutes for us to reach the mobile home park where Tucker Miles resides. The Willow Run RV Park is nestled in a treed area and partially obscured by a wooden privacy fence that's badly in need of repair. At first glance everything seems rustic and quaint, the kind of place where your grandparents might park their RV for the summer. The instant Tomasetti turns into the park, all semblance of charming grinds to an abrupt halt.

The first trailer is actually a camper set in the bed of a pickup truck that's jacked up on cinder blocks. I'm pretty sure the puddle beneath it is raw sewage. In the second lot, a blue and white trailer with a broken front window sits at a cockeyed angle. The condition of the homes disheartens me. The optimist inside me hopes this is a stop on the way to something better for the people living here. The part of me that is a realist—the part of me that has seen this scenario too many times to deny its existence—knows that for many, the buck stops here.

"Looks like ole Tuck is making all the right connections," Tomasetti mutters as he idles down the street. "What's that address?"

I glance down at the paper the waitress gave us back at the restaurant. "Robin Hood Lane. Lot fourteen."

"Here we go." He makes a quick right.

The curb at the second space we come to is marked with a faded LOT 14. An old van with a creased door sits in the narrow gravel drive. Tomasetti parks at the curb and shuts down the engine. "Home sweet home."

"Looks like he's there," I say.

Tomasetti eyes the trailer. It's a narrow rust bucket with a living room extension and a navy blue blanket covering the kitchen window. "You sure you want to do this?"

"We're just going to ask him a few questions, right?"

"You know those are famous last words, don't you?"

Casting him a grin, I get out and start toward the front door. I hear Tomasetti behind me as I take the steel stairs to the small landing. I wait for him to reach me before knocking.

A moment later the door swings open. I find myself looking at a thin man a few inches taller than me. He's got a receding hairline and gray hair that's pulled into a ponytail. He looks to be about sixty, but I suspect he's closer to fifty, his body and face ravaged by hard living. Pale blue eyes, the whites of which are shot with red capillaries skitter from me to Tomasetti and back to me.

"Can I help you?"

"I'm Kate Burkholder, the chief of police of Painters Mill over in Holmes County," I begin. "This is agent Tomasetti from BCI."

"I thought you guys looked like cops." He looks past me and sneers at Tomasetti. "What'd I do now?"

"We'd like to ask you some questions about Angela Blaine."

"What?" He cackles, the sound squeezing from his throat like a bubble through wet concrete. "Did you find her?"

I shake my head. "We're looking into her disappearance and we were wondering if you could answer a few questions."

"I don't know what I can say that I ain't already said a hundred times." His eyes narrow. "What are you? Some kind of cold-case squad?"

"Something like that," Tomasetti mutters.

"I understand you and Angela were in a relationship when she disappeared," I begin. "Is that true?"

"Yeah, man, we were together."

"Did you get along with her?" Tomasetti asks.

Miles frowns. "We had our ups and downs. Just like everyone else."

"When's the last time you saw her?" I ask.

"Day she went missing."

"Anything out of the ordinary happen that day?" Tomasetti asks.

Miles sneers at him. "No, man, it was just like any other morning. I was working first shift back then. She was still in bed when I left." He grimaces. "She was gone when I got home and I never saw her again."

"Where were you working?"

"I was a welder down to the Peabody Machine Shop in Canton. My old boss is still there if you want to check."

"Did Angela have a job at the time?" I ask.

"She was a waitress down to the Cracker Barrel off the highway. They closed up shop some ten years ago. Cops talked to everyone there."

For the span of several seconds the only sound comes from the ticking of the Tahoe's engine and the chatter of sparrows in the maple tree a few yards away.

"Do you have any idea what happened to her?" I ask.

His sigh is a tired sound that makes me wonder how many times he's answered that particular question and how many times he wasn't believed. "I don't know. I really don't."

"Any theories?" Tomasetti puts in.

Miles studies him as if trying to decide if it's a trick question. Tomasetti waits him out, retaining his best poker face, giving away nothing.

"She was pretty as hell," Miles tells us. "Friendly to everyone and kind of naïve. Bad combination, especially when the restaurant where she worked got plenty of highway traffic. I always thought some guy . . . you know." Another sigh. "I think that's the first time I been asked that particular question. Cops around here never much cared for my opinion."

"Any specific reason why you think something happened to her at the restaurant?" I ask. "Had someone bothered her there? Did she mention anything to you?"

He shakes his head. "I just know how people are."

"And how's that?" Tomasetti asks.

"Alls I'm saying is that there're some freaks out there, man. They see a pretty girl like that . . ." He lets the words trail as if the complete sentence is too troubling to speak aloud.

"Some people think you did it," Tomasetti tells him.

"I didn't," Miles snaps.

"You were a suspect," I point out.

"They were wrong. I loved her. I did."

"Is that why you beat the hell out of her?" Tomasetti asks amicably.

"That happened one time." Eyes flashing rage, he stabs his index finger at Tomasetti. "Just once! I was young and stupid and I wish to God it never happened."

"Were you jealous?" I ask.

Miles looks away. "I wanted her to quit her job

and she didn't want to. I didn't like the way all those scummy sons of bitches looked at her. Can't fault me for that."

"As long as you didn't take all that macho bullshit out on her." Tomasetti's voice is like steel.

"Is it possible she was seeing someone else?" I ask.

"She wadn't the two-timing type," he says. "Looking back, I just . . ." He lets his voice trail off.

"You just what?" I press.

"I guess I always wondered why a girl like her was wasting her time on a guy like me." He shrugs. "I was kind of a loser back then."

I hold his gaze, looking deeply into his eyes, seeking a trace of any of the things I was looking for when I knocked on the door. Lies. Sociopathic tendencies. My instincts usually serve me well when it comes to people, their agendas and the things they're capable of; I'm generally a pretty good judge of character. I'm surprised to find that while Tucker Miles isn't exactly an upstanding citizen or even a decent human being, I don't think he's lying about Angela Blaine.

"Thank you for your time, Mr. Miles," I say and we turn and walk away.

Back in the Tahoe, Tomasetti exits the trailer park and pulls onto the highway. "Not exactly a man-of-the-year candidate."

"I was ready to crucify him," I admit.

He slants me a wry smile. "Only you think he's telling the truth."

"Don't you?"

"I'm sure this will come as a shock to you, Kate, but I do."

I look out over a cornfield where yellow stalks shiver in the breeze. "So where does that leave us?"

"On vacation?"

I reach across the console to set my hand over his. He turns his hand palm up and squeezes mine. It's a small thing; the kind of simple gesture lovers have shared since the beginning of time. But for Tomasetti and me, there's nothing simple about it. It's huge, maybe because we're still finding our feet when it comes to the many facets of intimacy.

"I'm sorry," I tell him. "I know this isn't how you wanted to spend our weekend together."

"I guess that's one of the perils of falling for the chief of police."

"Or an investigator from BCI."

Glancing in the rearview mirror, he makes a quick left and pulls onto the shoulder of a little-used back road.

"What are you doing?" I ask.

"Something I can't do while I'm driving."

He puts the Tahoe in Park and turns to me. For an instant, we stare at each other. I see his nostrils flare and then he reaches for me. Cupping the back of my head, he pulls my mouth to his. The kiss isn't gentle this time, but I go with it, reveling in the sensation of his lips against mine. The essence of him surrounds me, and for the span of several seconds I'm lost in the moment.

He pulls away and sets both hands on the steering wheel. "I just wanted to toss that out, make a point."

"Duly noted."

We grin at each other.

"So what do you think?" he asks after a moment.

"I think you know how to kiss a woman silly."

"I mean about this cold case."

I laugh, then sober as I consider the question. "I think someone got away with murder."

"That's the thing about homicide." He puts the Tahoe in gear and pulls back onto the highway. "There's no statute of limitations."

The Portage County Sheriff's Department is located in a newish brick building adjacent to a small airport. With the exception of a couple of county vehicles, an old Volkswagen Jetta, and a sheriff's department SUV, the parking lot is nearly empty.

Tomasetti parks in the nearest visitor spot. "Looks like a slow afternoon for local law enforcement."

"Might bode well for us," I say.

We take the sidewalk to the double set of glass doors and go inside. A middle-aged woman with a head full of curly black hair slides open a Plexiglas window and greets us with a wide smile. "Hi, folks. How can I help you?"

We cross to the window and Tomasetti shows her his ID. "This is actually an unofficial visit," he tells

her. "We're looking into the disappearance of Angela
Blaine."

"Wow, that's a blast from the past. I haven't heard
that name in a while." She looks at me and arches a
brow as if to say 'and you?'

I show her my ID. "Agent Tomasetti and I worked
on some missing persons cases last summer over in
Stark County."

"That rings a bell. You talking about the Mast
case?"

I nod. "You heard about it?"

"Best story we've had around here since . . . well,
since Angela Blaine disappeared."

"We were wondering if we could take a look at the
case file," Tomasetti says.

"I can't give you the file, but you might still be in
luck. Jake Cornelius is with the detective division
and he's still here. Let me buzz him for you."

The detective doesn't make us wait. White haired
and barely over five feet in height, Jake Cornelius
looks more like somebody's grandfather than a detective. But despite his genteel appearance, he's got
a cop's eyes, direct and probing and just a little too
straightforward.

Introductions are made and we exchange hand-
shakes.

"Come on into my office and we'll have us a conversation about Angela."

We follow the detective to a decent-size office with
a single window that looks out over the parking lot.

He slides behind a desk adorned with a dozen or so photographs of children. He notices me admiring the photos and grins. "Grandkids. Twelve of them."

"You have a beautiful family."

"Thank you." He looks at Tomasetti. "Now that your partner here has got me properly buttered up, why don't you tell me what you want and I'll see if I can lend a hand."

We get a good chuckle out of that and then Tomasetti gets to the point of our visit. "We were wondering if we could take a look at the Angela Blaine file."

He takes the request in stride, as if it's not unusual for two out-of-town cops to ask to see a twenty-two-year-old file. "You folks just curious, or what?"

"We closed the Mast case last summer and thought we might take a look to see if we can help," Tomasetti tells him.

"Without stepping on anyone's jurisdictional toes," I add.

"I thought your names sounded familiar." He folds his hands atop the desk blotter and looks at us a little more closely. "Damn crazy case, wasn't it?"

"Nobody expected it to turn out the way it did," I tell him.

"Well, I hate to disappoint you, but the Blaine file is in archive at an off-site facility. I suspect you're not going to want to wait until Monday to take a look." He glances at his watch. "I'm happy to tell you whatever you want to know as long as it doesn't take more than ten minutes. Granddaughter has a piano recital in half an hour and I don't want to miss it."

Tomasetti scoots closer to the desk. "What's your take on the case?"

The detective grimaces. "I think that girl's long dead."

"What do you think happened to her?" I ask.

"I think that son of a bitch Tuck Miles did it." He studies me for a moment. "I couldn't prove it. Mainly because I could never poke any holes in that alibi of his. One of the most frustrating cases I've ever worked."

"Is it possible his boss lied?" I ask. "Covered for him?"

"It wasn't just his boss. It was the whole damn crew. Six men vouched for him."

"Could he have hired someone?" Tomasetti asks.

"I considered that, but I don't think so. Tuck was a real hothead when he was young. Couldn't keep a handle on that temper of his. If he killed her, it was a crime-of-passion kind of thing. Besides, he's always been kind of a lone wolf. No friends. Nobody trusted him enough to do something like that for him."

"If he was at work and six men vouched for him, why is it you think he did it?" I ask.

The detective's eyes slide from Tomasetti to me. "I always thought he slipped out when no one was looking and got back before anyone noticed. If you look at the logistics of it, the machine shop is twelve minutes from that bed-and-breakfast where her bloody clothes were found. I drove the route myself and timed it. I think Tuck left, drove to the bed-and-breakfast, lured her to the river, stabbed her to death, and returned to work before anyone noticed he was gone. At the end of his shift, he went back, picked up the body, and disposed of it."

"You guys check him for blood residue?" Tomasetti asks.

"He was clean." The detective shakes his head. "By the time those clothes were found, he could have showered twenty times over and tossed his clothes in the next county."

"What do you think he did with the body?" I ask.

Cornelius sighs. "The river was our focus for the first couple of days. We had dogs out there and even brought in a diver from Cleveland to check some of the deep pools. It had been a rainy spring and the water was high and swift." He pauses. "I think that's where we fucked up." Catching himself, he glances at me. "Sorry."

I smile. "How so?"

"Tuck didn't dump her in the river. I think he hid it somewhere nearby and while we were screwing around with divers and dogs, he picked up the body and buried it somewhere. That's why we never found her. Dumb shit outsmarted us."

I can tell by the way he says those words that the

case has haunted him all these years. That, as a cop, the disappearance of Angela Blaine might have been the biggest failure of his career.

"Miles was abusive to her?" I ask.

Cornelison nods. "We interviewed a lot of people. Every one of them said they believed he hit her a few times."

"Why did she stay with him?" The question comes from Tomasetti.

"I wish I could answer that." He shakes his head. "Angela Blaine was a pretty, smart girl with a lot of potential. I don't know why she stayed with him."

"Maybe she was afraid to leave him," I say.

"Maybe." The detective shrugs. "She was from a poor family. Single mom. They didn't have much. From what I hear, she didn't get much guidance from her mother. Maybe she thought Tuck was her ticket out."

As cops, all of us have seen those kinds of scenarios before. Even so, it doesn't make them any easier to accept.

"Did Angela have any close friends?" I ask. "Someone she might've confided in?"

"She had a lot of friends," the detective replies. "Everyone seemed to like her. We talked to all of them and, unfortunately, not a one could offer anything we didn't already know."

"Do you mind if we follow up with a couple of her friends?" I ask, ignoring the dark look from Tomasetti.

"Her best friend was Patty Lou Crosby. Name's

Lengacher now. Nice little gal who lives down on Sawmill Road with her husband and kids."

Most cops would have forgotten the names of witnesses involved with a case that's two decades old. That Cornelius remembers tells me this was no ordinary case and he carries the memory of it like a photo in his pocket.

The detective plucks a sticky pad from a small canister on his desk and scribbles an address. "Lengacher farm is the one with the big white silo just past the covered bridge. Not too far from the old railroad trestle."

We rise and the three of us shake hands again.

"Thank you for your time, Detective Cornelius," I say.

We leave him sitting at his desk, looking down at the leather blotter, a troubled look on his face.

By the time we're back on the road, dusk has fallen. The air is thick with humidity and filled with the promise of rain. Above the treetops to the west, black clouds spit spears of lightning at the ground.

I should be thinking about the evening ahead, spending the night wrapped in the arms of the man I love. Instead, I can't stop thinking about Angela Blaine and a mystery that's as tumultuous and dark as the storm bearing down on us.

"What do you say we pick up a bottle of wine and head back to the room?" Tomasetti says as he pulls onto the highway.

"That sounds suspiciously like an attempt at se-
duction." I smile at him. "I'm not complaining."

He gives me a sideways look. "Or maybe I'm trying to distract you from what you really want to do."

"You're not starting to think there's a downside to
getting involved with a cop, are you?"

"Not a chance." He shrugs. "Besides, you're not the
only cop getting sucked into this. Wouldn't take too
long to swing by the Lengacher place. Ask a few questions and we'll still have the entire evening ahead."

"Tomasetti?"

He looks away from his driving.

"Patty Lou Lengacher will still be there in the
morning," I tell him. "Let's call it a night."

We've just turned into the narrow gravel lane of the
bed-and-breakfast when the sky opens up.

Tomasetti stops a few yards from the front door.
"Go ahead," he tells me. "I'll grab everything and
meet you inside."

Pulling my jacket over my head, I slide out and
splash through the downpour. I reach the front door,
yank it open. I'm surprised to find the reception area
dark and silent. I glance at my watch to see it's only
seven-thirty P.M. Too early to close the front desk,
I think, and a ripple of unease moves through me.
I reach beneath my jacket and touch the .22 mini
Magnum I carry when I'm off duty. I may be on
vacation, but I've seen too much violence in the
course of my career to ever get caught unprepared.

"Mr. and Mrs. Hilty?" I call out.

I reach for the light switch and flip it up, but nothing happens. Shaking the rain from my jacket, I cross the reception area to the counter where we checked in. I stand there for a moment, listening, but it's difficult to hear because of the rain pounding against the roof. Outside, thunder rumbles like the growl of some prowling beast.

I call out again. "Hello? Is anyone there?"

To my right is a small sitting area. I can just make out a rocking chair silhouetted against the window. The outline of a lamp and a table. I start toward the double French doors, my boots seeming unduly loud against the hardwood planks.

The door behind me bursts open. Gasping, I spin. The silhouette of a man, shiny and wet, steps inside.

"You're not thinking about shooting me, are you?"

"Jesus, Tomasetti, you scared the crap out of me."

"Someone's a little jumpy tonight." I hear him flip the light switch. "Storm took out the electricity."

"I can see why you're a detective."

I hear him chuckle. "Kind of early to close up shop." He taps the flashlight against his hand and a dim light flickers on. "Even if they are Amish."

"Mennonite."

"That, too."

I glance at the dim yellow beam and shake my head. "Looks like your batteries are just about cooked."

"Just changed them."

A crack of thunder makes both of us jump and then we grin at each other, not sure if we're amused or embarrassed or both.

"Mr. Tomasetti? Chief Burkholder?"

We spin simultaneously at the sound of the voice. Harley thrusts a lantern at us, his eyes looking huge and owlish in the dim light. "Sorry about the electricity. I was just checking the fuse box off the back porch. Is everything okay?"

"Everything's fine," I hear myself say just a little too quickly.

"Did you replace the fuse?" Tomasetti asks.

"I did, but that's not the problem," Harley tells us. "Sometimes it's the transformer down the road."

"This happen often?"

"During storms. Electric company is usually pretty quick about getting us up and running."

"Harley?"

I turn to see Fannie coming down the hall, a small lantern in her hand. "Oh, hi, Kate." She nods at Tomasetti. "John. We didn't hear you come in." She goes to the counter, sets down the lantern and picks up a platter mounded with some type of pastry. "I baked some homemade apple turnovers earlier. Would you like to sit for a spell and chat? Or you're welcome to take a few back to your room if you'd rather retire. They're just about cool."

I smile at her. "Thanks, but we just had dinner."

Fannie nods. "In that case let me make some tea."

A few minutes later we're sitting at the dining

room table next to a blazing hearth. Outside the window, lightning flickers and rain lashes the glass. Beyond, the treetops sway in the gale. Fannie proceeds to pour tea into four cups.

"How was your dinner?" she asks.

"Prime rib was to die for," I reply.

"Good service, too," Harley adds. "You meet Sandy?"

The couple seems to lean just a little bit closer at the mention of our waitress.

Tomasetti eyes them suspiciously. "She gave us an earful about Angela Blaine."

"And Tucker Miles," I add.

Fannie glances down, folds her hands on the tabletop in front of her. "So what do you think?"

"About the case," Harley clarifies.

Tomasetti catches my eye, a ghost of a smile crossing his features. "We talked to Detective Cornelius."

Harley shoots his wife an I-told-you-so look. "Always liked Jake."

"We also talked to Tucker Miles," I add.

They look taken aback by the news, then Harley clears his throat. "You two don't mess around, do you?"

"Do you think he did it?" Fannie asks us, her eyes alight with curiosity.

I should be annoyed that they're trying to manipulate our interest in this cold case. But this couple is so sweet, so sincere in their motives, I'm not. "Look, Mr. and Mrs. Hilty, Tomasetti and I have worked a lot of cases. I know Tucker Miles isn't exactly what you'd call an upstanding citizen, but neither of us believes he murdered Angela."

"Detective Cornelius thinks he did it," Fannie says quietly.

"He could be right." Tomasetti shrugs. "Police work isn't an exact science. I just don't like Tucker as a suspect."

"Six men put him at the shop where he worked that night." I struggle to find the words that will explain the other, not-so-straightforward reasons why Tucker isn't at the top of our suspect list.

Tomasetti saves me the trouble. "After talking to him, I just don't feel he's smart enough to have pulled it off without getting caught."

"He's definitely not the sharpest knife in the drawer," Harley agrees.

The couple looks deflated, as if they'd been expecting us to cuff Tucker Miles and take him to the courthouse for an expeditious hanging.

"*Someone* killed that poor girl," Fannie says. "If it wasn't Tucker Miles, then who?"

No one knows how to answer that, and for the span of a full minute the only sound comes from the rain pelting the window and the growl of thunder in the distance.

"What can you tell us about Angela's friends?" I ask.

"From what I hear, she had lots of friends," Harley says, sipping his tea.

"She and her mama were poor," Fannie adds. "She didn't have all the nice clothes and things. No one cared because she was pretty, inside and out. Everyone seemed to like her, especially the boys."

"There were all kinds of rumors flying around about her back then," Harley says with a grimace. "You know how small towns are."

I'm the proverbial expert on small towns and gossip, but I don't mention it. I don't tell them that most of what they heard is probably bullshit.

"Tell us about the rumors," Tomasetti says.

"Nice as she was, Angela hung out with some wild girls," Harley begins.

"Do you remember their names?" I ask.

He shakes his head. "Just a bunch of party girls. Police questioned them after Angela went missing. No one knew anything."

"She liked to go to the bar," Fannie whispers. "Liked to dance. And she liked her whiskey." She lowers her voice so that we have to lean closer to hear the rest. "Not to speak ill of the dead, but I hear she liked her men, too."

A bitter aftertaste materializes at the base of my throat. I remember some of those same things being said about me, a mix of truths and fallacies that painted a not-so-flattering picture—and still rankle to this day.

"How do you two know all these things?" Tomasetti asks, truly baffled.

"Gossip mostly," Harley replies. "Some of it came

out after she went missing. People remembering things."

"Things that may or may not be true," I put in.

Harley looks away from us, but not before I see a shadow of guilt in his eyes. "Stories do have a way of taking on a life of their own the more they're told."

"That's true," Fannie admits. "We don't know these things to be true. No one who said them intended to be hurtful, including us. Everyone wanted to give the police all the information they needed to figure out what happened."

Thunder crashes loud enough to shake the windows, as if to remind us we're speaking of the dead and the things we're saying aren't kind.

"Were there any other males interested in Angela?" Tomasetti asks.

"Despite all the gossip, I never saw her with anyone besides Tucker Miles," Fannie answers.

"What about a best friend?" I ask. "A girlfriend. Was there someone she might have confided in?"

"She probably hung out most with the Crosby girl," Fannie says. "Angela and Patty Lou were friendly during high school."

"The police talked to her?" I ask.

"Lots of times," Harley replies.

"Detective Cornelius mentioned her," Tomasetti says.

"She's married with children now," Fannie volunteers. "Name is Lengacher."

I recognize the name as a common Amish name. "She's Amish?"

"Lord, no." Fannie huffs. "Husband was, but he left the fold years ago. Drives a truck for a bread company now. They live out on Sawmill Road down by that old railroad trestle."

Finishing the last of his tea, Tomasetti rises. I do the same and push back from the table. "Fannie, thank you for the tea," I tell her.

The Mennonite woman beams. "My pleasure."

Harley hands us his lantern. "Electricity might be out awhile. You're probably going to need this."

"There are candles and matches in the night table if you need them," Fannie adds.

Thanking them, Tomasetti and I take the stairs to our room.

"I think I'm glad I didn't grow up in a small town," Tomasetti says as he pushes open the door.

I laugh as I remove my jacket. "I suspect you would have given your contemporaries a lot of fuel for the fire."

"They were pretty tough on Angela Blaine." He sets the lantern on the night table and crosses to me. Putting his arms around my waist, he pulls me against him. "You know that in the eyes of a few we're going to burn in hell if we move in together."

It takes me a moment to digest that. "Are you asking me to move in with you, Tomasetti?"

"I'm thinking about it."

"You have a place in mind?"

"I'm working on it."

I look into his eyes, trying to discern if he's serious or teasing or somewhere in between, but I can't tell. "You'll give me a heads-up when you come up with something?"

"You'll be the first to know." He lowers his mouth to mine and for several minutes I'm lost in the sensation of him against me and the sweet promise of the night ahead. All of my reservations about becoming more deeply involved with him dissolve, replaced by the knowledge that we've created something precious and rare. Something to be nurtured and cherished, not feared or run away from.

I turn my head slightly and break the kiss. "Tomasetti, I want you to know . . . I'm glad we're here."

Lowering his mouth to mine, he walks me backward toward the bed. I collapse onto the quilt and he comes down on top of me. He pulls slightly back and looks down at me. "You make me happy, Kate," he whispers.

"Even when I'm being annoying?"

"Especially when you're being annoying." He kisses the tip of my nose. "I never thought I'd be happy again."

"I'm glad," I say. "You make me happy, too."

"I know it hasn't been easy," he tells me. "I mean, for either of us. It's not easy to put yourself out there when life has kicked you."

"I trust you," I whisper.

When he kisses me, the rest of the world ceases to exist. The storm fades and in the small span of time that follows, we're the only two people in the world and the only thing that matters is the moment between us and the night ahead.

The next morning dawns cold and rainy. Tomasetti and I had talked about packing a picnic lunch and hiking the trails along the river, but by the time we're showered and dressed, the rain is coming down in sheets.

"So much for a hike in the woods," Tomasetti says as we descend the stairs and enter the dining room.

At the table, he pulls my chair out for me and we help ourselves to a carafe of dark-roast coffee.

"Good morning!" Fannie enters from the kitchen with a tray of pastries, toast, and fruit. "I hope you two are hungry."

"Starved." Rubbing his hands together, Tomasetti scoots his chair closer to the table.

Fannie sets the tray in front of us. "Sorry about the weather. It's kind of unpredictable this time of year. Crazy weatherman is forecasting snow later!"

"I'm sure we'll find some way to fill our day." Tomasetti's voice is bone-dry as he helps himself to some blackberries.

I pour orange juice into a glass. "Fannie, where did you say Patty Lou Lengacher lives?"

"A couple miles down the road. Left on Sawmill Road. Their place is next to that old railroad trestle."

She pauses. "I hope Harley and I weren't too pushy with all this talk of Angela Blaine. It's just that with her disappearing here at our bed-and-breakfast, we feel a little . . . responsible."

Harley emerges from the reception area and walks up behind his wife and sets his hand on her shoulder. "Now, Fannie, we had no part in what happened to that poor girl. You just put all that guilt out of your head, you hear?"

"I know that." She reaches up and pats his hand. "It's just that . . . I never stopped wondering."

Across from me, I see Tomasetti frown.

For the first time I understand how profoundly the disappearance of Angela Blaine has affected them. I nudge Tomasetti beneath the table with my foot. "Maybe by the time we talk to Ms. Lengacher, the weather will improve and we'll have time to take that hike."

Fannie brings her hands together. "Well, I made quiche this morning. I'll put the leftovers in a picnic basket for you. There are some pretty places down by the river if you'd like to go down there for lunch."

Half an hour later, Tomasetti and I are back in the Tahoe. We reach Sawmill Road and he makes a right at the railroad trestle. From there, we take the gravel lane that dissects a cut cornfield. Outside, the rain has dwindled to drizzle, but the air is damp and cold.

A quarter mile in, he motions toward a white SUV parked near the house. "Looks like someone's home."

The lane curves left and then opens to a circular drive with the house on my right and a massive white barn to my left. A gooseneck horse trailer is parked adjacent to the barn. He stops next to the SUV and cuts the engine.

"You know this is probably a dead end," I tell him as I open the door.

"Since when did you become such an optimist?"

I get out of the Tahoe and slam the door. "At least we'll be able to finish this with the knowledge—"

My words are cut short when a massive Great Dane gallops toward me and slides to a stop at my feet. Tongue lolling, he looks up at me as if debating whether to jump on top of me or lick me to death.

I raise my hands to prevent a friendly mauling when I hear a lilting female voice. "Biscuit! You big lug. Quit that!"

I glance toward the barn to see a woman wearing a red barn coat and rubber muck boots tromping toward us. "Sorry about that," she says by way of greeting. "He's a little overzealous."

I pet the dog and my hand comes away wet. "He's cute."

"Wish he would have stopped growing fifty pounds ago." Grinning, the woman reaches us and puts her hands on her hips. "You folks lost?"

I guess her to be in her early forties. She's plump with a pretty face and a good highlight job on shoulder-length hair. I extend my hand. "I'm Kate

Burkholder, the chief of police over in Painters Mill."

Tomasetti introduces himself and they shake hands. "You Patty Lou Lengacher?" he asks.

Her expression goes from cheerful to wary, as if she's expecting something unpleasant. "Is everything okay?" she asks.

"Everything's fine," I reassure her.

"We're actually not here in an official capacity," Tomasetti clarifies.

"We're looking into the disappearance of Angela Blaine," I tell her.

"Oh." An almost imperceptible quiver goes through her body. Across from me, I sense Tomasetti watching her, and I feel my own antennae go on alert.

"We understand you were friends," he begins.

"We were friendly," she admits. "I mean, a lifetime ago. My gosh, I barely remember those days."

"We heard you were her best friend." I say the words quietly, holding her gaze.

"Barely knew her." Her eyes flick from Tomasetti to me. "I'm not trying to be rude, but I really need to get back to work."

Tomasetti isn't deterred. "Do you have any theories on what might have happened to her?"

"Everyone knows Tuck Miles did it." A note of hostility edges into her voice and she looks away to brush flecks of hay from her coat. "I don't know why you people can't just leave it alone, for God's sake."

"Ms. Lengacher, we just want to—"

The sound of a horse's shod hooves against gravel cuts my words short. Tomasetti and I turn to see a single-horse Amish milk wagon coming up the lane. It's the kind of rig dairy farmers use to deliver milk to local families. Unpasteurized milk more than likely, I think, which has been in the news lately due to an array of inflexible FDA regulations. Several Amish farms have been the target of raids. Farmers have had hefty fines levied against them.

"Well, Amos always did have a knack for bad timing." Shaking her head, Lengacher looks from Tomasetti to me, her expression resigned. "So what are you going to do? Arrest me for buying fresh milk for my kids now?"

"We don't care about the milk," I tell her.

"I heard that before." Turning away from us, muttering beneath her breath, she starts toward the buggy, the dog bounding at her heels.

Tomasetti shoots me a puzzled look. "What's the deal with the milk?"

I explain to him that it's against the law to sell unpasteurized milk and the FDA has deemed the Amish fair game.

"There's some bad PR for you," he says.

We stroll toward the wagon, keeping a respectful distance, and watch the Amish man carry an antique-looking milk can to the back porch and set it next to the door. When he returns to the wagon, Patty Lou Lengacher hands the man some bills. *"Danke,"* she says.

The Amish man glances at me and Tomasetti and then makes eye contact with Lengacher as he climbs into the buggy. "Tell them you're going to use the milk to make cheese," he tells her in Pennsylvania Dutch. "They can't fine you if you're going to use it for cheese making."

"We don't care about the milk," I call out to him in Pennsylvania Dutch. "That's not why we're here."

If the situation wasn't so serious, I might have laughed at the shock on their faces. The last thing they were expecting was for me to speak to them in their own dialect.

The Amish man backs up the horse and then starts down the lane. When he's out of sight, Lengacher approaches us. "Well, that got my attention." She tilts her head, giving me a close once-over. "How is it you know Pennsylvania Dutch?"

"I used to be Amish," I tell her.

Her eyes widen and she looks at me as if seeing me for the first time and in a completely different light. "My husband is former Amish," she tells me. "He left when we got married. I mean, with my being an *Englischer* and all . . . they put him under the *bann*. Even after all this time he still misses his family."

"I underst—"

"Mom!"

I glance toward the barn to see two teenage girls astride horses. One of the girls wears riding tights and boots. The second girl is wearing a black coat over an Amish dress, her sneakered feet in the stirrups of a western saddle.

"You girls get back in the barn!" A thread of alarm I don't understand laces Lengacher's voice. "I'll be there in a minute!"

"We're just going to ride down the road!" Ignoring the woman's command, the two girls walk their horses over to us, steel shoes crunching over gravel.

The animals' coats have been groomed to a high sheen. I can smell the coat conditioner and hoof polish from where I stand. Manes and tails are braided, the strands interspersed with colorful ribbon. I find myself smiling because as a young girl I spent many an afternoon primping our old buggy horse, much to my *datt*'s chagrin.

The English girl is a pretty blonde with blue eyes and chubby cheeks she hasn't yet grown out of. I look at the Amish girl and experience an unexpected flash of recognition. I feel as if I've met her at some point, but I know that's impossible. When I glance at Tomasetti, I'm surprised to see that same recognition on his face.

Lengacher thrusts her hand toward the lane as if to hurry the girls along. "Go ahead, but don't go far. I've got to take Ada home in twenty minutes. Now go on and watch for cars."

Laughing and talking, the girls nudge their mounts into a trot and head toward the road. We watch them disappear down the lane.

"Give a girl the opportunity to show off her horse, and she'll never disappoint you," I say.

Up until this point, Tomasetti has been silent, listening, watching intently. "Do you and your husband have many Amish friends?" he asks.

Lengacher looks at him as if he'd voiced a prying question that shouldn't have been asked, then shakes her head. Around us, the tempo of the rain increases; we're getting wet, but none of us seem to notice. All the while I feel something building in my chest. Some startling realization that changes everything I thought I knew about this case.

After a moment, Tomasetti shakes his head. "I'll be damned."

"That Amish girl—" I begin, but Lengacher cuts me off.

"I think you should leave," she snaps. "Both of you. Right now."

Neither of us moves. We don't look away. All we can do is stand there and try to absorb what none of us can deny.

"She's the spitting image of Angela Blaine," Tomasetti says after a moment.

Raising her hands, Lengacher backs away from us, an animal trapped and willing to fight to protect its young. "Please. Leave. Right now, or I'm going to call the police."

I finally find my voice. "After all this time, why did Angela let everyone believe—"

"Don't say it. Don't even think it." She shoves a

shaking finger at me. Tears fill her eyes, but they don't spill. "Just leave it alone," she says in a strangled voice.

Tomasetti never takes his eyes from Lengacher. "If Angela Blaine is alive, we need to know about it."

"You don't know what you're asking," she snaps.

"We know exactly what we're asking," he counters.

"I swore . . ." Lengacher's voice breaks. Anger, at herself—or at us—I can't tell, flashes in her eyes. "Tuck Miles is crazy and violent. If he finds out . . . My God, he'll go after the kids. I don't even want to think about what he'll do to—" She smothers the words by placing her hand over her mouth. "Ada looks more like her every day. I was afraid this would happen."

"Tuck won't find out," Tomasetti says firmly.

"For God's sake! One word and everyone in the county will know." She chokes out a sound that's part sob, part frustration. "She's going to hate me."

"You've protected her for twenty-two years," I tell her.

"It was supposed to be forever!" The woman wipes frantically at her eyes.

"Mrs. Lengacher," I say, "you can trust us."

"Why would I trust you?" She spits the words as if they're laced with poison.

"Because we care," I say firmly.

"Forgive me if I don't believe you." She says the words with bitter resignation, then puts her face in her hands and bursts into tears.

Before realizing I'm going to move, I step forward and set my hand on her shoulder. I wait until she looks at me before I speak. "Mrs. Lengacher, we understand that sometimes it's best to leave well enough alone."

"We're not going to tell anyone," Tomasetti says.

"Not even Angela," I tell her. "Your secret is safe. You have our word."

She blinks at me through her tears. "Why would you do that for me?"

"We're not doing it for you," Tomasetti says. "We're doing it for Angela."

By the time we roll into Cadiz, Ohio, half an hour later, the rain has transformed into snow. It's a pretty town with a quaint downtown area and a massive courthouse, made all the prettier by the big, fat flakes floating down from the sky.

"She faked her death to get away from Tucker Miles," I say.

"Wouldn't be the first time a woman went to extreme measures to escape an abusive relationship," Tomasetti replies.

Following the directions Lengacher gave us, he makes a left at the traffic light. A mile down the road, we pass a large hand-painted sign that reads: FRESH EGGS FOR SALE. "Here we go." He pulls into a long, narrow lane banked on both sides by a white rail fence.

It's a typical Amish farm. The front of the house

is shrouded by trees, firs and maples, the boughs of which are snow covered. We climb a hill and then the redbrick house looms into view.

Tomasetti parks in a gravel area between the house and a huge white barn where two buggies are parked just inside the sliding door. I get out and for a moment, I'm taken aback by the beauty of the place. The architecture of the old house and barn. The falling snow. The sight of a dozen cattle grazing in the pasture beyond.

The slamming of a screen door draws my attention. I glance toward the house to see an Amish woman step onto the porch and look our way. Behind her, two little girls stand at the door, peering out at us. Working a shawl over her shoulders, the woman starts toward us. "Are you here for eggs?" she calls out.

Tomasetti and I watch her approach. "Jesus," he says beneath his breath. "It's her."

I experience an odd moment of something akin to awe when I realize I'm looking at Angela Blaine. She's in her early forties now, and pretty in the way mature women are. She's got the same huge brown eyes, freckles on her nose, a full mouth that smiles easily. And a mole on the left side of her chin.

"I'm afraid we made a wrong turn," I tell her.

"Happens all the time out here," she says easily.

"Good place to get lost," Tomasetti says.

She hesitates an instant and then nods. "That it is. Where you folks trying to get to?"

"Back to the highway," he tells her.

She motions toward the lane from whence we came. "Just make a left at the end of the lane and go right on Abbottsville Road. Highway's four miles down. Can't miss it."

"Got it," he says.

"Mom?" comes a male voice. "Everything okay?"

I glance toward the barn to see a lanky young Amish man approach, an egg basket in his right hand, his gaze settling first on me and then on Tomasetti. He's wearing gray trousers and a black barn coat with a dark, flat-brimmed hat.

"Everything's fine," the woman says easily.

The young man is in his early twenties, and I can't take my eyes off him. Neither can Tomasetti. Maybe because he's the spitting image of a younger—and much less damaged—Tucker Miles.

No wonder Angela didn't want to be found.

As if realizing we're staring, the woman reaches out and gives the young man's arm a squeeze. "This is my oldest, Mark. Everyone calls him Bean."

The man ducks his head as if embarrassed by his mother's open affection, then raises the basket. "You folks need eggs?" he asks. "They're fresh and we got plenty."

I glance over at Tomasetti. "We could take a dozen back to the bed-and-breakfast."

"A dozen it is, then." He pulls out his wallet and looks at Angela Blaine. "How much do we owe you?"

"Three dollars ought to keep us in chicken scratch a few more days."

He hands her a five and tells her to keep the change.

"We got milk, too," the young man tells us. "It's fresh."

"We don't advertise," the woman says quickly, "since the government started citing the Amish."

"We don't need any milk." I offer a smile. "But your secret's safe with us."

The Amish woman tilts her head and gives me a closer look, her eyes narrowing slightly. "Is there anything else I can help you with?"

"I think we have everything we need now," Tomasetti replies and we start toward the Tahoe.

Tomasetti and I don't speak again until we're on the highway, heading back to the bed-and-breakfast. I break the silence with, "I wish there was some way we could let Harley and Fannie know Angela Blaine is alive and well."

He shrugs. "I think this is one of those times when the lost are better off staying lost."

"And Harley can continue to enjoy his ghost story."

"Case closed?" he asks.

I smile at him. "Definitely."

Glancing away from the road, he sets his hand over mine. "I guess that means you and I can get back to our vacation."

"Tomasetti, that's the best idea I've heard all day."

A HIDDEN SECRET

She thought she'd been prepared. What a fool she was, to think she could do this on her own. Stupid, stupid girl. If she hadn't been in such a dark place, she might have laughed at the magnitude of her own idiocy. At the moment, she didn't think she'd ever laugh again. Wasn't even sure she'd survive.

The pain was worse than anything she'd ever experienced in her life. Like a hand that had been thrust into her body, grasping at the very core of her, pulling and tearing until she was turned inside out. She screamed and panted and cursed. She writhed on her bed, crying uncontrollably, wet with sweat and twisting in the sheets. She'd sought relief on the floor, the hardwood cool against her face. She tried lying in a bathtub full of warm water, like she'd read in the books. Nothing helped. The pain only worsened as the night wore on. It became part of her, a vicious and unrelenting thing, beating her down, until she lay still, staring into the darkness, saving her breath for the next onslaught.

She'd never felt so alone. She'd never been so scared. Oh, how she wished he were here with her. Between the waves of pain, she talked to him. She cried for him; told him how much she loved him. How much she missed him. Then another surge engulfed her and she wished, not for the first time, that she was the one who'd died instead of him.

Twice, she almost called for an ambulance. Anything to end the suffering. Then she thought of her dad. How disappointed he'd be. She thought of her friends and how they would look at her if they knew. She thought of those who would never be her friend and she knew they'd turn this into something it wasn't. None of them would understand. She had to get through this. Alone.

An earthquake of agony tore through her. She bit down on the cloth between her teeth. She gave in to the urge to bear down. She pushed hard. Gave it her all. She just wanted it out of her body. She wanted this to be over. She wanted it gone so she could get on with her life.

Oh, God! Oh, God!

A final push. Animal intensity. Muscles quivering. Primal sounds squeezing from her throat. Sweating and grunting like a beast. The cruel fist clenching and tearing low in her belly. Her eyes fluttered. Her vision went dark. For an instant, she couldn't breathe. Couldn't hear but for the buzzing inside her head.

The pain shifted and eased. She sucked in a breath. Her senses returned. For an instant, she lay there, panting and exhausted, trying to absorb the magnitude of what she'd done.

After a moment, she sat up. A sob tore from her throat when she saw the bluish, bloody mass. A dark shock of hair matted with blood. Tiny hands and feet moving. Wrinkled red face. Little mouth mewling like a kitten.

She should have anticipated the blood. Warm and wet and slick on her skin. Bright red and shimmering against the floor. The sight of it terrified her anew. Not because it had come from her body, but because she didn't know how she would get it cleaned up before someone discovered her secret.

Panic nipped at her with sharp teeth. She'd read all the books; she knew what to do. Hands shaking, she grasped the scissors. Not thinking, not letting herself feel, she snipped.

More blood.

Another cry.

And the final tie was severed.

The bishop dreamed of repairing the fence. The one on the south side of the pasture that had been kicked last spring by that rambunctious bay colt, knocking the third rail off the post. His wife had been after him to fix it for weeks now. He'd never admit it, but it was getting harder and harder to keep up with all the chores around the farm these days. Kneeling, he set the bubble level atop the board, set the nail against the wood, and let the hammer fly with a satisfying whack!

Tap. Tap. Tap.

The old man startled awake. Disoriented, he sat up, listening, unsure what had roused him. A noise outside his window? One of the animals? He glanced over at his wife, sleeping soundly beside him, and sighed. It seemed the livestock always got into trouble at night. The horses. The milk cows. That little pygmy goat that had gotten separated from its mother last week. It didn't matter how secure the pasture or barn, they always found a way to escape. Might as well rise now and get a jump on the day's chores.

Tap. Tap. Tap.

The sound was faint, a barely discernible rap from downstairs. A neighbor stopping by to let him know that fat little goat had escaped its pen again? The little rascal was more trouble than he was worth. But the old man smiled as he swung his legs over the side of the bed. He was reaching for his clothes draped over the rocking chair when he heard the other sound. Not the goat, but the soft mewl of an abandoned kitten. Or a cat that had been injured, judging from the intensity of its cry. Whatever the case, it needed help.

He dressed in the darkness of the bedroom. Black

trousers. Blue work shirt. He pulled his suspenders over bony shoulders and then wriggled into his
black coat. On his way to the door, he plucked his flat-
brimmed hat from the hook on the wall.

The steps creaked beneath his stocking feet as he
made his way downstairs. The clock on the wall in
the living room told him it wasn't yet four-thirty. He
was thinking about a hot cup of coffee and helping himself to one of his wife's apple fritters as he
went into the kitchen and lit the lantern. He carried
it back through the living room to the front door. Setting the lantern on the table, he opened the door.
There was no one there. He looked down; surprise
quivered through him at the sight of the plastic laundry basket. A quilt inside. But who would leave an
injured animal on his doorstep?

Something moved within the quilt. The sound that
followed sent him back a step. Alarm fluttered deep
in his gut. He pressed his hand to his chest. He'd fa-
thered eleven children; he'd heard enough crying in
his lifetime to know this was no animal, but a child,
and a newborn at that.

Bending, he carefully peeled away a corner of
the quilt. Sure enough, the wrinkled red face of an
infant stared back at him. Tiny mouth open. Chin
quivering. Hands fluttering.

The old man's heart turned over. *"En bobli,"* he
whispered. A baby.

He figured he'd held a hundred or more babies

in the eighty-one years he'd been on earth. It had been awhile—even his grandchildren were older now—but holding one of God's children was something a man never forgot. Ignoring the arthritis in his knees, he knelt, plucked the child and quilt from the basket, and brought both to his chest.

"Vo du dich kumma funn?" he cooed in Pennsylvania Dutch. "Where did you come from?"

A rustle from the darkness beyond the porch startled him. Something moved on the other side of the lilac bushes that grew alongside the driveway. Cradling the baby, he stepped back and squinted into the shadows beyond the porch.

"Who goes there?" he called out.

He listened, thought he heard footsteps against gravel, faint and moving away. "Hello? Who's there?"

The only reply was the whisper of wind through the trees. Whoever had left this child on his doorstep was gone.

"Was der schinner du havva?" What've you got there?

He jolted at the sound of his wife's voice, turned to see her, still clad in her nightgown, a thick cardigan sweater draped over her shoulders, creeping down the stairs, a lantern in her hand.

Taking a final look outside, the bishop closed the door and started toward his wife. "I believe God has sent us a package from heaven."

She thrust the lantern toward him. Her step faltered; her eyes went wide when she spotted the baby.

"Oh Good Lord! *En bobli?*" She looked from the child to her husband. "Where did it come from?"

"The porch," he told her. "Wrapped in the *deppich,* inside a laundry basket."

Recovering from her shock, she set the lantern on the table against the wall. "Someone *left* it? But who would do such a thing?"

The bishop shook his head. "A mother who's lost her way."

His wife's eyes attached to the baby. "Oh, poor little thing." She held out her arms, and he slipped the child into them. Though they were old, they remembered how to handle a baby. He wondered how many times over the years they'd passed a crying infant back and forth as a young couple building their family.

"It's cute as a button," his wife purred. "Look at that little nose."

"Do you think it's *Amisch*?" the old man asked.

"The *deppich*"—the quilt—"is *Amisch*."

He looked toward the door. "I wonder how long it was out there in the cold."

His wife made a sound, as if the thought distressed her. "I bet it's hungry." She clucked her tongue. "I don't have a baby bottle in the house. But I do have some goat's milk in the refrigerator."

"Goat's milk?"

"Easier on the stomach," his wife told him. "I can use my finger and get a few drops in its belly."

Looking down at the child in her arms, she trilled.

"Witt du wennich eppes zu ess?" Want you a little something to eat?

The bishop stared at the tiny, wriggling infant and, despite the worry weighing him down, he smiled. "Don't fret, Little One," he said. "It's all part of God's plan."

He caught his wife's gaze. "The English police will want to know about this," he said.

"Es waarken maulvoll gat," she replied. There's nothing good about that. *"Ich bag nix dagege."* But I don't object.

He nodded. "So be it."

Cradling the child against her, his wife turned and started toward the kitchen.

A middle-of-the-night phone call is never a good thing when you're the chief of police, even in a small town like Painters Mill, Ohio. The *chirp* of my cell phone yanks me from a deep sleep. One eye open, I grapple for it on the table next to my bed. "Burkholder," my voice rasps.

"Chief, sorry to wake you."

It's my graveyard-shift dispatcher, Mona. She sounds worried.

"No problem." I push myself to a sitting position and shove the hair from my eyes. The clock on the nightstand tells me it's not yet five A.M. "What's up?"

"I just took a call from the Amish bishop," she tells me. "He says he found a baby on his doorstep about twenty minutes ago."

"A *baby*?" I'm out of bed and reaching for my bra draped over the chair, yanking a fresh uniform shirt from the closet.

"Yup. A newborn."

"Any sign of the mother?"

"Just the baby."

"Is it hurt? Or injured?"

"He didn't think so."

I consider that for a moment. "Call Holmes County Children's Services, will you? They've got an emergency number for after hours. Tell them to meet me out there ASAP. And let the ER folks at Pomerene Hospital know we're on our way."

"Got it."

"And call Bishop Troyer back. Tell him I'll be there in ten minutes."

"Sure thing, Chief."

I end the call, my dispatcher's words tumbling uneasily in my brain. *A newborn.*

"Kate?"

I look toward the bed to see John Tomasetti flip on the light. For an instant we squint at each other. "I caught the tail end of the conversation." He throws back the covers and steps into trousers. "What's up?"

I tell him about Mona's call.

"Abandoned?" he asks.

"Apparently." I feel the grimace overtake my face. "I've got to get out to the bishop's farm. If it's a newborn, it may need medical attention."

"You want some company?"

"You mean officially?"

"Or unofficially. Whatever works."

Usually, when dealing with the Amish, I prefer to do it alone. They're more likely to speak freely to me than to my counterparts, mainly because of my Amish roots and the simple fact that I'm fluent in Pennsylvania Dutch. But there's nothing usual about this call and I think it might be best to bring a partner along. Especially since John Tomasetti is an agent with the Ohio Bureau of Criminal Investigation.

I smile at him. "You think you'll manage to behave yourself?"

He snags a shirt from his closet and shrugs into it. "I'll do my best."

"That's a likely story." But I grab my equipment belt off the chair and buckle it at my hip. "Let's go."

Bishop David Troyer and his wife live on a farm just south of Painters Mill. I've known the bishop for as long as I can remember. When I was twelve, my *datt* caught me smoking a cigarette with a neighbor boy by the name of Brodie Mathis. It was a serious offense for an Amish girl, made worse by the fact that Brodie was five years my senior and an *Englischer,* to boot. It wasn't my first show of disobedience, and my *datt* delivered a robust "smacking" when he got me back to the house. The following Sunday after worship, he made it a point to put me before Bishop

Troyer, who proceeded to lecture me on the importance of obedience and the benefits of being a "good child." The bishop possesses a powerful presence and, in my twelve-year-old heart, he was the closest thing to God I'd ever encountered. It was a formative experience. After that day, my opinion of him hovered somewhere between terror and awe. It wasn't until I'd graduated into adulthood that I realized while he can be judgmental, his words sometimes harsh, he is also kind and generous and fair.

I take the long gravel lane of the Troyer farm with a little too much speed. Ahead, the windows of the old farmhouse glow yellow with lantern light.

"Any idea who might've left their baby here?" Tomasetti asks as I pull up beside a ramshackle shed.

"Since it was left with the bishop, I suspect she's Amish." I consider that as I put the Explorer into Park and kill the engine. "Then again, if an Amish woman or girl had an unplanned pregnancy and felt she couldn't handle a newborn, it seems like the most likely place to leave a baby would be with her parents."

"Unless there are problems at home."

I glance at him and nod. "Hopefully the bishop will be able to shed some light."

I grab my Maglite, and Tomasetti and I take the sidewalk to the back door. I've not even knocked yet when the door opens and I find myself staring at the bishop. Clad in black with a long, steel-wool beard, eyes as dark and penetrating as mica, he's still got that powerful presence that intimidated me so completely as a child.

"Katie." His usually stern face is a mask of worry this morning.

"Bishop." I look past him toward the kitchen. "Thank you for calling me."

"It seemed like the right thing to do." His eyes flick to Tomasetti.

Extending his hand for a shake, Tomasetti introduces himself, using his official title. "Is the baby healthy?" he asks.

"If that baby's cry is any indication, she's as healthy as a horse." Stepping back, the bishop ushers us inside. "This way."

The mudroom is dimly lit, too warm, and smells of coffee and frying scrapple, an Amish breakfast staple. The plank floor creaks beneath our shoes as we cross to the kitchen. I find the bishop's wife, Ada, standing at the sink, cradling a small, wriggling bundle against her generous bosom.

"*Guder mariye,* Ada." I bow my head slightly. Good morning.

She nods, but doesn't smile. "*Wie bischt du heit*, Katie?" How are you this morning? The elderly woman's eyes flick to Tomasetti and only then do I realize the discomfort on her face is due to the fact that she's wearing a plain flannel nightgown, with an oversize cardigan and well-worn socks.

I cross to her and look down at the bundle. Tomasetti holds his ground just inside the doorway. Ada opens a flap, exposing a tiny, wrinkled face and cloudy blue eyes. "She's a pretty little thing," the Amish woman tells me.

"A girl?" I ask.

The woman nods. "I checked. And brand-new, too. Cord is still attached."

I stare down at the small, alienlike creature and a combination of affection and uneasiness presses into me. I've not spent much time around babies. In fact, I'll be the first to admit I'm more than a little out of my element. Even so, there's nothing more heart-rending than to look into the eyes of such a tiny and vulnerable human being and know someone abandoned her.

"I'll just let you hold her while I get dressed."

Before I can object, the Amish woman places her gently in my arms. She must have sensed my hesitation—or maybe the instant of panic in my eyes—because she chuckles. "Keep her head in the crook of your arm to support it." Bending slightly— ignoring my discomfort—she coos at the baby. "Just like that."

Tugging the cardigan around her, she nods at Tomasetti and leaves the kitchen.

I'm staring down at the baby in my arms, relieved she's not crying. I'm already looking to hand her off to someone else. I'm aware of Tomasetti moving closer to get a look at her face.

"She doesn't look very old," he says.

For a second I wonder how he could know that, then I realize he was a father of two before we met. "How old?" I ask.

"If the cord is still attached"—he shrugs—"a few hours. ER doc should be able to narrow it down."

Bishop Troyer sidles up to me. "I'm very glad she stopped crying."

Alarm niggles me at the thought of holding a screaming baby, but I shove it aside. "Bishop, do you have any idea who might've left her with you?"

The three of us stare down at the baby. "I don't know," he says, looking baffled.

"Do you know of any expectant mothers who might've been confused or frightened about having a baby?" I prod. "Troubled marriages, maybe?"

"No, Katie," he tells me. "Nothing like that."

I nod, knowing that even in the Amish community, some secrets are tightly held.

"Bishop, can you take us through exactly what happened?" Tomasetti asks.

The old man relays the story from the moment he was awakened until he opened the door and discovered the laundry basket on the front porch. "I think there was a knock, but I can't be sure."

"Did you see or hear anything else?" I ask. "A car? Or a buggy?"

He nods. "When I stepped onto the porch, I heard something or *someone* on the other side of the lilac bushes. I called out, but they ran away."

I recall the tall bushes that grow alongside the lane. "Did you see anyone?"

He shakes his head. "It was too dark."

"Any idea how long the baby was on the porch?" Tomasetti asks.

"Not too long," the bishop replies. "Once I was awake, I got up right away and came downstairs."

Tomasetti nods down at the baby in my arms. "The quilt was with her?"

"Yes."

I look closely at the quilt. It's a pretty patchwork of rose and cream. "It's Amish," I tell him.

"A nine patch."

I glance up to see the bishop's wife approach, fully dressed and toting a second crib blanket. "To keep her from catching a chill."

"Ada, do you recognize the workmanship on this quilt?" I ask.

She examines the fabric. "Hmmm. I don't recognize the stitching. Or the pattern or color combination. And there are no initials. It's well made, though."

I turn my attention to the bishop. "Was there anything else with her?"

The Amish man picks up a wooden rattle off the table and hands it to me. "I believe this is *Amisch*, too. My uncle made several just like it for our children."

"Sometimes the women will crochet a little cover for the newborns," Ada adds. "Makes it softer for the tender gums since they like to put everything in their mouths."

The rattle is made of wood—maple or birch—and constructed with a four-inch-long smooth dowel with one-inch round caps on either end, and three rings around the center.

I turn my attention to the bishop. "We're going to need to take that."

Tomasetti reaches into an inside pocket of his jacket and removes a small evidence bag. He holds it open and the bishop drops the rattle inside. "Probably need the laundry basket, too," he says.

"Of course," the bishop says.

The infant in my arms begins to cry. I try jiggling her gently, but the movement feels awkward and unpracticed. The baby isn't appeased. Slowly, the cries transform to wails. I break a sweat beneath my jacket.

Everyone seems to take it in stride, but it rattles my nerves, and I realize everyone in the room has experienced this at some point in their lives. To me, this is as foreign as a trip to the moon.

I look helplessly at Tomasetti.

"You look like you could use some backup, Chief," he says in a low voice.

"The thought crossed my mind," I mutter.

"I'd take her off your hands, but I was going to grab the Maglite and take a look around outside."

I nod, hoping he doesn't notice the sweat beading on my forehead.

Finally, Ada takes pity on me. "I'll take her, Katie, if you need to do your police work."

"Thanks."

With the ease of a woman who's carried out the maneuver a thousand times, Ada sets both hands beneath the crying child and scoops her into her arms. "Come to *grossmudder*," she whispers. Grandmother.

Out of the corner of my eye I see Tomasetti go through the front door.

"Maybe she's hungry," the bishop offers.

Ada holds the child against her, rocking and humming softly. "I got a teaspoon or so of goat's milk down her earlier."

A knock sounds. Relief flits through me when I realize the social worker from Children's Services has arrived. The bishop leaves us to answer the door.

"Chief Burkholder?"

A young woman with curly red hair and a navy pantsuit walks into the living room in front of the bishop. "I'm Carly Travis with Children's Services."

She looks capable and professional in her chic suit and briefcase/purse slung over her shoulder. I introduce myself as I cross to her and we shake hands. "Thanks for getting here so quickly."

The social worker's face softens into a smile upon spotting the wriggling, crying bundle. "Oh, my." Her eyes meet the Amish woman's. "Can I have a peek?"

Smiling, Ada peels back a corner of the quilt. The

social worker actually giggles. "I think that's the cut-est newborn I've ever laid eyes on."

"They're not all pretty like this one." The Amish woman uses her pinky finger to tickle the little roll of fat beneath the infant's chin.

Leave it to a baby to bring the most unlikely people together, I think. "Carly, do you have a baby seat in your vehicle?"

"Never leave home without it."

I nod. "I thought we should get her checked out at the hospital first thing."

"Definitely." Carly makes eye contact with Ada and holds out her arms. "May I take her?"

"Oh, I kind of hate to see this one go." But the Amish woman relinquishes the baby.

Carly expertly takes the child into her arms. "Even when you haven't known them for long, it's always hard to let them go," she says softly. "Isn't it, pretty girl?"

"What will happen to her now?" the bishop asks.

"We'll take her to the hospital for a checkup," I tell him. "Once we make sure she's stable and healthy, she'll probably be placed in a foster home. In the meantime, I'm going to try to find her mother and father."

The old Amish couple exchange a look that betrays their concern. For the baby. Maybe for the mother, especially if she's Amish.

I nod at the social worker. "Tomasetti and I will follow you to the hospital."

Taking a final peek at the newborn, Carly flips the corner of the quilt over the baby's head. "Since we're getting a police escort, I'll get her buckled in."

I spend an hour in the emergency room of Pomerene Hospital in Millersburg with the abandoned newborn—now dubbed "Baby Doe." The social worker and I talk shop while the baby is thoroughly examined. A blood sample is taken from her little heel for DNA that will, hopefully, be matched with the mother's DNA when—or if—she's found.

Once the infant girl is deemed stable and given a clean bill of health, I leave her in the capable hands of the social worker and make my way to the OB department to speak with the RN on duty.

I find Louann Zeigler at the nurse's station, her fingers flying over the keyboard of a sleek laptop. I've met her a couple of times over the years in the course of my job. She's friendly, capable and, luckily for me, always seems to have a pretty good handle on the goings-on inside the hospital.

She looks up from her computer screen and smiles when I approach. "Hi, Chief Burkholder," she says. "How can I help you?"

I tell her about the abandoned newborn.

"I just heard," she says with a shake of her head. "Doctor Atherton—he's the head of pediatrics here at Pomerene—is looking at her now. He says you probably got her here just in time. Any longer and we might have been dealing with dehydration issues or even hypothermia."

"I'm wondering if you're aware of any expectant moms who were upset by their pregnancy or troubled or confused about having a baby," I begin.

"Not off the top of my head." Her brows knit. "Occasionally, we'll have a patient get upset when her pregnancy is confirmed. Usually, a case like that is a young woman who's not married or she's not ready for kids, and the pregnancy is unplanned. I've seen it happen to women in unhappy or abusive relationships, too."

She thinks about it for a moment and then shakes her head. "We're a relatively small department, Chief Burkholder. I come into contact with most of our maternity patients, and I can't think of a single woman who was in any way ambiguous or unhappy about her pending birth. Then again, women are good at keeping secrets when they feel they need to."

Disappointment ripples through me, but it's short-lived. I hadn't really expected her to relay much in the way of useful information. I'm pretty sure the woman who abandoned Baby Doe is Amish. While the hospital was the logical place to begin my search, I know this case isn't going to reveal its mysteries easily.

I drop Tomasetti at the farm. By the time I park in front of the Siess Kaffi baby shop on Main Street, it's nearly ten A.M. *Siess kaffi* is Pennsylvania Dutch for "sweet coffee." The term is born from the tradition in some Amish communities of a new mother serving coffee with sugar when she receives visitors after the birth of her baby. The shop is a tourist favorite and sells everything from crib quilts to bassinettes and just about everything in between.

On the passenger seat beside me the quilt in which Baby Doe was wrapped and the rattle found with her are sealed in evidence bags. Grabbing both items, I exit the Explorer and head inside.

The wind chimes hanging on the front door tinkle like tiny bells when I walk in. The aromas of vanilla and lavender greet me. A middle-aged Amish woman stands behind the counter manning an antique-looking cash register and chatting with a tourist who's just purchased an Amish-made stuffed lamb and a wooden sign that reads MY GREATEST BLESSING.

The shop is jam-packed with every kind of baby item a new mom or dad could possibly need, including old-fashioned baby bottles, handmade vintage toys and an entire wall of awe-inspiring crib quilts.

"Can I help you with something?"

I turn to see a second Amish woman standing a few feet behind me. She's wearing a gray dress with the requisite organdy *kapp* and wire-rimmed eyeglasses. I guess her to be about forty years old.

"Hi." I introduce myself and extend my hand.

"It's nice to meet you, Chief Burkholder." She looks at me over the tops of her glasses. "I'm Laura Schlabach. Welcome to Siess Kaffi."

"You have some lovely things."

"*Danki.* All made with *Amisch* hands, too," she tells me. "Hard to find that kind of workmanship these days."

"I'm investigating a case, Mrs. Schlabach, and I'm wondering if you might be able to identify a couple of baby items."

She's already peering down at the evidence bags in my hand, curious eyes prying. "I can try." Nodding, she turns and starts toward the counter. "Better light over here."

I follow her to the cash register, set the evidence bags atop the well-worn counter, and pull out the folded quilt. "Do you recognize the workmanship?" I ask.

She picks up the quilt and tilts her head back, gazing at it through her bifocals. "It's nicely made." She runs her fingers over the fabric. "Stitching is good and straight. And such pretty colors for a little one." She lowers the quilt and looks at me over the tops of her glasses. "I don't recognize the workmanship, though, and it didn't come from this shop."

"What about the fabric?"

The Amish woman shakes her head. "These pieces are old. See the fading there? The worn threads? The patchwork on this quilt comes from a lifetime of use."

Nodding, I tuck the quilt back into its plastic nest and pull out the rattle. "What about this?"

Laura takes the rattle, turns it over in her hands, looking at it carefully from all angles. "I've seen some like it over the years. The wood is nice and smooth. Probably *Amisch* made. The men are so good with the carving." She hands it back to me. "It didn't come from Siess Kaffi."

Disappointment presses into me as I slide the rattle back into the evidence bag. "I appreciate your time."

She offers a sage look. "Do you mind if I ask why you're so anxious to find out where those items came from?"

As the police chief of a small town where gossip can quickly grow into unwieldy half-truths or hurtful speculation, I'm careful how much information I pass along and to whom. But with this case—and since the cat is already out of the bag, so to speak— the community may be one of my best sources of information. "A newborn was abandoned early this morning," I tell her. "A little girl, just hours old. Someone left her on the bishop's front steps."

"Oh, Good Lord. A baby." The woman presses a hand to her chest. "Is the poor thing okay?"

"She's doing fine." I think of the tiny face that had stared back at me and, despite the situation, I find myself smiling. "We're calling her Baby Doe."

"Baby Doe." The woman looks at me over her glasses and smiles back at me. "Kind of catchy."

"Mrs. Schlabach, if you hear anything that might help me find the mother, will you let me know?"

"You think she's *Amisch*?"

"I don't know. Maybe."

"I can't imagine. The birth of a baby to an Amish family is always a happy occasion. Children are a gift from the Lord." She shakes her head. "I don't know what kind of woman would leave her own baby."

"A frightened one. A confused one." I shrug. "Someone who, perhaps, felt she couldn't care for a child at this point in her life."

"Well, I'll pray for the little one and her *mamm*," she tells me. "And I'll keep my ear to the grapevine."

Leaving her with my card, I gather the evidence bags and start toward the door.

Back in the Explorer, I call my first-shift dispatcher, Lois. "I need you to put out a press release on our newborn," I tell her.

"No luck finding the parents?" she asks.

"I think this is going to be one of those cases where the public might be able to help. Hopefully, someone knows something and will come forward."

"You think the mother is from this area, Chief?"

"I do. I think she's Amish or has some connection to the Amish. I just don't know what it is." I pause. "Don't put that in the press release."

She laughs. "Gotcha." We fall silent and then she adds, "You know, Chief, a pregnant belly isn't exactly an easy thing to hide."

I consider that for a moment. "But not impossible," I say. "Loose clothing. Minimal weight gain. A lack of suspicion by friends and family members. I suspect it happens more often than we think."

"I'll get the press release out immediately, Chief."

"Thanks."

The Care Cottage Birthing Center is located off the highway between Painters Mill and the Coshocton County line to the south. The facility is managed by several certified Amish midwives with a local ob-gyn on call. Local Amish women have been having babies here for as long as I can remember.

The birthing center is housed in a circa-1950s bungalow to which a drive-through portico has been constructed so buggies can pull up directly to the front door in inclement weather. There are two buggies in the parking lot, the horses still hitched, and a white van parked at the side. On the west side, there are two horse pens with a divided loafing shed and a big aluminum watering trough in case the father-to-be needs to spend the night. I park beneath the shade of a maple tree bursting with fall color and take the wide steps to the front door.

The interior of Care Cottage is homey and warm and welcoming. Instead of the medicinal odors I'd anticipated, the place smells of cinnamon and clean linens. The door opens to a large waiting area that looks more like an Amish living room. There's a blue sofa set against the wall and bracketed on either side by vintage end tables. A bay window with lace curtains looks out over a field where the corn has already been cut and bundled. A slightly battered coffee table is covered with magazines, inspirational books and *Es Nei Teshtament*, a Bible translated into Pennsylvania Dutch. Next to a recliner, a toy box full of wooden Amish-crafted toys—tops and a little dog on wheels that can be pulled with a string—invites fidgety youngsters to play while *mamm* is seeing the midwife.

An elderly Mennonite woman wearing a green print dress and small organdy head covering stands at the reception counter, her arthritis-bent fingers pecking at a computer keyboard. Her name tag tells me her name is Ruth and she's a volunteer.

"Hello," I say as I cross to the counter.

She glances up from her work and startles a little at the sight of my uniform. "Oh. Hello there." She chuckles. "Didn't expect to see a woman policeman."

I introduce myself. "I'm working on a case and was wondering if you could answer a few questions for me."

"I will if I can," she says. "Can't imagine what would bring a policeman to a birthing center, though."

I give her the rundown on Baby Doe and take her through the same series of questions I asked the RN at the hospital.

"I'm sure you know the majority of our clientele here at Care Cottage are Amish," she tells me. "We've had several *Englischer* women in the last few months; most were interested in a more natural birthing process. And of course we're more afford- able here than a typical hospital." Her mouth tight- ens and she gives a nod. "The birth of a baby is usually a happy occasion."

"What about a very young woman? Have you had any teenagers come in?" I ask. "Or perhaps an unmarried woman?"

"We had one unmarried Mennonite woman come down from Cleveland. That's been a couple of months ago, and to tell you the truth, she wasn't too concerned about not having a husband."

"Have any women come in for a prenatal checkup and not returned?" I prod. "Or do you know of any women who were in an unhappy or abusive relation- ship?"

"Oh, I sure do hate to think of that happening to a woman with a baby on the way." Her brows knit. "Chief Burkholder, I've been a volunteer here for eight years, and I don't recall anything like that."

I pull out my card. "If you think of something, will you give me a call?"

"I sure will." She sets the card next to her com- puter. "I hope you find what you're looking for, Chief Burkholder."

"Me, too," I tell her. "Me, too."

I swing by LaDonna's Diner for a BLT and a large coffee to go and take both to the police station. I'm sitting at my desk, paging through messages, when

Lois peeks her head in the door. "Sorry to disturb your lunch, Chief."

Swallowing coffee, I set down the sandwich. "It's okay. What's up?"

"Mrs. Stelinski is here to see you," Lois tells me. "She owns that fancy baby boutique down the street? Says it's important."

The name is vaguely familiar, but I don't recall ever meeting her and I've never been in the shop. "Send her in."

A moment later, a tall, delicately built woman decked out in Ralph Lauren and over-the-knee boots walks into my office. "Chief Burkholder?"

I stand. "What can I do for you?"

Offering a dazzling smile from lips the color of overripe plums, she strides to my desk, her perfectly manicured hand outstretched. "I'm Paige Stelinski. I own the Little Buckeye Baby Boutique just off of Main Street?"

The shop is a chic specialty store that caters to upscale clientele and sells every baby item known to mankind. It's a tourist magnet, one I'm sure has prompted many a new parent to lay down too much cash—and enjoy every minute of it.

"It's nice to meet you, Mrs. Stelinski—"

"Oh, call me Paige, please." I catch a whiff of Chanel No. 5 as she takes the chair adjacent to my desk. "I took one of my clerks to lunch this afternoon and she was telling me about that abandoned baby found

out at the Amish bishop's place? Well, I got to thinking and it reminded me of an odd incident that occurred at the shop a few weeks ago."

My interest piqued, I lean forward. "What kind of
incident?"

"Shoplifting." She tilts her head at me, her brows
raised nearly to her hairline. "Crazy, right? I mean
who steals baby things?"

"I don't recall my department taking a call for
shoplifting at your shop."

"That's because I didn't file a complaint. I came
this close." She raises her hand, indicating a small
space between her thumb and forefinger. "I mean,
stealing? Seriously? Ultimately, I chose not to
press charges against this young man. There was
just something about him. Earnest, you know? And
he was Amish. Clean-cut. He seemed truly embarrassed and, frankly, ashamed. Not just because he
got caught, mind you. But because he'd stooped to
the level of stealing. Like it went against his code of
honor or something. To top things off, he offered to
make it right by working off the cost of the items."
She laughs. "Just between us, by the time he finished
with me, I was putty in his hands."

I'm not holding out hope that this incident is
related in any way to Baby Doe, but I listen with
interest nonetheless. "What makes you think that
has something to do with the abandoned newborn?"

"That's what was so strange and pathetic about the whole thing. The items he took."

"What were they?"

"He had this cute little onesie. The yellow one with bears on it. And two pairs of newborn socks. A knit hat. Who steals stuff like that?"

"Did you get his name?"

"In a sad twist, Chief Burkholder, his name was Noah Fisher."

The words impact me like a sucker punch. Not too hard, but in just the right place. Six weeks ago, I worked a fatality farm accident in which a young Amish man driving a horse-drawn manure spreader fell and ended up under the wheels. He was killed instantly. It was one of the saddest and most disturbing accidents I'd ever worked. Noah Fisher was seventeen years old. An only child. And his parents were absolutely devastated.

Paige Stelinski is still talking. "Anyway, after I caught him and we talked, he spent the rest of the day cleaning the storage closet and the bathroom, too. I'm telling you, the place *gleamed* when he was finished. I let him have the items he wanted, and I threw in a pack of cute little bibs." She shakes her head. "I didn't give it much thought and just figured he had a little brother or sister on the way and his mom needed help. Just about broke my heart when I heard he was killed. Really nice boy and talented, too." She laughs. "A woodcarver, of all things. I ended up buying some toys from *him*." A wistful sigh escapes her. "I'm sure one day he would have been quite the businessman."

The mention of the wood carving garners my attention. "What kind of toys?"

"Kind of rustic, but interesting. I think there was a top. A little round teething toy. A couple of rattles. Even a toy box."

I pull the evidence bag containing the rattle from my desk drawer. "Do the rattles look like this one?"

Her mouth opens. "Exactly the same." Her eyes land on mine. "You think he's the—"

"I'd appreciate if you'd keep this between us for now," I cut in.

"I understand. Of course."

At the moment, she means it. But I've been around long enough to know it won't last. This is too juicy not to become gossip. At some point, she'll have a weak moment and spill her guts. The details of the story and the players involved will eventually get around. But if Noah Fisher was involved—if he's the father of Baby Doe—I want to let his parents know before they hear it from another source.

"I appreciate it," I tell her. "His parents have been put through the ringer."

"I can't imagine how devastated they must be. He was such a sweet kid." Rising, she smooths her hands over her midi skirt. "In any case, I don't know if any of what I've just told you is helpful, Chief Burkholder, but I thought it was my civic responsibility to let you know."

I stand and extend my hand for a shake. "I appreciate your coming in to talk to me, Ms. Stelinski. I'll let you know if anything pans out."

Willis and Miriam Fisher live off a dirt road a few miles east of Charm. The house and barn are plain, but picture pretty and well kept. A massive elm tree stands sentinel in the front yard. I park behind an Amish wagon loaded with hay, grab the evidence bags containing the rattle and quilt, and take the sidewalk to the front door. I knock and wait. Frustration presses into me when there's no answer. I'm in the process of leaving a note when I hear the *clip-clop* of shod hooves against hard-packed dirt. I turn to see a black buggy pull into the gravel lane.

Tucking the half-written note into my pocket, I leave the porch and meet them in the driveway. *"Guder nochmiddawks,"* I tell them. Good afternoon.

An Amish man with a shaggy red beard slides from the buggy. He's about fifty years of age, wearing a blue work shirt, dark trousers with suspenders, and a frayed black coat. His eyes are the color of a cornflower. As I draw closer, I sense those eyes had once been full of good humor and maybe a joke or two. Today, they're shadowed with the grief of a parent who's lost a child.

"Mr. Fisher?"

"That's me," he says.

I identify myself and offer my hand for a shake. He

gives it two firm pumps, eyeing me, and I realize he's just figured out I was one of the police officers here the day his son was killed.

The woman who'd been sitting beside him comes around the front of the horse and approaches. I nod and offer a smile. "You must be Mrs. Fisher?"

She smiles back. But I can tell it's a habit born of politeness. A sense of sorrow hangs in the air like a pall.

"Please call me Miriam," the woman says.

"What can we do for you, Chief Burkholder?" Willis Fisher asks.

"I'm working on a case," I begin. "Would you mind answering a few questions? It's about your son."

The Amish man's eyes narrow. "What kind of questions could you possibly have about a dead boy? Did he do something wrong?"

His wife reaches out and pats his arm. "Willis."

"I'm sorry," I tell them. "I know it must be difficult for you."

"We miss him every day," Miriam tells me. "His voice. His smile. The way he used to slam the screen door in the kitchen."

"We find comfort knowing Noah is with the Lord," her husband says. But the Amish man looks anything but comforted.

I hold up the evidence bag containing the rattle. "Do either of you recognize this?"

Willis's eyes flick to the rattle. His mouth opens slightly. A quiver runs the length of his body.

"Oh, my." Miriam looks from the rattle to me. "May I?"

I hand her the bag. Removing a pair of spectacles from her apron pocket, she slides them onto her nose. "Noah made this." She runs her fingers over the smooth wood. "I'm sure of it. He was a fine carver. He could make anything he set his mind to. Where did this come from?"

I don't want to answer that yet, so I hold up the bag containing the quilt. "What about this?"

"That's . . ." She takes the bag from me, handles it with reverence. "I made this quilt. Right before Noah was born. My goodness, I thought I'd misplaced it." She raises her gaze to mine. "Where on earth did you find it?"

I go to my next question. "Mr. and Mrs. Fisher, do you know if your son was seeing anyone? Did he have a girlfriend? Or someone he was courting?"

"A girlfriend?" Willis spits the words at me. "Why do you want to know something like that?"

Making a sound of discomfort, his wife sets her hand on his arm. "Now, Willis . . ."

"I understand it's a personal question," I tell him, "but it may be related to a case—"

"I'm going to unhitch the horse," the Amish man says abruptly. "I don't wish to speak of my son or disrespect his memory with questions about girls." Shaking his head, he grasps the reins and leads the horse toward the barn.

Miriam and I watch him walk away. When he's out of earshot, she lowers her voice and says, "Would you like a cup of coffee, Chief Burkholder?"

I can tell by the way she's looking at me that she's offering more than coffee. Something she'd prefer her husband not hear. "I'd like that very much," I reply.

A few minutes later, I'm seated at the big rustic table in her kitchen. Miriam fusses with an old-fashioned percolator, then sets a platter mounded with oatmeal cookies on the table while the coffee perks. Within minutes the aroma of fresh-brewed coffee fills the air. She places a steaming mug in front of me. I sip, find it strong and good.

"I know it must be difficult talking about your son so soon after his death," I begin.

"Some days I still can't believe he's gone. He was such a force and so full of life." She bows her head slightly. "To tell you the truth, I could talk about Noah all day. And I do, sometimes, to any-one who will listen." Her lips twist into a sad replica of a smile. "Willis took his death hard. Won't speak of it. Spends all his time in the barn, working." She chuckles. "I think we have the cleanest horse stalls in all of Holmes County."

We reach for cookies at the same time and smile at each other. I like this woman, I realize. She's kind and maternal and it's hard to look into her eyes and see so much pain.

"Noah was our only child," she tells me. "I had some problems with his birth and I was never able to carry to term again. Lost four little souls in the years that followed."

"I'm sorry."

"It was God's will."

I nudge her back to my question. "Mrs. Fisher, do you know if Noah was seeing someone?"

"I'm pretty sure he was courting a girl. There were a few times when he didn't come home. He was on *rumspringa,* you know, so we tried not to pry. Willis thought he was out drinking and raising cane with his friends." She looks at me from beneath her lashes. "But I knew. I knew because Willis acted the same way while he was courting me. Like he had a hundred dollars in his pocket and the world at his feet."

"Do you know her name?"

"I asked Noah about it once or twice." Another sad smile. "But he wouldn't speak of her."

"Any idea why he didn't want to say?"

She lifts her shoulders, lets them drop. "I don't know. For whatever reason, he wasn't ready, I suppose."

I struggle to find the right words to ask her about the possibility of a pregnancy. "I thought it was interesting that he carved a baby rattle. Do you have any idea why he would make something for a baby?"

"At first I thought it was for the money. I thought

maybe he was selling things to the shops in town." Her expression turns sage, and she sets down her mug. "Let me show you something."

We leave the kitchen. I follow her through the living room and up the stairs to the second level. Down a darkened hall toward a bedroom at the end. She pushes open the door and we walk inside. Like many Amish homes, there's no closet. Clothing and hats are hung on hooks or dowels set into the wall. Boots are left in the mudroom downstairs.

"This was Noah's room," she tells me.

I notice a hand-carved wooden yo-yo on the table next to the bed. The handmade wooden rocker in the corner. Above the steel frame headboard, a wood wall-hanging depicts the faceless images of an Amish boy and girl. "He made some beautiful things," I tell her.

Miriam goes directly to a wooden trunk at the foot of the twin-size bed and opens the lid. Something inside me quickens at the sight of the items inside. We kneel. With a certain reverence, she picks up a newborn's onesie. A wooden teething ring. A rattle much like the one in my evidence bag. A double pack of baby bottles. I recognize the bibs from the Little Buckeye Baby Boutique in town.

When I glance over at Miriam, tears are streaming down her cheeks. "I don't know why he had these things," she whispers.

"It's almost as if he was saving them for something," I say gently. "Or someone."

"In all the years Willis and I have been married, I've never lied to him. I've never kept anything from him. But I didn't tell him about this."

"Mrs. Fisher, did you hear about the newborn baby found on Bishop Troyer's front porch?" I ask gently.

"I heard." She lowers her gaze. "And I've been praying ever since."

For the first time I understand why she didn't want her husband to overhear our conversation. "I'm trying to find the mother," I say softly.

We stare at each other, a silent communication passing between us. A silent voice telling us now is not the time for certain words.

"Goodness." Forcing a laugh, the Amish woman brushes at the tears with both hands. "Would you look at me?"

"Miriam, is it all right with you if I take a look around Noah's room?" I ask gently.

Her gaze slides to the window. "I suspect Willis will be in the barn for a while. . . ."

"I promise not to leave anything out of place."

Giving me a decisive nod, she gets to her feet. "I'll fetch our coffee."

I begin my search with the trousers hanging on the dowel next to the window, but the pockets are empty. I check the windowsill, behind the curtains, but it's bare. I look beneath the cushion on the rocking chair in the corner. Next, I go to the neatly made bed. I peel back the vintage quilt and look beneath the pillow. I squeeze the stuffing, but there's nothing inside, either. I look under the bed and randomly check for loose floorboards. There's nothing there. Nothing tucked between the box springs and the frame. Finally, I slide my hands beneath the mattress. My fingertips brush something hard. At first I think it's a board someone added to shore up the frame for support. But the object is small and plastic. I know it's a cell phone even before I pull it out.

"What on earth is that?"

I look up to see Miriam standing at the door, a mug in each hand. "I found a cell phone," I tell her. "Under the mattress."

"Oh, my." She bites her lip. "I didn't know he had one."

It's an old-fashioned flip phone. The kind you can buy at any discount department or electronics store. "Any idea where it came from?" I ask.

She shakes her head. "Too many Amish youngsters are using the phones these days."

"Do you mind if I take it back to the station with me?" I ask. "I'd like to find out who he talked to."

"I have no use for a phone. But since it belonged to Noah, I'd appreciate it if you brought it back."

"Of course I will," I assure her.

Back at the police station, I take the phone directly to my office and flip it open. The first thing I notice is that while it has the capability to send and receive texts, Noah Fisher didn't utilize either. I page through the recent calls, sent and received, and I immediately notice nearly all the calls were to or from a local number, right here in Painters Mill.

Bingo.

If Noah Fisher were still alive and suspected of committing a crime, I'd have to secure a search warrant before looking through his cell phone to collect information. Since Noah is deceased and I received express permission from his mother, I'm free to use whatever information I find.

Picking up my desk phone, I dial the number in question. A girl's voice picks up on the third ring. "Hello?"

Young, I think. Teenager. Possibly pre-teen. "Hi," I begin. "I'm trying to figure out if I dialed the correct number." I recite the number back to her. "Who's this?"

"Chloe," she replies uncertainly. "Who are you trying to reach?"

"What's your last name, Chloe?"

She makes a sound of annoyance. "Why are you asking me that? How did you get that phone?"

"Chloe, this is Kate Burkholder, the chief of Police in Painters Mill. Is your mom or dad there? I'd like to speak with them."

A quick intake of breath and then the line goes dead. Either she didn't believe me when I identified myself, or she knew exactly why I was calling and panicked. I'm betting on the latter.

My interest piqued, I enlist the help of a reverse number lookup database and enter the number. Four dollars and ninety-nine cents later, I have a name and an address: Damon Atherton.

I've never met Chloe but her father, Damon Atherton, is a respected pediatrician at Pomerene Hospital. I've never met him, but I've heard the name. More recently, I recall one of the nurses mentioning him the morning I brought in Baby Doe.

I spend a few minutes digging up everything I can find on Chloe Atherton. She just turned sixteen years old. She's had her driver's license for two months. No citations. No arrests. She's on the Painters Mill High School track team and holds the record for the mile run. According to a recent newspaper story highlighting outstanding high school students, she's an honor roll student with a 4.0 GPA—and aspirations for med school. Just three months ago she was awarded the People Helping People Award for her volunteer work at the local retirement home.

Is it possible this girl—Chloe—is Baby Doe's mother? Did this young overachiever become pregnant, somehow hide the pregnancy for nine months, and give birth without anyone knowing? The scenario doesn't seem plausible. Especially with her father being a physician. But experience tells me it's not only possible, but it happens more often than most people realize.

Committing the Atherton address to memory, I grab my keys and head for the door.

In 2001, Ohio enacted a Safe Haven law, which basically allows any parent who feels they are unable to care for a newborn to leave the child with a peace officer or medical worker without legal ramifications. The law was adopted to keep mothers from leaving their newborn babies in places that might endanger the child.

I don't know if Chloe Atherton is the person I'm looking for. If she is, I need to be prepared. While Baby Doe was found healthy and unharmed, the infant was not left with a peace officer or medical worker. Still, Bishop Troyer claimed someone was there the morning he discovered her on his front porch. I suspect Chloe stayed to ensure that her baby was taken in immediately. That means something; it tells me she was responsible enough—that she cared enough—to make certain the vulnerable newborn was not left alone.

Chloe probably wasn't aware of the law's details. She may have simply left the child at the only safe place she could think of; the only place where she believed she could remain anonymous: the Amish bishop. It doesn't negate the fact that she didn't follow the law, but I know the county attorney will take all of the circumstances into consideration when—or if—charges are filed.

The Athertons live in the upscale Maple Crest subdivision. It's nearly six P.M. by the time I pull into the driveway and park behind a silver Land Rover. The house is a massive Tudor with a four-car garage, landscaping befitting a European castle, and an extravagant entrance covered with ivy. I take the curved flagstone path to the front porch and make use of the brass knocker.

I hear voices on the other side of the door. A girl calling out to someone. Laughter. The door swings open and I find myself looking at a tall, slender teenage girl with huge brown eyes, her dark hair cut into a messy bob. She's wearing loose-fitting sweat pants and an oversize Painters Mill Panthers sweatshirt Bare feet. Toenails painted blue.

"Chloe Atherton?" I say.

She steps back as if expecting me to reach in, grab her, and drag her away. Her mouth opens, a sound of distress escaping between perfect white teeth. Her eyes widen as she takes in my uniform. She looks over her shoulder. Her fingers twitch on the doorknob, and I know she's thinking about slamming it in my face.

"There's no one here by that name," she says quietly.

"Don't be afraid," I tell her. "Everything's going to be okay."

"You have the wrong house." She starts to close the door.

I put my hand out and stop her. "No, I don't."

"What do you want?"

"I just want to talk. That's all."

She glances over her shoulder again, and I realize her most pressing concern is her father. "Just go away," she whispers. "Please."

"Honey?" comes a male voice from somewhere inside the house. "Hey, the sweet potato fries are burning."

I look past her to see Dr. Damon Atherton approach. He's still in his work clothes. Custom trousers. Lavender pinstripe button-down shirt. Tie askew. Sleeves rolled up to his elbows. Big Rolex strapped to his wrist. He's probably just arrived home from the hospital after a busy day.

He looks perplexed by my presence. Slightly annoyed that dinnertime with his daughter has been interrupted. "Can I help you?"

I show him my badge and identify myself.

His gaze switches from me to his daughter and then back to me. "Is everything all right?"

"Everything is fine, sir," I tell him. "If you have a minute, I'd like to talk to you."

He blinks at me, surprised, but invites me inside. "Of course. Come in."

I enter a tiled foyer with an impossibly high ceiling and gleaming walnut floors. Overhead, a crystal chandelier dangles like a giant diamond earring. To my right, a console table holds a massive vase. I can smell the fresh-cut flowers from where I stand.

"You'll have to excuse the boxes," he tells me.

For the first time I notice several corrugated boxes stacked against the wall ahead. "You're moving?" I ask.

"I just accepted a chief-of-pediatrics position in Phoenix."

"Big change."

He grins. "Nicer weather."

I smile at his daughter. "Are you excited or bummed?"

She attempts to smile, but doesn't quite manage. "I'm ready."

"She's a trouper," he says affectionately.

"When's the big move?" I ask.

"Two days and counting." Smiling, he puts his arm around his daughter's shoulder and hugs her against him. "We can't wait."

Silence falls, a thin ribbon of tension slicing through it. "We were just making dinner," Atherton says. "I've got grilled chicken breast and some burned sweet potato fries." He smiles, but I can tell he's perplexed by my presence and growing concerned. "Still trying to get the hang of cooking, since it's just the two of us now."

"You're divorced?" I ask.

A shadow passes over his features. "My wife, Jane, passed away last year."

I wince. "I'm sorry," I tell him.

"We're doing okay now." He hugs his daughter again. "Aren't we, honey?"

The girl tries to match his smile, but fails, and ends up looking at the floor. "Yeah."

"I won't keep you," I tell him. "I know you were involved with Baby Doe at the hospital and I was in the neighborhood so I thought I'd stop in and update you on my progress finding the baby's mother."

"Ah. Of course." But I can tell he isn't sure why an update warrants a personal visit from the chief of police as opposed to a phone call or email. "We can sit in the living room if you'd like, Chief Burkholder." He looks at his daughter. "Honey, you want to bring the three of us some of that coffee I just made?"

The girl has barely taken her eyes off me since I walked in. "Sure, Dad." Reluctance rings clear in her voice, telling me the last thing she wants to do is leave me alone with her father.

"None for me, thank you," I say quickly.

He ushers me to a spacious living room where a fire crackles in a stone hearth. "I take it you've found the mother?" he asks.

"Not yet, but I'm working on a few leads," I say vaguely.

"I heard she's Amish. Is that true?"

"I thought so at first, but now I'm not so sure."

Chloe returns with coffee. She hands one of the mugs to her father and sets the other on the coffee table in front of me. I don't know if her father notices, but her hands are shaking.

"The social worker seemed confident that she'd be able to find a foster family in the next couple of days," I tell him. "She's looking for a couple or a family to permanently adopt her."

"It sounds like a happy ending for everyone."

I acknowledge the statement with a nod. "We're still hoping Baby Doe's mother will come forward."

He shakes his head. "I suppose these young mothers just don't know about the Safe Haven law."

I look at Chloe, including her in the conversation. "That's the law that was enacted to protect new mothers from prosecution, if they're unable to care for their baby and drop it off in a safe place."

"It protects both the mother and the baby." Atherton's brows go together. "Since this particular mother didn't relinquish her baby to a doctor or police officer, she could be in trouble. Will she be charged?"

I hadn't wanted the conversation to go in that direction; the last thing I want to do is frighten Chloe. "That'll be up to the county attorney, but I don't think so. I suspect this girl is young. Maybe even a minor. I think she may have recently suffered a devastating, personal loss and felt she couldn't deal with a new baby all alone." I look at Chloe. "Bottom line is, she did the right thing. She took her baby to a safe place. I think she even waited and made sure someone took in the baby. As chief, I'll do everything in my power to help her."

Chloe looks away, but I tilt my head, catch her gaze, and maintain eye contact. Her face is flushed, her forehead shiny with perspiration. "I know it sounds odd, considering the circumstances, but I think we're dealing with a courageous young woman. I think she cared for the well-being of her child, but needed some time to pull herself together and put all of this into perspective. I believe she's going to do the right thing and come forward."

"I hope so," says the doctor.

I didn't expect Chloe to admit to anything tonight. But if she is Baby Doe's mother—and I suspect she is—I wanted her to know that while the situation is serious, the repercussions may not be as dire as she'd anticipated.

Rising, I extend my hand to Dr. Atherton. "Thank you for your time."

"Thanks for the update, Chief Burkholder."

I smile at Chloe and offer my hand. "Good luck in Phoenix."

"Thanks," she mutters.

But her hand is cold and limp within mine.

After a long day, I'm looking forward to spending some quality time with Tomasetti at the farm, but thoughts of Baby Doe have been tugging at my brain all day; a little hand reaching out and touching me with tiny, soft fingertips. I know she's being well cared for at the hospital. Still, the thought of her being brought into the world, unwanted and abandoned, plucks at my heartstrings. Since the hospital is on my way home, I opt to make a quick stop to see how she's doing.

It's fully dark when I park adjacent to the ER entrance and make my way to the nursery. The ward is brightly lit, cheery, and bustling with activity. I see new mothers and fathers in homey birthing rooms as I pass. The mewling cries of newborns as they're taken to and from the nursery.

I'm on my way to the nurse's station when I spot the RN who was on duty when I brought in Baby Doe. She spots me and smiles. "I knew you wouldn't be able to stay away."

I smile back. "I thought I'd stop in to see how she's doing."

"I was just heading that way for a peek if you'd like to walk with me." Her practical shoes squeak against the floor as we walk to the nursery. "She's got a lot of fans here at the hospital."

"The police station, too."

"I hear the chief is particularly fond." Another hearty grin. "To tell you the truth, we're having a tough time keeping our hands off her. There's just something about her." She lowers her voice to a conspiratorial whisper. "Just between us, I think she's the cutest baby on the floor."

We're chuckling as we make our way to the viewing window. Inside, a dozen clear plastic bassinettes are arranged in three rows. There are six newborns; three girls tightly swathed and wearing pink knit hats and three boys, their little heads snugged in blue hats. Each infant has a name tag and a number affixed to their bassinette. Baby Doe is nearest the viewing window, a pale little face nestled in a yellow blanket. I get a twinge in my chest when I see that she's the only baby without a name, just a number.

"It's usually a little more crowded in there, but most of our babies are with mom at the moment," she tells me. "We encourage all our new moms to keep their newborns in their rooms while they're here, and send the babies to the nursery only when they want to sleep or take a shower."

For several minutes we stand outside the glass, watching the babies. Some are sleeping. Others are awake and looking around. The infant farthest from us is red faced and crying his heart out. I think of the new mothers and fathers standing here to *ooh* and *ahh*, and the babies being taken to mom's room for nursing and coddling, and it makes me sad that there's no one to do any of those things for Baby Doe.

"How is she doing?" I ask.

"She's eating and healthy. Once they find a foster home for her, she'll be ready to leave the hospital."

I make a mental note to contact the social worker first thing in the morning to find out what the status is on Baby Doe's foster family.

"This must be the happiest floor in the hospital," I say.

"Isn't that the truth? Who doesn't love babies?"

The question, intended to be flippant, makes me think of my own life. I feel like an outsider here. A foreigner looking into a world to which I don't belong—a world to which I may never belong. A part of me has always believed that having children is something other women do, a ritual other families partake in. I don't let myself think of it often. When I do, it's with some level of discomfort because I'm seriously behind the curve. I know that at some point, I'll need to confront the question of having a family, and the reality that Tomasetti and I are going to have to make a decision or else the decision will be made for us.

The nurse puts her face close to the glass and makes nonsensical baby noises. "Have you found her mama yet?" she asks.

"I've got a few leads I'm following up on."

She sighs, wistful. "I raised five, but I swear if I wasn't so old I'd take her myself."

"Thanks for taking such good care of her." I pull my car keys from my pocket.

"See you tomorrow, Chief."

As I walk away, I wonder how she knew I'd be back the next day.

I arrived at the farm to find that Tomasetti caught three decent-size bass earlier and cleaned them for dinner. Over fresh fish, we shared half a bottle of chardonnay and exchanged stories about our day.

He's working on a missing person case up in Geauga County, the outlook of which doesn't look good for the missing man. Painters Mill has been quiet, so over raspberry sherbet, I updated him on the Baby Doe case. It was nearly midnight when we went to bed.

I'm wakened from a fitful slumber by the *cheep* of my cell phone. Only half awake, I snatch it up and squint down at the lighted face. *Painters Mill PD.*

"Hey, Mona," I grumble to my third-shift dispatcher.

"Chief, I just took a call from Damon Atherton. His daughter is missing. He's worried she's going to hurt herself."

The words bring me bolt upright. "She's suicidal?"

"I guess they had some kind of an argument. She got upset. When he went to check on her, she was gone."

Rising, I pad to my closet, swing open the door. "Where is Dr. Atherton now?"

"Home."

"Call him and tell him to stay put. I'm on my way." I hit End, step into my trousers, and pull on my uniform shirt.

The light flicks on. I glance over to see Tomasetti rise and reach for his clothes. "Where are we going?" he asks.

I tell him about Chloe going missing.

"That's the girl you believe is the mother of Baby Doe?"

I nod. "I saw her earlier and she was scared, wouldn't admit to anything. I didn't push because I was hoping she'd come in on her own." I finish buttoning my shirt, yank my jacket off a hanger. "Her father thinks she might be a danger to herself."

Muttering a curse, he reaches for his coat. "Let's go."

The night is moonless and windy. The trees shake their fists at me as I fly down a backstreet toward Main. Leaves scramble across the road in the beam of my headlights as I speed toward the Maple Crest subdivision. Two minutes later, I pull in to Atherton's driveway and park behind his Land Rover. The porch light is on. The front door stands open, yellow light pouring out. Atherton is standing in the entryway, dressed, his smartphone pressed against his ear.

Tomasetti and I disembark simultaneously and jog to the house. "Any sign of her?" I ask when we reach him.

The doctor's hair is mussed. His shirt is untucked on one side. His hands shake when he drops the phone into his jacket pocket. "I searched the house twice. Her car is gone. Phone is gone. She's not answering."

"You had an argument?" I ask.

He sighs, nods. "I'm not sure what's going on with her. We were talking about Phoenix. She got upset. Started to cry. Things escalated, so I sent her to her room to cool off." He shrugs. "When I went to check on her later, she was gone."

"How long ago?" Tomasetti asks.

"Twenty minutes."

"Any idea where she is?" I ask. "Best friend's house? Boyfriend's place, maybe?"

"I don't know." He chokes out the words, his face crumbling. "I should know, but I don't. What the hell kind of dad doesn't know who his kid's friends are?"

I touch his arm, not only to reassure, but to keep him focused. "What kind of vehicle does she drive?"

"A 2016 Mustang GT. Red. I bought it for her for her sixteenth birthday."

I hit my lapel mike and put out a BOLO for Chloe and her car, with the added code for missing endangered. Then I turn my attention to Atherton. "You stated to the dispatcher that you believe Chloe may be a danger to herself?"

He stares at me, eyes wide and blinking, but his thoughts seem to turn inward. "She's been . . . depressed recently. Gained a lot of weight since her mom passed away. A couple weeks ago she actually said, 'I wish I was dead.'" He rubs a hand over his face. "I thought she was just acting out. You know, the pressure related to the move to Phoenix. School. Grades. The usual stuff teenagers face. And I know she's been missing her mom."

"Her mother passed away?" Tomasetti asks.

"A year ago," he says. "Breast cancer." He looks

down, then back at me. "I've been so tied up with work. So . . . damn blind. I should have seen this coming. I should have—" He bites off the word as if he doesn't know how to finish.

"We've got a BOLO out for her. Agent Tomasetti and I are going to get out there, too, and look for her." I pause. "Dr. Atherton, this may or may not be related, but it may help us find her and maybe fill in some of the blanks as far as her recent behavior, so I'm just going to lay it out for you. I'm not certain, but I have reason to believe Chloe may be the woman who abandoned Baby Doe."

"*Wh—what?*" He chokes out a sound that's part laugh, part sob. "But . . . that's not possible. She hasn't been dating regularly. How could she . . . ? She doesn't even have a boyfriend. For God's sake—"

"Has she been wearing baggy clothes recently?" Tomasetti asks. "Oversize shirts? Anything like that?"

For an instant, I think Atherton is going to argue the point. At the same time, I see his mind working, a terrible realization entering his eyes. "My God, the weight gain. I didn't . . ." He blinks as if waking from a nightmare. "She picked out an alpaca poncho when we were in Santa Fe a few months ago. Wears it all the time . . ."

"You're not the first parent this has happened to," I tell him.

"I'm a doctor. A pediatrician, for God's sake. How

could I not see it? Why didn't she talk to me? How could I—"

"The most important thing right now is that we find her and make sure she's safe," I tell him. "We can deal with the rest later."

He raises his hands, sets his fingers against his temples, and presses hard, misery etched into his every feature. "If you're right about the baby, maybe she's with the child's father."

The question pings in my brain. *Maybe she's with the child's father.* And suddenly I have an idea where to look first.

I glance at Tomasetti. "The Amish cemetery."

The doctor's eyes snap to mine. "Wait. The Amish boy? Noah Fisher? I knew they were friends, but . . . she never let on that they were . . . Oh, Dear God. No wonder she was so upset when he was killed. First her mom and then the boy . . . She must have been in so much pain. I was so busy with work I didn't notice any of it."

Tomasetti is already striding toward the door. "Let's go."

"I'll go with you," Atherton cries, following.

I reach the porch, glance over my shoulder at him, and raise my hand to stop him. "I need you to stay here, Mr. Atherton, in case she comes back or calls."

"But she needs me." He stops, but he doesn't look convinced.

"If she's there, we'll bring her home." I reach the Explorer, look at him over the hood. "I'll call you the instant we lay eyes on her. In the interim, try to stay calm and keep trying her cell."

"All right." He's already got his smartphone to his ear.

Giving him a reassuring nod, I get in the Explorer, crank the engine, and back onto the street.

Tomasetti punches numbers into his phone. "I'm going to call EMS."

"Tell them to meet us at the Amish cemetery. No lights or siren. I don't want to scare her. Tell them we need the hospital on standby."

I push the speedometer to seventy when I hit the outskirts of Painters Mill proper. The engine groans beneath the hood, the tires humming against the asphalt. I'm not sure what we'll find when we arrive; I'm not certain Chloe will even *be* there. But it's the only place I can think of where she might go to seek comfort. The place where her lover—the father of the child she abandoned—was laid to rest.

The *Graabhof* is located on the township road west of town. A gnarled bois d'arc tree stands guard next to the gate, a brave sentry scarred by hundreds of harsh seasons. The gate, which is usually closed, stands open. Beyond, a sea of plain headstones form neat rows before fading into the darkness like white-capped waves. It's a pretty place during the day, a peaceful and quiet sanctuary to reflect and pay homage to the dead. Tonight, the darkness is forbidding, the silence unbearably lonely.

Tomasetti points. "There's her Mustang."

Sure enough, parked in the shadows beneath the tree is a red Mustang. Neither of us speaks as I park in the gravel driveway, blocking in her vehicle, and shut down the engine. Reaching into the pocket next to my seat, I hand Tomasetti an extra Maglite and we exit the Explorer. The night closes over us like a black hand slamming down. The wind grabs at my jacket as we pass through the gate. I can hear the chain latch clanging with every gust. Our Maglites flip on simultaneously, twin beams illuminating hundreds of small white headstones that run in neat lines, parallel with the fence. In the darkness, they look like ghosts, restless souls rising from the earth.

This isn't the first time I've been here. My parents are buried just a few yards away, and I've attended several funerals over the years. I'm familiar with the general layout and use my Maglite to scan the south side where any new graves would most likely be located. I nearly miss the mound of freshly turned earth fifty yards away. A small heap on the ground next to the headstone.

"There," I whisper.

We break into a run, both beams focused on the small form huddled next to the headstone. A sick feeling augments in my gut when she doesn't move.

"Chloe!" I call out. "It's Kate Burkholder! Are you all right?"

"Doesn't look good." Tomasetti mutters the words beneath his breath.

I'm a few feet away when she raises her head. I

see the pale oval of her face. The shimmer of tears on her cheeks. She's lying on her side with her arms wrapped around the headstone, as if trying to keep it from sinking into the earth.

I reach her first, drop to my knees at her side. "Sweetheart, are you all right?"

When she raises her head and looks at me, her eyes are glazed and far away. "Noah . . ." she whispers. "He was here. Just a moment ago. I saw him." She looks around. "Noah . . ."

Tomasetti kneels beside her. "Chloe, honey, did you take any medication or pills?"

She looks away. "It doesn't matter. I just want to be with them. Noah and my mom."

Locating her handbag, he upends it on the grass. A wallet, makeup bag, hairbrush and, finally, a brown prescription bottle spill out. He snatches up the bottle, shakes it. "Empty."

I grab my lapel mike, put out the emergency call for the ambulance. "Ten fifty-two. Ten eighteen. Expedite."

"Noah wanted to marry me," Chloe slurs. "But I said no and he died before I could tell him I'd changed my mind. Why did that have to happen?" she asks. "He never knew."

"It's going to be okay," I tell her. "Everything's going to be okay. I promise."

Chloe begins to cry. "Tell my dad I love him. . . . He worries all the time. . . ."

Grimacing, Tomasetti looks at me over the top

of her head. "Let's get her to where the Explorer is parked. Speed things up." Even as he says the words, he lifts the girl into his arms, carrying her as if she weighs nothing.

We're midway to the gate when I see the ambulance pull in behind my Explorer. "Hurry," I say and we break into a run.

Three days later:

It's the end of my shift and I'm thinking about heading to the farm, where Tomasetti is about to grill T-bone steaks and break the seal on a bottle of cabernet. Not for the first time in the last few days, I'm reminded of how blessed I am to be loved by a good man and how lucky I am to know that we have a bright future to look forward to.

I've been thinking of Chloe Atherton on and off since Tomasetti and I found her at the Amish cemetery. She'd ingested all of her mother's painkillers. Luckily, there had been only five pills left. Her condition had been dicey for a few hours, but she pulled through. Her father didn't let her out of his sight the entirety of the two days she was in the hospital. There's no doubt in my mind his love for her is strong enough to get them through the challenges they face in the coming weeks and months.

On the outskirts of Painters Mill, instead of turning north toward the farm, which is located just outside Wooster, I make a detour and head east toward Charm. Ten minutes later I turn into the long lane of the Fisher farm, park adjacent to the barn, and take the sidewalk to the house.

Miriam Fisher answers a moment later and greets me in Pennsylvania Dutch. *"Guder ovet."* Good evening.

The aroma of frying bologna wafts through the open door and, for an instant, I'm transported back to my childhood, where fried bologna sandwiches were not only a staple, but a treat. "I hope I'm not disturbing your *ovet-essa*," I tell her. Your evening meal.

"I'm still frying and Willis is washing up, so I have a few minutes." Eyeing me guardedly, she opens the door wider. *"Witt du wennich eppes zu ess?"* Would you like something to eat?

I smile. "I'm tempted, but no thank you."

"Come in."

I follow her to the kitchen, stopping just inside the doorway while she goes to the stove and turns bologna sizzling in a copper skillet. "What brings you to our home this evening, Kate Burkholder?"

I tell her about Chloe Atherton without revealing the girl's identity or mentioning the incident with the pills. "Your son loved her, Miriam. He'd asked her to marry him. She was going to say yes, but she never got the chance."

She sets her hand against her stomach as if in pain. "Such a tragic, sad thing."

"She was devastated when Noah died, and terrified of raising the baby on her own."

She clucks her tongue. "Poor child. Can't blame her for being afraid, I guess."

"She's going to officially relinquish her parental rights so Baby Doe can be adopted."

Miriam goes back to her skillet, pushing the bologna around with a wooden spoon, but I can tell her attention is focused on me.

"Miriam, you understand that Noah is the father," I tell her.

The spoon stops. Without looking at me, she turns off the burner, sets down the spoon, and leans heavily against the stove. "I know. *Mein Gott.*" My God. "I know."

"I spoke to the social worker a couple of hours ago. She's still trying to find a permanent adoptive home for the baby. Since you and Willis are the child's biological grandparents . . ." I'm not sure how to finish the sentence, so I let the words dangle.

Finally, she turns to me, her mouth open and quivering. Tears shimmer in her eyes, but she doesn't let them fall. "I'd like to meet this girl. The mother."

"I can't reveal her identity. She's a minor, so a meeting between you will be up to her and her father. But I'll let them know."

She nods, but I see her mind working through all the possibilities. "There is a chance Willis and I could adopt and raise Noah's daughter? Is that what you're telling me, Kate Burkholder?"

I nod. "It'll probably have to go through the court

system," I tell her. "But I thought you'd want to know it's an option."

She glances past me; her eyes widen slightly. I glance over my shoulder to see Willis standing in the kitchen doorway a few feet away. Neither of us heard him approach. But I can tell by the look in his eyes he heard every word.

Without speaking, without making eye contact with me or his wife, he brushes past us and walks into the kitchen. For an instant, I think he's going to keep going and walk right past us, through the mudroom and back outside. Instead, he stops at the table, sets his palms against it, leans heavily, and lowers his head.

Miriam's eyes flick nervously to me, then to her husband. Grabbing the kitchen towel, she uses it to dry hands that are already perfectly dry. *"Sitz dich anne un bleib e weil,"* she says to her husband. Sit yourself down and stay awhile.

Staring straight ahead, Willis pulls out a chair and sinks into it. *"En kins-kind,"* he whispers. A grandchild.

"You heard?" Miriam asks him.

"My hearing is just fine." When he raises his head and looks at his wife, I see tears in his eyes. "It's been a long time since we had a little one in this house. Not since Noah."

"Well, I'm not so old that I can't manage a baby," Miriam huffs, but she's crying, too. "A mother never forgets."

"A father, too," he whispers.

Realizing this is a private moment that I'm no longer a part of, I pull the social worker's card from my pocket and place it on the table in front of Willis.

Back in the Explorer, I take a moment to calm my own emotions, trying in vain not to examine them too closely. In that instant, I'm keenly aware of my age. The passage of time. How easily the things we cherish can slip away. No matter how unflagging my denial of its existence, I know there is a silent clock ticking inside me. A clock that sets its own pace, one that cannot be sped up or slowed down or stopped.

Another deep breath and I'm steady enough to call Tomasetti.

"I hope you're not too far away," he says without preamble.

"You miss me that desperately, huh?"

"That, and I just broke the seal on that Cabernet you've been saving."

I laugh, but my voice is thick with emotion. I don't want him to know that I'm a little too caught up in this Baby Doe case. That I'm probably thinking a little too hard about my own life.

"Kate?"

Feeling like an idiot, I choke out a sound that betrays the tears waiting at the gate. "I'm leaving the Fisher place now."

"Everything okay?"

"I think the grandparents are going to adopt Baby Doe," I tell him.

"Good for them." His voice is warm. "Good for everyone involved." He falls silent and then asks, "So, are you coming home?"

Home.

I like the way the word rolls off his tongue. The warm impression it leaves in my chest. "John Tomasetti," I whisper, "You can count on it."

SEEDS OF DECEPTION

Zimmerman's Orchard was the last place fourteen-year-old Katie Burkholder wanted to be, especially with her older brother, Jacob. He was bossy and about as fun as a milk cow—one that kicked. But Mamm had insisted. She needed six bushels of apples for pies and apple butter, both of which she planned to sell. Katie had already finished the sign Datt would post at the end of their lane: HOMEMADE APPLE BUTTER $3.99. DUTCH APPLE PIES $5.99.

No worms, her *mamm* had told them as they walked out the door. *And keep your sister out of trouble.*

She'd just had to add that last line. As if there was trouble to be found in an orchard. Mamm was probably still angry with her. Two nights ago, Katie had been caught reading, huddled beneath her covers, using the flashlight she'd bought for a buck at the drugstore. The reading itself wasn't the problem, but the material was. It was the book her best friend, Mattie, had given her. A mystery novel in which the young heroine solved crimes and just happened to receive her first kiss. Katie had been enthralled with the story, but before she could finish Mamm had confiscated the book and tossed it in the trash. Now Katie was relegated to picking apples, with Jacob watching her every move.

Datt had hauled them to the orchard in the buggy and dropped them off. While Katie walked ahead, Jacob checked them in with Mrs. Zimmerman, who supplied them with bushel baskets, two wagons with hand pulls, and instructions on where to pick.

"Stop looking so dejected."

Katie glanced over her shoulder to see him pulling both wagons behind him. "I have better things to do than tromp around in this orchard picking apples with you," she said.

"Like what?" He smirked. "Read an English romance book?"

"It was a mystery novel," Katie defended herself, taking the handle of the second wagon.

"Same thing."

"You're just jealous because I read better than you."

"Better at filling your head with useless words maybe." He started down the row of trees. "Mamm says those books are trash."

Katie scooped a rotten apple out of the grass and threw it, hitting him solidly in the back.

Jacob spun, laughing. Katie couldn't help it; she laughed, too. Her brother might be older, but he still liked to have fun on occasion. When he wasn't try-ing to boss her around, anyway.

"Better not bite off more than you can chew," he warned. "I can throw a lot harder than you."

He had a point. Not that long ago, she'd been able to outrun him, throw the baseball farther than him, and outwrestle him. But not now. Jacob was nearly a foot taller than her and his muscles were the size of small hams. Of course, Katie knew he was too kind to ever hurt her. On the contrary, *she* was the one who'd been accused of possessing a mean streak.

He motioned toward the far end of the orchard. "I'll start a couple of rows over at the end and we'll work our way toward each other."

Glad to be rid of him, Katie watched him walk away, trying hard not to feel sorry for herself. It wasn't fair. Not only had Mamm taken her book, but she'd ripped it in half. That had hurt. Worse, she wouldn't be able to return it to Mattie. At least Mamm hadn't found the lip gloss she kept hidden in a sock in her drawer.

Resigned, she dropped the wagon's handle to the ground, went to the nearest tree, and plucked a shiny Ginger Gold apple off the branch, setting it carefully in the basket so as not to bruise it or nick the flesh.

Around her, the late August day was glorious and warm, with a breeze that held a hint of autumn. She daydreamed as she worked—the one thing she was good at, it seemed. She entertained forbidden thoughts about the boy who had helped her *datt* and brother cut and bale hay a few weeks ago. Daniel Lapp was Jacob's age, a good worker, and he had the face of an angel. Pretty eyes that sparkled when he smiled. It had been hot that day, and Mamm had asked her to take lemonade to them out in the field. Daniel hadn't said a word to Katie, but he'd smiled when she handed him the glass. Her legs weren't quite steady when she walked back to the house. Later that night, she'd dreamed of him.

She'd just twisted another apple off the branch when something hit her in the back hard enough to hurt.

Drawing back to defend herself from her marauding brother, Katie spun. "Mattie!"

The Amish girl doubled over with laughter. "You should have seen your face! Like you were under attack and you were going to beat the crap out of someone!"

The image struck Katie's funny bone and for a full minute the girls' laughter rang out. Mattie Erb had been her best friend for as long as she could remember. In the past, Katie had seen her at school, which made learning so much more tolerable, even though they'd gotten their knuckles rapped for speaking out of turn or laughing when they weren't supposed to. But the Amish only went to school through the eighth grade; both girls had finished last year. Katie didn't get to see Mattie as often now. She missed those easy, carefree days. Mattie was funny and pretty and, like

Katie, had a penchant for getting into trouble. They were a match made in heaven.

"What are you doing here?" Katie asked.

"Picking apples—same as you, dummy."

Dropping a piece of fruit into her basket, Katie walked over to her friend. Mattie wore an Amish dress like the gray one Katie was wearing, but maroon, and an off-white cardigan with the sleeves pushed up to her elbows. Like most of the other Amish girls their age, they wore sneakers and matching organdy *kapps*.

"Mamm needs three bushels for pies." Mattie tilted her head, her eyes sparking. "Is Jacob here?"

Mattie had a crush on Katie's brother—though he wasn't the only boy she had her eye on. It was one of the reasons Mamm didn't approve of their friendship. She said Mattie was "boy-crazy and wild." Of course, Katie loved her even more for it.

"He's two rows over at the other end," Katie replied.

"You're lucky to have such a cute brother," Mattie said breezily.

"Cute like a pig, maybe." But the blues that had been weighing her down all morning began to lift. Now that Mattie was here, the day was looking up.

"Have you seen anyone else we know?" Mattie asked.

"No such luck." Tugging an apple from a branch, Katie checked it for worms and took a bite. "Just us boring girls."

"Speak for yourself." Digging into her apron pocket, Mattie withdrew a tube of lipstick. "Peach Berry Dew is definitely not boring."

Katie watched as her friend swiveled the tube and glided the lipstick over her mouth. It was the color of a ripe, wet peach. It looked good on Mattie, she thought. And not for the first time, Katie found herself wishing she were as pretty as Mattie. Hopefully, it wouldn't be too much longer before her figure filled out.

"Where'd you get it?" Katie asked.

"Fox's Pharmacy. They've got the best colors."

Wearing makeup was forbidden by the *Ordnung*, which made Katie wonder if Mattie had bought it—or if the lipstick had somehow found its way into her pocket. She didn't ask.

Mattie offered the tube to Katie. "Try it."

Katie shook her head. "Jacob will tell."

"So wipe it off before he sees you. He'll never know."

Glancing toward the far end of the orchard and seeing no sign of her brother, Katie accepted the tube. Never taking her eyes from Mattie's, she applied the color. It glided on like silk. "It smells like strawberries."

"A little dark for you." Mattie reached out and touched the side of Katie's mouth, erasing a smudge with her thumb. "But you look good. Sexy."

Katie grinned and felt herself blush. "You, too."

Pulling their wagons, the girls strolled between

the endless rows of trees, picking apples as they went. Mattie wasn't quite as careful not to bruise hers. Every now and then she'd toss one aside with a little too much force. "Worms!" she'd exclaim and before long they were both throwing perfectly good apples and cutting up.

Katie had nearly filled her first basket when she heard the rumble of an engine. Scrubbing her hand across her mouth, she turned to see Billy Marquart and another *Englischer* boy on an ATV. The small vehicle's bed was piled high with tools—a chain saw, bags of mulch, some kind of sprayer, and two shovels. The boys were clad in work clothes, their shirts emblazoned with the orchard's logo.

Billy shut down the engine. "Now, ain't that a sight for sore eyes. Two pretty little Amish girls, picking apples."

Katie's interaction with non-Amish was limited; her parents were firm believers in the tenet of separation. But Painters Mill was a small town, and she'd seen Billy around in places where the two cultures intersected. The feed store. The horse auction. In town. He was a year or so older and good-looking, with black hair and brown eyes. But he was also a known *druvvel-machah*—troublemaker—with a smart mouth that, according to Jacob, he "ran a little too often."

Billy and Mattie had had some kind of run-in at the auction in Millersburg a couple of weeks ago while Mattie was working at the concession stand.

Billy had ordered hot chocolate, but accused Mattie of spitting in it. She denied it, but the owner, a Mennonite guy by the name of Zook, hadn't believed her and fired her on the spot.

Mattie slanted Billy a smile. "Look what the wind blew in," she said. "A piece of trash."

Billy's grin widened. "You're not still mad about that stupid concession job, are you, Matts?"

"I don't like liars," she said sweetly.

"Takes one to know one," he returned. "But hey, if I'd known you wanted to swap spit, we could have found a better way than you spitting in my frickin' hot chocolate."

Turning her back to him, Mattie picked an apple and held it out for Katie to see. "Oh, look, a rotten apple." She tossed the apple over her shoulder, and it struck Billy's leg.

Sighing, he turned his attention to Katie. "Nice lipstick."

Self-consciously, Katie reached up and touched her lips, her eyes flicking to Mattie. Her friend looked back at her and chuckled. "Just a little smear," Mattie whispered.

Katie wiped her mouth with her sleeve, her face heating in embarrassment.

The second boy said something beneath his breath and the two broke into laughter.

"Don't pay any attention to my friend Gavin." Billy smiled appreciatively at Mattie, his eyes bold as they skimmed over her body. "So what are you girls doing here, anyway?"

"Um, picking apples?" Mattie replied, adding a generous dollop of smart-ass to her voice.

"I reckon you're not going to let me off the hook until I apologize, are you?" he asked, trying to charm her.

Turning away, Mattie resumed picking apples. "I don't really care."

Billy addressed his friend without taking his eyes off of Mattie. "Hey, Gav, why don't you head down to the other end and get started on that branch? I'll meet you there in a few minutes."

"You got it, Bill."

Gavin climbed onto the ATV and started the engine. Giving the two girls a mock salute, he put the vehicle in gear and roared away.

When he was out of sight, Billy crossed to the girls, his focus riveted on Mattie. Katie didn't mind. She didn't like being the center of attention. And she didn't much care for the likes of Billy Marquart. He might be attractive, but he was also coarse and foul-mouthed, and she was relieved she wasn't the object of his affection.

"So, are you going to forgive me or what?" he cooed.

Mattie didn't even look at him. "Why would I do such a thing?"

Billy rolled his eyes in a self-deprecating way

that might've been charming if it hadn't been so rehearsed. "Because I'm irresistible?"

Now it was Mattie's turn to laugh. "If I had a mirror, I'd give it to you so you could admire yourself all day."

Shaking his head, he shifted his attention to Katie. "What about you?"

Katie liked to believe she was worldly enough to converse with an English boy, even an obnoxious one like Billy. But there was something in the way he looked at her that made her uneasy. Like he was privy to some secret joke that had been made at her expense—and only he understood the punch line.

Instead of coming back with some sharp, Mattie-esque retort, Katie found herself dry-mouthed and tongue-tied. "Mattie didn't spit in your hot chocolate," she managed, "and she doesn't want to trade spit with you."

"Yeah?" Billy assumed an amused countenance. "That's not what I heard."

"You should apologize to her," Katie said, "and mean it when you do."

"I did—"

"No, you didn't," Mattie cut in.

Wishing he'd go away, Katie yanked a scarred apple off the nearest branch and tossed it into her basket.

Smiling, Billy moved closer to Mattie and got down on one knee, as if he were about to ask her to marry him. "Will you forgive me?" he asked.

Mattie threw her head back and laughed a little cruelly, then picked another piece of fruit. "You're an idiot."

"I admit it. I'm an idiot. A big, stupid one. Now will you forgive me? Please?"

Mattie slanted him a look over her shoulder, her eyes alight with interest. "What are you going to do for me?"

Looking around, he shrugged. "Hey, I got cigs if you want one." He glanced toward Katie. "You, too. I got a whole pack."

Mattie looked intrigued by the idea. *Too* intrigued. Katie knew a bad idea when she heard one. If her brother didn't smell smoke on her, Mamm would. Her punishment would surely be something unpleasant, like mucking stalls for the next year or two.

"Jacob is working just a few rows over," Katie said. "And I have to get these baskets filled."

Mattie clucked. "Come on, Katie. Don't be such a stick in the mud. Just one?"

Shaking her head, Katie plucked another apple from the tree. "Can't."

Her friend shifted her attention to Billy and turned on the charm with a smile. Katie almost felt sorry for Billy; he didn't know it, but he wasn't nearly as smart as Mattie. He didn't stand a chance.

"Well, we can't smoke out here in the open," Mattie pronounced.

He motioned toward Zimmerman's old barn, a run-down structure tucked into the corner of the field.

"No one ever goes in the barn. The old man keeps the tractor and hay inside. I'm in there all the time." He passed her a cigarette. "Here you go."

"Going to cost you more than one." Turning up her nose at the proffered cigarette, Mattie held out her hand. "The whole pack."

Katie smiled inwardly at her friend's pluck and experienced a moment of envy that she didn't have the same confidence.

Billy shook out a couple for himself and set the pack in her hand. "You drive a hard bargain for an Amish girl."

"It's the least you can do after telling that big fat lie and getting me fired."

"I take it all back, babes." He stared at Mattie as if she were some exotic delicacy and he was famished. "Let's go."

Something in his eyes gave Katie pause. The flash of a thought or emotion she couldn't identify, but she knew it wasn't good. Fingers of worry kneaded the back of her neck as Mattie fell into step beside him.

"Mattie, I don't think you should go," she called out.

"Keep picking," Mattie said breezily, completely unconcerned. "Toss a few apples in my basket, too, will you? I don't want to fall behind."

"*Er is en leshtah-diah maydel,*" Katie said emphatically. He's a beast that blasphemes girls.

Mattie gave her an I-know-what-I'm-doing smile. "This won't take long."

Standing next to their wagons, Katie shook her head and watched her friend and Billy go through the gate, traverse the dirt track, and disappear inside the barn.

For an instant, she regretted not going with them. Not because she wanted to be in that dusty old barn with the likes of Billy Marquart, but because she didn't want Mattie in there alone with him.

The logical side of Katie's brain told her that Mattie knew how to handle herself, but the knowledge was little comfort; Katie also knew her friend didn't always use the good judgment God had given her. Billy had a reputation for kissing and telling. If Mattie let him take things too far, everyone in town—including the bishop—would know about it.

Sighing, Katie watched them disappear into the shadows. "I hope you know what you're doing," she muttered.

She picked up both wagon handles and pulled them a few feet down the row. Keeping an eye on the barn, she went back to working, but her mind wasn't on picking apples. There was a new presence dogging her now—worry—and Katie didn't like it.

"Where'd you get that second wagon?"

Katie startled at the sound of her brother's voice. She'd been so embroiled in her thoughts—so intent on watching the barn—that she hadn't heard him approach. She turned to see him ducking beneath the low-slung branches of two trees.

"It's Mattie's," she replied.

"Mattie Erb? No wonder you haven't gotten much done." He looked at her basket and shook his head. "Where is she?"

Katie blinked, her mind whirling. She was such a terrible liar . . . "Not that it's any business of yours, but she went into the barn for a pee break."

"Oh." He glanced away, trying not to look embarrassed. Served him right for being so nosy, she thought. "I know how you two are when you're together with all the talking," he said. "I've already filled two baskets and you've barely filled one. Datt'll be here shortly to pick us up."

Katie tried to keep her eyes off the barn, but it wasn't easy. She disliked lying to her brother—disliked lying to *anyone*—even if it was by omission. But there was no way Jacob would stand for Mattie going into the barn with a boy, especially Billy Marquart. If he found out, he'd surely tell their parents. Katie knew all too well that if that happened, she'd find herself in trouble, too, even though this time she hadn't done anything wrong.

"The only one I hear talking too much is you," Katie muttered.

Sending her a scowl, Jacob picked up one of her empty baskets and retreated toward the other end of the orchard.

For ten minutes Katie picked apples as quickly as she could. When the lower halves of the trees were picked clean, she moved the wagons farther down the row. She didn't like the growing distance between her and the barn. Mattie had been gone for nearly fifteen minutes. How long did it take to smoke a cigarette? Not *that* long, a little voice whispered. What else were they doing? Talking? Something else?

The tiny seeds of worry from earlier had grown into something dark and unwieldy. Not only was Billy a troublemaker, but Katie had heard stories about his temper, too. Rumor had it, he'd gotten into a fight at Miller's Pond last summer—and sent another boy from Coshocton County to the hospital.

The whisper of footsteps against the grass spun her around. Katie gasped. It was Billy walking fast, passing within a few feet of her. He didn't look happy, didn't make eye contact with her, and Katie was pretty sure he had a scratch on the side of his face.

"Where's Mattie?" she called out.

"That little bitch is all yours." He didn't spare her a glance as he followed the tracks of the ATV. "I'm outta here."

Katie watched him stalk away, alarm stealing through her. How did he get that scratch on his face? Where was Mattie? Had he done something to her?

She launched herself into a dead run toward the barn. "Mattie!"

She was midway there when her friend emerged. A quick once over told her Mattie was unharmed. But Katie didn't miss the tuft of hair that had been pulled from her *kapp*. That the *kapp* itself was askew. Her cheeks were flushed, her lips devoid of the lipstick she'd put on minutes before going into the barn.

"What happened?" Katie asked.

"Nothing happened, silly."

"But I saw Billy," she blurted. "He had a scratch on his face. He looked . . . upset."

Mattie huffed. "Billy Marquart is dumber than a chicken." Brushing hay from her dress, she headed for their wagons. "Looks like you've been busy."

Katie wasn't ready to let it go. "How did he get that scratch?"

"Probably ran into a tree."

"Mattie, you were in the barn for fifteen minutes. What were you doing? Why was he so angry? Did you argue?"

"*Er harricht gut, awwer er foligt schlecht.*" He hears well, but obeys poorly. "So I put him in his place.

Katie paused. "What did he do?"

"If you must know . . ." Mattie swung around to face her. "He tried to kiss me."

All Katie could do was put her hand over her mouth.

Mattie laughed. "Don't worry," she added. "I sent him packing."

"You're sure you're okay?"

A slow smile spread across Mattie's face, telling Katie she was not only unfazed by what had happened, but she'd enjoyed it. "Has anyone ever told you that you worry too much?" Mattie asked.

"Yeah," Katie muttered. "Me."

Elbowing her good-naturedly, Mattie motioned toward the wagons. "Come on. Let's go work down at the other end with Jacob."

"We've got plenty of apples to pick here," Katie returned.

"I want to say hello to him." Scooping up the wagon's handle, Mattie started toward the opposite end of the orchard. "Are you coming?"

Grumbling beneath her breath, Katie followed, but she was only mildly annoyed. Mostly, she was glad Mattie was all right—and Billy Marquart was gone.

Neither girl spoke as they made their way down the row of apple trees, the wagons bumping over tufts of grass and uneven ground.

They'd only gone a few yards when Katie caught a whiff of something burning. "I think you smell like smoke," she whispered.

Frowning, Mattie looked down at her clothes. "Do you have any perfume or hand lotion?"

"Did you really just ask me that?"

They'd nearly reached the end of the row when Katie spotted Jacob through the trees. A look at his baskets told her he'd already filled three—to her one.

"We'd best get picking," she said.

The girls set to work, barely speaking now to make up for their lack of productivity. Katie was still pondering the scratch on Billy Marquart's face and Mattie's nonchalant attitude about what had happened in the barn. She loved Mattie, but there were times when she didn't like her ways, especially when it came to boys. Mattie had known from the get-go that Billy was trouble, and yet she'd willingly gone into the barn with him. Worse, Katie didn't think she was telling the whole story about what had happened. But what could she do?

She'd just twisted an apple from a branch when she caught another whiff of smoke. Not cigarette smoke, but something stronger carried on the breeze.

"Do you smell that?" Katie asked.

Pausing, Mattie sniffed. "I bet someone is burning trash or brush."

The wind was from the south. Katie glanced that way. Uneasiness quivered through her when she spotted dark tendrils of smoke rising into the air. It seemed to be coming from the general direction of the barn.

"I think the barn's on fire!" Katie exclaimed.

"What?" Dropping the fruit she'd been holding, Mattie spun and looked. "Oh no!"

As if by mutual agreement, the girls ran toward the barn. They'd gone only a few yards when Katie saw orange flames leaping twenty feet into the air. Through the open barn door, she saw a good-size fire blazing inside the structure.

"What's going on?"

Both girls started at the sound of Jacob's voice. Katie glanced at him, but his eyes were fastened to the flames licking at the sky thirty yards away.

"I'm going to get Mr. Zimmerman." Jacob tossed

a hard look at Katie. "Stay here. Do not get any closer to the fire. Do you understand?"

She nodded.

At that, he took off at a sprint toward the Zimmerman house.

Katie and Mattie watched the flames expand, the smoke pouring like a twisting, writhing tornado into the clear blue sky. Though they stood a safe distance away, Katie could feel the heat against her face, the acrid stink of the smoke climbing into her nostrils.

It seemed like an eternity before the wail of sirens sounded in the distance. Relief swept through her when the first fire truck rumbled through the gate, emergency lights flashing. Two firefighters clad in protective gear dragged a hose from the truck and began to spray water onto the flames.

"It's a good thing you and Billy got out when you did," Katie said after a moment.

"That's for sure," Mattie replied.

"I wonder how the fire started."

When her friend didn't reply, Katie looked her way. "Mattie?"

Glancing left and right, Mattie lowered her voice. "I think Billy Marquart might've . . . done something."

Though she was sweating, the hairs on Katie's arms stood on end. "Done something like what?"

"When we were in the barn," Mattie began, "We smoked for a bit and then he . . . you know, tried to . . . kiss me. I pushed him away, and he got angry.

He . . . called me bad names and punched the wall with his fist."

"He didn't hurt you, did he?"

"No, but he scared me."

"Why didn't you tell me?"

"Because it was my fault for going into the barn with him in the first place." Mattie blew out a breath. "Bad idea, huh?"

A second fire truck arrived on scene. Two additional firefighters disembarked. Beyond, flames devoured the barn, the dry wood snapping and popping like firecrackers.

All the while Katie tried to absorb everything her friend had told her. "Did Billy start the fire?" she whispered.

"He was so angry with me." Looking miserable, Mattie shrugged. "He had a lighter. What if he did?"

A crash sounded, making both girls jump. Katie glanced over in time to see part of the barn's roof cave in, sparks flying high into the air, gray smoke billowing. The firefighters continued to battle the blaze. In the gravel driveway beyond, a sheriff's department cruiser pulled up next to one of the fire trucks.

"We have to tell someone," Katie said after a moment.

"You mean the police?" Mattie asked.

"They're probably going to want to talk to us anyway. All we have to do is tell the truth."

For the first time Mattie looked frightened. "Billy's going to be pissed."

Katie felt something protective rise up inside her. "I have a feeling the police are going to keep him busy for a while."

Twenty minutes later, Katie, Jacob, and Mattie stood in the gravel driveway of the Zimmerman home. They'd been instructed by the Holmes County sheriff's deputy to wait for their turn to be interviewed. Mr. Zimmerman was talking to the deputy, gesturing angrily toward the barn. Both men's faces were grim, their voices low.

A dozen yards away, the barn smoldered and steamed. The fire had been extinguished. The structure was still standing, for the most part, but the contents inside—a tractor, spray equipment, and a hundred bales of hay—had been destroyed.

Through the door, Katie saw the outline of the tractor listing at a cockeyed slant, the tires burned off. Once the firefighters had gotten the blaze under control, the deputy motioned them over and brought them here, to the driveway. Katie, Jacob, and Mattie watched, unspeaking, while the police had methodically talked to everyone—workers and customers alike. Billy Marquart was nowhere in sight.

The uniformed deputy approached them, his expression grim, his demeanor professional. "Is everyone okay here?" he asked.

"We're fine," Jacob told him.

"Was anyone hurt?" Katie asked.

The deputy shook his head. "Luckily, no one was inside."

He pulled a notebook from his shirt pocket. His eyes fell on Katie and then went to Mattie. "I understand you girls were picking apples near the barn. Did either of you see anything you want to tell me about? Was there anyone else around?"

Jacob interjected, his expression puzzled. "Did someone start the fire?"

"We don't know yet," the deputy hedged. "Fire marshal is probably going to get involved. But we think it's a possibility."

The cop's gaze slid to Katie. "Did you see anyone?"

Her heart began to pound. She swallowed hard, staring back at him. "The English boy."

The deputy's eyes narrowed. "Which English boy? What's his name?"

"Billy Marquart," Mattie put in. "He works here at the orchard."

He scribbled in the notebook. "Virginia and Bud's son." He said the words to no one in particular, frowning. Painters Mill was a small town, and evidently, he had some knowledge of Billy.

"Where did you see him exactly?" the deputy asked.

"Both of us saw him," Mattie replied. "In the barn."

SEEDS OF DECEPTION 151

Neither girl mentioned that Mattie had been in the barn with him.

Across from her, Jacob looked from Katie to Mattie, his eyes narrow and glinting with reproach.

"How long after you saw him in the barn did you notice the fire?" the deputy asked.

"A few minutes," Katie replied.

Grimacing as if he'd bitten into something distasteful, the deputy made another notation in his notebook. "Did you see anyone else?"

"No," Mattie replied. "Just Billy."

In her peripheral vision, Katie was aware of Jacob watching the exchange with interest. She didn't dare look at him, but she knew what he was thinking. That she and Mattie had been talking to Billy. That they'd been *flirting* with him. *That Mattie had been in the barn.*

The deputy asked for the exact time, but neither girl could say for certain. "What was Billy doing when you saw him?" he asked.

"Leaving the barn," Katie said.

"He was running," Mattie added. "He looked like he was in a big hurry."

The deputy snapped the notebook closed. "If we need anything else, we'll get in touch with your parents. You're free to go." Tipping his hat, he walked away.

Katie had hoped for a few minutes alone with Mattie, but she didn't get the chance to speak with her again because Datt arrived a few minutes later to take her and Jacob home.

On the buggy ride to the farm, Datt inquired about the fire. Jacob explained that Mattie had seen the *Englischer* boy who worked at the orchard and left it at that. Datt didn't press.

Katie decided she was going to be nicer to her older brother.

Early the next morning before worship, Katie went to the barn to feed the old Percheron draft horse her *datt* had charged her with caring for. She found Jacob already at work, mucking out the stalls.

"Did you hear about Billy Marquart?" he asked.

Katie cut the tie on the hay bale, pulled out a generous flake of alfalfa and dropped it into the feeder. "What did he do now?"

"The police arrested him. For arson."

The statement shouldn't have surprised her. Mattie had told her Billy might have set the fire. Katie had seen him walking away. The problem was, he hadn't been alone in the barn, and no one had told the deputy.

"How do you know?" she asked.

"Datt told me. One of his English friends works at the sheriff's department."

Katie went over to the hand pump, concentrating a little too hard on pumping water into the bucket.

"Billy claims he didn't do it," Jacob told her.

She stopped pumping. "Everyone knows Billy Marquart is a liar and a *druvvel-machah* to boot."

"Did you talk to him?"

She stopped pumping, her heart beating fast. "He came over to Mattie and me while we were picking apples. He was on an ATV with another boy. He asked me to go into the barn with him, and I told him no."

Jacob didn't look happy about that bit of information. He was protective of his sisters. Too protective, in Katie's opinion, and a lot more judgmental than he had a right to be. This morning, she sorely hoped he just let it go.

"What about Mattie?" he pressed. "You told me she went into the barn for a . . . break."

She stared at him for what seemed like an eternity. A lie dangled on her lips, but she couldn't bring herself to utter the words. "You'll have to ask her." Hefting the bucket, she carried it to the stall and hung it over the hook.

Her brother's eyes sharpened on hers.

"Stop looking at me like that." She closed the stall door with a little too much force. "I didn't do anything wrong."

"Are you sure?"

Katie didn't respond. There was no way she could defend herself without having to tell him more than she wanted to and risk getting her friend in trouble.

Leaving the stall where he'd been working, Jacob

crossed to her. "I see things, Katie. Things Mamm and Datt do not. Sometimes I don't like what I see when it comes to you."

"You don't know what you're talking about."

"I know you talked to Billy. I know you've talked to other boys, too, haven't you?"

"I don't see how that's any business of yours."

"You think I didn't notice the way you looked at Daniel Lapp? The way he looked at you?"

Heat flooded her face. Not because she was being accused of something she hadn't done, but because he was calling her on something she was, indeed, guilty of.

"I'm not a kid anymore," she snapped. "I'm fourteen years old. I'll be going to singings before long."

"I don't like Lapp. I don't like Billy Marquart. And I'm not sure I like Mattie Erb."

"You can't choose my friends," she spat, but her cheeks were still burning.

"Keep it up and I'll have no choice but to go to Datt."

Turning away, she started toward the barn door. "I have to get ready for worship."

"Billy says Mattie started the fire."

Katie stopped and swiveled to face him, her heart pounding. "*Sell is nix as baeffzes!*" That's nothing but trifling talk.

"He told the police *she* had a lighter. A pink one. The police searched Billy, searched his room, and guess what? They didn't find a lighter."

"That doesn't mean anything," she hissed.

"Billy told the fire marshal that he *saw* Mattie set that fire."

"I don't believe it. Mattie wouldn't—"

"Billy said she did it to punish him for getting her fired from her job at the auction."

"What else is he going to say?" Katie tried to laugh, but it didn't ring true. "Billy Marquart is a *liknah*." A liar.

"You seem to know a lot of them." Jacob moved closer, tilted his head to make better eye contact. "Maybe you ought to choose your friends with a little more care. I wouldn't want any of it to rub off on you."

"The only thing rubbing off on me is your suspicious attitude," she said.

Jacob sighed. "Datt told me the fire marshal is going to talk to Mattie again, if they haven't already. More than likely they'll be speaking to you and me, too."

A quiver of fear moved through Katie, but she didn't let it show. "I'm not worried," she said. "All we have to do is tell the truth."

"Hopefully, you will."

"I have to go." When she turned and walked away, her legs were shaking.

The day of worship is an important one for the Amish. It's a time of reflection and anticipation, but it's also a day reserved for rest and for socializing with friends, family, and neighbors. With the exception of caring for the farm animals, chores are set aside. The preaching service is held every other Sunday, not in a church, but in an Amish home or barn. Benches and chairs are brought in. Most of the women bring food. The service often lasts three hours or longer.

This week, worship was at the Stutz farm, and Katie couldn't wait to see Mattie. She'd been on pins and needles since talking to her brother. She couldn't get his words out of her head. *Billie says Mattie started the fire.*

Of course Billy Marquart was lying. That's what people like him did when they got caught doing something they shouldn't. They lied or blamed someone else. *Not this time*, Katie thought. She wouldn't allow it. If only she could silence the other, more disturbing voice whispering inside her head. That was the one that had her stomach in knots. The one that reminded her Billy Marquart wasn't the *only* one with a reputation. His was earned. Was Mattie's?

Katie knew better than anyone that her friend wasn't perfect. No one was. Yes, it was true that Mattie broke the rules and pushed boundaries—lots of people did, even among the Amish. It was one of the things Katie loved about Mattie. Her sharp mouth. Her quick laugh. Her devil-may-care attitude when it came to all those Amish rules. As far as Katie was concerned, most of those rules were too strict, anyway.

She'd never told a soul, but there were times when she entertained fantasies of leaving it all behind. Times when she knew in her heart that a life without books and music couldn't possibly be fulfilling. And what about college? What was so terrible about an education? How could those things keep you from getting into heaven?

Some days she was so filled with discontent that she dreamed about running away and never coming back. They were her private thoughts, thoughts she'd never shared with anyone.

Except Mattie.

One night last summer, Mattie had slept over with Katie. There was a new foal on the way and Mamm had allowed them to take their sleeping bags to the barn for the night. They hadn't slept a wink, instead staying up talking far into the night as they watched the mare and waited for the foal to come. They had shared their most personal hopes and secret dreams for the future. Not all those dreams included baptism, marriage, and children.

Mattie was the only one who understood. The only person brave enough to speak of such forbidden topics aloud and in the presence of another person. That was one of the reasons, Katie supposed, that not everyone liked Mattie.

She'd heard all the mean-spirited barbs. *The Erb girl is a boy magnet. That Erb girl will smile at a boy whether he's Amish or English. Her parents had better look out come her time for* Rumspringa!

Katie wanted to believe it was just idle gossip, a favorite Amish pastime. But as she'd entered her teens, she'd realized that harmless gossip was rarely harmless. The Amish may be pious, but they excelled at throwing the occasional petty jab, especially at their own.

Katie refused to give the cruel comments weight. She wouldn't listen and she wouldn't judge her friend. She loved Mattie and the loyalty she felt toward her was abiding and deep.

The preaching service seemed to go on forever. In the course of *Es schwere Deel*, or the main sermon, Katie had looked around and spotted Mattie on a bench three rows back. They made eye contact and a silent communication had passed between them. *Meet me at the swing behind the barn when this is over!* It was their usual rendezvous point, and Katie could barely wait.

It was noon by the time the closing hymn was sung and everyone was dismissed. Dodging the usual small talk, Katie snagged a plastic cup full of date pudding from the room where the food had been set up and made a beeline for the door. She marveled at the beautiful but crisp day as she made her way to the rear of the barn. At the base of a small hill, a stream trickled prettily. Next to it stood a towering cottonwood tree; someone had tied a swing to its lowest branch.

Mattie sat on the swing, swaying lazily and concentrating on her date pudding as Katie approached.

"Katie!" Mattie held up her pudding, motioning to the matching cup in Kate's hand.

Katie laughed despite herself. Raising her cup, she proclaimed, "Great minds!"

"I was beginning to wonder if Bishop Troyer would ever run out of breath," Mattie said between mouthfuls.

"The *Gottes-deensht* gets longer every time," Katie said, referring to the worship service. She set her empty cup on the ground. "Have the police or fire marshal people been to see you?"

"What?" Mattie stopped chewing. "The police? *Fire marshal?*"

Katie recapped the conversation she'd had with Jacob earlier. "Billy Marquart is trying to blame the fire on you. Jacob told me the police or fire marshal people are going to talk to you next."

Mattie tossed the rest of her pudding into the bushes. "What else did Billy say?"

"He told the police you're trying to get back at him for getting you fired from your job."

"Stupid liar." Looking worried, Mattie bit at a thumbnail. "This is all my fault. I should have known better than to go in the barn with him."

Katie shrugged. "You never know what some people are going to do."

"Especially people like Billy." Mattie sighed. "All this over an old barn no one cares about." She tried to slip into her usual cavalier persona, but Katie could tell she was concerned about this new bit of information.

Katie offered a kind smile. "Like my *mamm* always says: The truth will prevail. All you have to do is tell the truth, and you have nothing to worry about."

"What if the police believe Billy over me?"

"They won't. Come on. You're *Amisch*. They'll know you don't lie."

Mattie didn't look convinced. "I'll get into trouble for going into the barn."

"Which is a harmless thing." Katie paused. "Billy turned it into something dangerous and destroyed all that hay and equipment. Not you."

Tears shimmered in Mattie's eyes. "Thank you for believing in me. Not everyone does."

"That's because they don't know you the way I do." Reaching out, Katie laid her hand over Mattie's. "I have your back. Okay?"

A gust of wind rustled the branches of the cottonwood and Katie shivered. "I'm *so* going to miss summer."

"No more swimming."

"No more sunshine."

"Datt says we're going to have an early fall this year." Mattie removed her sweater and handed it to Katie. "Here. It'll keep you warm."

"I'm okay—"

But Mattie insisted. "You can give it back to me later."

Katie slipped the sweater on, smiling when she realized it smelled like Mattie, a mix of strawberry shampoo and her *mamm*'s hand lotion. "Hard to believe we won't be going back to school this year," Katie said.

"I'm not going to miss it."

The girls fell silent, thoughtful, listening to the metallic chirp of a nearby cardinal.

After a moment, Mattie rose from the swing. "Let's go get more date pudding."

Katie scooped her empty cup off the ground. "You talked me into it," she said and they started for the barn.

It was dark by the time Katie finished her chores and went to the bedroom she shared with her sister, Sarah, to get ready for bed. By the light of a single lantern on the night table, she unlaced her sneakers and was in the process of taking off Mattie's sweater when something clattered to the floor. Puzzled, she picked it up and held it to the dim light of the lantern. A chill scraped up her spine when she realized it was a lighter. Not just any lighter, but a *pink* one.

She stared at it, her thoughts scattering.

All the while Jacob's words about Billy Marquart rang hard in her ears. *He told the police she had a lighter. A pink one.*

Her brain refused to acknowledge the thoughts prying into it. The lighter didn't mean anything, she assured herself. Lots of people carried lighters.

When you were Amish, there were always lanterns or candles or stoves to light.

Katie held up the sweater for a closer look. It was the same sweater Mattie had been wearing the day of the fire. She remembered because before the boys came along Mattie had gotten too warm and hung it on a branch and they'd laughed because it looked so silly, like a headless scarecrow.

Was the lighter Mattie's? Was it significant? Did Billy drop it into her pocket so he could blame her for setting the fire? Even as the questions formed, a new and uncomfortable doubt reared its head. Katie loved Mattie; she didn't want to believe the worst about her. But she knew in her heart that sometimes her friend bent the truth to suit her own needs. And for the first time, Katie considered the possibility that Mattie had lied to her. *Is it possible Mattie is, indeed, guilty of setting the fire?* Was *she trying to get back at Billy for getting her fired?* Katie didn't like the answers coming back at her.

Katie slept little that night. By the time Mamm peeked into her room at 5:30 A.M. to rouse her for chores, Katie was already dressed. Mamm looked at her a little oddly, going so far as to press her wrist against Katie's forehead to check for a fever. "You look peaked," she said.

"Couldn't sleep," Katie muttered.

"I hope you're not coming down with something."

Just a bad case of worry, Katie thought.

She rushed through morning chores, feeding and watering the old draft horse. She tossed cracked corn to the chickens, dodging the rooster and stealing fourteen eggs while the hens were busy pecking at the ground. Mamm would be happy about the eggs. She saw Jacob mucking the buggy horse's stall, but she didn't pause to speak with him. The last thing she wanted to do was talk about Mattie, especially after finding the lighter. Her brother knew her too well. One look at her, and he would know something was wrong.

She spent most of the day in the kitchen with Mamm, helping her can the last of the season's tomatoes and green beans. All the while, Katie agonized over how to handle her doubts about Mattie.

Finally, at three o'clock, Mamm asked Katie if she wanted to ride with her to pick up Sarah, who'd taken on a part-time job at one of the tourist shops in town. Usually Katie was anxious to get out; anything to break up the incessant work and monotony of the farm. This afternoon, though, she had other plans. While Jacob harnessed the horse and pulled the buggy around for Mamm, Katie waited. Once the buggy had disappeared down the lane, she sprang into action.

Keeping an eye on the barn where Jacob was repairing a hayrack in one of the stalls, Katie went to the shed and pushed Jacob's bicycle to the gravel area. Mamm would be gone at least an hour. Datt wasn't due back from the auction in Millersburg until later. She should be able to make the trip to Mattie's house and get back before anyone noticed she was gone. A final glance over her shoulder at the barn, and she was off and pedaling hard down the lane.

It took her ten minutes to reach the Erb farm. Katie barely slowed the bike to make the turn into the long gravel lane. She passed by the old milk barn in need of paint, and then the lane curled right, taking her toward the house on the hill. She stopped just off the gravel and set the bike on its side beneath the shade of the maple tree outside the front window. Mr. Erb stood in the doorway of the barn and waved when he saw her. Katie waved back, but she didn't stop to chat.

The kitchen window was open, the blue curtains billowing out. Katie saw Mattie standing at the sink, washing dishes. When she spotted Katie, she stuck out her tongue and then disappeared inside. Katie ran past the clothesline, around the front of the house and vaulted the stairs to the porch. The two girls were moving so fast they nearly collided.

"Katie!"

"Hey," Katie said, realizing for the first time how out of breath she was from the physical exertion of the bike ride.

"What are you doing here?" Mattie stepped back and put her hands on her hips. "My goodness, you're all sweaty and breathless. Do you want something to drink? Mamm made iced tea."

Anxious to talk, Katie shook her head. "I have to talk to you."

"Let's sit down at least." Mattie motioned toward the steps and the two girls sat side by side. "Is everything okay?"

"I don't know." Katie took off the sweater and handed it to her friend. "You tell me."

"You rode your brother's bike all the way over here at the speed of light to return this old sweater?" Mattie gave an incredulous laugh. "What a good friend you are!"

"You left something in the pocket," Katie told her.

Looking puzzled, Mattie checked the pockets and pulled out the lighter. "This must be Billy Marquart's," she said, her brows knitting as she turned it over in her hands. "I wonder how it got there."

Katie watched her carefully, feeling guilty, because for the first time since she'd known Mattie, she was looking for a lie. "Billy doesn't seem like the type of guy to carry around a pink lighter."

Mattie's gaze snapped to hers, her eyes widening. "You don't *believe* me? You think it's *mine*?"

"I don't think anything." Katie's voice was strong, belying the nerves snapping beneath her skin, but her heart was beating wildly in her chest.

"It's not mine," Mattie said. "I had no idea it was there. The only explanation I can think of is that Billy put it there after he set the fire so he could blame it on me."

"Have the police or fire marshal people talked to you yet?"

"No."

"You have to tell them about the lighter," Katie said.

"The police already know Billy did it," Mattie said petulantly. "They probably don't even want to talk to me."

"Jacob told me they did." Katie sent a pointed look at the lighter. "You need to tell them about the lighter."

"If I do, they'll think I did it."

"The police aren't stupid," Katie told her. "You have nothing to fear from them."

Mattie looked away. "It's not the police I'm worried about."

The girls went silent and for the first time, Katie thought she understood. Still, she asked, "Did something else happen in the barn?"

Mattie was silent so long that Katie didn't think she was going to answer. Finally, she looked down at the ground and whispered, "I let him kiss me. I just . . . wanted to know what it was like, and he got all pushy and stuck his tongue in my mouth and . . ." She paused, out of breath and her face screwed up. "I don't want anyone to know!"

"Oh, Mattie."

"Katie, it's not the police I'm afraid of, it's . . . everything else. You know how the Amish are. You know they'll blame me."

Katie wanted to argue, but the words wouldn't come, because in some small corner of her mind she acknowledged that her friend was right. Some of the Amish *would* blame Mattie. For being in a place she shouldn't have been. For talking to someone she shouldn't have been talking to. For letting an older *Englischer* boy kiss her. Some of the Amish would gossip about her and whisper behind her back. But Katie also knew that those same Amish would be the first to forgive her.

As if reading her thoughts, Mattie said, "Billy set that fire, not me. But *I'll* be the one everyone will blame. *I'll* be the one everyone will condemn. *I'll* be the one they talk about because they have nothing else to say. I can hear their smug whispers already. *Did you hear what that wild Erb girl did with that* Englischer *boy?*"

It wasn't easy to admit, but Katie knew she was right. Oftentimes the truth was a far cry from fair. The Amish shared the same human flaws as their English counterparts. They made the same mistakes. But the Amish, it seemed, were invariably held to a higher standard.

Mattie got to her feet. "I don't want anyone to know I was in that barn with Billy. If they find out I let him kiss me . . . I'll never hear the end of it. My parents will know. The *bishop*." Her eyes filled with tears. "If you're any kind of friend, Katie Burkholder, you'll let sleeping dogs lie."

It was the first real argument Katie had had with her best friend, and it hurt a lot more than she thought it would. As she pedaled the bike down the gravel lane, Mattie's words echoed in her head.

If you're any kind of friend, Katie Burkholder, you'll let sleeping dogs lie.

Those were the words that hurt the most. The ones that had sunk into her heart like a knife.

Katie understood Mattie's reasons for not wanting anyone to know she'd been in the barn with Billy Marquart. But wouldn't it be worse for her to be accused of setting the fire? Katie didn't know what to do. She had no idea how to fix things between them. The only things she knew for certain was that she wouldn't let her friend be blamed for something she hadn't done and she had to make things right between them.

Katie was so embroiled in her thoughts that she didn't notice the ATV parked on the pullover outside the mouth of the covered bridge until she was already inside the structure. In the back of her mind she figured someone was down at the creek fishing or picking blackberries. The bicycle tires hummed over the wood surface as she flew through the bridge.

She'd just emerged on the other side when the figure came out of nowhere. One instant Katie was pedaling as fast as she could, determined to make it home before she was missed. The next she was being shoved violently sideways. The bicycle twisted beneath her, the front wheel jackknifing. Her body kept going. Vaguely, she was aware that someone had pushed her. That the impending landing was going to hurt.

She hit the asphalt hard on her hands and knees, scraping both palms, both knees, and then rolling, striking her right shoulder. Then everything went still. She was lying in the middle of the road, just a few feet from the mouth of the covered bridge. Her dress had ridden up to mid-thigh. The fabric was torn where her knees had ground into the asphalt. Already she could feel the burn of the abrasions, the ache of the bruises that would bloom later.

Jacob's bicycle lay on the asphalt a few feet away, bent at an unnatural angle. Standing over it, Billy Marquart and another boy Katie had never seen before smiled at her.

"Dang, didn't know Amish girls could fly." Billy smirked. "You okay?"

Katie got to her feet and brushed specks of gravel from her dress. Her heart pounded hard in her chest. Not because she was afraid Billy was going to do something else to her, but because she was angry he'd damaged Jacob's bike.

"I'm fine," she muttered, even though she was pretty sure he didn't care one way or another.

"Looks like she's got cut knees," his friend said.

"I reckon the Amish don't ride bikes any better than they drive cars," Billy drawled and both boys broke into laughter.

"I hear they lie, too," said the friend.

"Not to mention start barn fires," Billy added. "You know your friend Mattie's a fire bug, right?"

Two of the most important Amish tenets Katie's parents had instilled in her young mind were forgiveness and nonviolence. Important as they were, they were the two things she had the most difficult time adhering to.

Katie stared at the two boys, her temper pumping as hard as her heart. In the back of her mind, it registered that she was outnumbered. That they were bigger and probably stronger than her, not to mention meaner. She didn't like the way Billy was looking at her, with cruelty glinting in his eyes. But she refused to be cowed or bullied. At the very least she refused to let them see that she was afraid.

"If that bike is damaged, you'll be paying for it," she heard herself say.

Billy blinked, looking pleased and amused. Too late Katie realized she was giving him exactly what he wanted. He was looking for a fight. It didn't matter to him that she was an Amish girl. That she was fourteen years old and thirty pounds lighter. At the moment, the only things that mattered were that she was an easy target, they were alone on a back road frequented by few, and this was a prime opportunity to exact revenge.

Billy raised his booted foot and brought it down hard on the front tire's spokes.

"Stop it!" Katie cried.

"Why should I?" Billy shouted. "I ought to stomp this piece of shit bike into the ground just for the fun of it. You Amish bitches lied to the cops and got me into a shitload of trouble. They arrested me right in front of my old man and now I got juvenile court. Lying bitches."

All Katie could think about was Jacob's bike. Trying to think of a way to keep Billy from destroying it, she remembered the lighter and pulled it out, brandishing it like a prize. "But we didn't give your lighter to the police. We protected you. They can't prove you did it without the lighter. It's evidence."

She had no idea if that last part was true. But she couldn't let him ruin Jacob's bike. Her brother didn't deserve it. And Katie didn't deserve to spend the next six months paying for it.

Billy squinted at the lighter in her hand. "That ain't my damn lighter. Pink? Are you shitting me?"

"Take it." She thrust the lighter at him. "You can have it back. We won't tell anyone."

"I don't want that." He slapped it from her hand. It landed on the asphalt ten feet away. "It ain't mine."

"But . . ."

Again, he brought his foot down hard on the spokes of the front tire. Two of the spokes snapped. The sound of steel scraping against asphalt seemed unduly loud in the silence. He crushed the spokes so severely the wheel bent.

"Please!" Katie cried. "It isn't mine!"

"Aw . . . too bad," Billy whined. "Guess you'll think twice about lying to the cops next time."

"I didn't say anything to them."

"Lying bitch. You told them I started that fire. It was that bitch friend of yours who did it!"

His friend landed a kick on the bike's housing and the chain snapped off.

Billy crossed to her and stuck his finger in her face. "Tell your slutty friend she'd better come clean to the cops or I'm going to make both of you pay," he snarled. "Next time, I won't stop with the bike. You got that?"

The urge to hit him was strong; Katie was furious and upset. But some sixth sense warned her that if she did, he would retaliate in kind and the situation would deteriorate into something even worse.

She looked down at the bike. Tears burned at the back of her eyes at the sight of the mangled piece of steel, but she fought them. She would not give the likes of Billy Marquart the satisfaction of knowing he'd hurt her.

His friend landed a final kick to the handlebars, scraping off some of the paint, and the two boys walked away, laughing. Katie stood her ground, her bloodied palms and knees aching, not sure what to do next. She heard the engine of the ATV turn over. She glanced over her shoulder to see the two boys astride the vehicle, roaring through the bridge, screaming like banshees. Billy was driving and she knew he was going to take one last shot at her. For an instant, she considered stepping into the way. But she didn't think that would stop him so she stood there helplessly and watched him run over the front tire of her brother's bike.

When the boys were gone, she dropped to her knees and tried to put the broken pieces of the bike back together as best she could. The front tire was still attached, but it was badly bent. There was no way she could put the snapped chain back together. She didn't think she could get it home. Jacob was going to be so angry with her.

She was thinking about dragging it into the weeds so she could come back for it later and somehow haul it to a repair shop when she heard the *clip-clop* of shod hooves against the asphalt. She looked up to see a horse and buggy approaching. Her heart stopped when she realized it was Jacob, and for a moment she thought she might actually be sick.

"Katie?" He stopped a few feet away and quickly climbed down. "What happened to you? What—"

She stood her ground as he ran over to her. He stopped a foot away from her, his eyes taking in her bloody knees and torn dress. Reaching for her hands, he looked at her palms, his expression anguished.

"Who did this to you?" he asked.

All Katie could think was that he hadn't so much as looked at the bike, even though it lay completely demolished a few feet away. He didn't care about the bike, she realized—he cared about *her*. She didn't like crying in front of others. Overt demonstrations of emotion weren't the Amish way. But after the argument with Mattie and the incident with Billy Marquart, her emotions boiled over.

When she didn't answer, he sighed. "Did someone hurt you?"

She shook her head.

They both knew someone had. She could tell by her brother's expression that he knew the most serious wounds were on the inside where they couldn't be seen.

"Who did this?" he asked again.

She swallowed the knot in her throat. "Billy Marquart."

Her brother looked at the bicycle lying in pieces on its side, and for the first time in recent memory, she saw anger in his eyes. "What happened?"

She told him. When she finished the sobs came and she burst into tears. "I'll pay for it," she said. "I'll . . . get a job. Get it fixed for you. I had no right to take it. I'm sorry."

Jacob knelt beside the bike. "Help me load it in the buggy, and then we'll go home."

By the time they arrived at the farm, Katie had reined in her emotions. When Mamm arrived home, she sat

Katie in a kitchen chair and cleaned the bits of gravel from her scraped palms and knees. When Mamm asked what happened, Jacob told her the truth—Billy Marquart had pushed her off the bicycle. He didn't go into detail, and Katie didn't elaborate. Later, while Datt and Jacob repaired the bike, Katie asked her father if they should report Billy to the police. Datt didn't even look away from his work as he uttered the phrase she'd heard so many times. *This is an Amish matter.*

Katie wanted to think it was over. She could put her encounter with Billy Marquart and her involvement in the barn fire behind her. But she knew that wasn't true. The argument she'd had with Mattie hurt so much more than the scrapes and bruises. She couldn't bear to let things stand the way they'd left them, angry and unsettled. The problem was, she wouldn't see Mattie again until worship in two weeks. How was she going to wait that long to set things straight?

But the sense of urgency goading her wasn't confined to her need to make things right with her friend. There was another facet to the situation she had yet to acknowledge—a problem she hadn't yet fully defined in her own mind: Billy Marquart's reaction to the lighter.

That ain't my damn lighter. Pink? Are you shitting me?

Katie knew all too well that Billy was a bully and a liar and, as the Amish preferred to say, a *druvvel-machah*. But she also knew that some-times, even liars told the truth. When she'd pre-sented him with the lighter, he hadn't hesitated or minced words when he'd told her it wasn't his. In fact, he'd looked as surprised to see it as she'd been when she found it in the pocket of Mattie's sweater. Katie had even *offered* it to him—a po-tential piece of evidence related to a crime for which he'd been arrested and charged—and yet he'd shown no interest. Not even to destroy it.

She was plenty angry with Billy for what he'd done to her brother's bike; if he was guilty of setting the fire, she had no problem seeing him punished for it. But Katie wasn't so sure he was the guilty party. That left her with an even more troubling problem—and possibly threatened her friendship with Mattie.

She didn't want to believe Mattie had lied to her—lied to the police—to suit her own needs. But when Katie set her emotions aside and put all the evidence together, it was the only explanation that fit.

There was no way she would sleep tonight. She needed to speak with Mattie, and it wouldn't wait un-til worship. Good or bad or somewhere in between, she needed the truth. Tonight.

The late summer night was cool, but the upstairs bedrooms were uncomfortably warm from the pie baking earlier in the day. Katie huddled beneath her blanket, fully clothed, sweating and nervous. At nine thirty, she heard her father come up the stairs and turn in. Mamm liked to read—the Bible or sometimes a novel—and stayed up a little later. Katie waited, listening, her every muscle taut with tension.

Finally, at eleven, the stairs creaked. Through her partially open door, Katie glimpsed the flicker of the lantern in the hall. The door hinge squeaked as Mamm let herself into her bedroom across the hall. A *click* as it closed. Once again, the hall went dark. The house fell silent. In the bed next to hers, Sarah snored softly.

Still Katie waited.

At ten minutes after midnight, she tossed the covers aside. Sitting on the side of the bed, she quickly laced up her sneakers and tiptoed to the door. Beyond, the hall was quiet and deserted. She glanced left to see that Jacob's door was open about a foot, no movement inside. Through the closed door of her parents' room, she could hear her *datt* snoring. The sound reassured her as she crossed to the stairs. Cautiously, she made her way down them, avoiding the sixth step because she knew it squeaked. At the foot of the stairs, she went left toward the kitchen. Her hands shook as she tugged open the door, and then she was outside.

Around her, the night was windy, with just enough moonlight to keep her from running into things. Not giving herself time to debate the wisdom of what she was about to do, Katie jogged to the shed. She winced when the door squeaked, every sound seeming magnified in the silence of the night.

A quiver of guilt moved through her at the sight of the bicycle. Datt and Jacob had spent the entire evening repairing it. The front wheel had been so badly damaged, they'd had to replace it. The chain had been repaired. Three spokes were missing from the rear wheel, and the paint had yet to be touched up. But the bike was functional.

Katie was loath to take it yet again without her brother's permission. But when she thought of Mattie and how they'd left things, she figured she didn't have a choice.

"I'm sorry, Jacob," she whispered as she pushed the bike through the door and toward the driveway. Somewhere in the distance, a dog began to bark. Upon reaching the gravel, she hopped onto the seat and pedaled down the lane as fast as she dared. The skirt of her dress swished around her legs. The blackberry bushes and trees growing alongside the lane blurred past as she picked up speed. The wind was a cold slap against her face. The rear tire nearly slid out from beneath her when she turned onto the road. A glance over her shoulder revealed a darkened house, and another layer of relief slipped through her.

She pedaled hard in the darkness, mailboxes and trees whizzing past. She watched for headlights of approaching vehicles or buggies, but the back roads surrounding Painters Mill were deserted this time of night. The biggest threat would undoubtedly come in the form of a wayward skunk. Katie figured she'd have a tough time explaining the smell to her parents.

The thought sent a laugh to her lips, but it was a for-lorn sound as she pedaled the dark, deserted road.

Five minutes into the ride, she passed Zimmer-man's apple orchard. The windows of the house were dark. The reflectors on either side of the driveway stared at her like glowing red eyes. Katie hadn't planned on stopping. But she'd brought her flashlight along, and when she came to the inter-section, she veered right. *Just a quick look-see*, she told herself. *No time to dawdle. Probably a waste of time, anyway.*

The skeletal remains of the barn stood in silhou-ette against the moonlit sky. Katie stopped, her eyes skimming the scene. Someone had pulled the ruined tractor from the barn. It sat in knee-high grass like some massive beast downed by a hunter's spear. Be-yond, the endless rows of apple trees rustled in the breeze. The fire had long since died, but the smell of smoke lingered.

Katie got off the bike and leaned it against a tree that grew alongside the fence. Keeping her eyes on the road and the Zimmerman house a hundred yards away, she climbed the wire fence and made her way toward the barn. The stink of burnt rubber filled her nostrils as she passed the tractor. The sliding door had been knocked from its track and leaned at a pre-carious angle. The police had strung yellow caution tape across the opening. Standing in the doorway, Katie pulled the tiny flashlight from her pocket and shone it inside.

There wasn't much left. Every visible piece of wood was charred or burned through. One of the rafters had broken and angled down against the ground. The hay had been reduced to a pile of black ash. This was no harmless barn fire. The structure and equipment inside were a complete loss. She'd heard one of the firefighters mention how quickly the hay had ignited. If someone had been inside, they surely would have been hurt—or worse. The thought made her shudder.

Extinguishing the flashlight, Katie turned away from the barn and scaled the fence. Troubling questions plagued her as she pushed the bike onto the road and hopped on. She needed to know who'd set the fire. Once she knew the truth, she'd decide what to do about it.

A few minutes later, she turned into the Erb lane. Past the milk house, the driveway curved right. Another ten yards, and the big farmhouse loomed into view. Much to Katie's relief, the windows were dark. She knew which room was Mattie's. Tonight wasn't the first time she'd sneaked out to see her friend.

Hopping off the bike, she walked it to the maple tree and parked it. She scooped a handful of gravel from the driveway and walked to the side of the house where the dormer window of Mattie's bedroom looked out over the yard. She tossed a few pebbles at the glass and waited.

"Come on, Mattie," she whispered.

She was about to try again, when the screen slid

up and Mattie stuck her head out. "Katie? What on earth are you doing here?"

Katie let the pebbles fall to the ground. "I need to talk to you."

"Now?"

"I didn't ride all the way over here in the middle of the night because it can wait until morning," she whispered.

"Meet me in the milk house." Huffing her displeasure, Mattie closed the window.

Katie wandered to the old stone milk house and let herself in. Just enough light filtered in from the window for her to find a place to sit. She was sitting on the concrete ledge that separated the stanchions from the guttering, when Mattie entered a few minutes later. She wore a sleeping gown, no *kapp*, and—much to Katie's amusement—a pair of muck boots. Her hair was sticking up on one side like a rooster's tail.

Katie couldn't help it; despite the seriousness of her mission tonight, she grinned. "Boots look good with the nightshirt."

Mattie was grouchy. "If Datt wakes up and finds you here, we're going to have some explaining to do." Crossing to where a lantern dangled from a hook, she removed the globe and lit the wick. Yellow light rained down on them. "What's so important that it couldn't wait until morning?" Mattie plopped onto the ledge next to Katie and snuggled against her.

Both girls had their legs stretched out in front of

them. Katie pulled up her skirt slightly so that Mattie could see her knees. The abrasions looked black in the dim light, the bruises like shadows.

A sound of dismay squeezed from Mattie's throat. "What happened?" she asked.

Katie turned up her palms so her friend could see the abrasions there, too. "I ran into Billy Marquart on my way home this afternoon."

"Oh, no . . ."

Katie recounted the scene at the covered bridge.

When she was finished, Mattie put her hand over her mouth, her eyes anguished. "It's all my fault. He was angry with you because of me. I'm sorry."

Katie had rehearsed the conversation a dozen times in her head. Now that she was here, looking into her friend's eyes, none of the words she'd so carefully strung together over the last hours seemed right.

Taking a deep breath, she plunged. "Billy said the lighter isn't his."

"Even a dummy like Billy is smart enough not to admit something like that."

Katie held her friend's gaze. "Mattie, I was looking right at him when he said it. The look in his eyes . . . the way he said it . . ." Closing her eyes, she forced the words out. "I believe him."

"You believe him? A known liar? Over your best friend?" Mattie choked out a sound of incredulity. "After what he did to you?"

The girls fell silent, as if shocked by the words between them, unable to process the repercussions or put them in perspective.

Katie forged on. "You're my best friend and I love you like a sister. I'm on your side. Please tell me the truth."

Tears filled Mattie's eyes. "You have to believe me."

"I want to, but things aren't adding up. I don't know what to believe."

Lowering her head, Mattie put her face in her hands and began to cry.

The urge to comfort was powerful. It hurt to see her friend in pain. Twice, Katie leaned close to take her hand and tell her it was okay. Twice, she stopped herself before she could.

After a moment, Mattie raised her head. Tears streamed down her cheeks. Her eyes were ravaged, her nose red and running. "The lighter was mine," she whispered. "Are you happy now?"

Katie felt something tear inside her. A vital part of her had been whole and undamaged until now, and on some instinctive level, she knew that small part of her would never be the same. "No," she said softly. "It makes me sad."

"It's not what you think," Mattie told her.

"I don't know what to think."

Wiping her nose on the sleeve of her sleeping gown, Mattie shook her head. "It was an accident. A horrible, stupid accident."

"Tell me," Katie said.

"Billy and I were . . . smoking. Over by where

Mr. Zimmerman stored the hay. One minute we were just sitting there, talking and joking around and the next . . . Billy just . . . came at me and started trying to kiss me. Trying to . . . you know . . . put his hands on me." She touched her chest and shuddered. "I don't like him that way. The only reason I went into that barn with him was to . . . I don't know . . . show him an Amish girl could put him in his place. I guess I thought I could handle him. But when I laughed at him and tried to push him away, he wouldn't listen. He just . . . kept coming. We wrestled a bit, kind of awkward like, but then something happened to him. He got really mad and it scared me. I . . . must have panicked and somehow scratched his face."

Looking away, she drew up her legs and wrapped her arms around her knees. "When all that was happening, I dropped my cigarette between two bales of hay. I tried to get to it, but the bales were heavy, and Billy was still trying to . . . get at me, so I just left it. And I ran."

Katie stared at Mattie, her heart pounding, pain and guilt and doubt tearing into her like tiny, sharp teeth. "Billy came out of that barn before you did."

"After he left, I went back inside to make sure there was no fire and find that cigarette if I could. I looked for it. I swear to you, Katie, when I walked out of that barn there was no fire. There was no smoke. I figured Billy put it out. That's the honest-to-God truth."

"It was an accident," Katie said.

Mattie shrugged. "I'm not even sure it was my cigarette that started it. I mean, Billy had matches. I saw them. He was so angry and cursing at me. As far as I know, he lit those matches and tossed them inside just to spite me."

"Why didn't you tell the police?"

Mattie's eyes flashed. "Because I was scared. Billy was like a rabid animal, spitting and snarling. He said if I told anyone what happened, he'd wait until no one was around and finish what he started. I know it sounds silly now, but at the time . . . if you'd seen his face. I believed him. I still do."

Katie didn't know what to say. Guilt nipped at her conscience. For not believing her friend when she should have. For pressing her when she should have been patient. Worse, she didn't know how to make things right.

"I believe you," Katie said after a moment.

"I'm sorry I didn't tell you everything from the start. I should have. But it was such an ugly thing."

"Not easy stuff to talk about." Katie sighed. "What about Billy?"

"I don't know." Mattie bit her lip. "I don't know if he started the fire. Maybe he did. Maybe it was my cigarette." She shrugged. "What if he does that to another girl? What if he doesn't stop next time?"

The weight of the questions settled uneasily on Katie's shoulders. The truth of the matter was she didn't know what to do. The line between right and wrong seemed crooked and gray. Not for the first time she wished she could talk to her *mamm* or *datt* or even Jacob. But, of course, she couldn't.

"Maybe we ought to just let things play out with the police," Mattie suggested. "Maybe this is a lesson Billy needs to learn. Maybe he'll be a better person because of it."

Katie thought about what Billy had done to her earlier in the day. Pushing her to the ground and damaging Jacob's bicycle. After a moment, she nodded. "Maybe you're right."

"The English police know what to do with boys like Billy Marquart," Mattie added.

It wasn't the perfect solution, but it was the best one Katie could think of. She got to her feet. "I have to get back."

"Before someone misses you, sneaky girl." Rising quickly, Mattie threw her arms around Katie. "Thank you for believing in me."

Closing her eyes, Katie hugged her back and tried hard to ignore the little voice in the back of her head telling her that wasn't exactly the case. But it was close enough to the truth that Katie thought she could live with it.

"See you at worship," she whispered.

"See you then."

Three weeks later . . .

The old draft horse whinnied softly when Katie dropped the flake of alfalfa into his hayrack. She was in the stall, brushing the animal's coat when Jacob approached.

"Did you hear about Billy Marquart?" he asked.

Katie looked over her shoulder at him and smiled. "Billy who?"

Jacob didn't smile back. "He had juvenile court yesterday. The judge found him guilty of felony arson."

A sensation similar to nausea seesawed in her gut. "He's going to jail?"

"He got some kind of probation. And community service."

Katie still wasn't convinced Billy had started the fire—a doubt that still kept her up some nights. But when she weighed the question of his guilt against the things he'd done to Mattie—and the damage he'd done to Jacob's bicycle—she figured justice had prevailed, at least in a roundabout way.

She stopped brushing the horse and turned to face her brother. "Hopefully he learned his lesson."

"I think there were lessons in there for everyone this time." Jacob smiled at her kindly. "Come on, little sister. Let's go eat breakfast."

Giving the horse a final pat, Katie left the stall, closed the door behind her, and walked with her brother into the house.

ONLY THE LUCKY

Alma Fisher held up the mirror and smiled at her reflection. She'd bought the lipstick and mirror two days ago at the Walmart in Millersburg. Since both are forbidden by the *Ordnung,* she'd tucked them under her mattress where her *mamm* wouldn't find them. She especially loved the lipstick—it was shiny and pink and, according to her best friend, Irene, made her look like she was from New York City. Gazing into the mirror now, she had to agree.

Of course the lipstick wasn't the most important thing about the party tonight. She and Irene were going together, and later Alma was going to rendezvous with her beau, Aden Keim. Mamm and Datt didn't approve of his car—or its radio—but then Aden was on *rumspringa.* As long as he didn't bring the vehicle onto their property, he was allowed to pick her up. Usually, she just met him at the end of the lane. He would have picked her up tonight, but he had to work late.

Alma didn't care about any of that. She was in

love and all she cared about was spending time with
Aden. He was twenty years old—two years older
than she—and he was the most handsome boy she'd
ever laid eyes on. He was a hard worker. Not only
did he help his *datt* on their farm, but he worked for
a construction company in Millersburg and trained
buggy horses on the side. Best of all, he was de-
voted to the church and planning to become baptized next year. Even her parents liked him—less
the car, anyway.

The thought of him made her sigh. Every Amish
girl in their church district had her eye on Aden Keim.
Alma almost couldn't believe he'd chosen her. He'd
been courting her since the fall. He was smart and
funny—and he was the only boy who'd ever made
her heart pound. Two weeks ago after a singing at the
Borntrager farm, they'd shared their first kiss and it
had been a zinger. Alma hadn't told anyone yet, but
she was going to marry him.

She'd been hearing about tonight's party for weeks
now. All the Amish teenagers were talking about it.
Irene had a cell phone her parents didn't know about,
and the news was all over social media; everyone
would be there. The Amish boys on *rumspringa* with
vehicles were carpooling and driving in from as far
away as Geauga County. Rumor had it there would be
plenty of *Englischers* there, too. It was going to be the
best party ever.

"Alma!"

She turned at the sound of Irene's voice, nearly dropping the mirror and lipstick. "I'm almost ready!"

"Enough primping." Irene's eyes widened. "That lipstick looks good on you."

Alma couldn't help it; she grinned. "Makes me look like I'm from New York City."

"An actress from LA."

Both girls fell into laugher.

"Come on." Crossing to her, Irene reached for her hand. "I want to be gone before Mamm and Datt get back. It's going to be dark soon and we have a mile to walk."

Alma didn't mind walking. If anything, it might help settle her nerves. She was so excited she could barely stand it.

Hand in hand, the girls went through the back door and started down the lane.

It's dusk in Painters Mill, Ohio. The freshly plowed fields are as black and rich as dark chocolate. The dozen or so redbud trees lining the fence in front of the Stutz farm are in full stunning bloom. Their lavender-pink flowers make for a spectacular backdrop against the massive bank barn as I drive past in my city-issued Explorer.

My name is Kate Burkholder and I'm the police chief of this pretty little town, which is located in the heart of Ohio's Amish country. Friday evening is usually one of the busier times for my

small department, but the police radio has been un-
usually silent. In the last six hours I've made two
traffic stops and issued one speeding citation to the
sixteen-year-old driver I clocked doing eighty down
Hogpath Road. I talked to the boy's father after-
ward. Unfortunately, Doug Humerick thinks Doug
Jr. is just "feeling his oats"and "acting like any red-
blooded teenage male." Humerick wasn't there the
night seventeen-year-old Jimmy Stettler wrapped
his Mustang around a telephone pole, killing himself and his fourteen-year-old sister in the process.

I've just passed through the Tuscarawas covered bridge when my second-shift dispatcher hails.
"Chief? You ten eight?"

She's asking if I'm in service. Smiling, I pick up
the mike. "Last time I checked," I tell her. "What do
you need?"

"Aaron Yoder is here to see you."

Yoder is a local Amish farmer who raises sheep
and goats and does a little horse trading on the side.
"Any idea what he wants?"

"Not sure, Chief." Jodie lowers her voice. "Said
something about idle hands and the devil, so I thought
I'd let you get to the bottom of it."

"I'll be right there," I tell her and hang a U-turn.

I arrive at the police station to find an Amish buggy
parked in my reserved spot. Sighing, I pull up beside
it, shut down the engine, and head inside. I find Jodie
manning her post, speaking into the mouthpiece of

her headset. She's a pretty blonde, not yet out of her twenties, with zero interest in police work. But she's good on the phones and fast on her feet when things get hectic.

Aaron Yoder is sitting on the sofa against the wall looking uncomfortable and out of place. I went to school with Aaron, back when I was Amish. He's a year or so older than me, more than a little eccentric, and is married with a boatload of kids. The Amish, ever fond of nicknames, call him Crazy Red. Aaron has bright red hair cut into the typical Amish "bowl" and an equally red beard that reaches nearly to the waistband of his trousers.

My second shift officer, Chuck "Skid" Skidmore, is sitting in his cubicle, fingers pecking at the keyboard of his antiquated desktop.

"Mr. Yoder," I begin. "*Guder nammidaag.*" Good afternoon. "*Was cann ich du fadich?*" What can I do for you?

"There are bad goings-on out at the Davenport place," he tells me. "People coming and going. Buggies and motorized vehicles. *Un shtoahris.*"

"What kinds of stories?" I ask.

"There's all kinds of talk. Some say the devil will be there. *Schnell geiste.*" *Schnell geiste* is an Amish term for "quick spirit" a phenomenon associated with unexplained drafts that scatter papers and slam doors. "Lightning will strike them all."

I'm not sure what to make of any of it. Before I can ask him to clarify, his eyes slide left and right and he lowers his voice. "Something bad is going to happen."

"Something like what?"

He shakes his head. "I don't know. But the young people are talking in quiet voices. Planning things. Out at the old *spukhaus*." Haunted house. "*Sis at gottlos zammelaaf.*" It's an ungodly gathering.

"When is this event supposed to happen?" I ask.

Yoder looks at me as if I'm dense for not already knowing this. "Tonight. *Mitt-nacht.*" Midnight.

My eyes slide to the clock on the wall behind the reception desk. It's nearly 8:00 P.M.

The Amish man stands. "*Sis en veesht ding.*" It's a wicked thing.

"Thank you for coming in, Mr. Yoder." Rising, I extend my hand for a shake. "I'll head out to the Davenport farm and check it out."

He looks down at my hand, but makes no move to shake it. "Beware the *schnell geiste*, Kate Burkholder." Giving me a final look, he turns away and walks out.

Around me, the station has gone silent. Jodie is standing at the dispatch station, her mouth open. Having overheard, Skid emerges from his cubicle. An experienced cop, he's no stranger to the occasional odd encounter, but his expression is nonplussed.

"I guess that explains why they call him Crazy Red," Skid says.

"It *is* Friday the thirteenth," Jodie puts in.

When I frown at her, she quickly adds, "Not that I believe in all that superstitious crap. I'm just saying."

I turn my attention to Skid. "Have you heard any rumblings about something going on out at the old Davenport farm?"

"Not a thing," he says.

"Chief?"

Skid and I look at Jodie.

She clears her throat. "I heard there's going to be a rager out there."

Skid and I exchange looks. "A rager?" I ask.

"You know, one of those wild Amish parties," she tells us.

"Where did you hear about it?" I ask.

"Social media, mostly."

"Did it cross your mind that it might be a good idea to let someone here at the PD know about it?" I ask.

Her eyes flick from me to Skid and back to me. "I didn't think it was important. I mean, I thought everyone knew about it. Besides, it's just going to be a bunch of people listening to music and drinking. Right?"

"What could possibly go wrong?" Skid mutters.

Feeling . . . old, I smile at my young dispatcher. "Old man Davenport passed away a few years back. Find out who owns that land now and get me their contact info, will you?"

"You got it," she says.

I glance at Skid. "You game for a trip out there?"

He grins. "Hopefully that damn black cat I saw lurking outside the front door is gone."

I roll my eyes. "Oh brother."

But I'm not sure if he's kidding.

The Davenport farm is located a couple miles south of Painters Mill on a little-used stretch of asphalt that dead-ends where the Apple Creek Bridge washed out during a flood a decade ago. I think the property is still owned by the Davenport family, but no one has lived there since the old man died. His children are scattered all over the United States, and none of them have any interest in farming. The place has been left to the years and the elements.

I stop the Explorer at the mouth of what had once been a gravel lane. The gravel has long since been pulverized to dirt and overtaken by weeds as high as a man's waist. But the once-tall undergrowth has been crushed by the recent passage of a vehicle.

"Someone's been here," I say as I make the turn.

"A lot of someones," Skid returns.

There's just enough light for me to see that the front pasture is heavily treed; the house and barns are set back a ways. Neither is visible from the road. I make the turn and we bounce over ruts and softball-size rocks. Past a tumbling-down fence. We've only gone a few yards when Skid spots the hand-painted sign.

No drugs.

No underage drinking.

"Why do I have the feeling no one's going to pay attention to that sign?" I say.

"Because neither of us would have paid attention to it when we were teenagers," he replies.

The lane curves right and the old homestead looms into view. The farmhouse is a two-story frame structure with white paint that's gone gray and a rusty steel roof with several missing shingles. The back door hangs at a precarious angle. Every visible window has at least one broken pane. A large bank barn looks out over the fields at the rear of the property. The siding is the color of old bone. The big sliding door is gone and someone has stacked the wood into a pile that looks suspiciously like a future bonfire.

In the open area between the house and barn, someone has cut the grass. A huge meat smoker throws puffs of baby-back-ribs-scented smoke into the air. A travel trailer is parked a few yards from the smoker. An Amish man in his early twenties stands on the steel steps, a can of beer in hand, smoking a cigarette, watching us.

"Must be our host," Skid says.

I park a few yards from the trailer and keep my eyes on the young man as I get out. He comes down the steps and meets us midway between my vehicle and the trailer. "Help you?" he asks.

I identify myself and show him my badge. "What's your name?"

"Wayne Miller."

"You have an ID on you, Wayne?"

"No, ma'am."

"How old are you?"

"Twenty-two."

"Uh huh." I look around, noticing the generator parked at the end of the trailer, a cooler the size of a Volkswagen, and the string of lights still coiled and laying on the ground. "I understand there's going to be a party out here," I say amicably.

"Don't know nothing about no party," he mumbles.

I nod, look around, and motion toward the smoker. "Ribs smell good."

He glances at the smoker and actually sniffs the air. "Just smoking some meat for me and my friends."

"How many friends?"

"A few."

"You have permission to be here?" I ask.

"Yes, ma'am."

I give him a hard, lingering frown, and he looks away. "If I call the owner, he's not going to tell me you're trespassing, is he?"

"No, ma'am."

I turn and start toward the Explorer. Behind me, I hear Skid say, "Have a nice evening," and it makes me smile.

"That kid is up to no good," Skid says as he slides in.

"Judging from the size of that smoker and the cooler, he's got a lot of friends."

"Not to mention that generator and all those coiled lights."

I'm reaching for the radio to see if Jodie was able to obtain contact information for the owner when a code barks out at me. "Chief, I've got a ten fifty PI out on the west end of town." Ten fifty PI is the ten code for a traffic accident with property damage.

I pick up the mike. "Injuries?"

"That's affirm. Ambulance is en route. Sheriff's department, too."

"I'm on my way—"

"Chief, about that property damage . . . eighteen-wheeler took out a power pole and some kind of transmission line. We don't have any power here at the station. Looks like the whole town is in the dark."

A quiver of unease goes through me. "You know where the generator is?"

"Basement?"

"Think you can start it?"

"Mona showed me." But there's uncertainty in her voice.

"Let me know if you have any problems, Jodie. Skid and I are on our way to the accident."

"Roger that."

"Did you happen to get contact info for any of the Davenports?"

"Computer is down, but I'll get on it as soon as I get that generator going."

I rack the mike and glance over at Skid. "This has

absolutely nothing to do with this being Friday the thirteenth."

He raises his hands. "I didn't say it."

"You were thinking it," I tell him, and jam the Explorer into gear.

We arrive at the accident scene just as the ambulance pulls away. The area is an ocean of emergency lights. Two Holmes County sheriff's department cruisers, a fire truck from the Painters Mill volunteer fire department, and a state highway patrol vehicle. An eighteen-wheeler lies on its side, smoke swirling in the beam of a single headlight, yellow blinkers pounding through the semidarkness like a visual metronome. Beyond, a tangle of aluminum and steel from the electrical transmission tower lies across County Road 14, blocking both lanes.

"Looks like a damn war scene," Skid mutters.

I get a sinking sensation in my gut. "That's the tower for the main line that runs into Painters Mill."

Flipping on my emergency lights, I get out of the Explorer. The odors of burning rubber, diesel fuel, and scorched foliage offend my olfactory nerves. I'm midway to the fallen big rig when I spot Holmes County Sheriff Mike Rasmussen striding toward me.

"Kate." He reaches me and sticks out his hand. "Glad you're here."

"How's the driver?" I ask.

"Pretty banged up, but the paramedic says he's going to be okay."

"What happened?"

"I talked to the driver briefly. Says he fell asleep and took that curve too fast." He whistles. "Must have been doing sixty when he plowed into that tower."

"He's lucky."

"That's for sure." Tipping his hat back, he scratches the top of his head. "You guys without power in Painters Mill?"

I nod. "Dispatcher is firing up the generator now."

The sheriff grimaces. "Power company trucks should be here soon, but it doesn't look good." He motions toward the downed tower. "That transmission line went directly to the Buckeye Creek substation down near Clark. Lineman says it could be morning before power is restored."

Now it's my turn to grimace. "Mike, while we're on the subject of bad news, I may have a situation brewing out at the old Davenport place."

His eyes narrow on mine. "What kind of situation?"

"I'm still working on getting in touch with the owner, but I think some of the young Amish are planning a big party out there. I suspect we're going to have some problems with juveniles and alcohol."

"Bad combination," he says. "Any idea how many?"

"The young man I talked to wasn't very forthcoming, but it looks like it's going to be a big gathering." I don't have to remind him of the disastrous Amish party last summer when the sheriff's department made over seventy arrests. "You throw two hundred teenagers and an unlimited supply of alcohol together without supervision and things can get out of control pretty quickly."

"Just what we need."

"Hey, it's Friday the thirteenth, right?"

He groans.

When Skid and I are back in the Explorer, I make a U-turn and head back toward Painters Mill. Amish country is incredibly dark at night; there are no porch lights or streetlights. As we crest the rise overlooking Painters Mill, I can't help but notice the entire valley is black.

Painters Mill isn't exactly a bustling metropolis, but on most Friday evenings half a dozen businesses stay open past dark. The new upscale coffee shop on the corner. Two of the Amish tourist shops. The funky little thrift store. And, of course, LaDonna's Diner. Tonight, as I idle down Main Street, the town is as dark and deserted as some post-apocalyptic movie scene. I pull up to the police station, trying not to notice when a black cat skulks past the entrance and darts into an alley.

Skid makes eye contact with me.

"Don't say it," I tell him, but we both grin.

Pulling my Maglite from its nest, I head inside. The reception area is deserted. Jodie has lighted two candles along with a battery-powered lantern we keep on hand for this kind of scenario. My dispatcher is nowhere in sight.

"She's probably in the basement, trying to start that generator," I say.

"Pull cord is kind of hinky," Skid puts in.

We're midway through reception when the emergency lights blink on. The phone system beeps three times, and then one of the lines begins to shrill. I hear Jodie pound up the stairs.

I stride to the switchboard and pick up the headset just as she emerges from the hall. "Oh," she says. "Hey."

I nod at her as I answer the incoming 911 call. "Painters Mill Police."

"I just had a vehicle drive through my yard," comes an agitated male voice. "Left ruts a foot deep, went through my garden, and broke the damn dogwood tree clean in half."

I pick up a pen. "What's your name, sir?"

"Rick Sweeney."

"Where are you located, Mr. Sweeney?"

He rattles off an address that's just down the road from the Davenport farm.

I jot it down. "Did you get a look at the vehicle?"

"Hell yes I did. It was a damn buggy full of Amish kids and they looked like they was up to no good. I ran out and yelled at them and one of 'em flipped me the bird! Listen, I've had four buggies and a dozen cars come down this road in the last hour. I got puke in my driveway and beer cans in the ditch. They're playing loud music and making all sorts of noise. I'm sick of it. Gotta be one of them wild parties going on someplace."

"I'll send an officer out there now to check it out."

"I want someone to pay for that tree and clean up all the crap."

"Would you like to file a police report?"

"Hell yes I would!"

"I'll send someone to your location as soon as I have an officer—"

He hangs up on me.

I look up to find Jodie and Skid standing around the desk, watching me.

"I take it phones are up?" Skid asks.

I address Jodie. "You all set here?"

"Got it under control, Chief."

I turn to Skid and tell him about the call from Rick Sweeney. "He's right next to the old Davenport place."

"Looks like they started the party without us," he says.

"Get a statement from Sweeney and then meet me out there."

"You got it, Chief."

Alma had never seen so many people in one place. There were hundreds of them. Some were arriving in vehicles, windows down, radios blaring. A few were in buggies, the horses turned over to hostlers too young to partake in the festivities. The vast majority of attendees were Amish; most had traded in their dresses and suspenders for blue jeans and tee shirts. But there were a lot of *Englischers* in attendance, too.

It was the most exciting thing Alma had ever experienced in her life. Even more so because, in half an hour, she would be meeting Aden. He'd asked her to meet him in the old barn at nine thirty, when he got off work. She was pretty sure he was going to ask her to marry him tonight and the thought stole her breath.

Alma was so engrossed in her thoughts she didn't see the two boys, each carting a six-pack of beer, until she nearly ran into them. Luckily, Irene saw them coming.

"Look out!" Irene said, pulling her aside.

Alma sidestepped just in time. One of the boys turned and grinned at her as he passed. "Watch where you're going, cutie!" he called out.

The other boy dug two beers from one of the cases, jogged up to them, and handed the cans to them. "Enjoy yourselves!" he said, and continued on with his friend.

Alma and Irene looked at each other and burst into laughter. "He was talking to you!" Alma exclaimed.

"He was *looking* at you." Irene sighed. "You're the pretty one."

"Don't be silly." Alma slanted her friend a look,

saddened because she knew Irene was serious. She was a firm believer that beauty was on the inside of a person, not the outside. But she'd heard the cruel names the others called her friend. Names like "homely" and "stinky."

"You're pretty, and anyone who says otherwise is a *sau*," Alma said, using the *Deitsh* word for "pig."

Irene glanced down at the swell of her breasts, which were encased in a push-up bra beneath her tee shirt. "These are pretty, maybe."

Not wanting the topic to dampen their high spirits, Alma elbowed her. "A little bird told me Melvin Raber is going to ask you to the singing next week after worship."

Melvin Raber was a few years older than them. He was handsome and single and worked at the Amish furniture store near Charm. Alma didn't know for a fact he was thinking about asking Irene to the singing, but this was one of those little white lies women sometimes told to protect tender feelings.

"We'll see," Irene said, but she didn't look hopeful. "How are you supposed to find Aden with all these people here?"

"We're meeting in the barn at nine thirty."

"Let's drink these beers and I'll walk you over."

The girls popped the tabs on their beers and clinked the cans together. "Here's to a fun and memorable night," Alma said.

"And a boy for me!" Irene exclaimed.

"And beer for everyone!"

In unison, the girls tipped their cans and chugged.

I arrive at the Davenport farm to find a long line of vehicles parked on both sides of the lane. A dozen more are parked on the shoulders of Apple Creek Road. Illuminated by my headlights, a couple of Amish boys walk alongside the road, toting a large cooler between them.

Finding a spot behind an old F-150 pickup truck, I watch them make the turn into the lane and reach for my radio. "Ten twenty-three," I say, letting Jodie know I've arrived on scene. "I've got a hundred or so individuals out here. Skid, expedite that ten twenty-five when you finish up there, will you?" Ten twenty-five is the code for "meet me."

"Roger that," comes Skid's voice.

"Jodie, you got a number for the owner?"

My dispatcher rattles off a phone number. "Kent Davenport lives in Westerville, Chief."

"Thanks." Racking the mike, I shut down the engine, pull out my cell, and dial.

Three rings and a gruff male voice answers. "This is Kent."

I identify myself. "I'm calling from the property you own in Painters Mill. The farm on Apple Creek Road?"

"What about it?"

"Apparently, there's a party happening this

evening. I need to know if these individuals have permission to be there."

"Yeah, I got a call from Ralph Baker. He said he was going to smoke some ribs and have a few people out."

"Mr. Davenport, there are more than a hundred people here."

"I'll be damned. He didn't say anything about having that many. He'd better not leave any trash."

Since permission was indeed granted, I won't be able to disperse the crowd based on trespassing. But I'd bet my left pinky finger there will be a slew of other problems, including underage drinking and drug use.

"Mr. Davenport, I suspect there are some minor juveniles drinking alcohol out here this evening. Do you mind if I take a look around?"

"Help yourself. You let me know if those folks misbehave."

I thank him and slide out of the Explorer. The wind has kicked up, but it's a nice evening, balmy and cool. From where I'm standing I can hear the blast of country music. It's too far away and too dark for me to see, but it sounds like a live band. A dozen or so lights—spotlights and lanterns and flashlights—illuminate the area between the house and barn.

I start toward the chaos.

The beer was just going to her head when Alma stepped into the darkened interior of the old barn. She was a little early, but she didn't mind. A few minutes alone would give her nerves time to settle.

Anticipation pulsed inside her, keeping perfect time with the tempo of the music outside. She was so excited to see Aden she almost couldn't breathe. It made her think of the time her *mamm* told her that sometimes things could be *too* good and it was at that point when a good girl pulled herself back. But Alma knew there was no pulling herself back from this. She loved Aden and this was going to be the most wonderful night of her life.

Flipping on the little flashlight she'd bought at Walmart, she swept the beam left and right, taking stock of the interior. It was dusty and damp with a dirt floor, falling-down stalls, and a hayloft that sagged like a swayback horse. She shone the cone of light toward the rear of the barn where a rafter had broken loose from above and slanted down at a precarious angle.

Outside, the music pulsed with energy. She could feel the bass drum vibrate all the way to her bones. All of it was punctuated by the occasional shout of some rowdy boys or the yelp of a girl who'd had too much to drink.

A sound from the rear of the barn jangled her nerves. Heart leaping, she jerked the beam left. Dust motes flew within the cone of light. Was there a back door? Had the noise been the squeak of a hinge?

"Aden?" She laughed at herself when she saw the beam shaking. Her palm was wet on the flashlight;

she could actually hear her breaths hissing, feel the thrum of her heart against her ribs.

Alma took a long pull of beer, hoping the alcohol would calm her, and she moved toward the rear of the barn. "Aden? Is that you?"

A wide aisle lay straight ahead. Additional live-stock stalls lined both sides. Beyond, she could see the back side of the barn, huge beams, and the wood siding, all of it dripping with cobwebs.

Stepping over a fallen board, Alma walked into the aisle, peering over the tops of the gates as she passed stalls filled with junk. Rotting bales of hay. Miscellaneous pieces of farming equipment. A rusty fifty-gallon drum. All of it had her thinking about spi-ders, and she shivered. "Hello? Is someone there?"

Midway down the aisle, she shifted the beam and spotted the open door at the rear of the barn. Had someone come inside? Was Aden playing a joke on her?

"If you're trying to scare me, it's working!" But she could feel the fingers of uneasiness pressing into the back of her neck. "Aden! Come on! This isn't funny!"

Another sound spun her around. She swept the beam left. A shadow in the stall. Her beau's name on her lips. The blow came down on the top of her head with stunning force. Pain streaked across her scalp. Alma fell to her knees. Shaking her head to clear it, she looked up. Movement above her. She raised her hands to protect herself.

The second blow landed like a stone. Alma fell forward. The flashlight rolled away, crazy light playing against weathered wood. Her hands hit the floor. Her elbows collapsed and then she lay face-down, trying to make sense of what had happened, too stunned to move.

The final blow crashed against the back of her skull. White light exploded inside her head and then faded to red.

By the time I reach the area between the house and the barns I realize two things. I've seriously underestimated the size and scope of the party. And there's a hell of a lot more going on than underage drinking.

Several generators are running, producing enough electricity to light up the entirety of Painters Mill. Farther away, someone built a riser upon which a country band is performing, guitar and a decent voice echoing among the trees. The aromas of food—barbeque and smoked meat—float pleasantly on the night air, mingling with the unmistakable smell of marijuana. All of it punctuated by laughter and shouting, both in English and *Deitsh*.

A group of Amish boys, some seemingly no older than sixteen or seventeen years old, walk past me, gesturing and laughing, each with a can of beer in hand. My first instinct, of course, is to stop them and ask for identification, but common sense tells me for every teenager I stop, a dozen more will fill the void.

I'm reaching for my cell to call Sheriff Rasmussen for backup when it goes off in my hand. "Burkholder," I snap.

"Chief, it's Mona." Mona Kurtz is my third-shift dispatcher. As usual she's come in to work a few hours early. Usually, I'd take a moment to explain to her that I don't have the budget for overtime. Tonight I'm unduly relieved to have her on hand.

"What's up?" I ask.

"Traffic light is out on Main Street and a truck just plowed through the front window of the Butterhorn Bakery."

"Anyone hurt?"

"Driver's okay, but there's quite a bit of damage and Mr. Skanks is pissed."

Tom Skanks is the owner of the bakery. He makes the best apple fritters I've ever had the pleasure of devouring, so I'm inclined to cut him some slack. "Remind him that insurance will cover the cost of the repairs."

"Will do."

But I know Skanks can be a handful. "I take it power is still out?"

"I talked to the technician ten minutes ago and he said it's going to be a few hours before they can get that line repaired."

I need Skid here, but in order to avoid another potential accident, I opt to send him back into town to deal with the public safety issue. "Call Skid and tell him to set up a stop sign at the intersection and help Tom get the bakery secured for the night."

"Roger that."

"Mona?"

"Yeah, Chief?"

"Thanks for coming in early."

I can practically hear her smile come through the line. "You got it."

I hit End and thumb in the speed dial for Sheriff Rasmussen. "Mike, we've got a situation out at the old Davenport farm. There are a couple hundred people out here. A lot of juveniles and alcohol. Drugs, too."

He groans. "We're still dealing with that downed tower and power lines, Kate. As soon as I get someone freed up, I'll send them that way."

"Appreciate it."

"For God's sake, is there anything else that could go wrong tonight?"

"You might want to knock on wood when you say that."

Groaning, he hangs up.

I drop the phone into my pocket. Twenty yards away, the band breaks into a decent rendition of George Strait's *Amarillo by Morning*. The young Amish man manning the smoker is slicing a slab of brisket atop a butcher-block board. Beyond, a huge bonfire crackles and sparks, throwing flames ten feet into the air. It's a chaotic, raucous scene that a cop alone hasn't a snowball's chance of controlling.

I'm thinking about calling one of my other officers when my phone chirps. "What's up, Mona?"

"Chief, I just took a call from Aden Keim. He says he's out at the rager and there's been a serious accident."

"Someone hurt?"

"His girlfriend is unconscious. He says they're in the old barn on the property."

"I know it." I'm already jogging toward the structure, which is nestled in the trees a hundred or so yards from the house. "Get an ambulance out here, will you?"

"Already en route."

I disconnect just as I reach the barn. The interior is lit by a single lantern and at least one flashlight. There are several people standing in the doorway, mostly Amish, male and female. All of them look worried.

"Police!" I say as I enter. "Where's the injured party?"

A young man with long blond hair and a goatee looks at me as if I'm a ghost, raises a skinny arm, and points. "Back there."

Brushing past him, I pull out my Maglite. A young man with dark hair is on his knees next to a woman lying on the ground facedown. He looks at me as I approach. In the periphery of my flashlight beam, his face is ravaged.

"What happened?" I ask as I kneel beside the victim.

"I don't know!" he cries. "I found her . . . like this. I mean, I walked in and she was just lying there on the ground."

I shine my light on the girl. Though she's wearing blue jeans and a tee shirt, there's something about her that tells me she's Amish. No jewelry or piercings. Minimal makeup. No nail polish. I run the beam of my flashlight over her, looking for injuries or evidence of drug use. She's lost a shoe at some point.

"Has she been drinking?" I ask. "Doing any drugs? Anything like that?"

"No!" he cries. "She's . . . Amish. She . . . doesn't do those things."

As he says the words, I spot a bloodstain the size of a quarter on the shoulder of her tee shirt. A closer look reveals more blood matted in her hair at the back of her head.

He sets his hand on her upper arm as if to turn her over. I reach out and stop him. "Better not to move her," I tell him. "There's an ambulance on the way."

"But . . ." Looking anguished, he sets his hand against the side of her face, brushes hair from her eyes. "What's wrong with her?" He looks at me, demanding an answer. "Why won't she wake up?"

"What's her name?" I ask, aware that the people in the doorway are curious and getting closer.

"Alma Fisher," he tells me.

I hit my lapel mike. "What's the ETA on that ambulance?"

Mona's voice comes back at me. "Just pulled in to the gravel lane out there, Chief."

"Make sure they know the victim is in the barn."

"Roger that."

I'd been hoping the girl would regain consciousness by now, but she's not even stirring. Her face is slack. Her mouth open. A string of drool dripping onto the dirt floor. Her eyes are partially closed and I can see them rolling back white. Shit.

Movement at the big sliding door draws my attention. I glance over to see a paramedic enter. He's in uniform. Hands gloved. Nylon medical bag at his side.

Rising, I address the crowd, motion for them to move away. "Back up. Give him room."

The paramedic makes eye contact with me briefly before crossing to me. He drops the bag next to the girl and kneels. "What do we have?" he asks easily.

I tell him everything I know, which isn't much. "There's blood on her shirt there and on the back of her head."

"How long has she been unresponsive?"

"She was unconscious when he found her." I look at the Amish man.

"Five or ten minutes," he says. "I don't know! I found her like this. What's wrong with her?"

The paramedic quickly assesses her. "Bleeding is minimal. Airway is open. Breathing regular, but slow." He cranes his head and looks toward the door where his partner is standing. "I need a backboard and cervical collar."

He turns his attention back to the girl. "Hey, sweetheart. Can you hear me? Can you tell me what happened?"

No response. Not so much as a twitch.

I get a bad feeling in my gut. Anything could have happened, but the wound on the back of her head worries me. I don't think it happened in a fall.

The second paramedic joins us, and while the first supports the patient's head, he applies the collar. The two men carefully lift her onto the backboard. All the while the Amish man hovers, pacing, too close and getting in the way.

After the girl is strapped onto the backboard, the paramedics lift her and carry her to the waiting ambulance. The Amish man follows, but I stop him. "I need to talk to you," I tell him.

He barely hears me; he can't seem to take his eyes off the girl. "But she's all alone. I need to go with her."

Or maybe he's in a hurry to get away from me because he knows I'm about to ask him what happened. "Come over here," I say firmly. "Now."

Taking a final look at the door, he gives me his full attention. I look past him at the growing crowd in the doorway. "Stay put," I tell him and address the crowd. "You people need to clear out. Right now."

Since most of them are simply curious—and

would rather spend the rest of their evening partying instead of in this dusty barn with me—they begin to disperse.

I hit my shoulder mike. "Ten seven eight." Need assistance.

I turn my attention to the young man. He's about twenty years old, with dark hair. Brown puppy dog eyes. He's a good-looking kid. I can tell by the haircut he's Amish.

"What's your name?" I ask.

"Aden Keim."

"What's your relationship with the girl?"

"She's my girlfriend."

"What were you two doing here tonight?"

"I was supposed to meet her. When I got off work."

"What happened?"

"I walked in and . . . found her on the ground."

"Did she say anything?"

"No, she was . . ." His voice breaks. "She was just . . . unconscious."

"What happened to her?"

"I don't know!"

"Was there anyone else around?"

"I didn't see anyone." He looks over his shoulder, casts another glance toward the door. "Look, I need to get to the hospital."

"Do you know how I can get in touch with her family?"

"Andy and Edna Fisher. They live out on Otterbein-Ithaca Road."

I've never met the Fisher family, but I know of them; I've driven past their place a hundred times. "I need to take a look at your ID," I tell him. "I'm going to need to get in touch with you later."

He tugs a wallet from his pocket, yanks out his brand-new driver's license and shoves it at me, slings another look toward the door where the ambulance is pulling away. A boy losing sight of his mama in a crowded grocery.

Taking his license, I move away and speak into my lapel mike. "Ten twenty-nine," I say, which is the code for "check for wanted," and I recite Keim's driver's license number.

All the while he paces, looking repeatedly at the door. Anxious to leave. To get away from me and my questions? Or is he simply eager to get to the hospital to check on his girlfriend?

When his license comes back clean, I walk over to him and hand it to him. "Do you have any out-of-town trips planned, Mr. Keim?"

He looks at me as if I'm crazy. "No."

"Good, because I have some more questions about what happened tonight. Make sure you're available."

Snatching the license from my hand, he jogs to the door and leaves without looking back.

A few minutes later I'm standing near the spot where Alma Fisher had lain when my first-shift officer, Rupert "Glock" Maddox, saunters into the barn looking as if an Amish rager and city-wide power outage are business as usual. A former Marine, he's as sharp and competent as any big-city cop.

"Heard there was some excitement out here," he says as he approaches, and I notice the work light he's carrying. "Thought this might come in handy."

I have no idea how he arrived so quickly—on his day off no less—but I'm unduly pleased by his presence. "What are you, psychic?" I ask.

He grins. "Where do you want this?"

I motion toward the spot a few feet from the place where the girl was found. "I'm not sure what we're dealing with just yet so I'd like a thorough look around."

"Hello?"

Glock and I glance toward the door to see a young Amish man wheel in a good-size generator. "Where do you want this?" the man asks.

I make eye contact with Glock. "Is there anything you didn't think of?"

Another grin. "I thought about confiscating those ribs out there, but I was sort of worried about the whole police brutality thing."

Leave it to Glock to go there. Shaking my head, I address the man with the generator. "Over here."

He rolls it over to us and kneels beside it, flips a switch. "I appreciate your letting us borrow this," I tell him. "We'll pick up the cost of the gas."

"Officer Maddox said someone was hurt, so . . ." Rising, the Amish man bends and yanks the pull cord. The engine sputters to life.

Glock plugs in the work lights and suddenly the barn's interior is brightly lit.

"*Danki*." I shake the Amish man's hand. "We shouldn't be but an hour or so."

"I'll come back then." With a nod, he leaves the barn.

I get my first good look at the scene. There's no sign of a struggle. No blood. No weapon in sight. A woman's sandal lies on its side a few feet away. Pulling out my phone, I snap four photos of the shoe from different angles.

Glock holds his ground near the generator. Both of us are cognizant of footwear imprints, from the victim—or someone else—and we're careful not to disturb them.

"What's the story?" he asks.

I tell him what little I know. "Boyfriend found her."

He looks around, glances up at the rafters and farther back, the loft. "Too far away from the loft for her to have fallen."

"Even if she had help." I spot a two-by-four lying flush against the wall a few feet from where she was found. It gives me pause because it looks like someone put it there to keep it out of sight. . . .

Glock notices it at the same time. "That's interesting as hell."

I cross to the piece of wood and snap half a dozen photos from all directions. It's about two feet long and jagged on one end where it's been broken. When I'm finished, Glock joins me and we kneel for a closer look. Tugging on gloves from a compartment on my belt, I pick it up, hold it to the light. It's dusty and jagged and old. Suspicion stirs when I spot the hairs tangled on a rusty nail that had been hammered nearly flat.

"Hair," I murmur. The strand is about six inches long, shiny and brown—the same color as Alma Fisher's.

"Looks like blood, too," Glock says.

For the first time I notice the dark smear on the edge.

His eyes meet mine. "You think the boyfriend did this?"

"Someone did." We get to our feet and look around. "This was no accident."

Though the work lights emit a decent amount of illumination, there are plenty of shadows. I pull out my Maglite. "Footwear," I say. "Victim was wearing sandals."

"I got waffle sole here." Glock backtracks toward the door. "The boyfriend?"

I go to the imprint and pull out my phone. "Looks like work boots. Fits with the boots he was wearing."

"Easy enough to check." He looks around. "We don't know who else has been in here before tonight."

"True. Still, worth documenting."

I photograph the work boot imprint.

Glock aims the beam of his Maglite on the ground, sweeps it toward the door. "Dirt is pretty packed, but

ONLY THE LUCKY 225

it looks like he came in through the front door and went directly to her."

Keeping my eyes on the ground, I notice a smaller shoe impression. It has little in the way of tread, but has pointed toes and inch-wide heels. "Looks like a female shoe imprint here," I say to Glock without looking up.

He approaches with caution. "Or a dude with really small feet and a penchant for heels. "He sets a mini tape measure for scale next to the imprint.

I snap several photos. "Size seven or eight maybe." But there's only a single discernible imprint and it's been spoiled by other disturbances in the dirt floor—my own tracks included.

Knowing how quickly word travels in the Amish community, I decide to leave the scene in Glock's capable hands so I can drive over to the Fisher farm to let the girl's parents know what happened.

"Bag that two-by-four and courier it over to BCI," I tell him. "If you find anything else even remotely interesting, snap some photos and bag it."

"You got it, Chief."

"I'm heading over to the Fisher place."

He nods. "You want me to pick up the boyfriend?"

"Let's hold off on that until I talk to the doctor so we know what we're dealing with."

Hopefully, this won't become a homicide.

I call my significant other, John Tomasetti, on my way to the Fisher farm. He's a special agent with the

Ohio Bureau of Criminal Investigation. Not only is he a good cop and a good man, but he's also the love of my life.

"I'm not going to make it home tonight," I tell him.

"I heard about the power outage."

"The plot has thickened." I tell him about the Amish rager and the injured girl. "I'm on my way to talk to the parents now."

"Is there anything I can do to help?"

"You might pull out that nice bottle of Cabernet we've been saving. I'll let you know when to break the seal."

"I'm all over that."

Andy and Edna Fisher live on Otterbein-Ithaca Road in the southern part of Holmes County. It's a quaint little farm with a good-size sheep herd in the front pasture. The house is small and plain. I park next to a buggy and take the stone walkway to the front door and knock.

It's nearly 11:00 P.M. now, so I give them plenty of time to answer. I'm knocking for the third time when the door squeaks open. I find myself looking at a middle-aged Amish man with owlish, sleep-fuzzed eyes. He thrusts the lantern at me, his gaze skimming my uniform.

"Mr. Fisher?"

"What's wrong?" he asks, concern spreading across his face.

"Is Alma Fisher your daughter?"

"Yes."

"She's been injured and taken to the hospital."

"*Hospital?* Alma?" His eyes and mouth go wide. "What happened to her? Is she all right?"

His wife comes up behind him as I lay out what few facts I know. "I can drive you and your wife to the hospital if you like."

He shakes his head. "We will take the buggy." He looks down at the sleep shirt he's wearing. "I need to . . . harness the horse."

"I won't keep you, Mr. Fisher, but I need to ask you a couple of quick questions."

He stares at me, tension and apprehension pouring off him.

"Do you know where your daughter went this evening? Who she was with?"

His expression tells me he doesn't have a clue.

His wife steps in. "Alma went to the barbeque out to the Davenport place with her friend, Irene. She was going to meet Aden Keim when he got off work."

The Amish man blinks, as if still trying to absorb everything he's been told.

"What's Irene's last name?" I ask.

"Miller," she tells me. "The girls are best friends. She lives out to Dogleg Road with her *mamm* and *datt*."

I put the information to memory and ask, "What's your daughter's relationship with Aden Keim?"

"Aden is . . . courting her," Mr. Fisher tells me. "I suspect they'll get married."

"Do they get along?" I ask.

"I don't think they'd get married if they didn't get along," he says.

His wife interjects. "Alma is a good girl. Aden is a hard worker and a good boy. They're going to join the church soon."

I sigh, realizing I'll need to be careful because I don't want to frighten them unduly. "There's a possibility Alma was . . . assaulted. Can either of you think of anyone who might be angry with her? Someone she's argued with recently?"

"Assaulted?" Mr. Fisher recoils as if it couldn't possibly be true. "No."

"Does Aden have a temper?" I ask.

"No," the man says firmly.

Knowing sometimes women see things the men don't, I focus on Mrs. Fisher and raise my brows. "Mrs. Fisher?"

"He's a nice young man," she says. "Gentle and kind."

I give them a moment to add any additional thoughts, but I can tell they're too worried and anxious to check on their daughter. "I'll let you get on the road then."

I call the ER department of Pomerene Hospital as I pull onto the road. Quickly, I identify myself and ask about Alma Fisher's condition. The third-shift nurse on duty knows me, and since the girl's injuries are part of a police investigation, she's able to give me some preliminary information over the phone, even though I'm not a family member.

"I just talked to Doc McCoy, who's on call to-night, and I wish to God I had better news. The girl has suffered a traumatic brain injury. There's some swelling of the brain and she's slipped into a coma."

"How serious?"

"Still running tests, Chief, but it's not good."

"Does the doctor have any idea how such an in-jury might have occurred?"

"He knew you'd be asking. He doesn't believe it happened in a fall. In fact, he's pretty sure she was hit multiple times with a blunt instrument."

Like a two-by-four, I think darkly, but I don't men-tion it. "Her parents are on the way."

"She's going to need all the support she can get."

"Has she had any visitors?" I ask. "Anyone in the waiting room?"

"Just that nice-looking Amish boy. Been hanging around since shortly after she arrived. Comes up to the desk every ten minutes to ask about her." She makes a sound. "Can't tell him anything since he's not family, so I'm glad her parents will be here soon to fill him in."

I thank her and disconnect, wondering how Aden Keim will react when I show up.

Since I've already talked to Keim—and it could be beneficial to let him stew for a while—I call Mona for Susie and Perry Miller's address and then I head that way.

Despite the late hour, the windows of the Miller place glow with lantern light when I pull into the driveway. More than likely they already know about Alma Fisher. Word travels fast in Amish country, and when someone is hurt or ill, the Amish community shows up in force to help.

As I walk to the front door, I notice lantern light in the barn, too. I glance over to see an Amish man harnessing a horse. I continue to the front door and knock. A somber-faced Amish woman in her mid-forties answers quickly. She's wearing a light blue dress with a cardigan draped over her shoulders.

She doesn't look surprised to see me. "Can I help you?"

I show her my ID. "Is Irene Miller here?"

"Is this is about Alma?"

"Yes, ma'am."

"We're getting ready to go to the hospital." Stepping back, she ushers me inside and calls out in *Deitsh*, "The English police are here!"

Irene Miller enters the living room with the caution of a rabbit sneaking past the fox's den. She's short and stocky with dishwater-brown hair and eyes the color of pond moss. She's wearing a light blue dress that falls to mid-calf and a gauzy *kapp*.

Her gaze flicks from me to her mother and back to me. "Is she okay?"

"The doctor is still running tests," I tell her.

Nodding, she looks at the floor. "Poor Alma."

I cross to the girl. "You're friends with her?"

"More like *shveshtahs*." Sisters. "She's my best friend."

Now that I'm standing closer to her, I detect the aroma of wood smoke in her hair, confirming my suspicion that she'd been at the rager earlier. "You were at the party tonight?"

She doesn't look up, but nods. I'm betting her parents didn't know beforehand and probably wouldn't have found out if someone hadn't clobbered Alma Fisher with a two-by-four.

"Did you go with Alma?" I ask.

Another nod.

Remembering the footwear imprints that came from a female shoe, I send a covert glance to her feet, but she's wearing sneakers. Of course that doesn't mean she didn't change shoes. . . .

"How did you hear about the party?" I ask.

She looks down again. "Mary Zimmerman told me about it at worship last weekend. All the young people were going to be there."

I suspect there was a good bit of back and forth on social media, too, but I don't ask about it. Instead, I look at her mother. "Did you know about it?"

"We wouldn't allow such a thing with the music and beer." Clucking, she shakes her head in disapproval.

I turn my attention back to Irene. "Were you with Alma all evening?"

"We were only together for half an hour or so. Then she left to meet Aden in the barn."

"While you were with Alma, did the two of you talk to anyone else? Interact with anyone?"

"Just . . . some girls we know. We listened to the band for a while and some boys tried to get us to drink beer." She slants an anxious look at her *mamm.* "We didn't."

I suspect I'd get more out of her without her mother hovering, but since this girl is only seventeen years old, that's not an option. Yet. "Did Alma have any on-going disagreements with anyone? Any arguments or harsh words?"

The girl shakes her head. "No, she's very kind."

"Were any of the boys . . . forward? Or too interested in her?"

"All the boys want to marry Alma." She offers a sad smile. "None of them were mean to her."

"What about in the days or weeks before the party? Has anyone been bothering her? Has she mentioned anyone doing or saying something unpleasant or threatening? English or Amish?"

The girl's brows knit as she takes a moment to consider. Then she shakes her head. "No."

"Where did you leave Alma this evening?"

"I walked her about halfway to the barn. We hugged, and then I went back to listen to the band."

She shrugs and then her face screws up. "A couple hours later I heard she was in the hospital and I . . . didn't know what to do. So I came home."

"Did you go into the barn with her?" I ask.

"No."

"Was there anyone else in the barn with her?"

"Not that I know of. Just . . . Aden."

I nod, let the name hang. "We think someone may have attacked Alma while she was in the barn." I watch her carefully for a reaction, but the girl keeps her eyes downcast.

"Do Alma and Aden get along well?" I ask. "Did they ever argue?"

She raises her head. Her eyes widen as my words register. "He wouldn't. I mean, he's got a temper, but . . . he loves Alma." Tears threaten. "Too much probably."

"What do you mean by 'too much'?" I ask.

Her gaze hits the floor; she doesn't answer.

"Aden has a temper?" I press.

The girl hesitates, glances at her *mamm,* as if seeking permission to flee to her room. Her mother stares back as if wondering *how could she know of such things?*

"All you have to do is tell the truth," I say gently.

"He gets mad sometimes," the girl mumbles.

"About what?"

"He doesn't like other boys looking at Alma like they do."

"Was he angry with her tonight?"

Again, she avoids making eye contact with me. She studies the floor as if it's some enigmatic piece of art. "I think he was going to ask her to marry him."

I wait for her to elaborate, but she doesn't. "He was going to ask her to marry him tonight?" I repeat.

Just when I think she isn't going to respond, she raises her gaze to mine, tears shimmering in her eyes. "Alma was going to tell him no."

I call Glock on my way back to the station. "I want you to pick up Aden Keim and bring him in for questioning."

"You got it, Chief."

"Did you and Skid get that party dispersed?"

"Guy with the smoker just left. Hated to turn down all that brisket." A thoughtful pause ensues. "You think the boyfriend did it?"

I tell him about my conversation with Irene Miller. "He's my number one suspect at the moment."

He sighs. "Aren't they always?"

The statement echoes the sentiments of most cops. It makes the situation doubly sad because far too often it's the person women love most who would do them harm.

"Keep an eye on Keim," I say. "He's a big guy and from what I hear he has a temper."

"Suspect with a temper is my specialty," he says

with a chuckle. "Especially if they're a bully. See you in a few."

It's midnight when I arrive at the station. Mona is kicked back at the dispatch desk, studying a textbook while The Black Keys belt out a tune on the radio. She grins when I enter and turns it down.

"Any word on the condition of Alma Fisher?" I ask.

"As of ten minutes ago she was undergoing a CAT scan. Nurse told me to check back in an hour."

I pluck messages from my slot as I pass. "You can turn the radio back up now."

She dazzles me with a grin. "Oh, and you have a visitor in your office."

I enter my office to find Tomasetti sitting in the visitor chair across from my desk.

"I heard you have a felony assault on your hands," he says by way of greeting.

"And you learned about that in your sleep how exactly?" But I smile as I slide behind my desk.

"I'm not at liberty to disclose my sources. You know, BCI policy and all that."

I laugh outright. "Tomasetti, you're so full of shit."

"That's what everyone tells me."

I turn on my computer. "I'm bringing the boyfriend in for questioning."

"He have a record?"

"Not even a traffic ticket. But then he's Amish."

"You think he did it?"

I consider everything I know about the case, about Alma Fisher, about Keim. "I think we'll know a lot more after we talk to him. I asked Glock to pick him up."

"I'm glad I showed up."

"Me, too."

Twenty minutes later, Tomasetti and I are sitting at the table in the meeting room when Glock brings in Aden Keim. Even in the dim glow of the emergency lights, I can see the Amish man has calmed down since the scene in the barn. Glock unlocks the cuffs and motions him into a chair.

"Conduct yourself like a gentleman or I'll come back in here and put those cuffs back on," Glock tells him. "Do you understand?"

"Yes, sir," Keim mumbles as he lowers himself into a chair.

Glock is the only person who could pull that off with a smile and still be taken seriously. Nodding at Tomasetti and me, he backs from the room and closes the door.

"You're not under arrest," I tell Keim. "You are being questioned as a possible witness with regard to the assault that was perpetrated on Alma Fisher earlier. Do you understand?"

"I understand, but I don't see why we couldn't do this at the hospital."

Ignoring the statement, I identify Tomasetti and

myself before beginning. "Mr. Keim, I need you to tell me what happened in the barn this evening."

"Alma and I had been planning for days to go to the party together, but last minute I had to work late, so I asked her to meet me in the barn around nine thirty. I was a few minutes late. I found her on the floor, unconscious, and I called 911."

"Did you see or hear anyone else in or around the barn?" I ask. "Were there any signs that someone else might've been there?"

His brows go together as he considers the question. "There were people milling around outside. But the barn is old and dusty . . . I don't think anyone had been inside."

I think about the second set of shoe imprints. "You were alone?"

"Of course I was alone."

"Why did you want to meet in the barn?"

"I just . . ." He shifts in the chair, looking uncomfortable. "I wanted to be alone with her."

"Why is that?"

He looks away, seems to gather himself, then meets my gaze. "I was going to ask her to marry me."

"Did you?"

"I told you. She was unconscious when I got there. I didn't get the chance."

Tomasetti speaks up for the first time. "Or maybe something else happened."

His gaze snaps to Tomasetti. "Something like what?"

He leans forward and lowers his voice. "Maybe she said no and that pissed you off."

"What?" Looking indignant and trapped, Keim's gaze jumps from Tomasetti to me and back to Tomasetti. "That's not what happened! That's just crazy talk. I'd never hurt Alma and she would never say no!"

"Do you have a temper?" Tomasetti asks.

"No. I mean, no more than the next guy. And never with Alma."

Tomasetti keeps pushing. "That's not what we heard."

"I don't care what you heard! I didn't hurt her." He chokes out a sound that resonates with near panic. "You have to believe me! I love her and she loves me. When she wakes up, she'll tell you!"

It's an impassioned statement, but I know all too well that some individuals are born liars. I wish I could exclude the Amish altogether, but I can't.

I give him a moment to calm down and shift gears. "Did Alma have any enemies?"

"She's liked by everyone. I mean, she's that kind of person. Always smiling. She's humble and sweet and kind."

"Did she have any ongoing arguments or disputes?"

"No."

"Any jealous ex-boyfriends?"

"I'm her first." He says the words with a hefty dose of male pride, then lowers his voice. "My first, too."

To some people the words might seem corny. Knowing the Amish as I do, I find myself endeared by this young man despite the circumstances.

"Has she been approached or hassled by any strangers recently? Men or women? Amish or English?"

"Sometimes I see men look at her, but not in a way that worried me. I mean, she's so pretty who *wouldn't* look at her?"

"Can you think of anyone who might've wanted to hurt Alma?" I ask. "For any reason?"

He shakes his head. "Not a soul."

For the span of several heartbeats no one speaks. As if reminded of the situation, Keim shifts in the chair and looks longingly at the door.

"Do you have sisters, Mr. Keim?" Tomasetti asks.

The Amish man looks from Tomasetti to me and back to Tomasetti. "Four of them," he says. "What does that have to do with anything?"

"Are they younger or older than you?"

"Two younger, two older. I don't see what that has to do with—"

Tomasetti cuts him off, addressing me. "Any more questions for him, Chief Burkholder?"

"No."

Tomasetti gives Keim a poor imitation of a smile. "You're free to go. Glock will drive you home."

Looking suspicious of the easy escape, Keim rises. "I don't want to go home. I need to get back to the hospital."

When Keim is gone, I look at Tomasetti. Neither of us are a pushover when it comes to a sob story. We've heard them all, told a dozen different ways, some with a great deal of passion. But we also possess pretty good built-in lie detectors.

"I have a feeling you and I are on the same page," I say.

"The page that says 'he's either an award-winning actor or he didn't do it.'"

"Something like that." I tell him about the female shoe imprint left at the scene.

"That's interesting," he says. "Do you have photos?"

"Yep." I pull out my cell. "Server is down so they're only on my phone for now."

He comes around the desk and I scroll through the photos, enlarging each so we can see the detail. "Looks like some type of boot. With a heel."

"Tomasetti, you know your female shoes." I give him a questioning look.

"I'm going to have to take the Fifth on that."

I elbow him and he returns to the visitor chair on the other side of my desk. "There was definitely a female in the barn. The problem is we don't know *when*. She could have been there the day before any of this happened."

He thinks about that a moment. "Is there a shoe store in Painters Mill?"

"The Bootery." I feel a smile emerge. "Tomasetti, I'm really glad you decided to come in."

"Since the retail shops don't open until ten A.M. or so, we could head back to the farm to discuss the crime, and maybe grab a couple hours of sleep. Not necessarily in that order."

I know him well enough to know the crime is the last thing on his mind. "Since I have a teenage girl in a coma and a town without power I think I'm going to stick around here the rest of the night."

"In that case I'll take a rain check."

I call the hospital twice during the early morning hours only to learn there's been no change in Alma Fisher's condition. She's still in a coma, but stable. The nurse I spoke to informed me there were a dozen or so Amish in the intensive care waiting room. I'm not surprised; when someone gets hurt or is in need—even if they're English—the Amish turn out in droves to support them.

At 5:00 A.M. the electricity jolts on. Mona peeks her head into my office. "Do you think it's safe for me to turn off the generator?"

"It will be nice not to hear it," I tell her.

The day is looking up.

A few minutes before 10:00 A.M. Tomasetti and I are standing on the sidewalk outside The Bootery, Painters Mill's first upscale shoe store. It's a chic retail space set into an historic building with the original front door and an artful window display chock-full of everything from gladiator sandals to suede fringed booties. The bell on the door jingles when we enter.

"Good morning!" A white-haired gentleman with a precise goatee is standing at the counter behind an old-fashioned cash register. Wearing a double-breasted suit, a pair of square bifocals, and a bow tie, he looks more like a college professor than a shoe salesman.

I show him my ID and identify myself.

"Bart Wentworth." He sticks out his hand and we shake. "To what do I owe the pleasure?"

"Agent Tomasetti and I are wondering if you can help us identify the image of a sole."

He looks intrigued by the idea. "I've been in the shoe business since I was fourteen years old. If I can't identify it, no one can. What do you have?"

Pulling out my phone, I show him the image.

"Hmmm. Interesting." He tilts his head back and looks at it through his bifocals. "Exquisitely made shoe."

"A woman's?" I ask.

"Correct."

"Size?"

"If that tape measure next to it is correct . . . size eight. B width probably."

"Any idea where it came from?"

The old man's eyes sparkle. "I'd venture to say it came off that shelf right over there."

Tomasetti and I exchange looks as Wentworth saunters to a shelf, kneels, and pulls out a shoe-box. He brings it to us, sets it on the counter, and removes the lid with the flair of a chef revealing his greatest creation. "It's a summer clog. Wood sole. Leather upper. It was a big hit last year. Pricey, but the workmanship and beauty make it worth every penny."

"Do you have the names of people who purchased this shoe?" Tomasetti asks.

Wentworth nods, but his face is grim, as if in sharing the information he would somehow betray his customers. "Is it important?"

I tell him about the attack on Alma Fisher. "She's in a coma and we're trying to find the person responsible."

He makes a sound of distress. "In that case, let me take a look at my records."

It's not a speedy process since Wentworth's sales records are on paper and in a steel file cabinet in the rear office. Tomasetti and I pass the time perusing the merchandise. He picks up a sequined platform pump, turns to me, and raises his brows. "You'd look great in these."

Grinning, I shake my head. "What is it with you and women's shoes?"

"I'm a foot guy. What can I say?"

A few minutes later the curtain behind the counter parts and Wentworth comes through holding a short stack of sales receipts. "Here we go."

Sequined pumps forgotten, we cross to the counter.

"I've sold nine pair since last summer." Wentworth

sets the papers on the counter. "Names should be on the merchant copy of the receipt."

I page through the receipts. Some of the names are familiar. The mayor's wife. Jodie, my second-shift dispatcher. Three are from out of state.

"That leaves us with four names." Pulling out his phone, Tomasetti takes a photo of the receipts. I jot them down in my notebook.

When I'm finished, I extend my hand to Wentworth. "Thank you for getting the information for us so quickly."

"I hope the injured young lady is going to be all right."

By the time Tomasetti drops me at the station, my lack of sleep is starting to make itself known. Waving to Lois, my first-shift dispatcher, I grab a cup of coffee, go directly to my office, and dive into the list. It doesn't take long for me to call each of the four individuals—and strike out. All of the women have indisputable alibis for last night. No one borrowed the shoes in question. And none of the women donated them to charity.

"So how the hell did those footwear imprints get in the barn?" I mutter.

Realizing the footwear angle may be a dead end, I call the BCI lab only to learn there are no viable fingerprints on the two-by-four. The hair and blood samples have already gone to the lab for DNA testing, but I know both are probably from the victim.

My only hope is that a second interview with Aden Keim and Irene Miller will reveal some new bit of information. I'll also need to broaden my interview pool by including other individuals who were at the party and close personal friends of Fisher and Keim. I remind myself that most cases are solved simply because someone can't keep their mouth shut. Hopefully, someone will talk.

I decide to pay Keim another visit. Back in the Explorer, I call his cell and identify myself. "Where are you?"

"I'm at the hospital."

"Any change?"

"No."

"Stay put, I'm on my way."

He hangs up on me.

I call Bart Wentworth as I head north toward Millersburg. He answers with a cheerful "The Bootery, how can I help you?"

"Mr. Wentworth, it's Kate Burkholder."

"Was the information I gave you helpful?"

"Actually, I sort of struck out."

"I'm sorry to hear that."

"Is there any other way someone might have possession of those shoes? Are they sold by another merchant? Maybe you donated a pair to charity? Or gave them away?"

"No, ma'am. The only people who have—" He cuts off the words. "Oh, boy. Wait a minute. I just remembered. I sold a pair to one of my *employees* last spring. All employees get a twenty-five percent discount, so the receipts aren't filed in the same place as the others."

"Who's the employee?"

"Judy McNulty. Nice lady. She was with me for years."

My heart sinks at his use of past tense. "Was?"

"She retired last month. She and her husband moved to Florida."

"Do you have contact info for her?"

"Of course." Papers rustle on the other end of the line, and then he recites an out-of-state number. "I hope you find what you're looking for, Chief Burkholder."

"Me, too."

After thanking Mr. Wentworth, I pull over in the parking lot of Quality Implement, the local farm store, and make the call.

Judy McNulty answers on the first ring with an enthusiastic, "This is Judy!"

Quickly, I identify myself and get right to the point, giving her the fundamentals of the case. "I understand you purchased a pair of those shoes from The Bootery."

"Well, just between us," she lowers her voice, "the damn things were so uncomfortable I took them down to the thrift store with a bunch of stuff, right before Harry and I moved."

My heart takes another dive as the odds of my

locating the new owner shrinks even more. "Which thrift store?"

"That little shop on the corner, down from the Butterhorn Bakery."

Muttering a thank-you, I pull out of the parking lot and head back toward town.

If a thrift store is capable of achieving panache, Junky Delights has mastered the technique. The display windows are an imaginative mix of tarnished brass, dusty crystal, and antique hats, all of which somehow manage to make past fashion and decorating faux pas seem chic.

The bell on the door clinks gleefully when I enter. The aromas of potpourri, dust, and cinnamon greet me as I stroll to the counter, where a woman with purple hair is ringing up a sale for a twenty-something cradling the ugliest lamp I've ever laid eyes on.

"Be with you in just a sec," the clerk says to me with a wink.

"My mom's going to love this," the customer says to both of us, beaming.

With the lamp safely wrapped in brown paper, the customer makes her exit.

"What can I help you find?" the clerk asks.

I have my badge at the ready. "Some information, if you have it." I tell her about the shoes, describing them as best I can.

Her eyes light up as I describe the shoes. "I

remember them! They were clogs. Kind of 1970s retro." She sighs. "They were leather with wood soles and had those cool rivets along the side. I'd had my eye on them for a week."

"You sold them?"

"Yes, ma'am. A couple weeks ago."

"Can you look up the customer's name for me?"

"We don't keep their names on a list or anything, but I remember her just fine. I mean, she's freaking *Amish,* and I'm like, why does an Amish chick need—"

"What's her name?" I cut in, my interest jumping hard.

"Irene Miller. Let me tell you, seeing those clogs go out the door was a dark day for me, and the luckiest day of this girl's life. I mean, those shoes were *epic.*"

Ten minutes later, I'm standing on the front porch of the Miller home. Irene's mother, Susie Miller, opens the door and looks at me expectantly. I wonder if she knows why I've come back.

"Is Irene here?" I ask.

"You already talked to her."

"I need to talk to her again."

Suspicious of me now, she steps back and reluctantly motions me inside. Turning her head, she calls out. "Irene, *du havva Englischer bsuch ghadde!*" You have a non-Amish visitor.

She keeps her eyes on me. Not only is she wary, I realize, but anxious. Has her daughter told her something she didn't tell me last time I was here?

Irene skulks into the living room, stops upon spotting me, and looks at her *mamm*. "*Ich du nett vella shvetza mitt es.*" I don't want to talk to her.

"You don't have a choice," I say firmly. "We can do it here or I can come back with a warrant and take you to the police station. It's your choice. Do you understand?"

For the first time, the girl looks alarmed. She goes to her mother to stand beside her. Both women stare at me as if I'm the boogeyman and I've found my way into their home.

"Irene," I begin, "I need for you to tell me the truth about what happened last night when Alma was attacked, and I need for you to do it right now."

"But . . ." She chokes out the word as if it's a sharp bone stuck in her throat. "I already told you."

"You told me a story. This time, I need the truth."

She looks at her *mamm* for backup. When her mother says nothing, the girl turns her attention back to me. "I don't know what you mean."

"I know you went into the barn. I have proof. Why did you lie about that?"

She weighs her options, a panicked mouse trying to find its way out of a maze.

All the while, Susie Miller stares at her daughter as if realizing for the first time her daughter may not have told the truth. "You must tell the truth," she whispers in *Deitsh*. "Even if it's a painful thing."

The girl moves away from her *mamm*, looks left and right as if seeking a place to run. But there's nowhere to go, nowhere to hide, and she knows it. After a full minute, she raises her hands as if to fend me off, her hands shaking uncontrollably. "I didn't mean to hurt her!" she cries.

The girl's mother gasps and sets her hand against her chest. *"Irene?"*

"Tell me what happened," I say to the girl.

Irene breaks into tears.

Casting a horrified look at me, Susie goes to her daughter and guides her to the sofa, sits her down. "I think you'd better start talking," she says in *Deitsh*.

The girl looks at me, misery in her eyes, tears streaming. "I followed Alma to the barn, only I went in through the back. It was dark, but she had one of those little flashlights so it was easy for me to see her. She was just walking around. Waiting for *him*. I was on the other side of the stall; she didn't see me, didn't know I was there. There was a broken board right there, leaning against the wall. I don't remember picking it up. But then it was in my hand. I knew I had to stop her. Stop *them*. That's all I wanted to do. I didn't mean to hurt her."

Lowering her head, she puts her face in her hands and sobs.

Her mother makes eye contact with me, her expression stricken. For a moment, I think she's going to be sick. Instead, she puts her arm around her daughter and rubs her back gently.

"You hit Alma with the board?" I ask gently.

Choking back sobs, the Amish girl curls more closely into her mother and nods. "I only meant to do it once. But she wouldn't fall down. I was afraid she'd see me. I didn't want her to know. I got scared, so I hit her again."

Her mother lets out an anguished sob. "Oh, my daughter," she whispers. "Not Alma. You wouldn't . . ."

I ignore her. "Why did you do it?" I ask.

"Because she always gets the boy." Irene raises her head, cheeks and lips wet and shimmering with tears and snot. But there's anger in her eyes now, too. Anger—and jealousy. "It should have been me. I'm the one who introduced them, after all. Aden had eyes for me. I could see it. But Alma didn't care. She stole him, took him away, without so much as a single thought or regret. He should have been mine. But, no. He forgot all about Irene, the *ugly* one."

Her mother presses her hand against her mouth, but not before a sound of shock and grief escapes her. "You're not ugly, my girl."

I give them a moment and then address Irene. "You thought if Alma was out of the way, Aden would come back to you?"

The girl looks down at her hands, tangled and sweaty on her lap. "I don't know what I thought," she says. "I must have just gone a little crazy."

Sighing, I pull the cuffs from a compartment on my belt. "Irene Miller, you are under arrest for assault. Turn around and give me your wrists."

The solving of some crimes isn't always as simple or satisfying as one might imagine. While it's always a good thing to uncover the truth and get a dangerous individual off the street, too often the pain that's been caused lingers and the thing that's been done is irrevocable.

It's been twenty-four hours since I arrested Irene Miller for the assault of Alma Fisher. She spent a few hours in the Painters Mill jail, but was later picked up by a female officer with the Ohio Department of Youth Services and taken to a juvenile facility in Tuscarawas County.

Last I heard, Alma Fisher was still in a coma and Aden Keim hasn't left her side—not even to shower. A small stir of guilt goes through me at the thought, and not for the first time I remind myself that my cop's preconceived notions nearly got in the way this time.

A knock on my office door draws me from me reverie. I look up to see Tomasetti enter, a bag from LaDonna's Diner in one hand, a cardboard tote containing two biggie drinks in the other. "Mushroom and Swiss burger with a diet pop."

I watch as he sets the food and drinks on my desk and takes the chair across from me. "How did you know I needed cheering up?"

"I'm a special agent with BCI," he says as he takes the chair across from me. "I know these things."

I laugh.

"Okay, Lois told me you skipped lunch. Still . . ."

"And you just happened to be in the area."

"Actually, I took the afternoon off so I could drive the seventy miles from Richfield to Painters Mill and have lunch with you."

"Tomasetti, you're such a romantic."

"That's what all the female chiefs of police tell me."

The aromas of burgers and fries fill my office as we unpack the food. We've just settled in to eat when movement at the door draws my attention. I look up to see Aden Keim knock on the jamb.

"Chief Burkholder?"

"Aden. Hi. Come in." I rise, realizing I used his first name when I probably shouldn't have.

"Sorry to interrupt your lunch," he says.

"No problem," I tell him. "I figured you'd be at the hospital."

He enters my office, extending his hand first to Tomasetti and then to me. "My *mamm* told me I needed to go home and take a shower."

"We're glad you did," Tomasetti says deadpan.

It takes a moment for the Amish man to realize he's joking and he barks out a laugh.

"Any change in Alma's condition?" I ask, bracing because I can't discern if he's here to deliver bad news.

"She woke up a couple hours ago." A grin spreads across his face. "Doc says she's going to be okay. I wanted to tell you in person. And thank you for—" He struggles to find the right words. "For figuring out what happened."

I almost tell him I was just doing my job, but I think everyone in the room would know it's a lie. No matter how hard a cop tries to achieve emotional distance from a case, too often they simply don't succeed.

"I'm so pleased, Aden. Thank you for letting me know. I'm glad this one had a happy ending."

The young man can't seem to stop smiling. "She might get to go home tomorrow." Glancing at Tomasetti, he tries to curb the smile, but doesn't quite succeed. "Alma said yes, by the way. We're going to be married as soon as we're baptized." He reaches out again and I take his hand. "Thank you, Chief Burkholder. *Thank you.*"

"You're welcome."

Looking sheepish, his eyes flicking from me to Tomasetti, he pulls away and backs toward the door. "I've got to get back to the hospital." He dips his head. "*Gott segen eich.*" God bless you. And then he's gone.

"Young people in love." Tomasetti shakes his head, but he's smiling. "They're lucky."

"Middle-aged people in love." I match the smile with one of my own. "We're lucky, too."

"It's almost enough to make you forget about the cases that don't have happy endings."

"It is," I tell him. "It's enough."

IN DARK COMPANY

He was going to kill her.

She ran as she'd never run before. Arms pumping. Sneakers pounding the earth. Breathing hard between clenched teeth. Terror. Darkness all around.

She tore through cornstalks as tall as a man. Dry leaves slashed at her face like blades, stalks hitting her like clubs. At some point she'd lost a shoe. Rocks and clumps of earth and the gnarled roots of the corn punished her bare foot. No time to stop.

She darted left, burst into the next row. Trying to lose him. She ran another fifty yards. Lungs burning. Heart slamming against her ribs. She stopped and listened. Struggled to hear over her own labored breaths.

Then she heard the crack of breaking stalks. Boots pounding against the ground. He ran like some mammoth beast, crashing through brush, flattening everything in his path. He breathed like a bull, the occasional grunt of rage bursting forth.

Dear God, if he caught her . . .

She burst from the cornfield, stumbled into a ditch, nearly fell. A gravel road a few feet ahead. Breaths burning, a cramp in her side, she clamored up the incline and stopped, looked both ways. Darkness pressed down on her. A sliver of moon peeking through thin clouds. No headlights. No cars. No one to help her. She couldn't run much farther.

Then she saw the dim flicker of light in the distance. Through the trees, a farmhouse. Salvation. Her only hope. With a final look behind her, she started down the long gravel lane and prayed someone was there.

The buzz of my cell phone rattles me from deep sleep. Not bothering to open my eyes, I reach for it, press it to my ear. "Burkholder."

"Sorry to bother you, Chief," says Mona Kurtz, my third-shift dispatcher. "We've got a situation I thought you should know about."

I push myself to a sitting position. A glance at the clock on the night table tells me it's not yet 4:00 A.M. "What happened?"

"I just took a call from Noah Fisher out on Township Road 34. He says he's got a woman there at his house." She lowers her voice. "Says she's battered and scared. She thinks someone's trying to kill her."

"Kill her?" I swing my legs over the side of the bed and get to my feet. "How badly is she injured?"

"Not sure, Chief. Mr. Fisher says she's . . . confused."

"Is T.J. on scene?" I ask, referring to my usual graveyard-shift patrol officer.

"He's en route."

"Get an ambulance out there," I say as I go to the closet, pull my uniform shirt off a hanger. "Let Mr. Fisher know I'm on my way."

"Got it."

I hit End and glance over my shoulder to see my significant other, John Tomasetti, standing next to the bed, stepping into his trousers. He's an agent with the Ohio Bureau of Criminal Investigation and the love of my life.

"Caught the tail end of that," he says.

"Sorry to wake you."

"One of the hazards of living with the chief of police." He tugs a shirt off the chair and shrugs into it. "What's going on?"

I recap the call. "I'm hoping there's not some pissed off boyfriend around. I need to get out there."

"Want some company?"

It's Sunday, a day he usually has off. He'd been planning to start painting our barn. I'd been planning to help him. "Don't you have a date with a paintbrush this morning?"

"You're not trying to tell me something, are you?"

Grinning, I snag my equipment belt off the night table, buckle it, slide my .38 into its holster.

"Wouldn't dream of it," I say, and we start toward the door.

Ohio's Amish Country is incredibly dark at night. There are no porch lights or street lamps; most of the farmhouse windows are unlit. Contemplating the mystery woman's assertion that someone is trying to kill her, I fasten my eyes on the shadows as Tomasetti and I pull into the gravel lane of the Fisher farm.

Noah and Bonnie Fisher are Amish and run a dairy operation on a forty-acre spread just south of Painters Mill. They belong to the same church district I once did, back when I was an Amish girl. I've known them for two decades; they're one of the few who didn't denounce me when I left the fold. They're getting up in years now. I see them occasionally around town and I always make a point to say hello.

I take the driveway to the rear of the house. T.J.'s cruiser is parked adjacent a five-rail fence where a dozen or so cattle encircle a mound of hay. I pull up next to the cruiser and park.

"No other vehicles in sight," Tomasetti comments as we make our way to the front of the house.

"She was either on foot or someone dropped her off." In the back of my mind I wonder where the ambulance is.

We take the steps to the door. Before I can knock, it swings open. Noah Fisher squints at me, a lantern in his hand. "Katie, thank you for getting here so quickly."

"Hi, Mr. Fisher."

"*Kumma inseid.*" Come inside.

The man is about my height but outweighs me by a hundred pounds. He's wearing typical Amish garb: blue work shirt, dark trousers with suspenders, and a flat-brimmed straw hat. His salt-and-pepper beard hangs nearly to his waist. I glance past him to see T.J. standing in the living room. A young woman I don't recognize huddles on the sofa next to Bonnie Fisher. Late teens or early twenties. Blond hair. Blue eyes. She's wearing an old-fashioned dress that's not quite Amish. No head covering. Even in the dim light of the lantern, I discern her disheveled appearance. An abrasion glows red on her forehead. A smear of dirt stripes her left cheek. She's holding a mug of something hot with hands that aren't steady. Her knuckles are badly scraped. Dirt and grass stains mar a dress that's torn at the skirt. She's wearing a single nondescript sneaker; her other foot is encased in a sock that's covered with mud.

I make eye contact with T.J.

He crosses to me, nodding at Tomasetti, and we move out of earshot. "Fisher and his wife were sleeping," T.J. says in a low voice. "They heard pounding on the door and came downstairs to find this girl on the front porch. She claims someone's trying to kill her."

"You run her through LEADS?" I ask, referring to Ohio's Law Enforcement Automated Data System. "Check for warrants?"

"Uh, that's the thing, Chief." T.J. scratches his head. "She doesn't seem to know her name."

I look from T.J. to Tomasetti and back again, wondering if he's messing with me. "Is she impaired? Or refusing to say?"

"She seems . . . cooperative," T.J. tells me. "I don't smell alcohol on her. Eyes look normal. It's just that when I asked for her name, she said she couldn't remember."

I look at Tomasetti and he shrugs. "If this is some sort of domestic dispute," he says, "she could be trying to protect someone."

"I'll talk to her," I tell them. "In the interim, get me an ETA on that ambulance."

"Will do, Chief."

I lower my voice. "T.J., it might be a good idea to take a look around, make sure there isn't someone out there waiting for her."

"You got it."

Both men go through the door. I approach the young woman. She watches me with anxious eyes, clutching a knitted afghan that's draped over her shoulders.

Bonnie Fisher sits next to her, hovering like a mother hen. Noah busies himself lighting a second lantern in the kitchen.

"Hi," I say to the woman. "I'm Kate Burkholder,

the chief of police. Are you hurt? Do you need an ambulance?"

She shakes her head. "I'm fine," she says. "I'm just . . ." She lets the sentence trail as if she can't find the words to finish it.

"Can you tell me what happened tonight?" I ask.

The woman blinks. Her brows knit as if I've posed some complex math equation she hasn't a clue how to answer. She opens her mouth as if to respond, but doesn't speak. Her gaze slants toward the Amish woman sitting next to her, as if she's seeking help, then her eyes slide back to mine. "I don't know," she blurts.

"Let's start with something easy." I pull my note-pad from my pocket, flip it open. "What's your name?"

She stares at me as if I've stumped her. "I'm not sure."

"I need your name," I say gently. "You're safe. I'm a police officer, and I'm going to get you some help. Okay?"

Blinking, she shakes her head, as if trying to loosen the information from a brain that's locked down tight. "I don't know what's wrong with me. I mean . . . I should know my name. How can I not know who I am?"

I wait, looking for a lie, some sign of deception. The only things that come back at me are wide blue eyes filled with trepidation, stress, and fear.

"Did someone hurt you this evening?" I ask. "Or were you in an accident?"

Her eyes slant toward the door. "There was someone in the field with me. Chasing me. I was running
and lost my shoe." A shudder moves through her. She
grips the afghan more tightly, drops her voice to a
whisper. "He was so close."

"What's his name?" I ask. "Who is he to you?"

She gives a quick shake of her head, frustration
flashing in her eyes. "I don't know."

"Why was he chasing you?"

"I must have done . . . *something*." Her brows knit.
"He was angry with me. I was . . . scared." She raises
her gaze to mine. "I think he was going to kill me."

I feel Bonnie Fisher's stare, but I don't look at
her. I don't take my eyes off the woman. She's looking down at her dress as if she's never seen it before,
taking in the dirt ground into the fabric, the torn
skirt. Her eyes move to her stocking foot, the abrasions and scratches covering her hands, and the fear
in her expression augments to something closer to
panic.

"What happened to me?" she says, her voice rising. "Who did this? How did I get here? *Why can't I
remember?*"

I let the questions linger, allow her the time to think
them through and calm down. When she doesn't respond, I say, "Why don't you take a deep breath, and
then tell me what you *do* remember?"

Holding my gaze, the young woman obeys, drawing a breath, blowing it out slowly. She stares at me

for the span of a full minute, then her shoulders slump. "There's nothing there," she whispers.

"You're shaken up is all." Speaking in *Deitsh,* Bonnie pats the younger woman's arm. "It'll come back to you."

"It hurts . . . to think." The young woman raises a shaking hand to the back of her head and winces. Her fingertips come away smeared with blood. She stares at it and chokes out a sound that's part laugh, part sob. "I don't remember how that happened. How is that possible? How can I not remember?"

When you're a cop, you get lied to a lot. It's a fact of life. Over the years, I've developed a pretty decent built-in lie detector. Yet as implausible as this woman's claim appears, I see no sign of deception.

"I know how crazy all of this must sound," she says. "But I don't remember what happened to me. I don't know how I got here. I don't know who I am."

"There's an ambulance on the way," I tell her. "We'll have the doctor take a look at that cut on your head."

The woman's eyes go wide. "What if he's still out there?"

"My officer is looking around outside now. If anyone's there, he'll find them."

"He's going to kill me."

The woman whispers the words in *Deitsh,* but the dialect is unlike any I've heard. I'm fluent; in fact, I spoke *Deitsh* before I learned to speak English. And yet when she speaks, I understand only a few words, just enough to string together the gist of what she's saying.

Bonnie and I exchange a look, and I realize she's thinking the same thing.

"Where are you from?" I ask the woman.

The flash of uncertainty is followed by a too-long hesitation and then, "I'm not sure."

"Do you have a family?" I ask. "Is there someone we can call for you?"

Tears fill her eyes and spill onto her cheeks. "What am I going to do?"

She's getting herself worked up, so Bonnie pats her arm again and purrs in *Deitsh, "God is there to give us strength—"*

". . . For every hill we have to climb," the young woman finishes in *Deitsh,* and her eyes light up. "I've heard that saying before."

"Of course you have," Bonnie says. "You're *Freind-schaft.*"

I watch the exchange with interest. *Freindschaft* is a *Deitsh* word that means "friends and family," but it is sometimes used to include all Anabaptists—Amish, Mennonite, and Hutterite—across the United States and around the world. The young woman's reaction reflects her understanding of the word and the comfort it's intended to impart.

I turn my attention to Bonnie. "Her *Deitsh,*" I say. "Have you heard it spoken that way before?"

The Amish woman shakes her head. "She's not from around here."

"Chief Burkholder?"

I glance toward the door to see two paramedics standing in the doorway with a gurney.

Rising, I cross to them. "We need a transport to Pomerene Hospital," I tell him. "She's got a laceration on the back of her head."

"You got it, Chief."

While the EMTs take her vitals and load her onto the gurney, I meet Tomasetti and T.J. on the porch. "Did you find anything?" I ask.

"Looks like she came through that cornfield on the east side of the property," Tomasetti says. "On foot."

"Quite a distance," I say, wondering what would prompt a woman to run through a cornfield in the dead of night.

"There was a second set of footprints," Tomasetti tells me. "Probably male. Long stride. Deep imprint. Moving fast. At some point a vehicle went off the road." He looks past me where one of the paramedics is placing a cervical collar around the woman's neck. "It looks like there was a struggle. Grass is trampled. There's blood." Grimacing, he lowers his voice. "Evidently, she ran into the field to get away from someone."

"That jibes with what she told me," I say. "Which isn't much."

"The good news is we got tire tread," Tomasetti says.

"Imprints?" I ask.

"Maybe," he says. "You want me to get the crime scene truck out here? Get some plaster impressions?"

"Might be helpful to have them." I turn my attention to T.J. "Look, I don't know what we're dealing with here, but it might be a good idea for you to call the Maple Brook Mental Health Center in Millersburg and find out if they're missing a patient."

"You got it, Chief." He hefts two small clear plastic bags. "Found these items in the field."

I look down at the bags. The first contains a sneaker that matches the one the woman is wearing. Inside the second bag, I see what looks like a swatch of fabric. It's black with tiny white dots. A headscarf, I realize, and I find myself thinking about the woman's fluency in *Deitsh*.

Taking the bag, I study the headscarf. "This might help identify her."

T.J. cocks his head. "A scarf?"

"She's fluent in Pennsylvania Dutch, but I don't think she's Amish or Mennonite."

"Did she tell you that?" Tomasetti asks.

"Her dialect did; I've never heard anything like it. And the style of that dress she's wearing isn't Amish." I turn the bag over. "That's not to mention this scarf."

"Was she able to tell you anything, Chief?" T.J. asks.

"No," I reply. "I'm hoping once we get her to the

hospital, she'll calm down and things will start coming back to her."

Neither man has anything to say about that.

It's a little past 7:00 A.M. when I drop Tomasetti at the farm. From there, I head to Pomerene Hospital, which is just north of Millersburg.

The clerk at the information desk tells me "Jane Doe" was examined in the ER and admitted for "observation," and has just been settled into a room. When I ask about the woman's condition, even though I'm in full uniform and I've shown her my ID, because of confidentiality rules, all she can tell me is that her condition is listed as "good."

"Any chance I could talk to the doctor who treated her?" I ask.

"You're in luck. Doctor Brumbaugh is still on duty." She taps a few keys on the computer in front of her. "Let me give him a call and see if he can spare a few minutes."

Doctor Denny Brumbaugh has patched me up a couple of times over the years. He's about fifty years old with a neatly trimmed silver goatee and a kind, competent demeanor. This morning, he's wearing blue scrubs that are stretched taut over a middle-age paunch. His red-rimmed eyes tell me it was a busy night in the ER.

"You're here about the Jane Doe?" he asks as he slides behind his desk.

"I'm trying to identify her." I take the visitor chair adjacent him. "And find out what happened to her. Was she able to shed any light on either of those things?"

"After the paramedics brought her in, the nurse on duty asked her to fill out a couple of forms," he tells me. "We're talking basic questions like name and address. That young woman couldn't fill out any of it."

"You examined her?"

He nods. "The most notable injury was a laceration at the back of her head. It was a doozy and required four staples to close. There was a hematoma."

"Blunt force?" I ask.

"That's a likely scenario. Or she may have fallen and hit her head. Whatever the case, it was a forceful blow."

"Sexual assault?"

"No indication of it."

"She's claiming memory loss," I say.

"I'm aware." But he looks skeptical. "The CAT scan came back normal. X-rays look good. She may have a minor concussion, which is why I admitted her, but there's no indication of major swelling."

"What about alcohol or medication?" I ask. "Drugs?"

"I did a simple immunoassay screen and it came back negative. Blood work looks good." He glances down at the file in front of him. "She's covered with abrasions, scratches, and bruises. As far as I can tell, she could have been assaulted; she could have fallen, or those injuries might have happened in a traffic accident."

"I'm glad you're helping to narrow things down."

He laughs outright. "Anything to help, Kate."

"What about the whole memory thing, Doctor Brumbaugh? Is it possible?"

"I've been a physician for twenty-six years and I've never seen a case of true amnesia. Not one."

"Is she faking it?"

"I couldn't profess to know what's in her mind. All I'm saying is that true amnesia is extremely rare." He slides his glasses onto his crown and rubs his eyes as if the long hours are catching up to him. "That said, in light of her head injury she could be experiencing some form of transient amnesia."

"Transient amnesia?"

"All that means is that it's a temporary condition." His brows knit. "It's sometimes called retrograde amnesia."

"What's the treatment?" I ask.

"Time. If she doesn't start remembering basic things in the next twenty-four hours, I recommend she see a neurologist."

Doctor Brumbaugh's parting words ring in my head as I take the elevator to the third floor and head toward the nurse's station. I have my badge at the ready.

"I'm looking for the Jane Doe who was brought up from ER."

The young nurse motions down the hall. "Room 308," she tells me. "Last room on the right."

I find the young woman lying supine in the bed, her head turned away, staring out the window. She's not making a sound, but her cheeks are wet with tears. I give her a moment and then knock. "Hello."

She startles, swipes quickly at the tears as if she doesn't want anyone to see them, and pushes herself to a sitting position. "Oh, hi." The smile that follows is more polite than genuine. "I was wondering if you were going to come back."

"I'm a sucker for a good mystery." I enter the room, pull out the chair next to her bed and sit. "How are you feeling?"

"Fine."

The word hangs uneasily for a second. The enthusiasm in her voice so obviously doesn't ring true that she chokes out a laugh. "That's a ridiculous answer," she says. "I'm not fine. I'm scared because I'm lying here in this bed, wracking my brain, trying to remember something—*any-thing*—but it's all just a big fat . . . blank. How can someone just . . . forget their life?"

"According to Doctor Brumbaugh, you sustained a blow to your head. He thinks you'll start to remember within the next day or so."

"What happened to me?"

"The doc thinks you may have fallen or been in a traffic accident." I pause, watching her for a reaction. "Or someone could have assaulted you."

A tremor passes through her body with such intensity that I can see her shaking beneath the blanket. "Someone did this to me," she says.

"So you remember."

"Enough to know I didn't fall. *Someone* did this. The same person who was chasing me through that field." She tightens her mouth. "I just don't remember *who*."

"Are you sure about that?" I ask. "The doc also told me that amnesia is extremely rare."

Her gaze jerks to mine. "I don't blame you for not believing me. If I wasn't experiencing this myself, I wouldn't be buying into it, either."

"How do you know someone was chasing you?" I ask.

"I remember running from him." She taps her chest with her hand. "I still feel the fear of it here."

I take her through the same questions I asked earlier, posing them in different ways, trying to catch her in a lie or trip her up, but she's unable to answer any of them.

"If you're lying to me, I will find out," I tell her. "Do you understand?"

"I have no reason to lie." Looking defeated, she sinks more deeply into the pillows and pulls the covers up to her chin. "What am I going to do? What if I don't remember? Chief Burkholder, what will happen to me? Where will I go?"

"Chances are you have family and they're looking for you," I tell her. "You speak *Deitsh*. That's significant. It may help."

We fall silent, the only sounds coming from the ringing of the phone at the nurse's station in the hall and the squeak of rubber-soled shoes against the tile floor.

I look around the room, spot the small alcove closet in the bathroom. "Do you mind if I take a look at your clothes?"

"Sure."

Rising, I go to the niche and retrieve two clear plastic bags containing the clothes she was wearing when she was admitted. Someone has folded the dress and headscarf, and tucked them inside. A second bag holds a single sneaker. A sticker on both bags reads "Jane Doe. Room 308."

I didn't get a thorough look at the dress this morning, but I saw enough to know that while it isn't Amish, it's modest and traditional, both of which are likely culturally significant. I take the bags to the bed and pull out the dress. "Speak up if any of this jogs your memory."

She nods, looking a little too excited by the prospect of a breakthrough. "Okay."

The garment is blue plaid—a print that would not be worn by an Amish woman here in Holmes

County. It's sleeveless—another feature that tells me she's not Amish. A second garment I hadn't noticed spills out. It's a white blouse with elbow-length sleeves and a club collar. There's also an apron that matches the fabric of the dress.

I look at the young woman. "Are these clothes familiar to you?"

She can't seem to stop looking at the dress. "The blouse is worn under the dress," she tells me.

"Like a jumper?" I ask.

"Right."

I pluck the scarf from the bag. It's large; about two feet square. The fabric is black with tiny white dots. I hand it to her and watch as she folds it into a triangle, slips it over her head, and ties it at her nape.

Her eyes meet mine. "I've done that a thousand times."

"I can tell."

I'm about to fold the bag when I notice the key. Upending the bag, I let it fall into my palm. It looks like a typical house key. "Do you recognize this?"

She stares hard at the key, as if by the sheer force of her will, the memories will emerge. "Why can't I remember?" Putting her face in her hands, she begins to cry.

I give her a moment, and then say, "There are a couple of things I can do that might help."

She raises her head. "Like what?"

"For starters, I can take your fingerprints and run

them through AFIS, which is a law enforcement database system. If you've been fingerprinted—or arrested—your prints will be on file, along with the rest of your information." I watch her carefully for a response to the word "arrested," but she gives me nothing.

She brightens. "Let's do it."

"I can also use the media and circulate a photo of you," I tell her, "along with your story in the hope that someone recognizes you and steps forward."

She considers that a moment and then shakes her head. "What if whoever did this to me sees my photo? What if he comes after me?"

It doesn't elude me that she has consistently referred to her attacker as a male. "I'll talk to security here at the hospital." I tilt my head, snag her gaze. "If they're comfortable with all this, are you game?"

"I'll do anything." She offers a tremulous smile. "I just want to go home."

"Good girl." Tugging out my phone, I snap several photos of her, front and profile. When I'm finished, I hand her one of my cards. "I'll be sending someone in to fingerprint you."

"Okay."

"If you remember anything else, even if it doesn't seem important, call me. Day or night." Reaching out, I give her shoulder a squeeze and start toward the door.

"Chief Burkholder?"

I stop in the doorway and turn to her.

"What's going to happen next? I mean, I have no money. I obviously can't stay here at the hospital." She makes a sweeping gesture to encompass the room. "They're probably wondering how I'm going to pay my bill."

"We'll cross that bridge when we come to it," I tell her.

He spent the day pacing, icy sweat slicking his skin, nerves crawling. With every creak of the house, every car that passed, he imagined the police coming for him. By the time dusk fell, he was ready to jump right out of his skin. What was going on? Why hadn't they come for him?

It wasn't until he turned on the computer that the answer materialized. He almost couldn't believe his eyes.

Do you know who this woman is?

The Painters Mill Police Department is asking for the public's help in identifying this woman. "Jane Doe," as she has been dubbed, was discovered by a local Amish couple early this morning when she showed up at their farm with a minor head injury and no idea who she is or where she came from. Left without identification, she's counting on you for help. . . .

If he hadn't been so damn scared he might have laughed. What the hell? He read the article twice. In the back of his mind, he wondered if it was some kind of trap. But he didn't think so. Not in small-town Ohio. The cops simply weren't that sophisticated.

Everything wasn't lost. There was still time to salvage what he'd worked so hard for. All he had to do was find her. Finish what he'd started. In a town the size of Painters Mill, he didn't think that would be too difficult.

The police station is quiet most evenings and tonight is no exception. My second-shift dispatcher, Jodie Metzger, is at her station with the radio turned up a little too loud. I've spent most of the day working my Jane Doe case. I forwarded her photo to eight media outlets, including *The Columbus Dispatch, The Plain Dealer* out of Cleveland, and the radio station in Dover. I also contacted a social worker in the Holmes County Department of Job and Family Services. If worse comes to worst and Jane Doe's memory doesn't return, they'll assist her with housing and a job.

It's just past 7:00 P.M. I've spent the last hour hitting various websites in an attempt to identify Jane Doe's headscarf and clothing. It's a complex endeavor. There are numerous Anabaptist denominations and subgroups. They share many similarities, mainly the practice of adult baptism. But there are distinctive differences, too.

For example, most people know the vast majority of Amish eschew the use of electricity and motorized vehicles and dress traditionally. Most Mennonites, however, have no problem driving cars, using electricity and technology, and many forego traditional dress. The Amish do not proselyte; the Mennonites evangelize and are involved in missionary work around the world.

The tenet that differentiates the Hutterites is the practice of "communal" living. Most colonies consist of multifamily structures. The community prays, lives, and works together.

So far, my Jane Doe's dress and scarf most closely resemble the traditional garb of the Hutterites. The problem is, the nearest settlement is in Wisconsin; the vast majority is in Canada.

I'm reading an article on Ohio's German Baptist community when my cell phone erupts. Without looking away from the screen I pick it up, thinking it's Tomasetti. Instead, I hear a woman's frantic whisper.

"He's here! Chief Burkholder!"

Jane Doe. I stand up. "Where are you?"

"In my room. He's coming!"

"Where is he?"

"He walked by my door. He looked at me, but kept going. I'm scared. He's going to come back."

"Use your call button. Tell the nurses. Run out to the nurse's station if—"

A yelp cuts me off. The call drops.

"Are you there?" I say.

No answer.

"Shit." I call out to my dispatcher. "Jodie!" Then I hit the number for the hospital's security office.

Jodie slides up to my door. "Chief?"

"Get county out to Pomerene Hospital. *Now.* Room 308. Domestic situation."

"Got it." She runs back to her desk.

Snatching up my keys, I start toward the door. One ring. Two. "*Come on.*" Three rings.

"Security."

Quickly, I identify myself. "Get an officer up to room 308. Expedite. There's an unidentified male. Possible domestic situation."

In the background I can hear the bark and hiss of his radio. "On my way," he says.

I jog to reception. "You get county?" I ask Jodie.

"Deputy's a block away."

"Keep me posted. I'm on my way."

Then I'm through the door and into the night.

I arrive at Pomerene Hospital to find a Holmes County cruiser, lights blazing, parked outside the emergency entrance. I park just off the portico and run inside.

"Where's the deputy?" I ask the person manning the desk.

"Third floor."

The elevator is occupied, so I go to the stairwell and take the stairs two at a time to the third level. I'm breathless when I step into the hall.

The first thing I see is a Holmes County sheriff's deputy, two nurses, and a uniformed security officer standing outside room 308. All eyes fall on me when the stair door slams.

"Is Jane Doe all right?" I ask as I start toward them.

"She's okay." The deputy grimaces. "He got into her room. They struggled, but she made it out and ran."

"You get him?" I say.

He shakes his head. "Got away, Chief."

I peer into the room. Jane is sitting on the bed, shaking and pale faced, talking to a deputy and a nurse. I go back into the hall. "How did he get in?"

"We think he came up those stairs." He motions toward the illuminated exit sign at the end of the corridor. "Went out the same way."

"Anyone get a look at him?"

The nurse speaks up. "I saw a man in the hall, but we were busy and I didn't pay much attention to him."

I make eye contact with the deputy. "Anyone check with the clerk downstairs? If our intruder came in that way, he would have had to walk past her to get to the stairs."

"I talked to her," he tells me. "She saw him. Said

he came in as if he knew where he was going. Waved to her. By the time she finished her call, he was gone."

"Was she able to give a better description?"

"Male. Six feet. Two hundred. She thought he might've been wearing a hat."

I think about Jane Doe's traditional clothes. "Beard?"

"She didn't notice."

I turn my attention to the nurse. "How's Jane Doe?"

"Pretty shaken up, as you can imagine. She ran out to our work station like the room was on fire."

"Did anyone else see him?"

She shakes her head. "Most of the patients were sleeping. Nurses were busy. Sorry, Chief Burkholder."

I thank them and head toward room 308. I find Jane Doe fully dressed, standing next to the bed, tying the headscarf at her nape. Some kind soul has given her a pair of sneakers. She turns to me and her eyes meet mine. "I can't stay here," she tells me. "He'll be back. Next time he'll kill me."

"Do you remember him?"

She shakes her head and I notice the red marks on her neck. "All I know is I'm terrified of him."

Reaching out, I move the collar of her blouse aside with my finger. "He hurt you?"

She looks away, nods.

I pat the bed. "Sit down and tell me what happened."

Sighing, she lowers herself to the mattress. "The first time I saw him, he walked by my room and kept going. I called you. I was on the phone with you when he came back."

"What did he do?"

"He came in. Had this crazy light in his eyes. Like . . . rage. He closed the door behind him and he just came at me fast, pushed me onto the bed, put his hands around my throat." She runs out of breath, takes a moment to gulp air. "I could hear his teeth grinding." She closes her eyes, fingering her throat. "I couldn't move. Couldn't breathe. I'd hit the call button. When it buzzed, he scrambled off of me and ran."

"Did he say anything?"

"He was sort of snarling, but I think . . ." Her brows draw together. "He said something like, 'Keep your mouth shut.'"

I pull my notebook from my pocket. "What did he look like?"

"Older. Like Mr. Fisher. Heavy, but not over-weight. Dark hair. Gray on the sides."

I write all of it down. "What was he wearing?"

"A dark jacket." She shakes her head. "It happened so fast."

"Hat?"

"Black felt, I think."

"Beard?"

Her eyes find mine. "Yes. It was . . . trimmed. Gray. How did you know that?"

"Beards are traditional for some Anabaptist men."

We fall silent. She sags, looks around the room. "Chief Burkholder, what am I going to do?" she says quietly. "I don't think I can stay here. It's not safe, but I don't have anywhere else to go."

I'd decided earlier to take her to the women's shelter in Millersburg. But in light of the as-of-yet unidentified male who attacked her, I'm hesitant to leave her unprotected—and possibly endanger women and children, many of whom have already been traumatized.

"You got all your things?" I ask.

She frowns. "I'm wearing everything I own."

"Let me check with the nurses," I tell her. "I think I have a safe place for you to stay until we can get this figured out."

It's been two years since I moved into the farmhouse with Tomasetti. Before, I lived in a modest little house on the outskirts of Painters Mill. I put it on the market, but when it didn't sell quickly, our Realtor recommended we update the kitchen and try again—an endeavor we've yet to tackle.

I take a roundabout route to my old digs, cutting through a couple of different neighborhoods, keeping an eye on the rearview mirror in case some determined individual tries to follow.

"You used to live here?" she asks as I pull into the garage.

"Yep." I see her looking out the back window and add, "No one followed us."

She nods, but doesn't look too sure.

I park and close the overhead door. "I still keep some linens here, so we should be comfortable for a couple of days."

Leaning forward, she puts her face in her hands, uses her fingertips to wipe away tears. "Chief Burkholder, you didn't have to do this. You don't even know me. I don't know how to thank you."

"You can thank me by remembering your name."

She chokes out an emotion-laden laugh and we head inside.

I always experience a rise of nostalgia when I return to my old home. It was the first house I ever purchased, and it represented a fresh start when I moved back to Painters Mill to become chief. I love living at the farm with Tomasetti, but this place will always be special.

I find linens in the closet off the hall and unfold the sofa bed in the living room. Jane helps me with the sheets. "I'm not sure what to call you," I tell her as I slide a pillow into a case.

She shrugs. "The nurses called me Jane."

"Jane it is, then." I snap open a blanket while she tucks the base beneath the mattress. "You're welcome to take a shower. I might be able to drum up some soup if you're hungry."

"I'm starving." She smiles. "Thank you."

While Jane showers, I make up the bed in my former bedroom and then I call Tomasetti.

"I heard about the incident at the hospital," he says. "Any luck finding the suspect?"

"No. Rasmussen has a couple of extra guys on patrol. I told Skid to stay alert."

"You decided against taking her to the shelter?"

"In light of what happened at the hospital, I don't want to take a chance of him showing up there."

He's thoughtful for a moment and then he says, "I know you've got good instincts when it comes to judging people, but I'm obliged to ask, Kate. Are you sure she's telling the truth about her memory?"

"I had my doubts at first. Tomasetti, if I still did, I wouldn't be here."

"Good enough. Just do me a favor and keep your .38 handy tonight, will you?"

"You bet."

Jane and I bid each other good night at midnight. I lay awake in my old bedroom, the mystery of her identity and the unknown threat she faces weighing heavy on my mind. Storms and the first cold front of the season roll in a little after 1:00 A.M. with torrential rain and battering winds. Twice I get up to check out a noise; both times it's nothing more than the sounds of an old house settling.

I've just fallen into a fitful slumber when something sends me bolt upright. I listen, but I can't hear much over the pound of rain and rumble of distant thunder. Lightning flickers as I rise. I reach for my .38 on the night table. The hairs at my nape stand up when I hear the sound again. A thump coming from the general direction of the living room. Shit.

I sidle to the door. The hallway is silent and dark, so I take it to the doorway and peer into the living room. Dim light slants in through the window. The sound comes again. Banging coming from the kitchen. Someone trying to get in the back door?

"Jane?" I whisper.

No answer.

I enter the living room, my .38 leading the way. I glance at the sofa bed. No one there. Where the hell is she?

"Chief," comes a whisper from across the room.

I glance over to see her kneeling next to the chair. Hiding, I realize. "Someone's out there," she whispers and points toward the rear of the house.

"Stay put." I go to the kitchen doorway, peer around the jamb, expecting to see an open back door or a broken window. I see neither. Listening, I scan the room. There's an eye-level pane set into the door. There's no movement. Not even a shadow. I startle when something bumps the door.

Staying low, I steal across the kitchen, go to the door, set my left hand on the knob, and yank it open. Gun in my right hand. Wind and rain lash my face. I glance left, see the porch light hanging down, swinging in the wind, tapping against the door.

"What is it?"

I turn to see Jane standing in the doorway, her face a pale oval in the diluted light from outside. "Just the porch light," I tell her. "It must have come loose. The wind was blowing it against the door."

"Oh."

I flip on the light. We look at each other for a moment and then we both laugh. Nervous sounds that speak of released tension and relief.

"Sorry to wake you," she says.

"Couldn't sleep anyway."

"Me neither."

I glance at the wall clock to see it's going on 5:00 A.M. "I have an idea that might help us identify you."

"I'm all ears," she says.

"In that case, I'll make coffee."

At 7:00 A.M., Jane and I are in the Explorer heading east on US-62 toward Berlin. During the sleepless hours of last night, it occurred to me that there's one person who might be able to help identify Jane—via her clothes—and perhaps link her to a community.

Twenty minutes later I pull onto the lot of the Amish and Mennonite Heritage Center. We pass by an old Amish-style schoolhouse and an iconic bank barn, and then I veer left and park in front of the main office. The establishment doesn't open for business until nine, but I called the director earlier and explained the situation. Eager to help, he agreed to meet us.

I look over at Jane. She's staring at the low-slung

building, her hands knotted in her lap. "Do you think he's going to be able to tell us where I'm from?" she asks.

"I think there's a good possibility he'll recognize your clothes. Hopefully, that will at least point us in the right direction."

I reach for the door handle, but she stops me.

"Chief Burkholder, what if he tells me something I don't want to hear? What if . . . I'm not a good person?"

I give her a smile, hoping to reassure her. "After spending the last day or so with you, I don't think that's going to be a problem."

Offering a grateful smile, she opens her door.

The director greets us in the lobby. "Welcome to Behalt."

I met Mark Hochstetler a couple years ago when Tomasetti and I spent a Saturday afternoon here. He gave us an unforgettable tour of the cyclorama, which is a stunning floor-to-ceiling mural "in the round" that depicts the history of the Anabaptists. Their story begins with the first adult baptism in Zurich, Switzerland, in 1525 and follows the Anabaptist movement through centuries of persecution and martyrdom to modern day. The oil painting is a masterpiece that tells a powerful tale and an important history.

This morning, Mark wears his Sunday best— black trousers with suspenders, a white shirt, black jacket and hat. A studious and soft-spoken man, he possesses a palpable deep and abiding love for his brethren, and a perspicacious sense of humor.

"Good to see you again, Chief Burkholder," he says as we shake hands.

"I appreciate your making time to talk."

"It sounded important."

"History always is." I introduce him to Jane and explain the situation without going into too much detail. "We're hoping you'll be able to tell us something about her based on her clothing."

He nods thoughtfully at Jane. "I noticed your dress when you walked in." He looks around and then motions toward the door that will take us into the cyclorama. "This way."

I observe Jane as we enter the circular room. Her eyes widen as she takes in the breadth and scope of the mural. She walks along the wall awash with colorful depictions of the early Anabaptists, her face reflecting wonder and awe. Mark surveys her, too, and we share a moment of unspoken camaraderie.

Jane turns to us, her face reflecting some of the same emotions I experienced when I saw the mural for the first time. "This is amazing."

"Even more so," Mark says with a smile, "Because they are your ancestors."

Jane's eyes flick to mine, then back to him. "How do you know that?"

He motions toward her clothes. "The dress you're wearing is called a *dirndl*. It's Hutterite and is worn by all three denominations: *Dariusleut, Lehrerleut,* and *Schmiedenleut.*"

Jane stares at him, her mouth partially open, eyes filled with a mix of astonishment and reverence. "I'm . . . *Hutterer.*"

He nods. "I knew it the instant I saw you. But it was the *tiechl* that sealed the deal."

"My headscarf." Jane whispers the words, tears filling her eyes. "How did I know that? What does all of this mean?"

"The Hutterites, like the Amish and all Anabaptists, believe in adult baptism. What sets the Hutterites apart is their practice of living a community life." He addresses Jane. "Do you speak *Hutterisch?*"

"Yes." Laughing, she slants a look at me. "I don't know how I know that, but I do."

Shifting his attention to me, Mark gives me a knowing smile. "And you, Kate Burkholder, can only understand about half of what she says. Bet that drove you crazy."

I grin back at him and the three of us enjoy another moment. "Mark, we're trying to find out where she's from. Do you have any idea where we might start?"

"Most of our *Hutterer* brethren are in Canada. The nearest colony is in Minnesota, I think." He rubs his beard, mulling. "That said, I recall reading about a new Hutterite colony in the northwestern part of Ohio, near Coldwater."

"Do the Hutterites have anything similar to our Ohio Amish Directory?" I ask, referring to the eight-hundred-page tome that lists all the church districts and members for Holmes County and vicinity.

"They have a website." He starts toward the door. "Come in to my office and we'll take a look."

I'm not exactly sure how Mark skates the use of the no-technology rules set forth by the church district, but his office is modern. He keeps a lantern on his desk, but there's a relatively new-looking laptop right beside it. I know he's taken some flak for it over the years, but as director of Behalt—and taking into consideration the enlightenment he bestows on both Amish and English alike—using the computer and Internet seem like minor transgressions.

He slides behind his desk, taps a key, and begins to type. "Here's the website." He swivels the laptop so that Jane and I can see the screen. "You can search by colony, which I did. They are, indeed, building a new settlement in Coldwater, Ohio. No members or contact info listed on the website yet."

"There's a mother colony," Jane whispers.

Mark arches a brow. "Let's take a look." A few keystrokes and he arrives at the Regions page, then he clicks on Ohio. "You are correct."

I'm aware of Jane standing beside me, craning her neck, staring at the screen with a combination of curiosity and trepidation. She's gone silent, laser focus resonating in her stance.

"What is a mother colony?" I ask.

"When a colony gets too large, they move some of their members to start a new one." He clicks again. "Here we go. Castine, Minnesota, about an hour east of Fargo."

Another tap and he sets his index finger against the screen. "This one lists the colony manager, the *Prediger* or preacher, the farm boss—the colony is farm based—and the witness brothers. The *Zullbrieder*, which basically means—"

Jane cuts in. "The people who run the colony."

Mark smiles at her. "Exactly."

He reaches for a pad and scribbles a name and phone number on it. He slides it over to me and then looks at us over the tops of his glasses. "This might be a good place to start."

Jane doesn't speak as we make our way back to the Explorer. Once we're seated, she turns to me and the words begin to pour out of her. "I came to Ohio to help with the daughter colony," she says.

"You're remembering," I say.

"Not all of it." Her brows go together. "Big pieces of my life are missing. I know I was in Coldwater. But, Chief Burkholder, I wasn't alone. There was a man."

"Does this man have a name?" I ask.

She shakes her head. "All I remember are the construction workers. Five or six men. They're building the duplexes where all of us will live." She pauses as if breathless, sets a trembling hand against her chest and chokes out a laugh. "It's coming back to me. *It's coming back!*"

"Keep going."

"My name is Els." She repeats the name as if liking the feel of it on her tongue. "It's short for Elisabeth. I'm nineteen years old." She turns her gaze to mine, presses her hand to her mouth, and laughs, emotion ringing in her voice. "I think I got into some trouble."

"What kind of trouble?"

Her eyes widen. "There was a man in my life."

"Boyfriend?"

"I'm not sure. But I feel him." She presses her hand to her chest. "Here. He's kind and beautiful but . . . troubled."

I glance over at her. "Troubled?"

"There was some kind of conflict between us." Lowering her head, she pinches the bridge of her nose between her thumb and forefinger. "Something important and serious. Another man, maybe." She goes still and turns to me. "What kind of woman loves two men?"

"Els, you know that could be relevant to what happened to you."

She looks down at her hands. "I know."

"Tell me about the second man."

"He's . . . established. Successful. But . . . more of a father figure." Her cheeks flush. "I love him, but not in the same way."

I nod. "He's older?"

"Yes."

I think of the final tumultuous years I spent as an Amish girl and I feel an odd sense of kinship with this young woman. "What were you doing in Painters Mill?"

"All I remember is that the colony manager asked me to help with the daughter community in Coldwater. I think the preacher wanted to separate me from my boyfriend."

In the back of my mind, I wonder if what happened to her was the work of a jealous lover. Did her boyfriend become angry when she left him? Was he jealous of her relationship with the older man? Did he decide to do something about it?

"Do you remember your boyfriend's name?" I ask.

She shakes her head, her brows pulling together. "All of those things I should know . . . it's like a word that's on the tip of my tongue. So close, but for the life of me I can't pull them out of my brain."

"The good news is, you're remembering," I tell her.

"Not fast enough." Frustration furrows her forehead. "What do we do now?"

"We're three hours from Coldwater."

She sets her hand against her stomach, her expression a mosaic of hope and fear and dread. "Why does that scare me?"

"Only one way to find out." Pulling out my cell

phone, I glance down at the slip of paper Mark gave me, and I dial the number.

We hit rain east of Upper Sandusky. We've just turned south toward Lima when a blanket of fog settles over the flat farmland, hovering like smoke in the low-lying areas. We drive nearly blind through the Little Ottawa River basin. Though it's still early afternoon, the light wanes until it feels more like dusk.

Before leaving Berlin, I called colony manager Peter Decker in Castine, Minnesota, and obtained the physical address of the Coldwater settlement, the name of the manager, Leanard Stahl, and his phone number. I also asked Decker about Els. He informed me that her last name is Tsechetter. She's a delightful young woman, he exclaimed, in good standing with the community, and is the bookkeeper for the colony manager, handling payroll for the construction workers charged with building the planned duplexes. I got the impression he has no idea she'd run into trouble in Painters Mill.

Armed with new information, I asked my first-shift dispatcher, Lois Monroe, to run Stahl and Els through several law enforcement databases. There were no warrants, and neither Els nor Stahl has a criminal record. Sitting next to me, Els was stoic, but her relief was palpable.

I called Leanard Stahl twice. Both were met with voice mail—a result that solidified my decision to drive to Coldwater. Hopefully, someone there will be able to fill in the blanks.

As the miles fly by, Els talks, recounting every memory that comes to her. Some are mundane; she's allergic to shrimp, loves gardening, and she's never been married. Some of what she reveals is more pertinent. She lives in a mobile home and does most of the cooking and laundry for the construction crew.

"I was homesick for Minnesota," she tells me as we blow past Wapakoneta and head south. "I missed my boyfriend."

"What else?" I ask.

She makes a sound of frustration. "That's all I've got."

Whenever a cop pokes around in another jurisdiction, it's wise to give local law enforcement a heads-up. During a stop for gas, I call the Mercer County Sheriff's office and am connected to Chief Deputy Dale Light.

I identify myself and relay the basics of the situation.

"We're actively looking for Els Tsechetter," the chief deputy tells me. "Leanard Stahl filed a complaint two days ago alleging Ms. Tsechetter cleaned out the account of his foundation and then took off with her boyfriend." Paper rustles on the other end of the line. "Tyler Fournier."

I'm so taken aback by the news that for a moment I can't find my voice. I wonder if in the aftermath of making off with the cash, Els and her boyfriend had some sort of falling-out that turned physical.

"Does Fournier have a sheet?" I ask, referring to a criminal record.

"No, ma'am."

"How much money are we talking about?" I ask.

"Upwards of nine hundred thousand, according to Stahl."

"That's a lot of motivation."

"Which is why we're anxious to speak with them."

"Is there a warrant for Els Tsechetter's arrest?"

"For now we just want to talk to her."

"Do you have any idea where I might find Mr. Stahl?"

A weighty silence and then, "We're actually looking for him, too. He was supposed to come in this morning to meet with me, but Stahl was a no-show. I sent a deputy out to the colony, but there was no one there. We're kind of scratching our heads at this point."

"Where does that leave the investigation?"

"Until we can find him, we're sort of in a holding pattern."

Another pause ensues, then he asks, "How did a chief of police from Painters Mill get involved in all of this?"

IN DARK COMPANY 301

I give him the scant details of Els's appearance. "We're on our way to Coldwater now."

He doesn't mince words. "Do you want me to send someone to pick her up? Or do you want to bring her in?"

"Let me get a few things settled on my end and I'll bring her to you."

"Any idea when that might be?"

"Later this afternoon."

"All right, Chief Burkholder. I appreciate your cooperation."

My mind is reeling when I get back into the Explorer. I give Els a hard look. "You need to tell me what you know about the books you're keeping for Leanard Stahl's foundation."

Her eyes widen, dart left and right, as if she's suddenly realized she's in danger. "I don't know."

"What's your relationship to him?"

She swallows. "The name . . . Leanard. It's so familiar. I know him and yet . . . I don't see his face. I don't know who he is."

I deflect a rise of irritation. "Els, if I find out you're lying to me, I will come down on you so hard you'll wish you'd never set foot in Painters Mill. Are we clear?"

"I'm not a liar, Chief Burkholder. I wouldn't do that to you or anyone else, especially after everything you've done for me."

"Does the name Tyler Fournier mean anything to you?"

A quiver moves through her body. She whispers the name twice. She opens her mouth as if to speak, but she doesn't utter a word.

Finally, she says, "He's the one."

"The one who hurt you?"

"The one I love."

The words elicit a twist of dread in my gut. Did this young woman and her boyfriend steal money from some foundation? Is what happened to her back in Painters Mill the result of a struggle over the spoils?

"The Mercer County Sheriff's Department is looking for both of you," I say.

"But . . . why?"

"They suspect you of stealing funds from Leanard Stahl."

"I may not remember my life, Chief Burkholder, but I know one thing about myself: I am not a thief." She says the words with such conviction that I find myself wanting to believe her despite what I heard from Chief Deputy Light.

"One way or another—with or without your help—I'm going to get to the bottom of this," I tell her. "Do you understand?"

"When that happens, you'll know I'm telling the truth."

I pull back onto the highway without responding.

The village of Coldwater is a small farming community with a population of about 4,500. Els stares out the window, studying the countryside as if

certain all the things she so desperately needs to remember is about to come pouring back to her.

I entered the address of the colony into my GPS
during a stop for gas. A few miles west of Coldwater
proper, the female voice instructs me to make a
right. The map indicates the colony is located on a
barely there gravel track off of Siegrist-Jutte Road.
Several miles down, I spot the construction entrance
and a dirt lane that wends into a wooded area. A sign
dangles from a steel cable stretched across the narrow
drive: DANGER CONSTRUCTION PERSONNEL ONLY.

"I know this place," Els whispers. "I've been here."
She looks at me. "Can we go in?"

"It's not locked." I glance over at her. "The sheriff's
office knows we're here, so we're not trespassing . . .
exactly." I open the door. "Hang tight."

Light rain falls from a sky the color of wet gran-
ite. The temperature has dropped twenty degrees
since we left Berlin three hours ago. Fog drifts among
the trees. Trying to avoid the deepest areas, I wade
through mud and gravel to the cable and unclip one
end. Back in the Explorer, I pull through and start
down the lane.

A hundred yards in, the trees open to a large construction site. Four concrete slabs are laid out in a
semicircle. Two are framed. The others are a tangle
of plumbing pipes and rebar. To my left, a newish mobile home stares at us with blank eyes. A sign in the
yard identifies it as the Coldwater Colony Construction Office.

"No vehicles," I say. "No lights inside."

"Looks deserted," Els murmurs. "Where is everyone?"

"Weather, maybe."

I continue down the road, negotiate a curve that takes us through a stand of tall, winter-dead trees. We pass a graveyard of construction equipment. An orange skid steer. A wheelbarrow. Piles of boards and cinder blocks lying in the mud. There's a steel building in the back, some pens, and a chicken coop.

"I remember the chickens," Els says quietly. "I used to feed them." Wiping her hands on her dress, she gives a nervous laugh. "My palms are sweaty."

Ahead, I see another mobile home. It's surrounded by a picket fence with a freshly planted sapling off a newish deck. There's a Ford F-150 pickup parked in the concrete driveway.

"This is the trailer where I lived," Els says.

"Looks like you've got a visitor." I pull up behind the truck, work my cell phone from my pocket, and call Dispatch.

Lois answers on the first ring. "Hey, Chief."

I give her my location. "I need a ten-twenty-eight." I recite the license plate number. "Ten-twenty-nine."

Els gives me a wide-eyed look. "What do those codes mean?"

"She's going to give me the name of the person who owns that truck." I don't tell her the 10-29 was a check for warrants.

Lois comes back on the line. "Vehicle is registered to Tyler Fournier out of Minnesota."

"Thanks, Lois."

I shut down the engine. Beside me, Els stares at the mobile home as if expecting some flesh-eating monster to emerge and attack us.

"Do you still have that key?" I hold out my hand and she presses the key into my palm.

"It's going to fit," she says.

"Stay put." Then I'm out the door. Rain patters my face as I take the steps to the deck, open the storm door, and knock. I listen for footsteps or a radio or TV, but the interior is quiet and dark.

"Hello?" Calling out, I tap the door with my fob and identify myself. "Is anyone home?"

No answer.

I wait a full minute and then slide the key into the lock. The knob turns easily. I look back at Els, give her a sign to stay where she is, and then I go through the door. I'm standing in a tastefully furnished living room with wood grain laminate floors and modern furniture. The smells of heated air and candle wax mingles with the stink of garbage that should have been taken out days ago. There's a decent size kitchen ahead and a dining area to my left. A darkened hall to my right.

"Hello?" I say. "Is anyone there?"

No response.

I cross the living room to the kitchen and look

around. The door creaks behind me. I spin, startled, my hand falling to the .38 in my coat pocket, and I see Els enter. "I told you to stay in the car," I snap.

She doesn't respond; she can't seem to stop looking at the interior, touching things. "This is my home," she murmurs. "I'm sure of it."

"Does anyone live here with you? Boyfriend?"

"We're Hutterite, Chief Burkholder. The elders would never allow such a thing."

In the back of my mind I think: *Where there's a will, there's a way. . . .*

"I'm going to take a look around," I say. "Stay behind me. Don't touch anything."

I traverse the dining and kitchen areas and push open a door, find myself looking into a bedroom that's surprisingly large. I flip on the light. A full-size bed is draped with a hand-sewn quilt, colorful six-inch squares of corduroy, flannel, satin, and cotton. Not an Amish-style quilt, but the workmanship is superb. Another door opens to a bathroom with a window that looks out at the woods beyond.

I leave the bedroom, cross back through the kitchen and living room and head toward the hall that will take me to the other end of the mobile home. I hear Els behind me as I pass by a small bedroom. Like the rest of the trailer, it's orderly and neat with a twin-size bed swathed with a quilt, and a night table. The bedroom at the end has been transformed into an office. There's a faux-wood desk strewn with papers and files. I see an old-fashioned calculator and a landline phone. A four-drawer file cabinet squats in the corner, two of the drawers standing open.

I approach the desk, noticing the lamp's shade is cockeyed. A closer look reveals a broken bulb. On the other side of the desk I find a desktop computer and monitor on the floor. The monitor's screen has been shattered. A task chair has been toppled.

"What is this room?" I ask.

Els stands in the doorway, frozen in place. "This is where I work. I do the payroll. Pay the bills. Take care of the books for the foundation."

I turn and look at her. "What do you know about the foundation?"

"The Anabaptist Brotherhood Foundation," she murmurs. "Leanard started it years ago. It's a nonprofit dedicated to preserving the Hutterite traditions. He's planning to open a historical library. A place where we can store documents, bibles, and books. Some of the bibles are old and so some of the facility needs to be climate controlled, which is expensive. It was such a good cause—"

She gasps upon spotting the computer. "But . . . what happened? My computer . . ."

I take in the crinkled blinds at the window, and I realize the place was either broken into and ransacked—or there was a struggle.

"Something happened here," she says quietly.

Lifting the blind, I spy the broken pane; there's no glass on the floor, which means it was probably smashed from the inside. "Any idea what?"

"Something bad," she whispers.

Without saying anything else, she goes to the desk, runs her hand over the lamp, picks it up. She notices the broken bulb and her brows knit in confusion. Then she turns the lamp over so that the base is visible. That's when I glimpse several long strands of hair and the reddish-black stain.

Sliding my mini-Maglite from my pocket, I set the beam on the stain and I almost can't believe my eyes. "Looks like blood."

I hear her quick intake of breath. Looking sick, she sets down the lamp, takes a step back. Her eyes meet mine. "He came in here," she says quietly. "That last night. I was working. He was . . . angry."

"Who?" I ask. "Tyler Fournier?"

Pain flashes in her eyes. "Not Tyler."

"Then who?"

Without responding, she turns away and walks back out to the living room. I follow. I can tell by the look in her eyes that she's remembering something that's frightened her.

"Did Stahl do this?" I ask.

"I can't imagine. Leanard is gentle and kind." She presses her fingertips to her temples. "He wouldn't."

Someone did, I think, and I can't help but wonder how many times I've heard those words.

"Els, you said you'd had problems with a man in your life. If Stahl did this to you—"

"No, Chief Burkholder. This is . . . something

else." Lowering herself to the sofa, she leans forward and puts her face in her hands. "I just . . . it's so confusing. My head . . . I just can't remember. It was—" Her hands fall away from her face and she straightens. "Tyler isn't Hutterite. We were going to get married, but the elders wouldn't allow it. That's one of the reasons they sent me here."

"What does that have to do with what happened in your office?"

"I don't know."

I watch her, wondering if she's convinced herself of something simply because she wants it to be true. Or if there's something else going on that she simply hasn't remembered.

The door swings open. I start, turn toward it, set my hand over my .38. Els jumps to her feet, takes a step back. A young man of about twenty steps inside, eyes the color of a deep lake flicking from me to Els, back to me.

"I'm a police officer," I tell him. "Keep your hands where I can see them."

He can't seem to keep his eyes off of the young woman standing beside me. His expression softens as he takes in the sight of her. "Els, what happened? Where have you been? I've been looking all over for you." He starts toward her. "I've been worried sick."

"Keep your distance." I raise my left hand, set my right over my .38. "I need to see some ID. Right now. Slowly."

He halts. "What's going on?" Confusion clouds his expression. He looks at Els. "Why are the police here? Where have you been?"

I see Els in the periphery of my vision. She doesn't move, doesn't say a word, but I can hear her quickened breaths.

"ID," I tell him. "Now."

Keeping his eyes on mine, he pulls out a wallet, slides out a driver's license, and holds it out for me. "I'm Tyler Fournier."

I cross to him, take it, and give it a hard look. Tyler Fournier. Saint Paul, Minnesota. I hand it back to him. "What are you doing here?"

A laugh breaks from his throat. "I'm here to see her." He's staring at Els again; he knows something is askew. "Els, why are you looking at me that way? As if you don't know who I am?" His gaze drifts to mine. "What's wrong with her?"

I fill in the blanks. "Els showed up at a farm in Painters Mill, Ohio. She was injured. Took a pretty severe blow to the head."

"My God," he says. "How did it happen? Did someone hurt her? Was she in an accident? *What?*"

Els finally speaks, "I couldn't remember anything. Not even my name. I didn't know where I was from or how any of it happened."

He looks at her with a mix of astonishment and skepticism. "Are you okay now?"

"Thanks to Chief Burkholder." She looks from me to Tyler. "Things are starting to come back to me."

"What about me?" Uncertainty plays in his expression. "Do you know who I am?"

Letting out a cry of pure emotion, Els rushes past me and throws herself into his arms.

I call out her name. "Wait!"

Neither of them obeys my command; they don't even seem to hear me. I step back, watch as she falls against him. The young man wraps his arms around her. She buries her face in his shoulder and starts to cry.

"I've missed you," she chokes.

"Jesus, you're shaking." He looks at me, helplessly, as he strokes the back of her head. His hand freezes when he runs his palm over the laceration. "What the—" He extracts himself from her, eases her to arm's length. "Your head. It's cut . . . what the hell?" He looks at me, angry now. Protective. "Who did that to her?"

Els looks from Tyler to me. "That's what we're trying to figure out."

I watch the exchange, uneasy because I don't know this young man; I don't know if he's got an agenda or what he's capable of. I don't exactly know Els, either, though after spending so much time with her I don't think she's some hardened criminal. Even so, Chief Deputy Light's words scroll through my brain.

Leanard Stahl filed a complaint two days ago alleging Ms. Tsechetter cleaned out the account of his foundation and then took off with her boyfriend.

"You." I point at Fournier. "Sit down and do not

move." I motion toward the sofa. "Do you understand?"

Looking bewildered and annoyed, he takes a seat.
Els moves with him, lowers herself onto the cushion,
and curls against him.

I fix Fournier with a hard stare. "Where were you
night before last?"

"Home." He says the word without hesitation. "I
live in Castine. I left last night at midnight. Drove all
night. Got here around noon today."

"How did you know where to find her?" I ask.

He shrugs. "She told me. Last time we talked."

I look at Els and she nods.

"Why did you make the trip?" I ask Tyler.

"I don't know if you've realized it or not, Chief
Burkholder, but Els and I are in love. The problem
is, not everyone is happy about it."

I take the chair across from them. "Like who?"

"The elders," Els says quietly. "Tyler isn't Hutterite, you know."

"That's why they sent her here," he says. "To keep
her away from me." He sets his hand over hers. "She
loves them. Especially the old man."

"Old man?" I ask.

"Leanard Stahl." Pressing his mouth together as if
he's tasted something unpleasant, he looks from Els to
me and back to Els. "He's a controlling old goat. He
knows Els loves him and he uses that to control her."

"I've known Leanard since I was a child," she
says. "He's like a father to me."

Tyler looks at her as if she's betrayed him. "Tell her the rest, Els."

I watch her; wait for a response. The only thing reflected back at me is the guileless and troubled confusion of a young woman torn between loyalty and love. For a full minute the only sound comes from the patter of rain against the roof. The low rumble of thunder.

The last thing I want to do is add another complication to an already confusing situation. But if I'm going to get to the bottom of this, I have to ask all the questions, especially the hard ones. "What kind of relationship do you have with Stahl?"

"He's been a mentor," she says. "And a friend." The words come too quickly, with a little too much certainty that doesn't ring true.

Tyler mutters a curse. "That son of a bitch has been after her for weeks," he says. "She doesn't want to see it. But that's why I'm here. To get her away from all this."

Els lowers her gaze, but not before I discern the sick expression on her face.

I divide my attention between them. "Stahl went to the Mercer County Sheriff and told him the two of you stole money from him."

"*What?*" Tyler jumps to his feet. "That's a lie!"

"Sit down," I snap.

He sinks back onto the sofa cushion.

Els presses a hand to her mouth. "Why would Leanard do such a thing?"

"We didn't steal anything," Fournier growls. "Els has never stolen anything in her life."

"What about you?" I ask.

"I don't need his money," he shoots back. "I've got a good job in Saint Paul."

"Are we in trouble?" Els asks.

"We're going to ride over to the sheriff's department and get this straightened out." I look at Els. "Do you remember what happened back there in your office?"

Her expression pinches, the wheels in her mind churning. "I was working that evening. Like always. But there was something going on. I was upset because I'd found . . ." She presses her lips together. "Chief Burkholder, I think there was something going on with the books."

"That's the night she called me." Tyler's gaze slides from Els to me. "She was crying. I told her I was going to drive down. She asked me not to and we argued." As if realizing the words could be misconstrued by me, he raises both hands. "Not *that* kind of argument." He makes a sound of frustration. "I wasn't angry with her. I was frustrated because I wanted to be with her."

"What did you find?" I ask Els.

"The letters." She gets to her feet. "From clients who'd given Leanard money. To invest."

Tyler and I rise, too.

"How many people are you talking about?" I ask.

"Hundreds," she murmurs. "*Freindschaft.* Amish. Mennonite. And Hutterite."

Energized now, she starts toward the office; Tyler and I exchange glances and follow. I stop in the doorway and watch as she goes to the desk, rights the chair, and sits. She pulls open a drawer, then raises her eyes to mine. "They're gone."

Els closes her eyes, puts her face in her hands. "Chief Burkholder, what are we going to do? How could he do this to me? To us?"

"What did the letters say?" I ask.

"I don't—" She raises her head. "Wait." Jumping to her feet, she rushes to a small closet where a printer and office supplies are stored. Tugging out a stool, she steps onto it, and stretches to reach the top shelf. She pulls out a stack of crinkled papers bound with a rubber band, and then looks at it as if it's something grotesque.

"These are the originals," she murmurs. "The first one came about six months ago."

Peeling off the rubber band, she goes back to the desk and sets the stack on the blotter. Moving closer, I look down at the top sheet. It's a letter written in pencil on a wrinkled sheet of lined notebook paper. I pick it up and read.

Dear Leanard,
I hope this finds you well. Mary and I are
buying that new buggy. I need the $489.00
I invested with the foundation to pay for it.

Please send a check to our address in Ship-
shewana.

God bless,
Raymond Miller

I go to the next letter.

Dear Mr. Stahl,
Mamm passed last night. We are heartbroken,
but we know she is with God now and for that
we are happy. I need to withdraw my cash to
buy a new generator for our milking business.
Last I heard from you it was $898.00, but you
can just send me $600.00 or so.

God be with you and your family . . .

I flip through dozens of letters just like it. Some
are second and third requests for money they'd invested in the foundation. I look at Els.

"None of them got their money," she whispers. "At
first, I thought Leanard was taking care of it. He's
good with money. Always making wise investments
and letting his clients know they've made a good return. But when the letters started coming . . ." She
looks down at the stack and shakes her head. "They
broke my heart. I kept hoping I was wrong. That
Leanard would make it right. Those people *believed*
in him. They trusted him, and he stole from them."

"Did you confront him?" I ask.

Nodding, she looks down at her hands. "At first,

he told me he'd paid them, and I should mind my own business. For the first time in my life, I didn't believe him." She shakes her head. "Chief Burkholder, in all the years I've known him, I've never seen him angry. I've never heard him raise his voice. That night, he was a stranger to me, and I was afraid of him."

"Tell me what happened," I say.

"I called him around five o'clock or so and told him about the letters. He came right over. I was in my office, working. I figured he and I would work together and make it right, you know? Pay those poor people back. But he was furious. He demanded the letters. And then he fired me. Told me to get out. Go back to Minnesota. Keep my mouth shut."

Her voice breaks on the last word. "I was sitting at my desk, crying. He was pacing and ranting, saying the most ungodly things. I remember seeing him pick up the lamp." She shakes her head. "The next thing I know, we're in the car, out in the middle of nowhere. I had no idea where we were. He had a gun, and he was panicked. There's no doubt in my mind he was going to kill me. So I jumped from the car and I ran."

"Holy shit," mutters Tyler.

"All right." I look at them and nod. "I think it's time we talked to Chief Deputy Light." I'm reaching into my pocket for the Explorer keys when the lights blink and go out, plunging us into the waning light of dusk.

"Stay quiet." Tugging the mini-Maglite from my

pocket, I flick it on, averting the beam so it's not visible from the windows. "Don't move."

I take the hall to the living room, go to the front window, part the curtain, and look out. A cold, steady rain falls from a darkened sky. Tendrils of fog rise from the ground. My Explorer is still parked behind Tyler's truck. There are no other vehicles, no sign of anyone else.

"What's going on?" comes Tyler's whispered voice.

I glance over to see them coming down the hall. "Let's go."

The front door bursts open. I see a dark figure. Male. Six one. Two hundred pounds. A hot burst of adrenaline zings when I see the stainless steel .380 mini-revolver in his hand.

"If anyone moves, I will shoot you dead," he says in a deep voice.

The trailer rocks slightly as he enters. Stepping back, I ease my hand toward the .38 in my pocket. "I'm a police officer," I say. "Drop your weapon. Right now."

He shifts the gun to me. "You reach for whatever is in that pocket and I will kill you. Then I will kill them. Do you understand?"

"Leanard!" comes Els's voice from behind me. "What are you doing?"

"Stay put," I tell her. I'm thinking about the cell phone in my left pocket. The .38 in my right. I wonder if I can reach either before this crazy son of a bitch starts shooting.

"Leanard Stahl?" I say.

Using the revolver, he motions toward the living room. "Sit down. All of you. Keep your hands up."

Keeping my hands at shoulder level, I back toward the sofa. I'm vaguely aware of Els and Tyler moving with me.

"Not you," he says to Els. "Come here."

Sending an anxious glance my way, she walks stiffly to Stahl. "What are you doing with that gun?" she says. "This is crazy."

"Shut your mouth." He reaches into his pocket and produces a tangle of rope. "Tie them up."

Leanard Stahl is a far cry from what I expected. He's kindly looking with salt-and-pepper hair, wire-rimmed glasses, and a black felt fedora. He's using a walking stick, holding the curved handle in his left hand, but I don't detect a limp. I guess him to be in his mid-fifties. Outwardly, he seems as harmless as a grandfather, but I don't miss the glint of malevolence in his eyes. Something dark creeping around just beneath the surface.

"A deputy with the Mercer County Sheriff is on the way," I tell him.

"Shut up." He looks at Els, his mouth constricting into a snarl. "I would have given you everything. All you had to do was love me."

"I *do* love you, Leanard," she cries. "Please don't do this. It isn't our way."

"What do you know about our ways? Soiling yourself with a non-believer. Acting like some farm animal in heat." He tosses the rope at her. "Tie them up!"

I use the moment to get my first decent look at the revolver. It's a Taurus .380, double action, with five rounds. I'm looking for vulnerabilities, wondering if Tyler will be any help, wondering if I can get to my cell. . . .

Without warning, Tyler charges Stahl. He goes in low and head butts the older man's abdomen. Stahl reels backward. A roar of fury tears from his mouth. The two gunshots that follow deafen me.

Tyler drops to the floor. Els screams, but I tune it out. Focus on yanking the .38 from my pocket. I bring it up fast. Finger inside the guard. Seek center mass.

Stahl swings the cane. I squeeze off a shot as the wood cracks against my right temple, Hank Aaron slamming in a home run. Pain sings across the right side of my head from crown to jaw. Darkness closes in. My knees hit the floor. Vaguely, I'm aware of someone shouting my name. Then I'm laid out on the rug, some rude son of a bitch running a chain saw in my right ear . . .

"What have you done? *What have you done?*"

Screaming brings me back to full consciousness. I raise my head, glance over to see Els kneeling next to Tyler. Eyes wild with terror. Horror etched into her every feature. "*Tyler!*"

I have no idea how long I was out. At some point

Stahl bound her hands behind her back. Fournier lies supine, stone still. I see blood on his jacket. More soaked into the rug. *Dear God, he looks dead.* . . . I glance around for my .38, but it's nowhere in sight. I shift, realize my hands are bound, too.

Son of a bitch.

Rolling onto my side, I blink to clear my vision, look up at Stahl. "Sheriff's deputy is on the way," I lie.

The Hutterite man ignores me, stares at Els. "I would have loved you for all of eternity," he whispers.

She doesn't acknowledge him, instead focusing every ounce of her attention, her energy, on her fallen lover. "We were going to get married," she sobs.

I focus on the rope at my wrists, work it back and forth, trying not to attract attention.

Els leans forward, tears streaming, and sets her cheek against Tyler's. "We have to get him to a hospital," she sobs.

Stahl walks to the kitchen. Dread sweeps through me when he twists the four stovetop burners and the oven to the On position. Then he plucks off each knob and drops them into his pocket.

For the span of several heartbeats the only sound comes from Els crying and the hiss of gas. Then he turns to Els. "Get up. You're coming with me."

"I'll go to hell before I go anywhere with you!" she screams.

"As you wish." Eyes blazing, Stahl picks up the letters lying on the table. Removing a lighter from his coat pocket, he lights the corner, carries them to the window, and sets the curtains on fire.

"Don't do it, Stahl," I tell him. "Shut off the gas. Let her go."

"Too late," he says as he walks back to the living room.

I smell the rotten-egg stink of the gas as it creeps from the kitchen to the living room.

Els looks at Stahl. "You're a monster."

"And you, my dear, are a whore." Taking a final, lingering look at her, he crosses to the door, yanks it open, and then he's gone.

"Els! Get up!" I scramble to my feet, lurch over to where she's kneeling next to Tyler. "Is he alive?"

"He's breathing."

"We have to get him out of here. Gas is going to blow. Get me a knife. Cut this rope. *Hurry!*"

She darts to the kitchen, turns, and yanks out a drawer. I follow her, go to the stove, try to twist the knob assembly prong. It won't move without the knob.

I glance at Els, see the steak knife in her hand. "Cut my rope. Hurry!"

She crosses to me, spins so that we're back to back. Her entire body shakes against mine. As she saws, I'm keenly aware of the curtains burning, flames licking the ceiling, and smoke filling the room. I hear the hiss of gas pouring from the stove. And then my hands are free.

Snatching the knife from her, I spin her around,

set the blade against the rope. I slice hard, and it falls away. "Open the door!" I shout.

Vaguely, I'm aware of her running to the door. I go to Tyler. His face is the color of paste. Eyes partially open, unseeing. There's too much blood. Bending, I grab him beneath his arms. He's heavy, but my adrenaline is pumping, and I drag him to the door.

"Open it!" I shout.

"It won't open!" she screams.

I lurch to the door, twist the knob. Panic stabs me when it doesn't budge. Only then do I realize it's been jammed from the outside.

"Back door!" I say. "Help me."

Black smoke billows. To my left, flames devour the wall, a beast consuming everything in its path. Els and I grab Tyler's wrists and drag him toward the back door. He's dead weight, feet dragging, head lolling.

When we're a few feet away, Els rushes forward and yanks it open. Cold, clean air pours in. She goes through, onto the deck outside. Gripping Tyler's wrists, I haul him through the door. I've just stepped onto the deck when a tremendous roar shakes the trailer. The concussion slams against my back like a hot, cast-iron skillet. I pitch forward, lose my grip on Tyler, and tumble into space.

The fall knocks the breath from my lungs. I get to my hands and knees, see Tyler lying a few feet away. "Els!"

"I'm here!" She crawls toward Tyler.

Ten feet away, a window shatters. Flames shoot twenty feet into the air as the trailer burns unchecked. Taking Tyler's hands, we drag him to a safe distance. Only then do I reach for my cell and call the Mercer County Sheriff.

"Send an ambulance," I tell them. "I've got a gunshot victim. The shooter is Leanard Stahl. He's armed and dangerous."

Ending the call, I drop the cell into my pocket. Ten feet away, Els is sitting on the ground, holding Tyler's hand, her head bowed in prayer. I go to them, sit down beside her, and I take her other hand.

"Ambulance is on the way," I tell her.

"Tyler's going to be okay," she tells me.

"I know." I put my arm around her shoulders. "I know."

Sometimes it's the mundane cases that turn out to be unexpectedly perilous. The kind in which some unsuspecting cop misjudges the potential for danger and walks into it with her eyes closed. That was certainly the case with Els Tsechetter and our fateful trip to Coldwater. In retrospect, all I can do is chalk it up to experience with the hope that it will make me a better cop.

Ten days have passed since Els and I dragged Tyler Fournier from that burning mobile home. He survived the ordeal, despite a serious gunshot wound, and was released from the hospital four days ago.

According to Chief Deputy Light, Leanard Stahl was pulled over and arrested without incident by an Ohio State Police trooper a few hours after the shooting. He was booked into the Mercer County jail on a multitude of charges, including the attempted murder of a public official.

Chief Deputy Light transported us to the ER at the community hospital. Tomasetti showed up a short time later. He did his best not to look too worried. But he held me for a beat too long, and he stayed with me while my head was stitched and a CAT scan ruled out the possibility of a concussion. He wasn't happy that I'd ended up in the ER once again, though he couldn't tell me what I should have done differently. In the end we decided that hindsight is 20-20, and we left it at that.

This afternoon, I'm sitting at my desk at the police station, listening to the radio Lois has turned up a little too loudly.

"Chief?" Lois appears in the doorway of my office. "You've got visitors."

I'm about to ask who it is when Els Tsechetter and Tyler Fournier come up beside her. Both are grinning like fools and I find myself smiling back. "Thanks, Lois."

Rising, I motion to the visitor chairs adjacent my desk. "Come in and have a seat."

Tyler Fournier moves with the slowness of a man twice his age. He's lost a few pounds since I last saw him. But his color is good and the smile on his face tells me he's on the mend.

"Good to see you getting around so well," I tell him.

"I have a good nurse." He grins at Els.

Letting go of his hand, she crosses the short space between us, and encases me in a hug. "I just want to thank you, Chief Burkholder." She pushes me to arm's length and blinks back tears. "For saving Tyler's life. For giving me back mine. Thank you."

I bank an un-chief-of-police-like rise of emotion. "You know I was just doing my job."

She laughs. "That's a likely story."

Indeed.

"What brings you to Painters Mill?" I ask.

Els and Tyler exchange a look. "I wanted Tyler to see Behalt," she tells me. "I want to thank the director."

"He'll appreciate that." I turn my attention to Tyler. "You'll enjoy it."

"I'm leaving the colony," Els blurts.

"I asked her to marry me," Tyler puts in.

"Congratulations," I say.

A moment of silence ensues, and Els becomes thoughtful. "Chief Burkholder, I want you to know. What happened in Coldwater does not speak for my Hutterite brethren. It's not the reason I'm leaving the colony. I'm leaving because I love Tyler. I want to spend the rest of my life with him, and I can't do that and remain Hutterite."

Once again I'm reminded of my own heritage, my Amish past, and everything I left behind to follow my own path.

"You'll always be Hutterite." I tap a finger against my heart. "Where it counts."

"Thank you." Not bothering to wipe away the tears on her cheeks, she extends her hand to mine. *"Freindschaft,"* she whispers.

"Freindschaft," I echo.

Hand in hand, they go through the door.

IN PLAIN SIGHT

Darkness pressed down on him with an almost physical force. The wind had kicked up, hissing through the treetops, dry autumn leaves whispering as he passed. Lightning flickered on the horizon, telling him the storm would be here soon. Noah Kline wasn't worried about any of it. He'd walked this road hundreds of times. He knew every tree, culvert, and field along the way. Tonight, a tornado could swoop down from the heavens and he wouldn't care.

The only thing that mattered tonight was that he'd kissed the girl he loved. It was their first, a moment he'd anticipated for weeks, and he'd been grinning like a fool since leaving the high school. That had been twenty minutes ago and already he couldn't wait to see her again. Ashley Hodges was the sweetest, prettiest girl God had ever put on this earth, and Noah loved her more than his own life.

As perfect as all of that was, Noah wasn't so blind that he didn't see the troubled waters ahead. His parents disapproved of him dating a non-Amish girl. They hadn't come right out and said it, but he figured they were quietly hoping he'd break up with her once his *rumspringa* was over. As much as he hated the thought of disappointing them, that wasn't going to happen.

Ashley's parents were even less thrilled; he'd known it the first time he met her father and he'd started with the questions. *Did you graduate from high school? Do you have any plans for college? How are you going to get a good job and support yourself when you don't even drive a car?* Noah had answered as best he could, but it didn't take a rocket scientist to see that the man wasn't impressed.

It didn't matter. Ashley was his world, and nothing could change that. They were in love. Somehow, they'd make it work.

Noah was thinking about the kiss again when he noticed the headlights behind him. It was unusual to see a vehicle on this stretch of road so late. There were only a handful of farms out this way, most of which were Amish. It was probably Mr. and Mrs. Boedecker coming home from a movie—it was Saturday night, after all. Or else someone was lost.

Shoving his hands into his pockets, Noah moved onto the shoulder and kept walking. The farm where he lived with his parents and six siblings was a mile or so down the road. Hopefully, he'd make it home before the sky opened up. He picked up the pace. Headlights washed over him. Behind him, the vehicle's engine revved. Someone was in a hurry, he thought. Scooting right another couple of feet, he glanced over his shoulder. Bright headlights blinded him. The vehicle was moving fast. Too fast for this narrow, pitted back road. He sidestepped onto the grassy shoulder and kept moving.

Tires skittered on gravel, pebbles pinging in the wheel wells. Right behind him. Startled, Noah spun, blinded, threw up a hand to shield his eyes against the glare. "What the—"

The impact knocked him off his feet. Pain shot from his hip to his knee. His body cartwheeled. The world went silent for an instant. Then he sprawled face down in the ditch.

Noah lay still a moment, gasping and dazed, trying to get air into his lungs. Pain coursed through his leg, an electric pulse that zinged with every beat of his heart. Vaguely, he was aware that the vehicle had stopped, the engine rumbling. A groan squeezed from his throat when he rolled. A drumroll of pain in his arm. Nothing broken, so he struggled to his hands and knees and looked around. The vehicle idled thirty feet away. It must have done a U-turn because it was facing him, the headlights blinding.

Noah thought the driver would have gotten out by now to see if he was all right. In the back of his mind, he wondered if maybe the driver had been texting or drinking, and accidentally veered onto the shoulder.

"Hey." Noah raised his hand. "I'm okay!" he called out.

Dust swirled in the yellow shafts of the beams. No one got out. Noah got to his feet, a cymbal of pain clanging in his leg. He stood there, breathing hard, shaking. Squinting, he tried to make out the type of vehicle, but the lights were too bright. What was this guy doing?

The driver's side door swung open. He saw a silhouette as someone stepped out. "Hey, Loverboy!"

In that instant, Noah knew this was no random accident. He was keenly aware of how close the vehicle was. That he was vulnerable. Alone. He got a sick feeling in the pit of his stomach.

Never taking his eyes off the vehicle, Noah limped across the road to a safer distance, out of the glare of the lights. "I don't want any trouble," he called out.

Nothing but ominous silence came back at him.

There was a plowed field to his left, a fenced pasture to his right. Home was straight ahead. If he could get around the car on either side, he could make it. All he had to do was climb the fence or cut through the field.

Noah started toward the fence. He was midway there when the driver gunned the engine. Noah broke into a run, but he was hindered by his injured leg. The tires squealed against the asphalt. The vehicle jumped forward. Ignoring the pain, Noah poured on the speed, sprinting toward the fence a few yards away.

The vehicle roared toward him, closing in fast. It slid to a stop between him and the fence, missing him by inches, cutting him off. Noah pivoted, changed direction, and ran toward the open field, arms outstretched.

Behind him, the engine screamed. He glanced over his shoulder, saw the vehicle back up and skid sideways, mudslinging from the rear tires. Then it leapt forward.

Breathing hard, he sprinted toward the field, feet pounding the ground, boots sinking into mud up to his ankles. Loose cornstalks threatened to trip him. Headlights played crazily all around. The roar of the engine in his ears. No place to take cover. No fence or trees.

He tore through the field, feet barely touching the ground, pain zinging, arms pumping. Ten yards and he risked a look behind him. Headlights a scant few feet away, a giant beast about to devour him.

"Stop!" he shouted.

Noah cut hard to the left, tried to outmaneuver the vehicle. It tracked him, tires eating up the ground at an astounding speed, headlights bouncing over the rough terrain.

Noah swung right toward the trees a quarter mile

away. The vehicle stayed with him, mud flying, closing the distance in seconds. Noah zigzagged right and left, slid and nearly fell, then turned back toward the road. Not too far. If he could reach the fence he'd be home free. . . .

The bumper struck him from behind, a wrecking ball slamming into his backside. Noah's feet left the ground. He somersaulted across the hood, elbows and knees knocking against steel, the windshield. For an instant he was airborne, tumbling end over end. He hit the ground hard. Pain screaming through his body. Wet earth against his face. The taste of blood in his mouth.

Choking back a groan of pain, he rolled, got to his hands and knees, and crawled toward the fence. Just fifty feet to go. Behind him, the engine bellowed. He glanced back, saw the oncoming headlights, dirt and debris flying. The silver glint of the bumper loomed.

He raised his hands. "No!"

Thoughts of Ashley flitted through his brain.

The world exploded, and the waiting darkness sucked him into the abyss.

At seventy-eight years of age, Orin Schlabach figured he was old enough to know not to venture too far from the house, especially when his wife had just pulled a double batch of cinnamon rolls from the oven. He'd reached for one—just a little something to tide him over while the coffee perked—but she'd smacked his hand with the wooden spoon she kept next to the stove and told him to feed the cows first. Not a man to argue with a woman in charge of breakfast, Orin grabbed his coat and headed out to the barn. He was on his way back inside when he heard his birddog, Jojo, barking somewhere out in the front field.

Drizzle drifted down from an overcast sky; the temperature hovered somewhere around forty degrees. It was Orin's least favorite kind of weather. Unfortunately for him, Jojo loved it, the colder and wetter, the better.

Standing in the driveway between the house and barn, Orin looked out at the field. Sure enough, a quarter mile away, Jojo was barking at something on the ground. Some debris or trash that had blown in with the storm last night. Orin put his hand to his lips and whistled.

"Jojo! *Kumma inseid!*" Come inside.

The dog was usually obedient, especially during breakfast when more than likely he was in store for table scraps. This morning, he didn't even look back. In fact, if Orin wasn't mistaken, the dog's barking seemed frantic. What was he barking at? And what on earth was that on the ground?

Muttering beneath his breath, Orin crossed the driveway, opened the gate, and started across the field. He was thinking about cinnamon rolls and the possibility of scrambled eggs when he realized the dog wasn't barking at some flapping piece of trash. At first, he thought maybe a deer had come into the field and died. At forty yards, he realized that wasn't the case at all.

Concern twinged in his gut, and he broke into a wobbly old-man run. "Hello?" he called out. "Who's there? Are you all right?"

The person on the ground didn't move. A young man. Just a boy, in fact. The hat and suspenders told him he was Plain. He was sprawled on his side, one arm thrown over his head, legs splayed.

Jojo looked up at Orin, tongue lolling, tail wagging.

"Good boy, Jojo."

Ignoring the arthritis protesting in his knees, Orin knelt beside the boy. Recognition kicked him hard enough to shake his innards when he got a look at his face. *"Noah,"* he whispered. A quiver of fear went through him when he noticed the blood. It was on his shirt. More matted in his hair. On the side of his face. Dear Lord, what had happened?

"Noah?" He set his hand on the boy's shoulder, found it cold and wet to the touch. "What happened, son? Can you hear me? Can you move?"

No answer. No movement. Not even a shiver or twitch. *No sign of life.* For a terrible moment, Orin thought the young man was dead. Relief skittered through him when he saw the boy's chest rise. At least he was breathing. Working off his coat, he draped it over the boy.

"You just stay there and get warmed up." He

patted the boy's shoulder and looked around. "I'll get help."

The old man struggled to his feet and took off at a lumbering run for the neighbor's house.

My name is Kate Burkholder, and I'm the chief of police of Painters Mill, a pretty little township in the heart of Ohio's Amish Country. I've just pulled into my parking spot outside the police station when my cell phone vibrates against my hip. The screen tells me it's my graveyard-shift dispatcher, Mona Kurtz, who also happens to be a part-time patrol officer, and she hasn't yet left for the day. "Hey, Mona."

"Chief, I just took a call from the Amish pay phone out on Township Road 4. Orin Schlabach says the neighbor's son, Noah Kline, is injured and unconscious in his field."

It's not the kind of call I'd expect at 7:00 A.M. on a Sunday morning. "How seriously is he hurt?"

"Orin says it's bad. He went back out to the field stay with him."

"Do Noah's parents know?"

"Not yet. No one has a phone out there, except the Boedeckers." The couple are the only non-Amish who live on the township road.

"Get an ambulance out there," I tell her.

"They're en route."

"Tell Skid to meet me there," I add, referring to

Chuck "Skid" Skidmore, my officer on duty this morning. "I'm on my way."

The Schlabach farm is on a township road that's more dirt than asphalt and dead-ends at Painters Creek. There's an ambulance parked on the shoulder when I arrive, red and blue lights flashing. An Amish man and two paramedics are standing in the field fifty yards away. Skid's not arrived yet. A dog sniffs around in the distance. I park behind the ambulance and head toward the men.

I reach them as the paramedics are loading the patient into the ambulance. The young man is draped with a Mylar blanket; there's a cervical collar wrapped around his neck and an IV drip in his arm.

"What's his condition?" I ask.

"We've not been able to rouse him, Chief," the EMT tells me as he slams the rear doors. "He's got visible injuries about his head. Compound fracture of his arm. He suffered some kind of trauma. Pulse and heart rate are extremely slow. If he's been out here long, chances are he's hypothermic."

They're in a hurry to get their patient to the hospital, so I don't hold them up.

I've met Orin Schlabach a few of times over the years. I bought pumpkins from his wife last fall. The couple are well into their seventies, but they still run their farm and are active in the community.

"Can you tell me what happened, Mr. Schlabach?" I ask as we shake hands.

He's about six feet tall with a salt-and-pepper beard that reaches nearly to his waist. He wears traditional Amish garb—flat-brimmed hat, trousers with suspenders, blue work shirt, and a black barn coat—along with about fifty pounds of extra weight.

"I went out to feed the cows. Jojo started barking." He motions toward the dog. "That's when I spotted the boy on the ground."

"Noah Kline?"

He nods. "My neighbor's boy. The oldest, I think. Nice young man."

"Did he say anything?"

"He's been out cold the whole time."

"Any idea what happened?"

"I can't imagine." The Amish man shakes his head. "I see that boy walking along the road couple times a week. He don't drive, you know. And we don't get any traffic out this way."

"Have you talked to his parents?"

"I called you first thing, Chief Burkholder, and then I came back to stay with him."

We're standing in a cornfield, about fifty feet from the road. The corn has already been cut and harvested. Leftover dried yellow stalks litter the ground. A small circle of blood has soaked into the dirt where Noah Kline had lain. On the other side of the road is a tumbledown fence. Beyond, a wooded area that runs along the floodplain of Painters Creek.

I take a moment to walk the scene, trying to figure out what might've happened, when Skid's cruiser pulls up behind my Explorer, lights flashing. He meets me in the field, and I brief him on what little I know.

"How's the kid?" he asks.

"Not sure," I tell him. "Hasn't regained consciousness."

"That's not good." He looks around. "Any idea what happened to him?"

"I thought we might walk the scene, see if we can figure it out."

We fall silent, thoughtful, eyes on the ground. That's when I notice the tire ruts.

"Those look fresh," Skid says.

We follow the tracks. Sure enough, twin furrows cut deeply into the wet soil. Farther out, there's a place where the driver may have done "donuts," turning the steering wheel sharply while accelerating so that the rear wheels spin and the vehicle turns in a tight circle.

"Looks like a vehicle left the pavement at a high rate of speed," I say, motioning toward the deep ruts and mud that's been slung onto the asphalt.

"Braked hard there." Skid gestures.

"Did a donut there," I say.

"Goofy damn teenagers." He looks at me and shakes his head. "Could this be a case of car surfing?" he asks, referring to the practice of someone riding on the roof or hood of a vehicle, often while said vehicle is traveling at a high rate of speed.

"Maybe. But why would they leave him like this?"

"If they were drinking they may have panicked."

I move closer and kneel. "I've got footprints here."

"Someone was on foot." He kneels next to me, leans over the nearest imprint. "Judging from the depth of that print and the length of the stride, I'd say he was running."

Mindful of the possibility that this may not have been a case of teenage antics gone wrong, I look at the ruts in relation to the footprints and try to get a sense of what might've occurred. Was this a case of "car surfing" as Skid surmised? Or was this something more sinister? Road rage that led to an altercation? A hit-and-run?

Rising, I walk back to Orin Schlabach. "Did you or your wife hear or see anything unusual last night?"

The old man shakes his head. "Not a thing."

It's too soon to know how severe the young man's injuries are. In the course of my career, I've seen more than my share of traffic accidents—and worse. A head injury can go from minor to fatal in a heartbeat. Keeping that in mind, and knowing Noah Kline didn't get hurt without help, I call my significant other.

"I hear you've got a possible hit-skip on your hands," he says without preamble.

John Tomasetti is an agent with the Ohio Bureau of Criminal Investigation. He's also the love of my life. We live on a small farm a few miles out of Wooster, north of Painters Mill.

"Word travels fast," I say.

"Especially when you have a police scanner."

I recap what little I know. "It might be overkill, but I'm wondering if you know someone in the area who can come out and take a look at this scene. Depending on what happens with the victim, this could get serious, and I may want some plasters of the tire tread."

"You thinking drunk driver? Foul play?"

"Not sure." I tell him about the tire ruts and footprints. "Some teenagers may have been horsing around and had an accident."

"Wouldn't be the first time."

I think about Orin Schlabach saying that Noah Kline walked this road on a regular basis. "Tomasetti, I don't know if I'm right, but it looks like someone ran this kid down with a vehicle."

"I know a guy," he says. "Give me half an hour."

Mervin and Rhoda Kline are Swartzentruber Amish, a conservative sect that adheres to the old traditions with an iron fist. No windows or slow-moving vehicle signs for their buggies. Some don't use gravel in their driveways or even have indoor plumbing in their homes. The Klines live with their seven children on a dairy farm just down the road from the Schlabach place.

I drive up the long lane to find Mr. Kline hitching the buggy horse in the muddy area between the house and barn. His expression tells me he's already realized his son isn't at home. That he's worried about him and likely hitching the buggy to either use the Amish pay phone down the road or to look for him.

"Mr. Kline?" I cross to him.

He meets me halfway, glad to see me, which usually isn't the case, but he's apprehensive, too, afraid I may be the bearer of bad news. "You bring word of my son?"

We shake hands. "Your neighbor, Mr. Schlabach, found Noah unconscious in his field this morning."

"Unconscious?" The Amish man gapes at me, steps back, putting a hand to his chest. "He is injured?"

"He was taken to the hospital about twenty minutes ago. I don't have word just yet on his condition."

"I saw the police lights." His brows furrow. "What happened to him?"

"That's what I'm trying to figure out. If you could answer a few questions, it would be a big help."

"Of course. Come, while I finish here." Without speaking, he turns back to the buggy and resumes hitching the horse, working quickly now, anxious to get on the road.

"I can drive you and your wife to the hospital if you'd like," I tell him.

"We will take the buggy."

I can tell by the stiff set of his shoulders that the news has shaken him. I give him a moment and then ask, "When's the last time you saw Noah?"

"Last night. When he left. Around seven o'clock."

"Where did he go?"

"The high school," he mutters.

Surprise ripples through me. "Homecoming?"

He nods, his mouth tightening, telling me he isn't happy about it.

Having grown up in Painters Mill—having grown up *Amish*—I know firsthand how unusual it would be for a Swartzentruber boy to attend a typically "English" social rite of passage like homecoming.

"Who was he with?" I ask.

He doesn't look at me. "*Es maydel.*" That girl. He says the words with a generous dose of distaste. "The one he's been seeing. The English girl. Ashley Hodges."

Another layer of surprise settles over the first. Ashley Hodges is the daughter of a high-powered local attorney, Craig Hodges. The family was in the news recently when the *Columbus Dispatch* profiled his law firm, Hodges and Hodges. According to the piece, they're Painters Mill's wealthiest family.

"They've been seeing each other?" I ask. "Dating?"

He gives me a withering look. "Noah is on *rumspringa.*"

He says the word as if it explains everything. In a way, it does. *Rumspringa* is the *Deitsh* word for "running around." It's the time in a young Amish person's life, usually their late teens, before they commit to the church. A time when they're allowed to break all those Amish rules while their parents do their best to look the other way.

"I knew nothing good would come of it," Mr. Kline says.

"Why is that?" I know the answer, but I'm obliged to ask anyway.

He looks at me as if I'm dense. "She is English."

"Does Noah own a vehicle?" I ask, knowing many times young Amish men will purchase a vehicle during *rumspringa*. "Does he drive?"

The Amish man glares at me over the horse's back as he smooths the leather. "No."

"How did he get to the school?"

"He walked, like always."

"Do any of his friends have access to a vehicle?" I ask. "Amish or English?"

"Ben Weaver bought a car a couple of months ago." Clucking his tongue, he shakes his head. "Lives over in Killbuck now with a bunch of boys."

I write down the name. "Are Noah and Ben close?"

"They were up until a few months ago."

"What happened?"

The man sighs. "They had some kind of falling-out. Don't see each other much anymore."

"What was the falling out about?"

"You'll have to ask them." He makes a sound of disapproval. "You know how young men are during *rumspringa*. Drinking beer and staying out all hours. Dumb as a herd of cows."

"Do you know how Ashley got to homecoming?"

He shrugs. "I wouldn't know."

I think about that a moment. "Mr. Kline, has your

son had any arguments or disagreements with anyone recently?"

His hands go still on the harness. He looks at me
over the top of the horse's back, his eyes narrowing
on mine. "What are you asking me, Chief Burkholder? Did someone do something to my son? Hurt
him? On purpose?"

"I'm just asking questions that need to be asked
so I can get this figured out."

"Noah is *Amisch.* He has no enemies." He resumes
harnessing, yanks a strap tight. "No telling about that
girl, though."

"What do you mean by that?"

"You figure it out, Kate Burkholder. You should
know, with your being English and all."

I wince inwardly, curb a pang of an emotion I don't
want to identify. "Is there anything else you can tell
me that might help me figure out what happened?"
I ask.

Kline finishes with the harness and glances back
toward the house. "We have to leave for the hospital
now. Our business is done."

The Hodges family lives in the Maple Crest Subdivision, an upscale housing development that's Painters
Mill's rendering of location, location, location. Set
on lushly landscaped lots, the homes are spacious,
tasteful, and expensive.

Two turns and I pull into the driveway of a spectacular Tudor-style mansion and park behind a white

Escalade. A flagstone path takes me past a sculpted boxwood hedge to massive double wood doors more befitting a Scottish castle. I ring the bell and wait.

A pretty blond woman of about forty answers. She's wearing yoga pants and a snug T-shirt, distracted, her cell phone tucked into the crook of her neck. She does a double take upon noticing my uniform. "Oh." Ending her call, she motions me into the foyer. "I thought you were the pool guy," she says a little breathlessly. "Is everything all right?"

I give her a quick summary of what happened to Noah Kline.

"Noah? Oh my God." She presses a hand to her throat. "Is he all right?"

"I'm not sure what his condition is at the moment. I'm trying to find out what happened." I pause, giving her a chance to respond. When she says nothing, I add, "Ashley Hodges is your daughter?"

"Yes, of course." She sticks out her hand and we shake. "I'm Belinda Hodges."

"I understand Ashley was with Noah last night."

"They went to homecoming together."

I give her a thoughtful smile. "Must have made quite a stir."

She smiles back. "I'll say."

"Did either of them have any problems with anyone?"

"I talked to Ashley briefly when she got home and she had a wonderful time."

"Your daughter is fifteen?"

"Fifteen going on twenty." She blows a breath through her bangs. "A sophomore this year. She's an honor student. Captain of the volleyball team. She volunteers at the retirement home one night a week."

"How well do you know Noah?"

"I've only met him a couple of times, but he seems quite nice." Her eyes meet mine as the meaning of my questions sinks in. "You think what happened to him wasn't an accident?"

"At this juncture, I'm just trying to figure out what happened," I say, keeping the point of my visit as innocuous as possible. "Does Ashley drive?"

"She just got her temporary permit. So far, so good. Knock on wood." She taps her knuckles against the door. "Jason, my son, got his last year, and boy do I worry. They're responsible, but you know how kids are."

I let the silence ride. She fiddles with the Fitbit on her wrist, glances toward the kitchen. Ready to be rid of me so she can get on with her day. More concerned about her schedule than Noah.

"Would it be all right if I talked to Ashley, Mrs. Hodges? I'd like to ask her a few questions."

She blinks, hesitates. "She's still sleeping."

It's after 8:00 A.M., early for a teenager who was up late the night before, but not an unreasonable time, especially in light of the circumstances. "I'm sorry to wake her, but I'd really like to speak to her to see if there's anything she can add."

"Sure, let me get—"

"I'm right here, Mom," comes a sing-song voice.

I turn to see a pretty, blond-haired girl trot down the curved staircase.

"I got dibs on pancakes!" Behind her, a slightly older boy wearing a Painters Mill High football hoodie pounds down the steps. Both of them are giggling. At the landing, he elbows past his sister, descends the remaining steps in two big strides. He doesn't notice me until he reaches the base. He freezes, giving us a deer-in-the-headlights stare. Not expecting to find the police standing in the foyer first thing in the morning.

The girl's stride falters when she notices my uniform. "Oh. Hi."

Ashley Hodges is slender and athletically built, with blue eyes and sooty black lashes. Wearing ratty sweats, her hair pulled into an untidy ponytail, and not a stitch of makeup, she's model pretty, in a girl-next-door sort of way. She reaches the base of the stairs, eyes darting from me to her mother and back to me. "What's wrong?"

Belinda Hodges smiles at her children. "Chief Burkholder, this is my daughter, Ashley. And my son, Jason."

The two teenagers exchange looks, then move cautiously toward us. Belinda leans to kiss both of them on their cheeks.

Ashley's eyes flick from her mother to me and back. "Is everything okay?"

"It's Noah, honey." Belinda Hodges puts her arm around her daughter. "He's in the hospital."

"What?" The girl presses both hands to her cheeks, her eyes meeting mine over her French-manicured fingertips.

"Whoa," mutters Jason. "What happened to him?"

"How bad is he hurt?" the girl asks, the pitch of her voice rising. "Is he okay?"

I recap the basics, keeping it vague.

"Oh my God. Mom." She looks at her mother, her expression ravaged. "I have to go see him. Please."

"Sure, honey."

Jason touches her arm. "I can take you if you need a ride, squirt."

I address the girl before she can turn away. "I understand you and Noah went to homecoming last night."

Though she's visibly shaken by the news of Noah's hospitalization, happiness flashes on her face at the mention of his name. "It was our first real date. We just danced and talked all evening. He's incredibly sweet. We had a great time."

"How did you get to the school?" I ask. "Did someone drive you?"

"Dad drove me. Noah walked, like always."

"What did Dad do?"

The four of us turn at the sound of the male voice. I see Craig Hodges emerge from the kitchen. Wearing sleek running gear—tights and a windbreaker, with headphones looped around his neck—he's sweating and flushed as if he just arrived home from a morning run. He does a double take when he sees me and his expression sobers. "Is everything all right?"

I tell him about Noah Kline.

"An accident?" he asks.

"We're not sure what happened just yet." I turn my attention back to the girl. "Ashley, were there any problems last night? Any disagreements with anyone? An argument? Anything like that?"

"Everyone was so sweet to Noah. I mean, he didn't know a soul and he wasn't exactly comfortable. I introduced him around, you know, and everyone went out of their way to make him feel welcome."

"What time did you leave?" I ask.

"I picked her up around midnight," Craig inserts.

"What about Noah?" I ask.

"I offered to drive him home," he says. "It had been raining on and off." The man shrugs. "He said he'd walk, so I let him."

"You should have asked a little more nicely," Ashley says, pouting.

Her father shrugs. "He's a big boy."

"Here we go," Jason mutters, rolling his eyes.

Ashley's eyes fill with tears. She looks up at her mother. "Mom, please, Noah doesn't have a phone. I just want to see him. Please. Can we just go?"

Craig sets his hand on his daughter's shoulder. "Of

course, sweetheart. Let me walk Chief Burkholder to her car. You grab a quick breakfast, get dressed, and then we'll go."

He makes eye contact with his wife, then me, his expression letting me know he's got more to say that he doesn't want his daughter to hear. Jason catches his father's silent message. The three of us head outside.

When the front door closes behind us, Craig says, "Ashley's too naïve to understand, but I thought you should know, Chief Burkholder. She had a boyfriend before Noah came along."

Jason nods, his expression sober. "Doug Mason. He's on the football team. I always liked him, but he's kind of a jerk."

"Doug wasn't happy when she broke up with him." The lawyer grimaces. "Even less so when he found out she was seeing this Amish kid."

"Some people at school think it's weird that Ashley's going out with an Amish guy," Jason tells us. "They think the relationship is cringey. But Doug's a bully."

"He got into trouble for hazing one of his freshman teammates last year," Craig says.

I divide my attention between the two of them. "Has Doug Mason had problems with Noah Kline or Ashley?"

The two exchange a look, then the attorney scowls. "I saw some changes in Ashley right about the time they broke up. She wouldn't talk about it. Said everything was fine." He sighs unhappily, his expression contrite. "I went through her phone. I just about hit the roof when I saw the texts Mason had sent her. That little shit called her a few choice names."

"Like what?"

"Uppity bitch. Cocktease." He growls at the back of his throat. "Once I got myself calmed down, I talked to Doug's father and it stopped."

"How long ago?"

"A couple months." He heaves another sigh. "Look, I'm not a big fan of her relationship with this Amish kid. He seems decent enough and I don't have anything against the Amish, but those people are backward. They only go to the eighth grade. The boy doesn't even drive. None of that bodes well for a successful career."

"Some of the Amish make a good living," I point out. "Farmers. Cabinet makers. Furniture makers. Builders."

"Yeah, well, that's not the future I have in mind for my daughter. Honestly, I don't know what she sees in him."

I call Pomerene Hospital on my way back to the scene. After being put on hold twice, I finally get the emergency department. Due to HIPAA laws and privacy concerns, the nursing supervisor can't tell me much. But because I'm law enforcement working an open case—and she knows me personally—she's able to give me enough information so that I can proceed with the investigation.

The news isn't good.

"Doctor Romer ran a CT scan and some x-rays upon arrival," she tells me. "The boy's got a skull fracture, Chief. Likely a traumatic brain injury. He's in a coma."

"What's his condition?"

"Critical."

My heart stutters in my chest. "Is he going to make it?"

"It's going to be touch and go for the next twenty-four hours. They don't want the brain to swell. That's the main concern. That's all the doc can say at this point."

I wonder if Noah's parents have arrived at the hospital. If they've heard the news. I think about Ashley Hodges. In the back of my mind I'm reminded that if the boy dies from his injuries, the investigation will take a much more aggressive path.

I thank her as I make the turn onto the township road. Tomasetti's Tahoe and a Ford Focus I don't recognize is parked on the shoulder. The men are standing in the field, a measuring tape stretched between them. I meet them at the spot where Noah Kline was found.

"This is Kyle Holloway," Tomasetti says, motioning toward the man on the other end of the measuring tape. "He's a patrol sergeant with the Wooster PD and specializes in accident reconstruction."

"Thanks for coming." I extend my hand and we shake.

Holloway is casually dressed in khaki slacks, rubber boots for the mud, and a plaid shirt covered by a Wooster Police Department windbreaker. He grins. "I owed John a favor."

I give Tomasetti a look. "Lots of people owe you a favor."

He shoots me a half smile. "How's the kid?"

I tell him. "Things are going to heat up if he doesn't pull through."

"Especially in light of what we think happened here," Holloway adds.

I look from man to man. "That sounds like maybe this isn't a likely case of car surfing gone awry."

Putting his hands on his hips, Holloway makes a sound of bemusement, and strides toward the road. "I've reconstructed hundreds of accidents in the thirty years I've been a cop, Chief Burkholder. In this case, I don't have much in the way of skid marks or even a vehicle to look at. That said, we're not operating completely blind, either. Judging from the tire ruts, the footprints, the other indentations and marks where I believe someone was on the ground, and the location of the blood, I think we're dealing with extremely dangerous and irresponsible behavior."

From his place on the shoulder of the road, Tomasetti indicates the skid marks in the gravel. "Vehicle went off the road here. Went through the ditch and entered the field."

"There's no indication he tried to stop, at least initially." Holloway takes it from there, motions toward the ground where he's standing. "I pick up the victim's footprints here. He's running. Moving fast. It looks like the vehicle came at him from behind." He walks about twenty feet and points out a place where the mud is smooth and slightly compressed. "There's no way to tell exactly what happened, but I believe the victim was struck at least twice by the vehicle. There are marks in the mud where he went down. There's blood."

For the span of a full minute the only sound comes from the caw of crows from the greenbelt and the bawling of a cow at the back of the Schlabach farm.

"Are you saying the driver of the car purposefully ran him down?" I hear myself ask.

Holloway nods. "I think that's a likely scenario."

"Is it possible this was a bunch of teenagers clowning around?" Tomasetti asks. "An inexperienced driver? Maybe they'd been drinking? Something like that?"

"Absolutely," Holloway says. "This isn't an exact science. We don't have a lot to work with, so this is basically theory."

"It would be helpful to see the vehicle," Tomasetti says.

Holloway sighs. "Whatever the case, we're dealing with a hit-and-run. Someone struck that kid and left him lying in the field. If he dies, even if this was an accident, the driver could be facing a vehicular homicide charge."

Half an hour later, Tomasetti and I are in the Explorer heading toward Painters Mill. We left Skid at the scene. Over the next few hours, the BCI crime scene investigator will photograph and videotape the area, and plaster the tire ruts in an effort to pick up tread and any marks that are unique to the tires. If at some point we're able to identify the driver or the vehicle, we'll have the plasters on hand to run a comparison.

I call Mona and ask her to set up a tip line. "There's a five-hundred-dollar reward for any information that leads to an arrest and conviction."

"Got it, Chief."

"Thanks." I end the call to find Tomasetti contemplating me.

"Tell me about Doug Mason," he says.

"He's the ex-boyfriend of the girl Noah Kline was with last night."

"He the jealous type?"

"And a bully, evidently." I tell him about the text messages Craig Hodges found on his daughter's phone.

"Nasty stuff," he says.

"Especially after two months have passed."

"Long time to stew."

"Or boil over."

Doug Mason and his parents live in Painters Mill in a nicely renovated older home set on a large lot with a dozen or so mature trees. I park curbside and find two teenaged boys and an adult male throwing a football in the front yard.

"Someone's got some nice wheels." Tomasetti points to the silver muscle car sitting in the driveway. "Looks just washed."

"Not the kind of vehicle a dad would drive," I say as we get out.

The three men stop what they're doing and watch us approach.

"Christopher Mason?" I say when we're a couple yards away.

The man tosses the football to one of the boys, his eyes flicking from me to Tomasetti and back to me. "I'm Chris Mason."

I show him my badge. "I'd like to talk to you and your son, Doug, if you have a few minutes."

"What's this about?"

"There was an incident on Township Road 4 last night involving Noah Kline," I tell him, keeping it purposefully vague. You never know when someone you're talking to is going to volunteer information they couldn't know—unless they were at the scene.

"Heard about that," the man says. "How's the kid?"

"Critical. It's serious."

He jerks his head knowingly, suspicious of us now, unsympathetic about the injured boy. "I figured you'd show up sooner or later."

Tomasetti speaks for the first time. "Why's that?"

"Evidently, you talked to Craig Hodges."

Neither Tomasetti nor I say anything.

As if on cue, Chris Mason keeps talking. "Look, just because Doug dated Ashley doesn't mean he had anything to do with what happened to that Amish kid. Doug's a good boy. He learned an important lesson with Ashley, and he's moved on."

"Do you mind if we ask him a couple of quick questions?" I ask.

I see him working that over, trying to come up with an excuse to refuse. Before he can say anything, the two boys saunter over to us, expressions curious. They're close in age, physically fit, their dark hair damp with sweat and sticking to their foreheads.

Still holding the football, the oldest of the two boys eyes us suspiciously. "What's going on?"

Chris Mason introduces him. "This is my oldest son, Doug." He's a nice-looking kid with baby blue eyes, ham-sized shoulders, and a face that exudes boy-next-door charm.

"And this is Duke, my youngest."

Duke is wearing a Painters Mill High School Football jersey. He's the taller of the two, with angular arms and legs, and feet he hasn't quite grown into.

Both boys mutter an unenthusiastic hello.

Tomasetti jumps into good cop mode. "That's a nice-looking GTO," he says motioning toward the muscle car. "1969?"

Doug Mason perks up. "Seventy." Though he's apprehensive about our presence, he grins, his pride in his car shining through the veil of nerves. "Me and Dad restored it."

"Four fifty-five?" Tomasetti asks, referring to the size of the engine.

The boy's chest puffs out. "Four hundred."

Tomasetti whistles and smiles back, his new best friend, rapport successfully built.

"Looks like you just washed it," I say.

"Been raining, so . . ."

The father sighs, letting us know he's not pleased with my comment.

"Doug, can you tell us where you were last night?" I ask.

"What?" The boy looks from me to his dad.

"Noah Kline was in some kind of accident," his father tells him.

"Oh. Wow." The boy's forehead wrinkles. "How bad?"

"He's in the hospital," I tell him.

"Shit." As if realizing the response is inappropriate, he ducks his head, slants a look at his dad. "Sorry."

I repeat the question.

Doug shrugs. "I went to homecoming like everyone else."

"Alone?"

"He's got a girlfriend," his younger brother interjects. "Laura Simms. You can check."

Doug shoots his brother an annoyed look. "Jeez, shut up, dude."

I watch both boys for any telltale signs of deceit, but see nothing overt. "After homecoming, what time did you and Laura leave?"

"Eleven or so. She had to be home by eleven thirty."

"Where did you go after you dropped her off?" I ask.

Duke makes a sound of irritation. "Are you saying my brother did something to Noah Kline?"

Tomasetti skewers him with a dark look.

"Doug is so over Ashley." The young man rolls his eyes, teenager style. "Look, everyone's wondering why she's going out with some Amish dude. I mean, she's straight fire and he doesn't even drive a car."

"That's enough, son," Chris Mason says mildly.

"Maybe they ought to look at Ashley's old man," the boy says. "I don't want to throw shade on the guy, but Jason says his dad hates it that Little Miss Perfect is going out with someone who only went to the eighth grade."

"Jason?" I ask.

"Ashley's brother," the boy tells me.

"Duke, go inside and help your mother with lunch." Chris Mason points at the house. "Now."

Giving us a final, withering look, the boy starts toward the house.

The elder Mason watches his son depart and then turns his attention back to us, his expression penitent. "Sorry, he's a little protective of his brother."

That's not the way I would describe the boy's behavior, but I hold my silence. Tomasetti and I turn our attention to the other boy.

Doug Mason swallows. "Am I in trouble?"

"Where did you go after homecoming?" I ask.

"Me and Laura sat in the driveway for about fifteen minutes. Uh . . . you know . . ." He blushes. "Then I drove back into town and met a couple of guys at the sub place. We ate and goofed off." He rattles off the names of his friends.

I jot them down. "You went home after that?"

"Well, the engine was ticking, so I drove around a while. You know, listening, trying to figure out what it was." He shrugs. "Then I went home and hit the sack."

"What time was that?" I ask.

"Twelve thirty or so."

About the time Noah Kline was walking home.

"Have you ever had any problems with Noah Kline?" I ask. "Any arguments or disagreements?"

"No, ma'am."

"What about Ashley? Did the two of you ever argue?" I ask, aware that Tomasetti has made his way over to the car. He runs his hand over the gleaming hood as if in admiration, but I know he's checking for damage, dents or chips in the paint—or blood.

The boy glances from Tomasetti to his father, and shifts his weight from one foot to the other. "Look, I didn't like it when we broke up. I was pissed when I found out she was seeing Noah Kline. I mean, he's frickin' *Amish*. So I sent her a couple of texts. I don't see what the big deal is."

"Did you break up because of Noah?" I ask.

He grimaces, looks down at his sneakers. "She broke up with me, so you'll have to ask her."

"Were you jealous when you realized she and Noah were going out?" I ask.

"No, ma'am." He says the words with gusto, but he's not a very good liar.

"Were you on Township Road 4 at any time in the last twenty-four hours?" I ask.

"I don't go out that way." The boy's eyes go wide. "You think I ran him over?"

"I think I want you to answer the question."

"I didn't do anything wrong." He steps back, looks up at his father. "Dad? What the hell?"

"You got your answer, Chief Burkholder." Chris Mason sets his hand on his son's shoulder and squeezes. "Doug had nothing to do with the Kline boy getting hurt. If you have any more questions, we'll do this with an attorney present."

I close my notebook. "Thank you for your time."

A few minutes later, Tomasetti and I are back in the Explorer. "What do you think?" I ask.

"I think he just reminded me why I don't trust any male under the age of thirty," he grumbles.

"Jealousy can be a powerful motive."

"Teenagers don't have the strongest impulse control to begin with."

"In light of the texts he sent Ashley Hodges, I'd say he just moved to the top of my suspect list."

According to Mervin Kline, Benjamin Weaver had once been best friends with Noah, but the two boys had some sort of falling-out. Located ten miles west of Painters Mill, Killbuck is a small village with a population of about eight hundred souls. Benjamin lives a few miles out of town in a small house nestled in the hills along scenic State Route 520. The driveway is a gauntlet of potholes and the occasional piece of junk. An older sedan sits next to a beat-up-looking Jeep Grand Cherokee. A chain-link fence encloses the front yard that's been stomped to dirt. A sorrel gelding watches us from a loafing shed surrounded by livestock panels at the back of the house.

"Jeep is covered with mud," Tomasetti says as he opens the door.

He gets out and starts toward the vehicle. I'm on my way to the house when a twentysomething man wearing insulated coveralls and a ski cap comes through the door. He does a double take upon spotting me.

"Can I help you?" he asks.

I have my badge at the ready. "Benjamin Weaver?"

His eyes flick from me to Tomasetti, who's a few yards away looking at the Jeep, and back to me. "I'm Ben."

"Do you know Noah Kline?"

"Yeah, I know him." He grimaces. "I heard what happened. You guys find out who did it?"

I'm thinking about the grapevine, how quickly news travels, and I wonder if it's common knowledge that the incident wasn't an accident—or if this young man knows more than he should. "We're talking to everyone who knows him." I pause, watching him. He seems more interested in Tomasetti and his proximity to the Jeep.

"How do you know Noah?" I ask.

His gaze shifts back to me. "I've known Noah since we were kids. We grew up together. We've been friends for years."

"When's the last time you saw him?"

"A couple of months ago."

"That's a long time not to see your best friend," I say.

A cognizance flits across his expression. "I reckon you talked to his *datt*."

"I understand you had an argument with Noah."

"It's a little more complicated than that." He heaves a sigh of resignation. "Yeah, I'm pissed at Noah. But I had nothing to do with what happened to him."

"Where were you last night?"

"I drove down to the Brass Rail, had a few drinks, and played some pool."

"Alone?"

"Yeah, I was alone."

Tomasetti climbs the steps to the porch and joins us. Ben looks at him, curious, a little intimidated. Tomasetti doesn't identify himself, never takes his eyes off the young man, saying nothing about the Jeep.

"What was the argument about?" I ask.

"He courted my little sister, Loretta, for a while." The corners of his mouth turn down, as if he's swallowed something foul. "She was only sixteen at the time. Shy. Sweet. He was her first boyfriend and she was crazy about him. I was cool with the whole thing. I mean, Noah's a good guy, right?" Shaking his head, he looks down at his work boots. "Or so I thought."

"What happened?"

"He slept with her." Emotions akin to anger and shame flash in his eyes, and I think about how deep some Amish mores go. "She thought they were going to get married. Then all of a sudden he's with that English girl and it's like my sister doesn't exist. It just about killed her, and it sure didn't do shit for her reputation. You know how the Amish are."

"Did you confront him?" I ask.

"I called him out on what he did. If you want to call that a confrontation, go for it."

"Did the argument get physical?"

"No, but if he'd pushed it, I'd have happily beat his ass."

Tomasetti rolls his eyes. "How did your Jeep get so muddy?"

"I went coyote hunting down to the wildlife area two nights ago. Got stuck out by the creek."

"Anyone go with you?"

"Nope." He looks from Tomasetti to me and back to Tomasetti. "Like I said, I didn't have nothing to do with what happened to Noah."

"So you say."

"So I say." He looks away, zips up his coveralls. "Look, I gotta get to work. Are we done here?"

Ashley Hodges was running late. Usually, she left her volunteer job at the Buckeye Ridge Home for the Retired at 6:00 P.M. Tonight, Mrs. Henderson, who was legally blind and her favorite resident, had wanted her to read the final chapter of the mystery novel they'd been reading for the last week and Ashley hadn't been able to say no. Though it was nearly dark now, Ashley didn't mind. She'd been enjoying the book, too. Besides, staying busy kept her mind off Noah.

She worried about him every minute of every day—and she missed him so much she could barely stand it. She'd called the hospital four times today. Each time the news was the same: He's in critical condition. Since she wasn't family, it was all they could tell her. Tomorrow, she was going to ask her mom to drive her out to the Kline farm so she could talk to Noah's parents. If only he would wake up so she could talk to him, see his smile . . .

She was a few blocks from home, walking fast, embroiled in her thoughts, backpack straps digging into her shoulders, when the shadow came at her out of nowhere. Strong arms wrapped around her, trapping her arms at her sides, and swung her around with such force that she lost her balance.

Ashley yelped. A thousand thoughts raced through her mind. She hit the ground on her back, the backpack jabbing her spine. Then the man was on top of her, straddling her. Panic sparked and then a steady stream of terror had her struggling mindlessly against a heavy body and muscles that were incredibly strong. A tidal wave of horror washed over her at the sight of the mask. It was a skull mask with black eyes and hit-or-miss teeth.

She screamed, but it was cut short when he slapped a leather-clad hand over her mouth hard enough to cut her lip. "Shut the hell up and listen!" he hissed.

Heart slamming against her ribs, adrenaline pumping pure fear through her blood, Ashley tried to dislodge him. She lashed out, grabbing the material of his coat, and shoving at him with both hands—to no avail.

"Cut it out!" Drawing back, he slapped her.

Ashley went still, breathing hard.

He shoved a finger in her face. "You keep your fucking mouth shut or we will shut it for you permanently," he snarled. "You got that?"

Ashley stared up at him, comprehension and dread snaking through her. She could barely see him through the tears, the veil of shock. Still, she knew what he wanted, and she nodded.

"Say it." Giving her face a final, vicious squeeze, he removed his hand. "Do it!"

"I won't tell," she choked.

He got to his feet, looking at her, the mask macabre in the semidarkness. He pointed at her, a silent and effective threat, and then he turned and ran.

I'm in my office at the police station, running the names of the players involved in the Kline case through OHLEG and LEADS, law enforcement databases that will tell me if any of them have criminal records. Noah Kline. Ashley Hodges. Doug Mason. Duke Mason. Benjamin Weaver. Not a single one of them has ever been in trouble with the police.

I've filled several pages of my legal pad with names and motives and possibilities. The name that keeps bubbling to the top of the list is Doug Mason. The jealous ex-boyfriend. Is he vindictive enough to have run down Noah Kline? The two boys he claimed to be with at the sub shop after homecoming corroborated his story. Still, there's an hour or so that's unaccounted for. Did Doug drive around, listening to some mysterious "tick" in his car? Or did he go looking for Noah Kline and act on some dark impulse he couldn't control?

"Chief?"

372   Linda Castillo

I look up to see my second-shift dispatcher, Jodie
Metzger, standing in the doorway. "I just took a call
from Ashley Hodges. She's in the park. Hysterical.
Says someone attacked her."

I get to my feet. "Is she hurt?"

"Says she's just shaken up."

"How long ago?"

"A minute."

Grabbing my keys, I head toward the door. "Who's
on duty?"

"Skid."

"Tell him to meet me there."

Creekside Park is a pretty little green space that's
been around as long as I can remember. There's a
playground complete with a swing set, a slide, and
old-fashioned monkey bars. A fountain featuring
a giant catfish spurting water draws kids to splash
around in the summer months. A small, trickling
stream spanned by a wood footbridge cuts through
the park's center. All six acres of it is jam-packed
with stately hundred-year-old trees.

I'm not sure what to expect when I arrive. Generally speaking, Painters Mill is a safe town; parents
don't hesitate to let their kids play outside or walk to
and from school. My first thought is that whatever
happened to Ashley Hodges is related to what happened to Noah Kline. But how?

The final vestiges of dusk hover above the treetops

to the west when I pull into the park. The shadows swallow me as I idle along the narrow asphalt roadway. There's no sign of Skid. I hit my high beams and keep an eye out for Ashley.

I find her walking alongside the road, huddled in a hoodie, her arms wrapped tightly around her middle. She startles upon spotting my headlights, then recognizing my vehicle, raises both hands and runs toward me.

I stop and pick up my radio mike. "Ten twenty-three," I say, letting Dispatch know I've arrived on scene. "I've got her. Stand by." I'm about to hail Skid when his flashing lights appear in my rearview mirror.

Grabbing my Maglite, I get out and start toward Ashley. "What happened?" I ask. "Are you all right?"

She stumbles toward me, sobbing. "Chief Burkholder!"

I set the beam of my flashlight on her, catch a glimpse of a ravaged face streaked with tears. A thin line of blood on the right side of her mouth. She reaches me, throws her arms around my waist and clings.

"Someone attacked me," she chokes.

Her entire body trembles. Wanting to get a better look at her, I ease her to arm's length. "Are you injured?"

"No," she says in a tremulous voice.

Vaguely, I'm aware of Skid coming up behind me,

listening, the beam of his flashlight illuminating the surrounding trees and brush.

"Do you know who it was?" I ask.

She shakes her head. "He wore a mask."

"Did he have a weapon?"

"I don't think so."

"How long ago?" I ask.

"Just a few minutes."

"Where did he go?"

"He ran into the park." She motions toward the playground.

"What was he wearing?" I ask.

"I don't know," she cries. "Just . . . a skull mask. And a hoodie, I think. Dark. Blue or black."

I glance at Skid. "Go."

Nodding, he takes off in the direction she indicated.

I speak into my radio and hail the sheriff's department. "Ten forty-eight A," I say, using the code for suspicious person. "Male. Dark hoodie. Skull mask. Creekside Park."

I turn my attention back to Ashley. "Did you call your parents?"

"My mom's on the way." She swipes tears from her face. "I can't believe this happened."

The sound of tires alerts us to an approaching vehicle. I turn, see the white Escalade pull up beside my Explorer. The door swings open and Belinda Hodges gets out.

"Mom!"

"Sweetheart!" The woman runs toward us, heels clicking against the asphalt. "What on earth happened?"

She reaches us, gets a look at her daughter's face, and gasps. "Oh my God! Your lip is bleeding." Pulling her daughter into her arms, she looks at me. "Who did this?"

As the girl tells her mother about the attack, a Holmes County sheriff's deputy rolls up behind my Explorer. I go to him, give him the basics, and ask him to stay with the women while I assist Skid.

I take off at a jog and enter the trees, speaking into my shoulder mike. "Skid, what's your twenty?"

"At the fountain, heading west."

"I'm ten seven-six," I say, letting him know I'm on my way.

I catch up with him at the footbridge that spans the creek. "Anything?" I ask.

"Nada," he says.

Our boots echo hollowly against the wood planks as we cross the bridge, the twin beams of our flashlights bobbing, not quite penetrating the shadows. I hear the gurgle of water below. Around us, the trees whisper and sway.

On the other side of the bridge, we pause, listening, shining our flashlights into the thick darkness ahead. We've just started down the trail when a flicker of light through the trees snags my attention.

"Kill your light," I whisper, dousing my own.

Skid reacts quickly, and we're plunged into darkness. He comes up beside me. "I saw it," he says quietly. "Fifty yards, straight east, on the path."

We watch for a moment and sure enough the light flickers again. "He's running," I whisper. "Let's go get him."

We charge into the darkness. Skid pulls ahead quickly. I let him, speak in a low voice into my lapel mike. "Ten seven eight," I say, using the ten code for need assistance. "Ten eighty-eight." Suspicious activity. "Subject is on the west side of Creekside Park. Past the footbridge. Westbound. Unit intercept at Weisenbarger Street."

Skid reaches the end of the asphalt and keeps going. It's too dark to see, so I flick on my Maglite. Trying to anticipate where the subject will go next, I cut slightly right, plunge headlong into the ditch, and enter the woods. Branches tear at my jacket as I run. The beam of my flashlight bounces with every stride, light playing crazily over the ground and brush and branches. I can't see Skid, but I catch the occasional flicker of his light; I hear him breaking through brush a few yards ahead and to my left.

I'm running full out when I reach a secondary trail, and I pour on the speed.

"Stop!" I hear Skid shout. "Police Department! Stop!"

He's fifteen yards away from me now, outrunning me. I follow the sound of his footsteps. Thrusting my

Maglite forward, I squint into the darkness, trying to spot the subject through the thick foliage.

"Halt!" Skid shouts. "Painters Mill PD! Stop!"

The curse that follows tells me our subject doesn't heed the order.

Weisenbarger Street lies a hundred yards ahead. It's a through street with easy access to the highway. Chances are, the son of a bitch is trying to reach a vehicle, either his own or someone is waiting for him.

I run another hundred yards, fight my way through a tangle of low-slung branches. I'm out of breath, a stitch forming in my side. The sound of an engine roars in the distance. I look up to see the flicker of headlights through the trees.

I reach Skid, who has stopped. Huffing and puffing, he bends, sets his hands on his knees, speaks into his shoulder mike. "Subject is on Weisenbarger," he pants. "In a vehicle. Southbound."

A Holmes County deputy's voice cracks a response over the radio, letting us know he's still a mile or so away.

"Damn." Skid shakes his head, his eyes meeting mine. "Son of a bitch runs like a damn cheetah."

"Or else we're old and out of shape."

He laughs. "Not a chance."

Using our Maglites, we head back toward our vehicles. Midway there, I spot something shiny and out of place on the ground, half buried in fallen leaves.

I shift my beam to the object. "What's that?"

Skid toes away the leaves. "Pocketknife. Blade is

out." His gaze meets mine, unspoken words floating between us.

"He was armed." I kneel for a closer look. It's an expensive-looking knife, about eight inches long, including the handle. "Nice of him to leave it for us."

"I was just thinking the same thing." He shifts the beam of his flashlight. "What's that on the blade?"

"Some kind of inscription." I move closer and read. *"Savage."*

We exchange a look.

"What the hell does that mean?" he asks. "A name?"

"Maybe." Pulling out my cell, I snap several photos. Then I remove a small paper bag from my duty belt and use my gloved hand to work the knife into it.

I look at Skid. "Check to see if there are any residents in Painters Mill with that last name."

"You got it."

"I'll check with the knife shop in the morning. See if it was purchased there."

As we walk back to our vehicles, I find myself thinking about Ashley Hodges. I don't believe this was a random attack, but why would someone accost her? What was their motive? Is the incident related to what happened to Noah Kline? If so, why is someone targeting this couple? I think about the people who may have had reason to harm Noah Kline—or at least want him out of the picture. Doug Mason. Ben Weaver. Maybe even Craig Hodges. All of them are likely physically fit enough to outrun the likes of Skid and me. But how does the name Savage fit into the equation? Or does it?

The Cutting Edge knife shop is located in downtown Painters Mill, a block from the police station. I'm waiting for the owner when he opens the doors at 10:00 A.M. It doesn't take long to ascertain he sold the knife.

"It's a Smith & Wesson first-response drop-point plain-blade pocketknife." He takes the bag containing the knife and turns it over in his hands. "Very popular, especially around Christmas."

"Do you recall who bought this one?" I ask.

"No, but I can look." He disappears into a back room behind the counter and returns with a sleek iPad tablet. He slides his index finger over the screen. "Here we go. Christine McDowell. Lives right here in Painters Mill. She bought five of them."

"That's a lot of knives." I think about that a moment. "Were all of them inscribed?"

He taps the screen. "I engraved all five knives for her."

"How were the other four engraved?"

"That's why I remember the sale. I thought it was odd that all five knives had the same engraving: Savage."

Christine McDowell is eighteen years old and lives in a small apartment on Ivester Court two blocks off the traffic circle. She graduated from Painters Mill High in the spring and works as a cashier at Fox's Pharmacy.

It's nearly 11:00 A.M. when I park in the driveway behind an older Camry, take the steps up to Apartment 2, and knock.

A muffled "shit" sounds from the other side of the door. The dead bolt snicks and I find myself looking at a petite redhead with large blue eyes, fifteen pounds of extra weight stuffed into faded bell-bottom jeans, and an expression that has bad attitude written all over it.

She sighs. "Look, if this is about the parking tickets—"

"This isn't about tickets," I cut in. "Can I come in?"

"Um." Her eyes flick sideways as if she's trying to remember if she left anything unseemly in plain view. "Sure."

I enter a slightly messy apartment that smells of fast food and the barely there redolence of cigarettes. I cut to the chase. "I understand you bought some knives from The Cutting Edge a few months ago."

"Knives?" She blinks, tries to assume an innocent countenance, but she doesn't quite manage. "Hmmm."

I pull out my cell and show her an enlarged photo of the knife. "You purchased five of them. Including this one."

"Oh, that." Her laugh is as phony as the innocent

expression. "They were on sale for twenty-five bucks each. I sold them online for forty. Made a nice little profit."

"Who did you sell them to?" I pull out my notebook and pen. "I need names."

"I don't remember." A wiliness flickers in her eyes followed by a flash of amusement. She's playing with me, enjoying this. "It was months ago. I sell a lot of stuff."

"Did you keep any paperwork?"

"I'm not a paperwork kind of girl." One side of her mouth curves. "Sorry."

"If you bought them to sell, why did you have them engraved?"

"I dunno." She lifts a shoulder, lets it drop. "Makes them more valuable."

"All five knives were engraved with the name Savage. I don't see how that could make them more valuable."

"People like stuff like that. You know, badass."

I stare hard at her. "You realize I don't believe a word that's come out of your mouth."

"I'm sorry you feel that way." Her lips twitch.

"You know it's illegal to lie to the police, don't you?" I slide the notebook back into my pocket.

She shrugs. "I'm not worried."

"Do you know Noah Kline?"

"Never heard of him."

I nod, take a moment to look around the apartment

on the outside chance I'll spot something illegal—a joint or some drug paraphernalia—but there's nothing there.

I turn my attention back to the girl. "If I were you, I'd take care of those parking tickets."

I arrive at the police station to news that Noah Kline is still in critical condition and shows no sign of emerging from his coma. I hope this case doesn't turn into a homicide investigation.

In the last hour, I've run Christine McDowell through LEADS to check for warrants and any criminal history, but her record is clean. I even braved her social media accounts in the hope she posted something that might be helpful to the case, but there was nothing there.

Who the hell runs down an eighteen-year-old Amish kid, leaves him for dead, and attacks his girlfriend?

I pick up my cell and look at the photo of the knife. *Savage.* What does it mean?

"Chief?"

I look up to find my first-shift dispatcher, Lois Monroe, standing in the doorway of my office. "You've got a visitor."

Ashley Hodges appears beside her. The first time I met her, she looked like the all-American high school girl: bright-eyed and engaged, as if she didn't have a care in the world. Now, there are dark circles beneath troubled eyes. A bruise next to her mouth. She looks as if she hasn't slept in days.

"Come in and have a seat." I nod at Lois and then turn my attention to Ashley, motioning toward the visitor chair adjacent to my desk. "Did your parents bring you?" I ask.

The girl settles into the chair and shakes her head. "I rode my bike."

I nod and wait.

Folding her hands in her lap, she looks down at them. "I think I screwed up."

"How so?"

A pause follows, as if her list of mistakes is so long she doesn't know where to begin. After a moment, she glances toward the door, as if she's frightened someone might overhear what she's about to say, and then she whispers, "Someone is sending me notes."

"What kind of notes?" I ask.

Reaching into the pocket of her hoodie, she removes two folded scraps of paper and passes them to me. "I only have two. I threw away the first one."

The paper is plain and unlined, torn from a notebook, and folded once. Using the tip of my pen, I open the one on top and read.

WE DON'T APPROVE.

The words are printed in what looks like black marker. All caps. "Any idea who it came from?" I ask.

Without looking at me, she shakes her head. "No."

"Where did you find it?"

"One was in my locker at school. The other one was tucked into my American History book. I don't know when or how it got there. The first one—the one I threw away—was in a regular envelope in the mailbox at home."

I go to the second note. *YOU'RE A DIME. DITCH THE CRINGEY AMISH.*

I look at Ashley. "Dime?"

She frowns, rolls her eyes. "It's kind of a slang word for 'a perfect ten.'"

I stare at the words, something tickling the back of my brain. *CRINGEY.* I've heard the word before.

"Do you recognize the handwriting?" I ask.

"No."

"How did your parents react?"

"I didn't tell them."

"Why not?"

A brief hesitation and then she raises her gaze to mine. "It would just give them one more reason to forbid me to see Noah. They already don't approve. My dad hates him because he's Amish. He has all these plans for me. College. Law school."

I sigh. "Is that why you didn't come to me until now?"

She jerks her head. "This is all my fault. If I'd come to you right away, maybe none of this would have happened."

I give her a moment, then ask, "What did the first note say?"

"Something like: *We got eyes on him.* I'm paraphrasing, but . . ." Leaning forward, she puts her face in her hands and begins to cry. "I never dreamed someone would actually *do* something so awful."

"Ashley, can you think of anyone who might've written those notes?"

She gives a vigorous shake of her head. "Who does something like that, Chief Burkholder? I mean, Noah is incredibly sweet." Fierceness and defiance flash in her eyes. "He may have only gone to the eighth grade, but he's smart. And as far as his career? How many seventeen-year-old kids have built a room full of beautiful furniture with their own hands?"

Something akin to admiration flutters in my chest. I think of my own teen years and try to recall if any of my early relationships were ever so crystal clear.

I touch the note with the tip of my pen. "Ashley, do you know anyone with the last name Savage?"

The girl goes perfectly still. She looks at me, her expression startled, her mouth open slightly. "No," she says after a moment.

For a full minute, neither of us speaks. I let the silence ride, watching her grow increasingly uncomfortable.

"You're not a very good liar," I say.

She drops her gaze to her hands, her fingers tangling nervously in her lap.

I dig my cell from my pocket, swipe to the photo

of the knife, and hold it out for her to see. "I found this on the trail the night you were attacked. The knife was open. He had a weapon, Ashley. If you have any idea who this might belong to, you need to tell me right now."

"It's not a name." She whispers the words without looking at me.

"What then?"

"It's a . . . clique. At school. The Savages. I mean, it's an urban legend kind of thing. A ghost group or something. Everyone knows about them, but nobody knows who they are or if they really even exist."

"I need names," I tell her.

"No one knows who they are."

"What kind of group are we talking about?"

"They're haters. Bullies. A lot of what they do is online. Anonymous, you know."

"Who do they bully?"

"Anyone they don't like. Take your pick." She gives a sour laugh. "They're equal-opportunity haters, Chief Burkholder. It doesn't matter who they are. Anyone who rubs them the wrong way or crosses them or pisses them off. They're vicious and secretive."

"Have you ever been threatened?"

"Not until now." She can't quite hide the shiver that runs through her. She raises knowing eyes to mine. "Do you think they're involved in what happened to Noah?"

"Maybe. Or what happened to you."

She looks at her hands again, saying nothing.

Something there, I think. Something she doesn't want to talk about.

"Do you know Christine McDowell?" I ask.

"I know *of* her." She makes a face. "She graduated last year. She's kind of sketchy."

"Does she have anything to do with the Savages?"

"I don't know."

"Is there anyone else I might talk to?"

"I just don't know." She sighs. "I'm sorry."

"All right." I motion toward the phone on my desk. "Call your parents. I'll load up your bike and drive you home."

I try to get Ashley to open up and talk to me during the drive to her house, but she doesn't bite. I suspect she knows more than she's telling me—about the Savages or maybe even the attack in the park—but every time I broach the subject, she shuts down. Why would a young woman who claims to be in love with the victim of a crime refuse to tell the police what she knows?

I'm in my office at the police station, thinking about the case. I'm missing something, but it's on the edge of my brain. My conversation with Ashley Hodges keeps running through my mind.

. . . it's an urban legend kind of thing. A ghost group or something. Everyone knows about them, but nobody knows who they are or if they really even exist.

I pull the two notes that were sent to her from my desk drawer and set them on my desk.

WE DON'T APPROVE.

YOU'RE A DIME. DITCH THE CRINGEY AMISH.

Ashley told me she threw away the first note, but it said something like:

WE GOT EYES ON HIM.

Were they threatening Noah Kline because he's Amish? Because he's Amish and dating a popular non-Amish girl? Something else?

Opening my desk drawer, I pull out a photo of the knife and set it beside the notes. I look at the engraving.

SAVAGE.

Not a name, Ashley had told me, but a group of people. A gang. A clique. The Savages. When I asked her for more, she'd clammed up.

"What don't you want me to know?" I say aloud.

I open the folder containing my notes. Starting at the beginning, I read. I'm midway through my initial interview with Ashley when I remember where I heard the word "cringey." It was when I spoke to her father, Craig Hodges, and her brother Jason, after they walked me to the front porch. Jason said something to the effect that people at school thought his sister's relationship with an Amish boy was "cringey."

"Her older brother," I whisper as I flip to the next page.

Jason had all but pointed the finger at Doug Mason. I think about Ashley's clamming-up and I realize if her older brother is involved in something iniquitous, she would likely try to protect him.

Is it possible Jason Hodges, the son of a prominent and well-respected attorney, is a member of some shadowy high school clique?

Only one way to find out. Grabbing my keys, I head for the door.

A few minutes later, I'm standing outside the ornate doors of the Hodges' home. I've knocked twice, but no one has answered. A glance at my cell tells me it's not yet 5:00 P.M. More than likely, both parents are still at work. I consider calling them, but realize this is a conversation I need to have in person. The same holds true for Jason. All the better if he doesn't know I'm coming. I resolve to try them again in a couple of hours.

I'm nearly to the station when a call comes in from my dispatcher. "Chief, I've got a ten fifty PI," she says, which is the code for traffic accident with a personal injury. "County Road 13, just past the railroad trestle."

"Get an ambulance out there. I'm ten seven-six," I say, letting her know I'm on my way. "Tell Skid to meet me there."

"Ten four."

Flipping on my emergency lights, I pull into the

parking lot of the Lutheran Church on Main, hang a U-turn, and head out of town. I crank the speedometer up to sixty, blow the stop sign at Hogpath Road, and make the turn onto CR 13. The railroad trestle is a mile ahead, an ancient structure that stretches over the road like the skeleton of some long-dead dinosaur.

As I draw closer, I realize there's no vehicle in sight. No sign that anyone is here at all. In the back of my mind, I wonder if Dispatch or the reporting party got the location wrong. I slow as I pass beneath the trestle. I'm reaching for my radio mike when my windshield explodes. Glass pelts my face, my jacket, shards clattering onto the dash. Something thumps onto the passenger seat. I stomp the brake. The Explorer skids into a spin. The ditch and trees loom. Too close. Too fast. I turn into the skid, but I'm not fast enough. The vehicle whips across the ditch, ends up in the field, facing the wrong direction.

Shaken, I unsnap my seat belt, take a quick physical inventory. My face stings, probably due to small nicks from the glass. Otherwise, I'm uninjured. A section of railroad tie lies on the passenger seat, looking ominous and out of place. Someone threw it from the trestle. . . .

I've ended up in a field in a foot of mud. The engine has died. I set my hands on the wheel, turn the key, but nothing happens. "Shit," I mutter and get out.

This road dead-ends a couple of miles ahead. There's not much through traffic. A chill scrapes up my spine when I realize it's the perfect place for an ambush.

I hit my shoulder mike. "Skid. Expedite. Ten eighty-eight," I say, reciting the code for suspicious activity. "Ten thirty-nine," I add, letting him know it's an emergency.

"ETA three minutes," comes his reply.

I cross the ditch and step onto the road. There's no one around. No accident. No sign of the ambulance yet. It's so quiet I can hear the whisper of wind as it ebbs and flows through the trees. I glance up at the trestle. It's about twenty feet high and has been abandoned for years. Northbound, the tracks head back to Painters Mill. South, they end up in Coshocton. In both directions, the tracks intersect roads. If someone tossed that piece of railroad tie, and wanted a quick getaway without being seen, all they would have to do is park to the north at Hogpath Road.

I hit my radio as I start up the steep embankment. "Skid, check for a ten forty-eight," I say quietly, using the ten code for suspicious vehicle. "Railroad tracks at Hogpath Road."

"Roger that," he says.

The embankment that will take me up to the tracks is steep and tangled with high grass, bramble, and saplings. I'm midway up when I hear the pound of footsteps. Using my hands, I scramble to the top, glance left to see a figure running away. Adult male. Moving fast.

"Stop! Police Department! Halt!"

I break into a sprint, shout into my lapel mike. "Suspect northbound on the tracks! Moving toward Hogpath Road! Male! Dark hoodie!"

Vaguely, I'm aware of my radio lighting up with traffic. The sheriff's deputy is en route. Skid is nearly to Hogpath Road. For now, I'm on my own.

"Stop!" I shout to the running man. "Painters Mill Police! Halt!"

He doesn't even break stride.

I'm no slug when it comes to running, but he's young and fast and pulls away from me at an astounding rate. He flies over the tracks, long strides, arms pumping, tossing the occasional glance over his shoulder. I'm thirty feet behind him and losing ground. In the back of my mind, I'm hoping Skid can get to him before this guy reaches a vehicle.

The man throws a look at me over his shoulder. His foot strikes a broken railroad tie that's sticking up. He goes down hard enough to send gravel flying. He recovers quickly, scrambles to his feet. But the fall cost him precious seconds. I close the distance between us.

"Police!" I pant the word, not enough breath to shout. "Stop! Stop!"

The intersection is two hundred yards ahead. No sign of Skid. I'm just feet behind my suspect now, running full out. I pour on a burst of speed, dive for him, reach out, wrap my arms around his waist. He drags me a few feet, so I jam my shoulder into the small of his back and take him down in a flying tackle.

He hits the ground with so much force he skids through gravel. My chin slams against his spine. I try to lock my arms around him, but his sweatshirt rides up. My hands slide on skin slick with sweat. He twists, raises his leg, shoves me with his foot, and I lose my grip.

"Stop resisting!" I make another grab for him, miss, my hands fisting his shirt.

Fabric tears. He writhes, cursing, and tries to dislodge me. His knee comes up, slams into the side of my face. Pain zings along my jaw.

He flops onto his backside, raises both feet to kick me. I get my first good look at his face. Jason Hodges. I see panic and rage. Lips peeled back in a snarl, teeth clenched, spittle flying.

"Jason!" I shout. "Stop!"

The next thing I know Skid comes down on top of him, flattening him, using his momentum and weight to overpower him. "Turn over, dude," he says. "Face-down. Relax. Do it now."

The boy tries to twist away, but we scramble, get him flipped onto his stomach. Once he's prone, Skid sets his knee against the boy's back. I grasp one of his arms, Skid gets the other and cuffs him.

"I didn't do anything!" the boy shouts.

"Get up." Skid rises.

Taking the boy's arm, I help him to his feet. The

three of us stand there for a moment, the only sound coming from our labored breathing. A few yards away, a Holmes County deputy approaches us from the trestle.

"Your parents aren't going to be happy with you," I say to the boy. "Neither is Ashley."

The boy hangs his head. In shame or defeat, I can't tell. Or maybe he's downcast simply because he got caught.

"I think I need a lawyer," he mutters.

"Yeah, I think you do, too," I tell him.

Skid glances at me, touches the side of his face to indicate mine. "You're bleeding, Chief. You need an ambulance?"

"Just a few nicks." I tell him about the railroad tie being thrown from the trestle and shattering my windshield. "I could use a ride into town, though."

"You got it," he says and we start toward his cruiser.

A few hours later I'm sitting at my desk at the police station finishing my arrest report, trying to ignore the headache that's taken up residence behind my left temple. Tomasetti sits in the visitor chair adjacent to my desk, trying not to rush me, not quite succeeding. I'm not sure who called him and told him what happened on County Road 13—that a railroad tie was thrown through my windshield—but he got there in a matter of minutes. I'll never forget the look on his face when he laid eyes on me. He's playing it cool now, but he hasn't let me out of his sight.

A subdued Jason Hodges was transported to the juvenile detention center in Wooster. He admitted to throwing the railroad tie off the trestle. More important, he admitted to running down Noah Kline. All for the simple fact that he didn't want his sister "wasting her time on some stupid Amish boy." He claims he didn't mean to hurt anyone; he'd only wanted to scare him. With the exception of his parents, no one believes him, including me.

The one subject he wouldn't discuss was the Savages. As the reality of his situation sinks in, I believe he will eventually come clean and name names. Even if he doesn't, I've no doubt I'll get to the bottom of it and bring their shady little operation to an abrupt and final end.

In the coming days, Jason will likely be charged with a multitude of serious crimes, including aggravated assault of a peace officer and failure to stop after a motor vehicle accident with serious physical harm. That he's a minor will be taken into consideration. Still, he's facing serious charges that will affect him for a long time to come, possibly the rest of his life.

In the good news department, Noah Kline emerged from his coma a few hours ago. According to the nurse on duty, he's conscious and asking for food. I figure that's a good sign.

I would have finished my reports and corresponding paperwork by now, but I've had a slew of visitors in the last hour, including every member of my small department. I played down what happened. All of us know it could have been a hell of a lot worse.

I've just shut down my computer when Tomasetti leans forward and closes my laptop for me. "What do you say we head home, pull out a couple of steaks, and open that nice bottle of Carménère I've been saving?" he asks.

Rising, I loop the strap of my laptop case over my shoulder and round the desk. "I think that sounds like a good way to end what has been a very long day."

"Has anyone ever told you you're easy?"

"Just you."

"In that case." Taking my hand, he pulls me close for a kiss and we go through the door.

ONE WEEK LATER:

I'm in my cruiser, idling down Township Road 4 when I spot the buggy a quarter mile ahead. The sight of it makes me smile, so I head that way and pull up beside it.

The buggy stops. Noah Kline sits on the passenger side of the bench, grinning from ear to ear. His arm is in a cast. A bandage peeks out from beneath his hat at his left temple. Next to him, Ashley Hodges grips the leather reins, looking a little too excited to be in the driver's seat. Her grin is as brilliant and wide as Noah's.

"I heard they sprung you," I say to Noah.

"Nurses got tired of feeding me, I reckon," he replies.

I turn my attention to Ashley. I've only talked to her once since her brother was taken into custody a week ago. She gave me the names of some students who may be involved with the Savages. It wasn't a pleasant exchange, but she stepped up to the plate and told me what I needed to know. The Savages no longer exist. Those who were part of the group know they're on my radar—and had better keep their noses clean.

The arrest of Jason Hodges has been tough on his family. I'm hoping all of them have learned something. I hope Jason will take all of it to heart and get off the path he's taken.

"Noah's teaching me to drive the buggy," Ashley announces.

"I see that." I look at Noah and smile. "How's she doing?"

Putting his arm around her, he hugs her against him. "She's a natural." His grin widens. "The horse likes her almost as much as I do."

Ashley elbows him and I realize she isn't wearing her usual hoodie, but a longish skirt with sneakers and a plain coat. It's not exactly Amish, but it tells me she'd dressed to please Noah's parents. The thought makes me smile. Young and with a lot to learn—but in love.

"Chief Burkholder." Ashley sobers. "I owe you an apology. And an explanation."

I nod, waiting, saying nothing.

"I didn't know my brother was involved with that group. I mean, early on." She seems to struggle through the words, figuring them out as she goes, trying to get them right, as if knowing they're important. "Mom says I was probably in denial. I just couldn't believe he'd get involved with a group like the Savages. By the time I faced the truth, it was too late to warn you."

She pauses as if she wants to stop there, leave it at that. Noah touches her arm, his expression urging her to continue. "If you'd been hurt when my brother threw that railroad tie off the trestle . . . I wouldn't have been able to live with myself."

I nod. "When did you figure out he was involved?"

She draws a deep breath, lets it out slowly. "The night I was attacked. I recognized Duke Mason, even though he was wearing that mask. He's on the football team with Jason. Duke's younger, but they're friends. That's when I knew, when I should have told you. I'm really sorry I didn't."

I've already talked to Duke's father. I didn't pull any punches, and Chris Mason was concerned and furious. If he holds to our agreement, and I have no reason to believe otherwise, Duke Mason has already relinquished football for the school year in exchange for volunteer "community service" work in and around Painters Mill.

"Sometimes it's difficult to believe when someone we love makes a mistake," I tell her. "Especially if it's ugly."

"I don't blame you for hating me. I don't—"

I cut in before she can finish. "Hate never entered into it," I say, meaning it.

She looks down at her hands. "What's going to happen to my brother?"

I've been in contact with the juvenile court personnel in Wooster. Jason hasn't yet been released to his parents, but he will be soon. "Once he's released, he'll have to return for some court appearances. The rest is up to the judge and juvenile court system. He may be incarcerated for a time, or he may get off with community service. The one thing I can tell you is that the judge and the court will be fair."

She doesn't make a sound, but tears begin to roll down her cheeks. "Okay."

I give her a moment, use the time to get my words in order, hoping she'll listen. "I learned a valuable lesson when I was about your age," I tell her.

The girl raises her gaze to mine.

"You can't control what other people do. The one thing you can control is how you react." I let my expression soften. "It's a good rule of thumb."

She offers a tremulous smile, swipes the tears from her cheeks. "Thank you, Chief Burkholder."

I can't help but think about the challenges that lie

ahead for this young couple. Even more if the relationship lasts and she becomes more involved with the Amish.

"Where are you two headed?" I ask.

Noah motions toward his parents' farm ahead. "Ashley's going to help me unload hay."

"Since his arm's in a sling," she says, "I figure it's the least I can do."

"In that case, I'll let you get to work." I nod at Noah. "Tell your parents hello."

He tips his hat at me. "I'll do it."

The two young people exchange a grin and the buggy pulls away. I'm smiling when I put the Explorer in gear and head toward Painters Mill.

Read on for an excerpt from

FALLEN
A Kate Burkholder Mystery
by Linda Castillo

Chapter 1

She knew coming back after so many years would
be difficult, especially when she'd left so much hurt
behind. She'd hurt the people she loved, never wasting a moment on the notion of regret. She'd sullied
relationships that should have meant the world to
her. She'd blamed others when misfortune reared
its head, never admitting she might've been wrong.
Mistakes had always been the one thing she was
good at and she'd made them in spades.

Once upon a time she'd called Painters Mill home.
She'd belonged here, been part of the community, and
she'd never looked too far beyond the cornfields, the
quaint farmhouses, and winding backroads. Once,
this little town had been the center of her universe. It
was the place where her family still lived—a family
she hadn't been part of for thirteen years. Like it or
not, her connection to this place and its people ran
deep—too deep in her opinion—but it was a link
she could no longer deny no matter how hard she
tried.

This saccharine little town with its all-American main street and pastoral countryside hadn't always been kind. In the eyes of the seventeen-year-old girl she'd been, Painters Mill was a place of brutal lessons, rules she couldn't abide by, and crushing recriminations by people who, like her, possessed the power to hurt.

It took years for her to realize all the suffering and never-lived-up-to expectations were crap. Like her *mamm* always said: Time is a relative thing and life is a cruel teacher. It was one of few things her mother had been right about.

Painters Mill hadn't changed a lick. Main Street, with its charming storefronts and Amish tourist shops, still dominated the historic downtown. The bucolic farms and back roads were still dotted with the occasional buggy or hay wagon. Coming back was like entering a time warp. It was as if she'd never been gone, and everything that had happened since was nothing more than a dream. The utter sameness of this place unsettled her in ways she hadn't expected.

The Willowdell Motel sure hadn't changed. Same trashy façade and dusty gravel parking lot. Inside, the room was still dressed in the same godawful orange carpet. Same bad wall art. Same shoddily concealed cigarette smoke and the vague smell of moldy towels. It was a place she shouldn't have known at the age of seventeen.

If life had taught her one lesson that stood out

above the rest, it was to look forward, not back. To focus on goals instead of regrets. It took a lot of years and even more sacrifice, but she'd clawed her way out of the cesspit she'd made of her life. She'd done well—better than she ever imagined possible—and she'd forged a good life for herself. Did any of that matter now? Was it enough?

Tossing her overnight bag onto the bed, Rachael Schwartz figured she'd waited long enough to make things right. The time had come for her to rectify the one wrong that still kept her up nights. The one bad decision she hadn't been able to live down. The one that, for years now, pounded at the back of her brain with increasing intensity. She didn't know how things would turn out or if she'd get what she wanted. The one thing she *did* know was that she had to try. However this turned out, good or bad or somewhere in between, she figured she would simply have to live with it.

The knock on the door came at two AM. Even as she threw the covers aside and rolled from the bed, she knew who it was. A smile touched her mouth as she crossed to the door. Recognition kicked when she checked the peephole. The quiver of pleasure that followed didn't quite cover the ping of trepidation. She swung open the door.

"Well, it's about damn time," she said.

A faltering smile followed by a flash of remembrance. "I didn't think I'd ever see you again."

She grinned. "No such luck."

"Sorry about the time. Can I come in?"

"I think you'd better. We've a lot to discuss." Stepping back, she motioned her visitor inside. "I'll get the light."

Her heart strummed as she started for the night table next to the bed. All the words she'd practiced saying for months now tumbled in her brain like dice. Something not quite right, but then, what had she expected?

"I hope you brought the wine," she said as she bent to turn on the lamp.

The blow came out of nowhere. A sunburst of white light and sound, like a stick of dynamite igniting in her head. A splintering of pain. Her knees hit the floor. Shock and confusion rattled through her.

She reached out, grabbed the night table. A sound escaped her as she struggled to her feet, teetered left. She turned, spotted the bat, saw the other things she'd missed before. Dark intent. Buried rage. Dear God, how could she have been so naïve?

The bat came down again. Air whooshed. She staggered right, tried to escape it. Not fast enough. The blow landed hard on her shoulder. Her clavicle snapped. The lightning bolt of pain took her breath. Mewling, she turned, tried to run, fell to her knees.

Footsteps behind her. More to come. She swiveled, raised her hands to protect herself. The bat struck her forearm. An explosion of pain. The shock pulsing like a strobe.

"Don't!" she cried.

Her attacker drew back. Teeth clenched. The dead eyes of a taxidermist's glass. The bat struck her cheekbone, the force snapping her head back. She bit her tongue, tasted blood. Darkness crowded her vision. The sensation of falling into space. The floor rushed up, struck her shoulder. The scrape of carpet against her face. The knowledge that she was injured badly. That it wasn't going to stop. That she'd made a serious miscalculation.

The shuffle of feet on carpet. The hiss of a labored breath. Fighting dizziness, she reached for the bed, fisted the bedsheet, tried to pull herself up. The bat struck the mattress inches from her hand. Still a chance to get away. Terrible sounds tore from her throat as she threw herself onto the bed, scrabbled across. On the other side, she grabbed the lamp, yanked the cord from the wall.

The bat slammed against her back. A sickening wet-meat punch that took her breath. An electric shock ran the length of her spine. Unconsciousness beckoned. She swiveled, tried to swing the lamp, but she was too injured and it clattered to the floor.

"Get away!" she cried.

She rolled off the bed, tried to land on her feet. Her legs buckled and she went down. She looked around. A few feet away, the door stood open. Pale light spilling in. If she could reach it . . . Freedom, she thought. Life. She crawled toward it, pain running like a freight train through her body.

A sound to her left. Shoes against carpet. Legs coming around the bed. Blocking her way. "No!" she screamed, a primal cry of outrage and terror. No time to brace.

The bat struck her ribs with such force she was thrown onto her side. An animalistic sound ripped from her throat. Pain piled atop of pain. She opened her mouth, tried to suck in air, swallowed blood.

A wheeze escaped her as she rolled onto her back. The face that stared down at her was a mindless machine. Flat eyes filled with unspeakable purpose. No intellect. No emotion. And in that instant, she knew she was going to die. She knew her life was going to end here in this dirty motel and there wasn't a goddamn thing she could do to help herself.

See you in hell, she thought.

She didn't see the next blow coming.